# DESIRES

## Holly J. Gill
## Nikki Blaise

**Erotic Romance**

**Secret Cravings Publishing**
www.secretcravingspublishing.com

**A Secret Cravings Publishing Book**
Erotic Romance

DESIRES
Copyright © 2012 Holly J Gill/Nikki Blaise
Print ISBN: 978-1-61885-594-7

First E-book Publication: December 2012
First Print Publication: March 2013

Cover design by Dawne Dominique
Edited by Julie Reilly
Proofread by Marja Salmon
All cover art and logo copyright © 2012 by Secret Cravings Publishing

**ALL RIGHTS RESERVED:** This literary work may not be reproduced or transmitted in any form or by any means, including electronic or photographic reproduction, in whole or in part, without express written permission.

All characters and events in this book are fictitious. Any resemblance to actual persons living or dead is strictly coincidental.

**PUBLISHER**
Secret Cravings Publishing
www.secretcravingspublishing.com

# Dedication

Thank you to my wonderful husband Nigel and my three fantastic children, Rhys, Victoria and Alisha for allowing me to write. Love you all with my heart.

Thank you to my friends, Sonia and Donna, for believing in me and prompting me to fulfil my dream when there were dark days. Your support has been wonderful.

And a special thank you to Nikki Blaise.

# DESIRES

**Holly J. Gill**
**Nikki Blaise**

Copyright © 2012

# Chapter One

Stacie walked up the three wide steps leading to the large entrance porch of the imposing Georgian building. The bitter winter air made her nose hairs cringe and seemed to batter its way in between the buttons of her thick wool coat. She took a deep anxious breath wondering, not for the first time, why on earth she was there. She glanced back at the car park, overhung by snow-clad trees. Her little car glimmered in the pale light of the winter moon. She could just walk back to the still-warm haven and drive away. But her feet wouldn't obey the sensible part of her brain that told her to go, and go now! The snappy wind blew her hair into her face. She brushed it away and turned her attention back to the innocent-looking door.

There was an intercom situated on the right hand side of the old oak double doors. Her life had to change—she knew that. She had to try, or she'd be forever wondering.

Stacie stepped further onto the porch and glanced at her reflection in the darkened glass pane inset into the door. She tried to peer through, but could see nothing. *It's like the privacy glass on celebrity limousines*, she thought, then shrugged. She fumbled in her handbag, and brought out her lip gloss, applying a quick sweep. It did nothing to calm the expression of trepidation on the face she saw reflected back to her, but at least now she had shiny lips. She tried to gulp down the nervous lump in her throat, and pressed the buzzer.

There was a pause, then a woman's voice came over the intercom. "Hello. How may I help you?"

She started to speak, but nothing came out of her suddenly tightened throat. She cleared it and tried again, whispering, "Stacie Clifford. I have an appointment."

"Have you got your code?"

"Oh, um, yes, one second."

Stacie began digging in her bag for her phone. She accessed her emails and found the reply they'd sent to her initial enquiry. She stared at the innocuous-looking four-digit code they'd included in the reply, and her stomach churned. Was it dread or excitement?

"Hello? Are you still there?"

The tinny voice brought her back. "Yes, sorry." She read the code aloud to the woman and exhaled. It was done.

The door lock released. Stacie pushed on the heavy door and walked through, letting it swing shut behind her. The welcome warmth of the establishment hit her cold face as she stared around, ingenuously open-mouthed. She stood in a large high-ceilinged hall. The floor was ancient satiny polished wood, probably the original flooring. The walls were decorated in a deep warm red, lined with huge oil paintings. Small tables bearing large houseplants were tucked into corners.

Stacie made her way down the hallway, her footfalls echoing in the passageway. Several oak doors led off the hall on each side. She wondered what lay behind them. Hopefully she would soon find out. Then her attention was caught by a large picture. As the subject matter registered, her mouth fell open again. It pictured a group of people having what could only be described as an orgy. They sat naked around a table laden with food and drink, some sitting and eating, others embracing each other, or sprawled on the floor, doing what came naturally. Gluttony and lust exemplified. Well, what had she expected?

The hallway opened out into a lobby. Two women in black business suits were seated behind a large reception desk. There was a waiting area opposite the desk with two large, black leather couches and a coffee table bearing a fan of leaflets and a flower arrangement.

Stacie edged toward the reception desk. The pit of her stomach ached. One of the receptionists was flirting into the phone and ignored her. The other looked at her with a welcoming smile and rose from her chair. She was a pretty woman in her early twenties with long dark hair tied in a high ponytail.

"Good evening, Stacie," she said. "Angel will be with you shortly. Would you be good enough to fill out this questionnaire whilst you're waiting, please?" Stacie wordlessly took the proffered clipboard, made her way to one of the leather couches and sat down.

"Would you like a drink? Tea? Coffee?" Stacie heard the receptionist ask.

"No, thank you, I'm fine," she managed to say.

She gazed around the eighteenth-century reception area. Twin staircases with black iron spindles curved down into the reception area from a balcony above.

Situated to her right and left were two sets of double oak doors with massive black iron handles and hinges. She could see another set between the staircases far behind the reception desk, and a corridor led off behind the staircases to both sides.

Stacie turned her attention back to the questionnaire. The first few questions were straightforward, name, address etc., but she paused at the next set.

- Why do you wish to join the club?
- What do you want to gain from your experience?
- What are your sexual likes and dislikes?

Stacie didn't know. She didn't even know what kind of experience to expect here, let alone what she was going to gain from it. That was what she was here to find out, wasn't it?

She scribbled quick vague answers. The questionnaire probably didn't really matter anyway.

Between questions, she looked up at the receptionists, who were talking to each other in low voices. She tried to listen in on their conversation, but they were speaking too quietly.

The young receptionist glanced up and arched a perfectly threaded eyebrow. "Is everything okay?"

She blushed, caught eavesdropping. Not wanting them to know she was baffled, she lied. "Everything's fine, thank you." Feeling like a kid caught slacking in class, Stacie dropped her chastened gaze back to the questionnaire.

As she continued with her non-answers, Stacie still felt numb with astonishment that she was actually here. It had taken her months to gain the courage just to contact the club.

Anxiety struck her again in the pit of her stomach. Was she doing the right thing? What should she expect? Maybe when she spoke to Angel it would help her make a final decision.

Then, Stacie heard high heels tapping on the dark wood floor. She raised her head. The noise was coming from the corridor behind one of the staircases. The sound drew nearer and Stacie saw a woman appear—young, slim, twenty-something, with a shimmering sheet of black hair rippling down her back. She wore a formal business suit, and black-framed glasses perched on her finely-shaped nose, but even in the severe attire, she was stunning. She was tall and her height was further enhanced by her towering platform heels. Stacie shrank into herself. This woman was the epitome of confidence, everything she admired, yet lacked herself.

*She looks frightening, dominating yet beautiful. Is this Angel?*

The woman smiled at Stacie. Stacie forced her mouth into a terrified rictus back at her. She took a calm deliberate breath as the woman approached her.

"Hello. You must be Stacie Clifford?" Her voice was soft and calming.

Stacie gulped and gave a jerky nod.

"Lovely, I'm Angel. May I have your questionnaire and then, if you'd like to follow me, we can have a little chat somewhere more private." She held out her hand and Stacie handed her the clipboard, feeling more nervous than ever.

Angel walked to the reception desk, stopping to have a few words with the receptionists.

Stacie pushed herself up, with difficulty, off the squashy leather couch that seemed to have swallowed her bottom. She straightened her clothes and followed Angel. She walked like a model, her perfectly-shaped derriere swaying hypnotically.

As they walked down the corridor, Stacie saw more raunchy paintings on the walls. These were far more in-your-face than the ones in the outer reception area. Whip-wielding dominatrices wearing black leather cupless corsets and crotchless thongs stood over their willing victims, who lay bound and naked awaiting their punishment. Small spotlights shone on each picture, highlighting them further. A large stained glass window was situated at the end of the corridor, an incongruous reminder of this building's more dignified past.

They approached another of the ubiquitous wooden doors. "Come in, please. Take a seat," Angel said, holding the door open for Stacie to follow her through.

Stacie entered the office and her eyes widened at the room's surprisingly masculine decor. Dark panelling covered all the walls, illuminated by several small lights placed strategically throughout the room. A large, old, oak desk dominated the space, sitting against the far wall. The only nod to femininity was several vanilla candles, which scented the room with their subtle fragrance. The office was immaculate.

The desk held only a phone and a laptop. Behind it was a large leather swivel chair that looked as if it would swallow the slim woman.

Angel indicated a leather couch, a twin of those in the reception area. Stacie went to sit down and sank further than she expected. She shuffled her bottom forward unobtrusively—she hoped—before perching uncomfortably on the front of the sofa. She looked at Angel sitting on her leather swirl chair, wearing an amused look. Stacie wanted to cross her knees, but when she tried she found her body sinking back in the seat, so she was forced to plant her feet firmly on the floor just to stay upright. She could feel the strain in her thighs already.

As she waited for Angel to begin, she took a further furtive look around the room. Shelves lined one wall—a few were filled with books and the others held a display of erotic figurines in compromising positions. Stacie found herself twisting her head to figure out what one particular couple, no, threesome, were doing.

"Right then, Stacie." Angel's voice snapped her back. Stacie turned to see her looking at the clipboard, which she had placed on top of her closed laptop. Angel leaned forward over the desk, the posture deepening her already impressive cleavage. Stacie found herself wondering if she was wearing anything underneath the jacket. "I've ordered some drinks for us," Angel said.

"I'm fine, thank you," Stacie replied.

Angel's sharp glance made her uncomfortable. "I insist. I want you to feel comfortable. I don't bite," Angel said. She paused and glanced down at the clipboard. Stacie swallowed. Angel looked back up at Stacie and smiled. "Okay, Stacie. Firstly, welcome to Desires. You know what our club does, so I don't need to give you any details about that. Secondly," she tapped Stacie's questionnaire with a long fingernail, "this is shit, and you know it." Stacie flushed miserably. There was that back-at-school feeling again. Angel paused before continuing in a more gentle voice. "I'm sorry, I don't mean to upset you. But these questions," she flourished the offending document, "are vital for me to give you the best experience of Desires I can, and your answers don't really help me do that. I need to ask you, why are you here? What is it you are looking for?"

Stacie stared at her, dying with embarrassment, but knowing the awkward questions had to be asked. Maybe Angel would help.

"I am just wanting to…" Stacie paused to think hard about her answer. "I am looking for help in regaining my confidence in myself and in…in…" *Say it, woman!* "in…sex."

Angel picked up a pen and wrote on Stacie's questionnaire, after very obviously scoring through Stacie's original answer. "What are your likes and dislikes?"

Stacie was unsure how to answer. "It depends what you offer me."

"Well, we can come back to that one. So, you want to gain confidence in yourself and enjoy sex?" Stacie had barely begun to nod when a knock came at the door. She jumped and felt her pulse fluttering in her throat.

"Enter," Angel called.

The young receptionist pushed open the door, balancing a tray bearing a bottle of white wine and two glasses. She placed the tray on the desk and poured a glass, before starting to pour a second.

"Sorry, I'm driving…" Stacie began, holding out a hand to stop the young woman, who glanced at Angel in enquiry.

"Trust me, it will relax you. Just make it half a glass for Miss Clifford," she said to the receptionist, who nodded and obeyed before leaving the room quietly. "How did you find out about Desires?" Angel asked, folding her arms over the clipboard.

"I was clearing out some of my ex-husband's stuff and I saw an advert in one of his magazines."

"You were shocked, right?"

Stacie nodded. "Very much so. It was a, you know, one of *those* magazines." Her face felt so hot she was amazed it wasn't setting off the fire alarm. "I only looked through out of curiosity. I'd never seen anything like that before."

"And you saw our advert."

"Yes."

"So what made you decide to make contact?"

"I was intrigued. I kept the advert in my underwear drawer for months. I kept taking it out and looking at it, then losing my nerve and putting it back."

"What changed?"

"Well, I guess I thought I needed a little fun back in my life."

"But you're still not sure, are you, Stacie?" Angel's eyes were keen and all-seeing. Stacie gave a tiny shake of her head. "Why not?"

"I just don't know if this is the right kind of fun for me," Stacie answered, deciding to be blunt. "No offence, but it's all a bit…well…icky."

"I see." Angel smiled. "Well, only you can decide on whether Desires is right for you. You're right. It's not for everyone. But you've told me what you are looking for and, if you decide to stay with us, we will make sure you receive it. You need confidence. I can clearly see that by the way you are dressed."

Offended, Stacie glanced down at her work suit, seeing nothing wrong with it. "What's wrong with the way I'm dressed?"

"You're covering up all your best assets. Your blouse is almost around your neck, your skirt is far too long and I bet you are wearing tights rather than stockings."

Stacie's eyebrows shot up. *How did she know?*

"So," Angel continued without a break, "tell me a little about yourself, your personal life and the last time you had sex, as well as your turn-on points."

Sex. Even the word scared Stacie. She needed to answer Angel's questions but her mind had gone blank. *Maybe I should just leave. Just stand up and walk out. That's the easy option. But if I give up now, that's one more thing I've failed at. I have to do something.*

Stacie gathered the courage to answer Angel's questions. "I work for a fashion magazine. I've worked there since leaving college. I was married to a violent monster who drank himself stupid, and demanded sex. He also hit me till I was black and blue. I have no children, thank goodness, and no friends. I live for my work. It's the only thing that keeps me sane. The last time I had sex was with the monster. What turns me on? I have no idea." *There, that should shut her up.*

Angel didn't miss a beat. "You must have some idea what turns you on." Stacie stared at Angel, full of puzzlement. Angel leaned back in her leather chair and played with her pen.

"Do you like your breasts played with or do you like the man to dive straight into your knickers?" Angel gave as an example, staring at Stacie.

Stacie glared back at Angel's abruptness. "First I have to get to know him."

"Good point, so you like…what, chat?"

"I guess…No…yes…I like to get to know him before…you know."

"So you're not a quickie girl?"

"God, no…I like romance with a meal, dim atmospheric lighting, a bit of flirting and sweet talking." Stacie's eyes misted at the fantasy before Angel's sharp voice interrupted.

"You like a bore, then?"

"No…I like chitchat. I am not the kind of girl to open my legs that quickly."

"So you like the build up? You want respect?"

"I want to be respected. Yes."

"Then what, chat, coffee and sex?"

"Not on the first date!" Stacie answered, annoyed.

"But why?" Angel fired back.

"Don't you think that's desperate?"

"Not necessarily. It depends who you are and what you're after. Some girls aren't bothered about who they are with, it's what's inside the trousers. Other girls, like yourself, prefer the build up. Also, it depends on whether you're just after a one-night stand or a relationship," Angel said, leaning back in the leather chair before continuing, "Now. Turn-on points, breasts or—"

Stacie decided it was like going to the doctor with something embarrassing. *Best just to say it.* "I like my breasts to be caressed."

"Excellent. I need to make a few notes," Angel started to write on the clipboard. "When was the last time you masturbated?"

*Okay, now that really was too much!* This woman was just too intrusive. Stacie stuck out a mutinous chin.

"I need to know, Stacie, or I can't properly help you."

*Oh God!* "Quite a while ago. I have completely lost interest."

"Because of your ex-husband?"

"I guess so. In the beginning of our relationship it was okay, but then once the ring went on my finger he changed. Out went the romance and flowers. Along came the booze, drugs and violence. I guess I've forgotten what love-making is."

"Sounds like he did an amazing job of messing you up. He's made you feel worthless and abused you mentally as well as physically. I give you full credit for gathering the courage to come here and attempt to regain what I call the joy of life. Love-making is the most amazing feeling with the right person, and I promise you, we *will* help you." Her brisk tone had gone, to be replaced by gentle compassion that made her seem an altogether nicer person. "However, there is one thing. You are here to be taught and not, and I repeat not, to fall in love," Angel said, sitting forward and looking Stacie directly in the eye.

"I will match you with a tutor who will help to give you confidence in both self-stimulation and also intercourse. He will not treat you like dirt, but with respect. The tutors in this place are paid by sessions and won't do the romantic build-up that you like, but I will chat with your tutor first, make him understand your feelings and relax your tension. He will treat you well and he will care for you. I have seen women in your position fall in love with their tutor, thinking he feels the same because he is caring. But he's just doing his job. And the women are inevitably disappointed."

Stacie found herself nodding. She could see how that could happen.

Angel continued more briskly. "Now, on a different note, everyone likes different things sexually and what works for one person may not work for another. If there is anything, and I mean anything, you are not happy with please say and it will be stopped instantly. You're not here to be unhappy or feel as if you have to do anything. Your happiness and satisfaction is paramount to us.

Let Desires bring back your life, fun, love and enjoyment of being who you are. It's Stacie-time now."

Angel then reached in her top desk drawer. "Here is our contract," she said, pushing some papers across the desk toward Stacie. Stacie stood up and moved forward to take them from her, glancing over the paper as Angel continued speaking.

"You'll note the clause stating no emotional involvement with your tutor or tutors. This is strictly forbidden. They are here to teach you only. You sign here…" Angel said, pointing on the contract where to sign.

Stacie skimmed the contract, sipping her wine, and then sat back on the edge of the sofa.

"The prices are listed on the second sheet. You can decide whether to book a whole course in one go, or book individual sessions. There is a discount for block bookings, but I expect you'll want to see how it goes first of all. See how you feel later once you've met your tutor. I have put on your sheet that you need to start from scratch, which includes masturbation. Is that okay with you?"

Stacie swallowed the mouthful of wine she'd just taken, nodding convulsively. It was all so…business-like.

"It also states there will be no secret meetings with any of your tutors. Anything said outside could lead to court action. Payment is either up front or you can set up an account, which one of the girls can take you through later if you prefer. All equipment and all relevant instruments must be left on these premises unless you have permission from your tutor to have them. All items need to be signed out. Does that seem fair to you?"

"Totally." *Equipment? Relevant instruments?* She hadn't realized there was going to be homework! Stacie suppressed a hysterical giggle.

Angel stood up and walked toward the door. "I'll just let you have a look through those. I'll be back in a moment." She left and Stacie leaned back on the squashy sofa for a minute, feeling somewhat stunned. She read through the contract and glanced over the price list. It wasn't cheap, but it would be worth it. If she did as Angel suggested and just did individual sessions to begin with, there was no commitment. She could just stop coming if it wasn't working for her. She levered herself up off the sofa and walked over to Angel's desk, contract in hand. She exhaled slowly and then quickly picked up Angel's pen and scribbled her name on the dotted line. She left the contract on the desk, but kept hold of the price list. A minute later Angel came back, smiling when she saw the signed contract.

"Welcome to the Desires family. I'm so happy to have you with us."

*And my money*, Stacie thought but said nothing.

"Okay. I'll talk to you briefly about what you will encounter and then I'll assign you your tutor. Firstly, you need help and guidance with understanding your body sexually and finding your way around it. You will learn your own likes and dislikes, how your body works, your turn-ons and turn-offs and, most importantly, your tutor will help you gain confidence. Each time you achieve a goal, you and your tutor will make the decision on the next stage."

Stacey just nodded.

"If there's anything you feel unsure about, just tell your tutor and he will advise or talk you through anything you don't understand. Any questions?"

Overwhelmed with the information she'd been given, Stacie couldn't think of anything to ask. "No, not at the moment."

"Well if you think of anything please do not hesitate to ask either myself or your tutor…"

As Angel was speaking, something popped into Stacie's mind. "Will I be treated like a whore?"

"Absolutely not. Well, not unless you want to be."

"Want to be! Why would anyone want that?"

"As I said, everyone likes different things. But from what you've said that's not your thing. Your tutor will look after you through your journey here at Desires and make sure you get the best treatment," Angel reassured her.

"What if I don't like my tutor?"

"You will, trust me. But if you don't, I'll assign you someone else. Here's an information booklet I need you to read. It's just some information about the building and where the fire escapes are, that sort of thing. Health and safety, you know. I'll leave you for a few minutes while I talk to your tutor. I will give him your details and make sure the room is ready," Angel said. She stood up and headed for the door, pausing to give Stacie a reassuring smile before leaving the room.

Stacie skimmed through the booklet, taking in the salient information before putting it to one side.

Indulging her curiosity, she wandered over to the bookshelves, glancing at a few of the books. She shouldn't have been surprised to see they were variations on a theme. There was one on bondage, one devoted to masturbation, and one about sex positions. She opened the sex positions book, leafing through the pages. Every page was a full-colour photograph depicting men and women in various coital positions. And they weren't just couples either. There was one woman being penetrated by three different men in three different orifices. On another page, a man was penetrating a woman while he himself was being penetrated by another man. Shocked and embarrassed, she put the book back.

Stacie trailed her finger along the long line of books about every possible aspect of the sexual act, from basic anatomy to fetishes she'd never heard of. The club was into serious business.

She sat back down on the edge of the sofa waiting for Angel to come back. At least she wouldn't have to get into any of the weird stuff. *Just simple nice sex, with, hopefully, a nice caring man.*

Angel swept back into the office. Stacie had to admire her. She bet Angel never had a problem speaking her mind, or telling someone they were wrong, unlike Stacie. Maybe one day she would have an ounce of the confidence Angel seemed to ooze.

"I've met with your tutor," she was saying as she rested her curvaceous bottom on the edge of her desk. Stacie snapped her awareness back to Angel. "He's called Dan and he's twenty-three years old."

*Twenty-three?*

"Is there a problem?" Angel said, a look of concern flitting across her face.

"Don't you think he's too young?"

"No, not at all. He's exactly what you need. Dan's not your typical young immature man. If you have a problem with him, I will select someone else. But I wouldn't worry. Dan is perfect for you. Trust me."

There was that phrase again. *Trust me.* Stacie wasn't convinced. Surely someone her own age, or older, would be more appropriate to teach her, not some kid eight years younger than her.

"Are you ready to meet him?" Angel said, standing up and walking toward the door.

"I guess."

"You don't sound keen." Angel turned back.

"Sorry…I'm just concerned."

"Don't worry. If you don't like Dan, I can assign you someone else, or you can just leave. I won't tie you down. Unless you want me to." Angel waggled her eyebrows and Stacie couldn't help but smile.

Stacie inhaled a deep breath, and stood up on wobbly legs. Angel held the door open for her and they went back out into the corridor.

Stacie's imagination took over. Images of what her twenty-three-year-old tutor might look like filled her mind. He could be ugly, covered in tattoos, piercings, have weird hair or those stretched ears. Perhaps the fire exit might be the better option. And now she knew where they were, thanks to the health and safety booklet.

They headed back to the reception area and up one of the staircases. Stacie glanced down at the receptionist who smiled at her encouragingly. At the top of the stairs, there was a long corridor with many doors off it. Angel headed off briskly down the carpeted passageway. There was a chair outside each door. More explicit pictures decorated the walls with small wall lights highlighting them. There were no other lights in the corridor so the effect was warm and calming. Halfway down the corridor there was a statue of a couple embracing. The man's hands caressed the woman's breasts. One of her hands surrounded his impressive cock while the other was twined round his neck.

Stacie was staring at the pictures so intently she didn't notice Angel come to a halt, and bumped into her.

"You okay?" Angel asked.

"Sorry, just admiring the artwork." Stacie felt her face flush, but Angel just smiled.

"No problem. Are you ready?"

"I guess so," she said. Her mouth felt dry and her heart beat so loud, she felt sure Angel could hear it.

Angel opened the door for her then called, "Dan."

"Hello," Stacie heard a male voice answer. His voice sounded sweet, not too deep.

"Dan, I would like you to meet your new client, Stacie," Angel said.

Stacie moved closer to the door as it opened wider from the inside. The most beautiful, for there was no other word for him, and so very young man stood before her, with a smile so sweet and gentle her knees crumbled. Her body quivered at the sight of him. She felt embarrassed that she had worried about what he might look like, her embarrassment quickly replaced with worry over what he might think of her. What would such a stunning young Adonis think of having to service a distinctly average and ordinary woman like her whose bits had already started to head south?

Stacie tried to return Dan's welcoming smile, but she knew it lacked conviction.

Angel continued the introduction. "Stacie, this is Dan, your tutor. I think you'll be happy, but if you have any concerns, you know where I am." Stacie only vaguely registered Angel's words. She was lost in Dan's eyes.

Stacie entered the room, holding her head low. She felt like such a fool. What had she been thinking?

Angel left the room without another word. The door closed quietly behind her. Stacie tried to look anywhere except at Dan.

"Hi," he said easily. She glanced at him, making eye contact for as brief a moment as possible. He was perfect in every way possible. He wore black jeans and an open-necked purple shirt. His hair was such a dark brown as to be almost black. It had a little unruly curl to it, making Stacie want to wind those silky curls round her fingers. He had warm brown eyes, and pouty, sexy lips. He was lean in build, about eleven stone and about six foot tall.

Stacie couldn't believe her luck. However, the memory that this angelic-looking young man had to teach her how to masturbate elbowed its way back into her conscious mind. Her face felt as if someone were blasting a blowtorch at her and she turned away to hide her cherry-red cheeks.

A few seconds went by and in the utter silence that fell between them, she heard the faint sound of him moving toward her. She kept her eyes downturned and shivered when she realised he was so close she could almost feel his body heat. He'd come round to face her—she could see his feet. She forced herself to look up at him, seeing only happy welcome in his gentle smile, not a trace of the half-hidden disappointment, resignation, or even revulsion she had feared she would see. He was a very good actor. Then she braced for impact as he came toward her and landed a gentle kiss on first one cheek, then the other. He smelled of chocolate and spices.

"It's fantastic to meet you."

Stacie's mouth was bone dry as she tried to speak. "Nice to meet you too," she managed to croak. "Could I possibly have a glass of water?"

"Of course." He stepped away—Stacie felt both relief at the cessation of his disturbing nearness, and a keen sense of loss at his absence—and went to a small table on which stood a jug of water and two glasses. He poured her a glass and brought it to her and the relief she felt on his return shocked her. For heaven's sake, he had only gone across the room. Gathering together her courage, she made eye contact and smiled at him as she took a sip. He smiled back. Then she started as he moved suddenly away from her toward the bed.

"I'll show you round the room, if you like," he said, not waiting for her to agree. He pointed to two large red round buttons situated on either side of the bed. "These are panic buttons. If, by any remote chance, you need urgent help, they will alert reception."

Stacie couldn't imagine under what circumstances she would need a panic button. It wasn't like he was going to rape her. But, once there, the thought persisted and uneasiness crept in. What might happen in here that would necessitate the installation of panic buttons? He opened the top drawer of a large dresser by the window.

"There is a phone in here." He pulled it out to show her. "You can ring zero for reception or two for the kitchen. There's also a menu for food and beverages if needed," he went on, pulling them out of the drawer to show her.

Stacie gazed around the dazzling room. The large four-poster bed dominated. It was adorned with a deep purple duvet, shot through with black and gold. Matching cushions were arranged on the bed, and the canopy above was hung with purple and gold voiles. Heavier purple curtains hung at the large window. There were two black leather tub chairs with a small table between them, and buttery-gold wallpaper completed the look. There was no ceiling light. Instead, the room was illuminated by several wall lights which were dimmed to a cosy level. The aroma of vanilla permeated the room, presumably from the bowl of pot pourri on the table.

He continued. "There are two large wardrobes if you decide to book one of the weekend packages," he said. Her gaze obediently followed where he pointed, and she cast her eyes over the wardrobes, which matched the lovely old oak of the antique dresser.

Dan moved to a door to the far right. Stacie followed him, noticing his cute, perfectly-shaped bottom enticingly encased in the black denim.

"The en-suite is through here and again there is a panic button," he said, opening the door and allowing Stacie to step in before him.

The bathroom was spacious with a large Jacuzzi and a shower big enough to take several people. *Now where did that thought come from?* Stacie was shocked at herself and forced her thoughts back to a civilized level. The room was decorated with cream patterned tiles and earth-toned stone floor tiles. Soft luxurious cream towels were piled on a side table and candles were placed strategically around the room.

She followed him back out into the bedroom and Dan led the way to the seating area. He sat down in one of the tub chairs and indicated the other. "Please, take a seat."

She sat down and turned her attention to Dan sitting directly opposite her. She tried her best to meet his direct gaze, but his eyes overpowered her. She gulped, and turned her head away, suddenly very, very uncertain.

"Angel told me you need to start with the basics."

Stacie looked down at the floor in embarrassment, her cheeks flaming.

"When was the last time you masturbated?"

"I don't know. Maybe five years ago," she said miserably.

"Five years?" His perfectly-shaped eyebrows flew up. *Did he wax them?*

She felt such a fool, babbling in her haste to try to explain. "My husband didn't like me to pleasure myself. He thought women masturbating was insulting. He wanted to do it all." *Not that he ever managed to.* "So I never...did that...when we were married. And since my marriage ended, I dedicated myself to my work. I work overtime as much as possible and spend my time off doing housework or visiting family."

"So you hardly make any time for yourself?"

Stacie tried to look at him without blushing. The furnace flaring in her cheeks told her she had failed. "No. It didn't really seem important."

Dan thought for a few minutes. "I have a few options here for you. Stacie, what your husband did to you was disgraceful and has left you in shreds. You are my client and you are paying for me to help you. Think of me more like a therapist than anything else. You will take the lead in everything we do. I might make suggestions, but the end decision is up to you. For now, we can either talk for a while and get to know each other a little, to build up your trust in me, or we can get down to business straightaway. It's entirely up to you. I am yours to command." He smiled and spread his hands out.

Stacie gazed at him, liking what she heard. *Therapist, hmm?* That sounded a bit better than anything else she could think of to describe his role. She focussed on her handbag where she had left it on the floor, wondering how much *therapy* she could afford.

"What would happen if I said let's begin now?" she asked in a small voice, still staring at her handbag.

"What I was thinking, and I want to run this all by you, was that we would go back to the complete beginning. You would learn to touch yourself, stimulating your senses and enjoying your body, not being ashamed of it."

She inhaled deeply, trying to listen to her heart. Stacie still felt acutely anxious about the whole experience. But she reminded herself of the final stimulus that had made her send that email—a hysterically giggly conversation between her work colleagues recently, sparked by a sexual survey in some women's magazine someone had brought in. She'd listened to them burbling about their sexual acts both with and without their partners and she'd realized her sexual organs had been made redundant. That was why she was here. Yes, it was deeply embarrassing, but going to the doctor was embarrassing and if this young man, no matter how gorgeous he was, thought he could help her, then…

"Where would you begin?" she said, suddenly eager.

"That's up to you. On your notes you said you liked your breasts being touched, maybe…totally up to you…but maybe we could begin there," he said.

Stacie panicked. "You would see me?"

"That's for you to decide. It would be better if I did, but it's your choice, Stacie," he said.

Stacie's sudden bravado fled. "May I use the bathroom?"

"Of course."

Not wasting a second she headed into the stunning en-suite. She closed the door and pressed her back against it, feeling a total wreck.

Her head filled with concerns. She was wavering, not altogether sure of the right thing to do. Her breathing became rapid and panicky. She pushed herself off the door and sat down on the closed toilet lid, taking deep breaths to try to calm herself.

"Come on Stacie, sort yourself out. Yes, he's gorgeous, nothing like you expected, but you're paying for the session with him. This is a sex club. What did you expect?" she muttered to herself, keeping her voice low. She didn't want him to hear her talking to herself. He probably already thought she was enough of a fruit loop.

Stacie headed over to the sink and stared at her own petrified face in the mirror.

"Right, girl." She glared at herself right in the eye. "You've come here to get help. You either walk and be boring and alone for the rest of your life, or you have that nice young man out there teach you." She gazed back at the bathroom door, with Dan the other side of it. Acid panic splashed about in her stomach, and a lump the size of Everest rose in her throat, but she knew what she had to do.

Stacie opened the bathroom door and stepped out. Dan still sat in the same place. He looked at her with a question written clearly on his face. She smiled and his face relaxed. He grinned back.

Dan watched Stacie make her way to the bed. She removed her jacket and sat down, wearing just her too-high blouse and too-long skirt. He stood up and walked toward her. "Are you sure?" he said.

"I am. Let's do it."

He pulled out the stool from under the dresser and sat down.

"Put out your arm," he instructed her.

Stacie gazed at him, feeling like an idiot. She did what he asked, however, and held out her arm. "Now, lightly place your fingertips along your arm and feel the sensitivity." Stacie did so, drawing her fingernails along her skin.

"How does that feel?" he said to her.

"It tickles."

"Did you like it?"

"Yes." She looked into his deep brown eyes.

"Good. We can begin there. I want you to lightly touch yourself across your hips, waist, thighs, and your breasts."

Another surge of embarrassment flooded her face. God, she was going to have to get over this.

"Are you okay?" he said.

"It's just weird."

"How so?"

"Having another man look at me."

"Don't think of me as a man. Think of me as a professional. I'm here to help you achieve your goal." He paused and his eyes flicked over her body. "You've nothing to be ashamed about, you know. You look great, you've just got a little side-tracked in your life and forgotten about number one."

Stacie jumped as he rose up from his chair and came toward her, but he just sat down beside her on the bed and took her hand.

"Look, I do understand what you're thinking, but I really want to help you. I want you to be confident about yourself and enjoy who you are. Don't allow your ex to win, Stacie. You are a very attractive woman who needs help in regaining her self-esteem, and I am more than happy to get you back on track."

*Oh my God...how sweet are you?*

She knew he was right and her ex had wasted her life, but she struggled to believe the words he said. Did it matter if he was lying about her being attractive? Did it matter if he was just saying it to make her feel better about herself? That was his job, right? And he was just doing it.

"Do you feel you can begin?" she heard him say.

Stacie glanced into his eyes, seeing them filled with concern. For her? Or for potentially losing a client?

*I can't allow this chance to slip away.* Her heart pounded as she gave a tiny little nod of assent, wondering what the gorgeous Dan was going to do with her. He smiled, a big wide happy smile and stood up. Stacie grinned back slightly hysterically, feeling more sorry for him having to tutor her. *I hope I'm not going to be his worst client.*

"Right, let's begin."

He sat back down on the stool opposite her but pulled it closer, so their knees touched.

"Close your eyes, Stacie," he said softly.

Stacie closed her eyes tightly and awaited further instructions.

"Place your hands on your tummy and slowly move your hands around your body."

She obeyed, moving her hands gradually across her stomach and gliding them toward her waist. A crop of goosebumps spread out over her skin under the thin short-sleeved blouse, and she shivered. She kept her breathing steady, allowing her own touch to relax her. She slid both hands down over her thighs and back up again.

Stacie glided her fingertips over her naked arms, the sensation sending quivers throughout her body. Her tension trickled away, her shoulders dropped and her breathing slowed down. Stacie felt her inner vaginal muscles tighten of their own volition.

She began to move her hands more quickly over her body.

"No, Stacie, take it slowly and enjoy the sensation," she heard him say in a quiet voice.

She listened to his command, placing her hands back on her tummy to knead the area. The lower part of her body jiggled with pleasure. How could she be turned on just by touching her own stomach and arms?

"Where would you like to touch yourself next?"

*My breasts*, was her immediate thought. *Here it is. Can I really play with my own breasts in front of a total stranger?*

*Pretend he's not there,* she advised herself. *But he is,* she argued back. In the end, her hands, despairing of her pathetic indecisive brain, decided the matter and headed north by themselves. One brush of her fingers against her sensitive nipples and she wondered why she'd ever doubted Dan. Her breasts were swollen and responsive. She let out a tiny involuntary noise as she cupped both breasts together, squeezing them, sending pulses running around her body like shockwaves. An image came into her head of Dan moving behind her, taking over, touching her, fondling her. The thought shocked her to the extent that she almost stopped, but after a second, decided to go with the fantasy. Fantasy Dan placed his hands on either side of her waist, sliding them across her stomach and up to her breasts. He caressed her breasts and lifted them up, rubbing his thumbs over them.

Then she nearly jumped ten feet in the air when she felt real, warm, man's hands on her waist. "Keep your eyes closed," she heard him say. She felt Dan's fingers stroke her waist through her blouse, then his fingers moved away. She almost protested, but then she felt him start to unfasten the buttons of her blouse. Her own fingers froze.

"Are you okay with this?" he said, pausing.

*Am I?* Stacie wasn't sure, but her head nodded all by itself and Dan continued with the buttons. Her only thought then was that she wished she'd worn a sexier bra, but then she'd thought she was coming here for an appointment. She hadn't expected to start straightaway. The blouse slithered off her shoulders and she wondered if Dan would take off her bra also. Dread and hope warred within her, and the disappointment when he made no move to do so cut deep.

Stacie kept her rhythm, moving her fingertips over her lace-encased flesh, the sensations even more intense through one less layer of material. Her nipples poked hard through the bra cup and she tweaked them between her fingertips. She found herself grinding into the bed, pussy twitching, whilst her fingertips ran over her ultra-sensitive skin.

She wished Dan would come back. She wanted to feel those warm hands on her again. She half-opened her mouth to ask him, then chickened out.

But there was no stopping her fantasies. Her mind ran crazy, as she continued to touch and knead and caress her breasts. She heard Dan moving away from the edge of his stool and her heart almost leapt out of her throat. Stacie held her breath.

She felt him move behind her on the bed. *Touch me!* her mind screamed. She felt his hands on her back, unclasping her bra. Stacie moved her hands from her breasts, allowing the bra to drop onto her lap. *Now. Touch me now!* She leaned back into him, feeling the heat of his body behind her. But he still made no move to touch her so she seized her own breasts, imagining him lowering her to the bed and taking her. She floated her fingertips over her aroused nipples sending white-hot sensations bolting around her body. She pinched harder, the pain pleasurable. Her pussy throbbed almost unbearably, seemingly on a direct link from her breasts.

She couldn't stop one hand from dropping to her pussy, rubbing wildly through her skirt. Instantly, her body was overwhelmed with arousal. She lunged her hips forward, shuddering with eruption. Stacie ground her lower pelvis against her hand whilst pinching her nipple with the other. Her hips lunged high off the bed and sweat prickled over her body. Her entire body was on fire and out of control.

Stacie let out a shuddering exhale as the peak died away and she flopped back against Dan, trying hard to catch her breath. She felt her racing heartbeat begin to slow.

She felt Dan's hands patting her upper arms, then he put her forward slightly and moved away from behind her. Stacie could hear him rummaging around. She lay on her side, taking deep breaths to calm her body down. With reluctance, she opened her eyes, staring directly in front of her. How could she look at him?

"I think you need this." Dan sat back down on the little stool opposite the bed and passed her some water. "How was that?"

Stacie took the glass from him. She had a sip of the water, and let her gaze flick briefly to his before resting on the floor again. There was no repugnance on his face, no ridicule, just a soft, happy smile.

"It was amazing. It blew me away." Stacie found her embarrassment draining.

"Good. You did really well."

## Chapter Two

Stacie hadn't slept a wink. Her mind churned with thoughts of last night, and Dan.

Stacie stared at the phone. Should she call the club? Impulsively she picked it up, then tossed it back on the bed and threw her head back on her pillow. Thoughts of last night once more filled her mind and she sat back up. The phone drew her eye again, sitting innocently, and yet enticingly on the bedside table. "Oh God, what am I doing?"

She grabbed the phone as if it might suddenly disappear, found the number for Desires and pressed the call button, only to stop the call as soon as it had begun to ring.

"Come on, Stacie, sort yourself out…do it…call the damn place," she chastised herself, frustrated with her own indecisiveness.

She dialled again and waited for the reply.

"Desires, how may I help you?" said a young female voice.

"Hi…sorry…I was wondering…I was at the club last night and well…I had my first session. And I was wondering if I could book again?"

"Of course. Could I have your name and identity code?" Stacie gave the receptionist the information. "You were with Dan?"

"Yes. Do you know when the next session would be?"

"I'll just check his schedule for you," the woman told her. Stacie anxiously waited for her answer. "Well, he's not down for working at the club tonight…" she began.

"Oh," Stacie blurted, disappointed.

"But I could call him to see if he can come in to see you," the woman said.

"Okay. It isn't urgent or anything."

"It's not a problem. I'm sure he'll be happy to see you if he can. What did you have in mind?"

Stacie paused. She wanted more than just a quickie. She wanted to spend time with him, get to know him. "How much would it cost from dinner this evening through to lunchtime tomorrow?"

"I will just check for you."

Stacie wasn't entirely sure if she was doing the right thing, but she knew if she walked away from the club that would be it. She would slip back into her boring life and be alone and never have the confidence to do anything.

"That would be eight hundred pounds."

"Pardon?" Stacie knew it would be expensive but eight hundred…?

"Eight hundred pounds," the receptionist obligingly repeated.

Stacie was suddenly unsure. It was a *lot* of money.

"Are you still there, Miss Clifford?"

"Sorry…just thinking. Just…just give me a moment." Stacie considered her options. She had the money. She'd got a decent chunk from the divorce settlement and she'd been working shedloads of overtime this last year with very little time to spend it. *Just do it!*

"Okay, I'd like to book that please, if Dan's available."

"No problem," the receptionist replied. "I will call Dan, and get back to you as soon as possible, Miss Clifford."

Stacie made herself go into the kitchen and make a cup of coffee. Sitting by the phone waiting for it to ring was a little bit sad.

It rang just as she was pouring the hot water into the mug. She dashed into the bedroom and threw herself across the bed to pick it up before it stopped. "Hello, Stacie Clifford," she answered breathlessly.

"Hello, Miss Clifford, it's Shannon at Desires here. I have spoken to Dan, and he's available for you in two hours."

"That soon?" Stacie was shocked.

"Would you like me to call him and make it later?"

"No…that'll be fine," Stacie said, suddenly excited to see Dan sooner than she had thought.

"When you arrive, you can use your identity code to gain access to the building, now you're a member. If that's everything, Miss Clifford, we will see you soon."

Two hours! Stacie didn't have much time to get ready. She jumped in the shower and scrubbed herself clean. She blow dried her hair then straightened it. Make-up could wait till she got back. She had to buy some new underwear and clothes. It was surprising how one evening had made her totally rethink her dress sense. She had to get some sexier bras. She threw on some clothes, downed her now-cold coffee with a grimace and grabbed a cereal bar for breakfast, before heading out to the shops.

She picked up a couple of matching lingerie sets, one in classic red and black, and one encrusted with diamantés. It looked like it might be a little scratchy, but the effect was stunning.

She dithered over the 'right' sort of clothes for a while. Angel had said she hid all her best assets. Her skirt had been too long and her blouse too high. She didn't want to go too far the other way, but perhaps she could show off a little more. She found a flippy little red skater skirt which hung to just above the knee and accentuated her waist whilst hiding her little belly. She'd never thought of herself as fat, but Graham had used to poke her tummy and call it her "beer belly". He used to wobble it and yell, "FAAAAAAT," as she lay in bed. And, if she got upset, he'd turn over in a huff and say he was only joking and she needed to get a sense of humour transplant.

She found a close-fitting black top with cap sleeves and a sweetheart neckline that showed a little more boob than the tops she usually wore, especially with her new push-'em-up-and-squash-'em-together bras.

She looked at stockings in the hosiery department, but lost her nerve at the last second. Maybe she could do stockings another time.

Stacie headed back to her rented one-bedroom, second floor flat. The décor was typical of a rented flat, white bathroom, and the open-plan living, dining and kitchen area painted uniformly magnolia, as was her plain bedroom. Dull, dull, dull, unlike the sumptuous rooms at Desires.

Stacie dashed into the bedroom and quickly applied some make-up before pulling on her new outfit. She twirled in the mirror. She actually looked pretty good. It was a long time since she had taken so much care in getting ready for a man.

At the beginning of their marriage she used to get dressed up for Graham on the rare occasions they went out, but when she came downstairs looking pretty, his lip would curl. He'd mutter something about mutton dressed as lamb, and he didn't know who she thought she was trying to impress. One memorable time, he'd gone to the toilet and a man had come over to talk to her. She'd been polite but when Graham came out and saw her smiling at this other man, he had gone ballistic. He'd taken her home and accused her of sleeping with him. When she stuttered that he only asked her the time, he grabbed her by the neck and pushed her up against the wall. How dare she lie to him? She was a slut, a whore. Just look at the way she was dressed. She'd obviously encouraged this man. It was clear she was up for the taking. Then he dragged her upstairs and…well, she didn't like to think of what he'd done to her. It was his right, as her husband. He'd told her that afterward.

She'd never dressed up for him after that.

Stacie pushed the disturbing memories from her head and concentrated on the future, on her forthcoming time with Dan. But her happy thoughts were marred by the memory of what Angel said to her. "No feelings for your tutor…"

Confused, Stacie examined her feelings. Dan was a nice young man and she had enjoyed spending time with him. It was no more than that. It was normal to have some sort of feelings surely. How could she not have some form of feelings for a man she was showing her body to? It wasn't as if she was going to spend time with someone she disliked.

She packed a few changes of clothing and some toiletries into her small overnight case. Forget Angel. She would have a fantastic day and evening with Dan. Excitement fluttered in her belly as she wondered what his next session would involve. After her initial embarrassment, she was stunned to realize how much she had enjoyed the previous session. She was ready for more.

Stacie threw her bag in the car and drove to Desires. She parked her car and regarded the old Georgian building. Once more a tiny niggle of doubt lurked in the corner of her mind, but she squashed it. *Come on, girl, we're over this now.* She climbed out the car and grabbed her handbag from the back seat, deciding to leave the case in the car.

It was another cold day and she quickly made her way to the main entrance, digging out her phone for the identity code. She punched it in and the door released. Her steps more confident than yesterday, she walked down to the reception area.

A different receptionist greeted Stacie. This one had short dark hair, black-framed glasses similar to Angel's, and wore a pinstripe suit. "Good afternoon, Stacie, how are you today?"

After a surprised moment that the receptionist knew her name, Stacie realized the identity code on the intercom must be linked to the computer. She smiled. "Fine, thank you." The receptionist discreetly handed her a piece of paper, which she realized was an invoice.

The credit card transaction was completed quickly. "Dan will be ready for you shortly. Would you like to take a seat?" the receptionist said, giving Stacie her receipt and card back. Stacie sat on the leather couch and waited, her knee jiggling impatiently.

It seemed like forever, but was probably only a few minutes later when the receptionist said, "Miss Clifford? Dan's ready for you."

"Thank you," Stacie said, leaping to her feet and picking up her bag.

"It's the same room as last night. Do you remember your way?" the receptionist asked with a smile at Stacie's eagerness.

"Yes...Yes I do, thank you," Stacie told her, trying not to run to the staircase.

"Have fun," she heard the receptionist say. Stacie decided not to comment.

Stacie made her way up the fabulous staircase. Her heart raced and her tummy knotted. Was it nerves or excitement? She arrived at the first floor and looked down the corridor. Dan was waiting for her at the door. He smiled when he saw her. "Here we go," she murmured to herself, before plastering on a smile that was mostly genuine and making her way toward him.

Halfway down the corridor, another door opened. A woman stepping out wearing a robe, looking as if she'd had a bad night, or at least an eventful one. She looked rough and her makeup was smudged.

"Afternoon," the woman said, approaching Stacie. She staggered and lost her balance, almost falling on top of Stacie. The woman's breath smelled fusty at such close quarters and Stacie recoiled.

"Afternoon," she replied, hesitantly.

Stacie turned to watch the woman walking down the corridor, losing her footing as she went. She shook her head and turned back to where Dan was waiting for her when a sound from behind her drew her attention again. Stacie turned back around to see the woman had walked into the naked statue. She stifled a semi-horrified giggle then continued quickly to where Dan waited patiently.

"Hello Stacie," he said, taking a few steps to close the distance between them. He leaned forward to give her a kiss on the cheek, placing his hands briefly on her waist as he did so. She inhaled his delicious chocolaty smell.

"Hi," she said back. They walked to the door together and he held back to allow her to enter first. The smell of fresh flowers greeted her as she walked in. It came from a large colourful bouquet arranged attractively in a vase which sat on the small coffee table, along with a basket of fruit and a chilled bottle of Cava in an ice bucket.

"I thought you might like a drink as you've booked to stay overnight. My treat."

Stacie turned to look at him. He was sporting the lumberjack look today, wearing a red and white checked shirt, which hung open, showing off his lean yet muscular chest and his youthful six-pack. His faded blue jeans sat just below his waist showing a Calvin Klein waistband. He hadn't shaved but instead of looking unkempt, his stubble made him look sexier than ever, and a little dangerous. She never usually went for the rough look, but with Dan she could definitely be persuaded.

"How are you feeling today? You look amazing," he said as he closed the door.

"I'm feeling pretty good actually, considering how nervous I was yesterday."

"That's great. It's pretty normal to be nervous though, don't worry."

His tone was authoritative and Stacie wondered for a brief second how he knew, before she realized he had probably done this before, with other women. The thought disturbed her. *Jealous, Stacie? This is a man who is paid to have sex with women. He's not your boyfriend. Get over it.*

"So you have me booked until lunch tomorrow," he was saying when she dragged her thoughts away from the worrying turn they had taken.

"That's okay, isn't it?"

"Of course it is."

*Of course it is, Stacie. You're paying him.*

Trying to calm her tumultuous thoughts, Stacie walked over to the small table and pulled a grape off the bunch. She popped it in her mouth and placed her handbag on the floor.

Dan walked across the room and pulled out the stool again, placing it to face the bed, in the same position as before.

"So, how did you find last night?" he asked.

"Interesting. But nice," she said, glancing at him to see his reaction.

"Good. What I thought we could do this session is move a little further on."

*How much further?* Stacie wanted to ask, but her mouth wouldn't work.

"When you are ready, I'd like you to sit on the bed like yesterday."

Stacie removed her coat and draped it over the back of one of the chairs, then walked over to the bed and sat, positioning her knees between his thighs. Not as nervous as yesterday, she found it easier to make direct eye contact with those stunning chocolaty eyes. He placed his hands on her knees and she shivered.

"Are you feeling anxious?" he asked.

"A little."

"Why?"

"I don't know."

"You're in charge, remember. Anything you don't like, we stop instantly."

Stacie nodded, barely listening, watching his mouth move as he spoke, wanting to taste those full lips, wanting to...*oh, he was talking again!*

"We're going to do the same as last night only this time you're going to get hotter."

*How much hotter? I want to shag you. Can I shag you?*

He pushed her skater skirt up to reveal her bare thighs. "I want you to close your eyes and stroke between your inner thighs, but don't touch your pussy." Stacie obediently closed her eyes tight and began to stroke up and down her own thighs. She relaxed, enjoying the tickling, tingling sensations. Her pussy tightened but she obeyed his restriction, enjoying the feeling of anticipation she was giving herself by delaying.

Then the sound of a mobile phone startled her.

"Damn," she heard Dan say as he stood up abruptly. "I am so sorry, Stacie." She opened her eyes and watched him get his phone from the pocket of his coat, which hung on the back of the door.

"Sorry. I'm supposed to have it turned off—I forgot." He chuckled as he looked at the display. "It's my mate sending me a rude text. Would you like to hear it?"

Stacie smiled. "Go on."

"There's a guy in hospital with sixty percent burns. The doctor says, 'Give him two viagras.' The nurse asks, 'Do you think it will help?' Doctor replies, 'No, but it'll keep the sheets off his legs.'" Stacie burst out laughing.

Almost immediately, the phone bleeped again.

"I am so sorry about this," he said. "I'll turn it off straightaway." He checked the phone first, then chortled. "You'll like this one though," he told her. "A couple just got married and on the night of their honeymoon before they made love, the wife tells the husband, 'Please be gentle, I'm still a virgin.' The husband was shocked and replied, 'How is this possible? You've been married three times before.' The wife responds, 'Well, my first husband was a gynaecologist and all he wanted to do was look at it. My second husband was a psychiatrist and all he wanted to do was talk about it. And my third husband was a stamp collector...oh, do I miss him!'"

Stacie giggled. If he'd told her those jokes last night she wouldn't have laughed, but found them vulgar. She remembered way back in the dim distant past when she'd found dirty jokes funny too. But Graham didn't like them. He thought they were crude and crass. His attitude had made her question her own. Without noticing it, she'd turned into a prude.

"I've turned it off, so we won't be disturbed again," he said and put the phone back in his coat pocket. He came back over to the stool and sat down, taking her hands in his. "Where were we?"

Stacie gazed deep into his eyes, seeing kindness and pleasure there. He was gorgeous, but there was much more to him than that. He was sweet and funny and genuinely seemed to care about her well-being. And she had him right through until lunch-time tomorrow. Panic spiked at the thought of leaving Dan, but she shoved it down. She was here now and determined to enjoy herself.

Dan released her hands and put his hands back onto her knees where they had been before. "Close your eyes and feel your breasts through your top."

Stacie cupped her breasts in her hands, curling her fingers and rubbing her nails lightly over her nipples which hardened and thrust out through the fabric. She pushed them together and imagined Dan lowering his face to lick them.

She felt him move closer to her, feeling his breath hot on her face. He pulled her top out of her skirt and lifted it slowly and gently up and over her head.

With the thrill of disobedience, she opened her eyes to watch him, wanting to kiss him badly, and feel his body pressing against hers. She inhaled his scent and felt her body quiver.

"Close your eyes," he reminded her, with not a hint of sternness.

She squeezed her eyes shut and relished the brush of his hands on her flesh as he exposed her to his view. Stacie inhaled deeply, pushing out her chest toward him, knowing that he had full view of her cleavage bursting out of her sparkling bra.

Stacie placed her hands back on her breasts, squeezing and kneading the soft lush flesh. Her mind filled with flickering random images. Dan kissing her, Dan touching her, Dan making love to her while she screamed in ecstasy. Her pussy quivered and she squeezed her muscles, feeling pulses shooting directly from her nipples to her core. How much longer could she wait for him to touch her?

Desperately, she moved her hands up and down her hips and waist. Then back to her breasts, squeezing them tight, feeling more eager than ever, feeling frustrated. She wanted, needed to be naked, to feel flesh against flesh.

Again Stacie felt Dan come back close to her. He wrapped his arms around her reaching for the back of the bra to unclasp it. All he had to do was lower her back against the satin cover and she would let him take her, then and there. Stacie quivered. She was ready.

The bra fell to her lap. Stacie inhaled his fragrance, wanting to reach out to touch him, aching for the feel of his hard cock in her hand, but he hadn't said she could. She reined in her temptation, instead squeezing and rubbing her naked breasts.

She felt him pull away from her and was bereft. She heard rather than saw him sit back in his seat. *Patience. Do what he says.* Stacie continued to knead, covering her nipples, not allowing him to see them. *Let him be frustrated for a change.* She held her breasts tightly, tweaking the nipples between her fingers. She thrust her pelvis forward and back to try to ease the ache within, wanting to fall back onto the bed and touch herself below, but knew he would give her the command to do so when he felt it was the right time.

Stacie looked at him from under her lashes. His eyes were focused on her, watching with great interest. She moved her fingers to reveal her nipples, wanting to lunge forward and kiss him. Stacie began to gently twist her nipples, her hyper-sensitive nerve endings sending their message straight to her pussy.

"Stand up, Stacie," she heard Dan say softly.

She opened her eyes, seeing him still sitting on the stool. Stacie rose to her feet. Dan unzipped her skirt and pulled it down over her bottom, revealing her sparkling thong.

"Now sit back down." She did so. "I want you to slowly caress around your thighs, stomach and waist without touching your genitals."

Stacie felt a twinge of annoyance. She wanted to touch herself. Nevertheless, Stacie slid her hands up and down her waist then across her tummy, feeling her body twanging with anticipation.

She moved her hands down between her smooth inner thighs, tickling the sensitive skin near her labia, wanting to move further up. Would Dan tell her off if she attempted to touch her pussy after he'd said not to? She decided to get as close as she could without actually going near. She threw herself back onto the pillows, spreading her legs, getting as close as she dared to her swollen pussy.

"I want to touch," she cried out, unable to bear it any longer.

"Not yet."

Stacie nearly sobbed with frustration, but she obeyed. She turned her attention back to her breasts, kneading and moulding them hard, causing her tender flesh to ooze out between her fingers. She thrust her hips off the bed. One hand squeezed her breast whilst the other ran wild all over her body, everywhere except the one place she was forbidden, the only place she wanted. Stacie shoved both her hands between her inner thighs and squeezed. She wasn't sure how much longer she could hold back her anticipation. She was bursting with frustration, wanting so much to touch her pussy. She wiggled her hips and waist all over the bed—needing so much to touch, but desperate to hear him allow it.

Stacie took her hands away from her body, thrusting her bottom high off the bed, begging, "Please!"

"Not yet," came the gentle command.

Stacie almost hated Dan at that moment. She felt ready to burst at her seams. She had never been so frustrated, feeling out of control and desperate to touch herself. Her heart pumped fast, her body seemed made for one purpose only—for sexual pleasure. Her pussy dripped, drowning her thong. She felt as if she would die if she didn't come right then.

"Stacie, I want you to listen to me, very carefully, but don't stop."

Dan moved closer and then whispered in her left ear, his breath tickling her hair.

"Put one hand in your thong slowly…"

Stacie widened her thighs as far as they would go. She slid her right hand down over her pubic mound and down toward her craving pussy. A great gusting exhale escaped her lips as she placed one finger within her labia, feeling her damp flesh quiver in response to her touch.

He whispered quietly in her ear. "Can you feel your pleasure?"

"Yes."

"Slowly dip your finger in," he authorised her.

Stacie did as she was told, dipping her finger between her pussy lips, feeling her heat and slickness. Her hips thrust against her hand, seemingly of their own accord.

"Don't put your finger in too much, just feel your excitement."

Her body was more aroused than it had ever been before. She slid her finger into her vagina, clenching her muscles around the digit, getting as much sensation out of it as possible.

He whispered in a very soft tone. "Take your finger in and out."

She responded to his order, holding her breath, ramming herself with her finger, feeling her juices coat it, wishing it was Dan's cock. She cried out aloud with pleasure. Every part of her body was on fire. Her hips bucked her body high off the bed. Daringly, she inserted two fingers inside her entrance—her juices flowed in delight, while her body shuddered.

His voice sounded again softly. "Take your fingers deeper."

Stacie didn't need telling twice, shoving her fingers in as far as they could go. The sensation overwhelmed her forcing her to cry out.

"Stacie, raise your bottom," he commanded her.

Stacie obeyed, then she felt Dan pulling her sodden thong down. She froze.

"It's okay, don't be shy."

After the realization that she was being ridiculous, after all, she'd just been writhing about riding her fingers in front of him, Stacie allowed him to continue.

Dan took hold of her hand and placed it on her clitoris. "I want you to find where it's most sensitive. Move two fingers lightly in a circular motion. Use your juices to keep it moist."

Stacie covered her fingers in her juices to lubricate her clitoris, feeling her heart racing whilst moving her fingers around the clit area, finding the most sensitive spot. She let out an involuntary, "Oh God!" when she found one spot that made her brain seem to explode. She began making small circular movements, at first, closing her eyes and throwing her head back as she thrust her pelvis against her hand.

She squeezed her vaginal muscles, tormenting the sensitive nerve endings while keeping the circular motion going on her clit. Her whole body became hot and sweaty. Her breathing sped up while her clit burned with sensation. She could feel it building within her. Instinctively she began to rub harder and faster.

Her head became light, her breathing quickened. She kept her fingers in motion, even when her entire body exploded. She lunged her hips high off the bed and screamed aloud, her body lifted to a whole new world. She rubbed as long as the sensation lasted, wave after wave of elation filling her. It seemed as if it would never end before finally the waves began to ebb and she dropped her body back to the bed, exhausted.

"Breathe, Stacie," Dan said.

"Wow," Stacie managed, on a breath. She closed her eyes and felt her body relax into the bed, utterly enervated. She touched her clit, and flinched away. It was bursting with so much sensitivity that it was now actually painful to touch. She had never felt so satisfied before. She couldn't even remember having such a feeling with Graham.

"I'll be back in a minute," Dan told her.

She felt him move away and opened her eyes to see him disappearing into the bathroom.

Stacie stayed where she was. She couldn't have moved if she'd tried. Her body was totally drained of all desire to do anything except sink into the mattress and sleep for a million years. She'd forgotten how good it felt to play with her body intimately. What had she been doing all those years? She hated Graham for doing what he had to her. He had stolen everything away from her, fun, sex, confidence, self-esteem and life. She despised him.

Stacie stretched luxuriously. Her heart-rate and breathing had started to return to normal. She rolled over onto her side and glanced at the bathroom door, thinking about Dan. He turned her on so much and that was with his clothes on. She could hardly wait to get him naked, feel his skin against hers and his cock sliding in and out of her. The thought caused her pussy to quiver again.

She closed her eyes and imagined Dan coming out, naked, his cock stiff and ready, saying how much he wanted to make love to her right now…

The bathroom door opened. She opened her eyes eagerly, but far from being naked, he was very much dressed with a slightly flustered look on his face.

"Do you fancy some lunch?" he asked.

"Yeah sure, that sounds great."

He walked over to the dresser and opened the top drawer, pulling out the phone and menu. He passed the menu to her to look at.

"I thought that we could grab something light now and have something more special later on."

Stacie perused the menu. There was a section labelled Lite Bites which listed sandwiches and wraps of various kinds. She didn't want to order anything too pungent and end up with stinky breath for him.

"I'll just have a chicken salad sandwich," she decided in the end.

"Good choice." Dan phoned their order down to the kitchen, ordering the same for himself.

"How are you feeling now?" he asked, putting the phone down on the dresser and sitting down on the end of the bed.

"Fantastic, I feel like a school girl who has just discovered her body." Stacie lay back on the pillow, trying to entice him with her eyes.

"Good. Good. So you are feeling happy about the sessions?"

Stacie rose onto her elbows grinning like a fool. "Yes I am, totally."

He smiled back at her, then got up and went over to the table, clearing the fruit basket and the vase of flowers off it, presumably for their impending food.

Stacie climbed off the bed to get a robe from the bathroom. It was a bit silly to be embarrassed about being nude. He had just watched her masturbating and dripping and screaming all over the bed. Nonetheless, she headed into the bathroom and wrapped her body in one of the soft white robes which hung from the hooks on the back of the bathroom door. She wandered over to the mirror and checked her appearance, licking her finger to rub the smudges of eyeliner from under her eyes. Her cheeks were pink and her face wore a satisfied look.

A knock at the bathroom door startled her.

"Food's here," Dan called through the door. Stacie quickly finished freshening up and came out, taking a seat at the small table as Dan placed their plates on two woven wicker placemats that hadn't been there before. *They must have been in the dresser drawer*, she decided. She watched him pop the cork on the bottle of Cava, laughing as it flew across the room.

She gazed dreamily into his gorgeous brown eyes, until he looked at her with a cock-eyed smile. Embarrassed, she flicked her gaze to one side, not wanting him to see just how attractive she found him. The Desires contract flashed through Stacie's head.

Dan poured a glass of Cava for them both, waiting for the froth to settle before topping the glasses up. Stacie took a sip, hoping it might calm her nerves. In the back of her mind, common sense put its hand up hesitantly, warning her not to have too much. She blithely ignored it. She wasn't driving. One glass wouldn't hurt.

"How are you feeling?"

"I'm great."

"Good," he said. He flashed his perfect white teeth at her—*someone's had some dental work done*—and she melted.

"So, what do you think of Desires so far?" he asked her, just as she took a mouthful of sandwich. She chewed quickly, struggling to empty her mouth while he waited for her reply.

"Well, from what I have seen so far, it's pretty incredible."

"Are you pleased with the way I am teaching you?"

"Oh, definitely yes," she replied, gazing into his eyes. "Have you been working here long?"

"I really shouldn't answer that question."

"Sorry, is that private?"

"Yes, I can talk to you about anything to do with Desires, what kind of activities there are in the building, and what sorts of services we offer to clients, although names of clients are strictly confidential, naturally."

"Naturally." *I certainly wouldn't want anyone at work to know I was coming here!*

"I can tell you about my training, but I'm afraid that my personal life is off limits."

"I understand. I just find it a little strange why a young man like you would work somewhere like Desires." Stacie could hardly believe what had just come out of her mouth. Would he be offended?

"'What's a nice boy like you doing in a place like this,' you mean?" Dan asked, smiling broadly. Stacie wriggled uncomfortably. *Is that how it had sounded?*

Dan continued, his face dropping into more serious lines. "I love sex, I enjoy everything about sex. As long as I respect my clients and myself, no one comes to any harm. I always use protection, so I can't see a problem," he replied, maintaining eye contact. "The human body is amazing. It can give such pleasure and so many women never experience that. I believe that everyone should know how to respect and use it. Sex is wonderful and special with the right person and what your ex did to you was…well, there are no words for it."

"Don't you find it degrading?" Stacie asked.

"Degrading?" Dan sat back and regarded her. "Degrading is a very strong word."

"I guess it is, but some people take sex too far."

"Too far?" He seemed to pounce on her words.

"Well, to the limits of disgracing themselves," she said, feeling uneasy at his reaction, yet determined to remain strong in her convictions.

"It all depends on the act and how they expose themselves. It doesn't mean they are bad, some people are more extravagant than others. Some people keep it strictly to the bedroom and others prefer to go out and about. It's more of a thrill to get caught out, whereas the bedroom's safe. Desires gives people the opportunity to play out their fantasies in a controlled environment, rather than out in the wild as it were. We are all different and like sex in different ways. So long as everyone's happy and no one gets hurt, it's not a problem."

"So what is Desires all about?"

"It's a very open-minded club. There's nothing legal that cannot be done within these walls. It's where your sexual fantasies come alive. And no one judges anyone."

"So, if I suggested—not that I ever would as I find it repulsive—a threesome?"

"Then that would happen."

Stacie widened her eyes, wondering if the club was the right place for her. It sounded like a freak show and she again found herself asking the question—*should I really be here?*

"So, the woman I saw coming out the room earlier, who looked rough to say the least, could've been up to anything, a threesome or maybe even more?" Stacie asked.

"She could've done anything. She's paying for a certain fantasy and she will get whatever she requests."

Stacie looked at him, shocked.

"Stacie, I am here to help you regain your confidence and self-esteem, and to teach you to enjoy your body after what your ex put you through. I want you to get your life back on track, meet new people, have fun. It doesn't matter what other people want from Desires. It only matters what you want."

"So, I only get what I request."

"Absolutely. Nothing will happen in this room that you haven't agreed to."

She smiled at him, feeling reassured and they finished their food in companionable silence. Stacie's mind wandered back to the thought she'd had earlier. What would happen if her secret came out at work?

Stacie's job was time-consuming, but through choice. When she was married to Graham, she used to make any excuse to work overtime. Since she'd left him, nothing had changed. Except now she worked to keep herself busy, not to avoid going home. She had forgotten there was more to life than working, which was another reason she'd contacted Desires. She wanted to change her lifestyle, she just wasn't sure how.

Her day was, get up, quick shower, coffee, breakfast, work till it got dark, home, maybe an hour of television, then bed. She couldn't even remember the last time she'd even had a long soak in the…

"Dan, is it okay if I have a bath?" The big Jacuzzi had suddenly flashed into her mind's eye and the thought of a nice long soak in hot bubbly water was very appealing.

"Of course, I'll run it for you."

She watched Dan stand up and walk toward the bathroom. Stacie had serious doubts about Desires. The only thing keeping her there was Dan. It was time she admitted it to herself, she had the makings of a serious crush. He was adorable. She hadn't felt this way about anyone for years. If anything she feared him, scared of what his thoughts about her were. Did he think she was pathetic and naïve?

"Your bath is ready," he told her, popping his head around the door.

Stacie entered the bathroom. Dan was standing proudly beside the steaming Jacuzzi. He had lit the candles she'd noticed before and the fragrance of vanilla filled the air.

"This is lovely."

"Good," he told her, checking the water temperature.

"Oh," she said, turning and heading back to the bedroom, rummaging in her bag for her car keys.

"What's the matter?"

"I left my overnight bag in the car."

"I'll get it," he said, snagging the keys from her hand and heading to the door.

"You don't have to," she said but he was already off, coming back quickly with the bag. Stacie pulled her clothes out of the bag, and laid them out on the bed. She set her makeup on the dresser, and then took her beauty products into the bathroom, arranging them on the side of the Jacuzzi.

The steamy room smelled of a mixture of vanilla and orange blossom, which emanated from the bubbles piling up in the Jacuzzi. She placed her hands on the sash of her robe, then hesitated, looking at Dan.

"Is everything all right?" he asked.

"It's perfect, thank you," she replied. In a rush, she slipped the robe off and let it drop to the floor, turning her back to Dan as she climbed into the bath. The temperature was perfect and she couldn't help letting out an, "Mmm," of pleasure as she slid down into the enfolding warmth. She gathered the bubbles together to hide her breasts, before daring to meet Dan's eyes. He raised his eyebrows and she felt silly for feeling embarrassed.

Dan moved closer to her and knelt at the side of the bath. He gazed deep into her eyes and then deliberately looked down at where her breasts were hidden under the cover of bubbles. His mouth was inches from hers. She could just lean forward and kiss him.

"How would you feel about playing with yourself in the bath? You could use your shower gel to soap up your breasts to start."

Stacie looked at him, stunned, and glanced at the bottle of shower gel.

*Well that wasn't quite what I had in mind.*

Stacie looked back at him. Was he waiting for her to begin? "With you watching?" she said, just to clarify.

"Yes, of course. I need to keep an eye on you. I have a feeling if I don't keep watching, as soon as my back's turned you'll forget why you're here." His tone was teasing.

The idea was intriguing. *What the heck? Why not?* She raised her upper body up and slowly brushed off the bubbles so her breasts were on show to him. They gleamed from the water, and steamed slightly as they came out into the open air. Her smooth pink nipples crinkled and shrank in protest.

She watched Dan watching her breasts. His eyes flicked up and he gave her a smile, not abashed in the slightest. This close up, she could see details in his face she hadn't noticed before. His lips were perfect and kissable, his cheekbones high and well-shaped. There was a slight scar, thin and about an inch long, on his right cheek. Stacie wondered how he had got it. His nose was elegant and his eyes looked like pools of chocolate framed by the kind of thick, dark eyelashes girls paid far too much money for. His gelled hair was styled in rough spikes and his stubble just cried out to have fingers rubbed over it. He was delicious.

She closed her eyes and dunked her head under the water, coming back up with her hair shiny and slick, plastered to her head. She felt like a mermaid. She ran her hands over her head and gazed at Dan, deliberately catching her lower lip between her teeth as she'd seen other women do. She didn't want him to just be doing his job. She wanted him to *want* her.

Dan's eyes were fixed on her. The candles in the room flickered in the damp atmosphere. Stacie took a bath puff from the side and squeezed a generous amount of shower gel onto it.

She lay back in the bath, bringing out her left leg from the water. Steam evaporated from her leg and she let Dan gaze at it for a second before leisurely applying the bath puff to her gleaming skin. She ran it down her thigh, then bent her knee, bringing her knee up to her chest and smoothing the bath puff down her calf, pointing her toe the whole time.

In her peripheral vision she could see Dan watching her keenly.

She repeated the process with her right leg, enjoying the golden glimmer the candles and water created on her limbs. The flickering light reflected tiny rainbows off the tiny bubbles sliding over her skin.

Stacie lowered her legs back into the water to rinse the soap off. Her breasts rose out of the water like iridescent islands. Her nipples were quiescent and flat. She ran the fingers of one hand around the nipple area of one breast, deliberately avoiding the nipple itself. Even though she hadn't touched it, her nipple rose and hardened in response. Dan's eyes were huge in the candlelight, fixed on her breasts. His breathing was audible in the silence. She lifted her breasts and pushed them together. Water drained away in shining rivulets.

She picked up a glass from the side of the bath. She dipped it into the water and poured it slowly over her boobs, jutting her chest out as much as possible, so the water ran over her breasts like a waterfall.

She placed the glass back and cupped her boobs in both hands, pushing them together and kneading them until her slick flesh squeezed out of the gaps between her fingers. A gasp escaped and she threw her head back. Not taking his eyes from her breasts, Dan reached for the shower gel and passed it to her. He didn't have to tell her what he wanted.

Stacie reached out to take the shower gel. Dan didn't let go, caressing her wet fingers with his before releasing the bottle. She shivered in delight at his touch then, flipping the lid open, she lay back in the bath. She held the bottle high above her chest and squeezed, watching the liquid pour out. The gel was cool as it hit her skin.

Stacie put the bottle back on the side and placed her hands where the gel had fallen at the top of her boobs. She began to spread it around, inscribing deep circles around her entire breast area, her fingers sliding on her glistening soapy flesh. She still didn't touch her nipples, eager to stretch out the anticipation. She lifted her breasts to bounce them in the water, feeling an answering thrill in her pussy. She looked at Dan, unable to read his expression. He was watching her avidly. Was his cock thick and hard within those blue jeans? She couldn't see. The panel of the bath was between them. Would this be the time he couldn't resist?

She tipped a small amount of gel into the palm of one hand, then rubbed it against the other so both palms were coated. She placed her hands directly onto her nipples, massaging in circles, feeling the buds tighten under the skin of her palms. She began to pinch and tease her nipples, letting out a little moan, looking at Dan to test his reaction.

She pushed her breasts together, creating a deep cleavage, flicking her fingers over the ultra-sensitive buds. Graham would have loved this. When it was her time of the month and he couldn't have sex with her, he would slather lube all over her boobs and give her a titty-fuck, always aiming his cum at her face to finish. It had never done anything for her, but if Dan had suggested it right now, she'd be up for it in a second. She imagined him sliding his thick cock between her breasts, her licking the salty tip on every thrust.

*Why won't he touch me?* Stacie's pussy throbbed with need.

She turned her head to her left, staring at Dan. His eyes were firmly fixed on the entertainment. Stacie smiled, seductively she hoped.

She sat up, reaching for the glass, and rinsed the shower gel off her breasts. Her nipples were erect and achingly tender. Just the feel of the water on them made her inner muscles squeeze involuntarily.

"Squeeze and twist your nipples," Dan said, his voice husky.

Desperate to obey his order, Stacie pulled hard on her nipples, clasping and twisting. The sensation sent shockwaves down to her pussy. She tugged her nipples again, making her body jerk, and cried out with pleasure. She knew without touching that her pussy would be moist and ready, begging to be filled.

She stood up in the bath, standing before him nude, water streaming off her. She imagined herself a modern-day Botticelli Venus, wishing her hair were long enough to twine round her body. In the mirrors around the room, she could see her body shining in the candlelight. She ran her hands up and down her waist then up to her breasts, taking her hands slowly over her breasts, making her rose-coloured buds send spasms down to her pussy.

Stacie placed her hand down her body, gliding them across her tummy and down to her neatly-trimmed pubic mound. The idea of having a Brazilian flitted across her mind. Graham used to try to persuade her to try one, but she'd always refused. She'd consider doing it for Dan, though. She continued, her right hand sliding between her thighs. When she touched her clitoris, pulsating with desire, Stacie wailed aloud, the delicate mound bursting with sensitivity.

She sat down on the side of the Jacuzzi facing Dan, her feet still in the water. Dan's face was expressionless, his eyes almost black in the dim light. She knew she had his full attention.

Stacie closed her thighs together, sitting straight up, keenly aware of the drop behind her. She stared at Dan. His eyes were fixed to her body. She ran her hands slowly from her knees up to her pelvis, then spread her legs and rose up onto her toes in the water unashamedly showing him her pussy. Instead of feeling embarrassed, the rush of desire and excitement robbed her of breath.

Desperate to touch her pussy, instead, Stacie took hold of her breasts, squeezing them together. She brought her right nipple up to her mouth, darting out her tongue to lick it. It tasted wet and clean. She did the same to the other breast, flicking her tongue from one nipple to the other, wishing it were Dan.

Only when she could stand it no longer did she drop her hand to her crotch. She placed her fingers onto her clit, feeling her whole body erupt. Every nerve ending jerked, sending electrifying pulses around her already twanging body. Her pussy was awash. Stacie took her two longest fingers and began circling around her clit, closing her eyes, trying her hardest to remember what Dan told her earlier.

Stacie began to rub the tiny nodule from side to side, teasing it, throwing her head back as she lost herself in the wonderful sensation. Astounding how this tiny protrusion of flesh could produce such pleasure. She rubbed harder, slitting her eyes so she could watch Dan watching her.

She dipped her fingers into her eager awaiting hole, covering her fingers in her juices, and used them to lubricate her clit. She felt the climb begin, concentrating hard on her pleasure, her free hand spasmodically grabbing at her breasts as she worked her way to the pinnacle.

Stacie was torn between wanting to hold the feeling as it built more, and wanting to be there at the top. The build up intensified, her body jerked. She felt it coming fast and hard. Her nerve endings were throbbing to the rapture, sending her into eruption. She cried aloud as she felt the spasm, thrusting her hips forward, and feeling her juices spilling. Her head became light and her body throbbed and jolted with the aftershocks. Once quiescent, she slid back into the bath, trying to calm her breathing.

She turned to look at Dan. He raised a smile.

"How did that feel?"

Stacie couldn't answer at first. How had she missed out on such an amazing feeling for so long?

"That was mind-blowing," she said eventually, wrapping her arms around herself.

He leaned toward her, placing a kiss on her left cheek. Stacie froze. Her mind was kidnapped.

"You're improving so quickly, Stacie."

She responded with a smile, not daring to tell him the truth that it was his company making her so hot and horny. On impulse, Stacie moved her head so their lips touched, but Dan pulled away. He stood up, heading to the door abruptly. Stacie was left baffled and upset, her heart bounding with disappointment. That bloody no feelings rule. Of course, he wasn't allowed, but she had expected…what? *What did you expect, Stacie?* she demanded of herself, angrily.

Stacie didn't expect Dan to drop to one knee, but a little bit of something back would be nice.

"I will leave you to your bath," he said, turning at the door, his face unreadable.

She didn't wish to answer him. She felt cheap, tacky and slutty. However, she had signed the contract for "no emotional feelings". Dan was just doing his job. It wasn't his fault if she had developed feelings for him. But the realisation that he had no feelings for her whatsoever made her feel ten times worse.

Dan exited the bathroom, pulling the door shut behind him.

Stacie curled up in a ball, not feeling too good about herself. She was supposed to be here to build up her confidence. Instead, she felt like a stripper. Even Graham had never made her feel like that.

Stacie knew she was taking it all too much to heart. She'd had no idea what to expect from Desires. Maybe she had taken on far too much, and got too involved.

She climbed out the bath, switching on the main light and blowing out the candles. She had a quick shower, rinsing off the bubbles and trying to scrub away her shame. What would the next lesson entail? Did she want there to be a next lesson? Maybe she should just cut her losses and go home.

Robed and towel-turbaned, Stacie headed back into the main room. There was no sign of Dan. As he'd promised, he had left her to it. She sat down at the dresser to dry her long brown hair, considering her next move. She straightened her hair, re-applied her makeup then sprayed her body in her favourite perfume.

She put on the other lingerie set she had bought. The bra was a powerful push and plunge one. Her boobs were already a good size, but a little help never hurt. The matching knickers were French style, all in lace. On went her grey straight-legged jeans with a roll neck, deep red sweater that clung to her slender figure and had the added benefit of making her breasts look bigger.

Stacie was finishing off the final touches when the door opened. Reflected in the mirror, she saw Dan enter.

"How was the bath?"

"I ended up in the shower," she told him bluntly.

He paused, looking at her reflection keenly. "Is everything all right?" he said, walking behind her to sit on the edge of the bed.

"Everything's fine."

"You sound annoyed."

Stacie didn't bother replying.

"What would you like to do next?" he asked cautiously, while she touched up her lip gloss.

"I quite fancy getting out for a little air."

"We can take a walk around the grounds," he said, standing up easily. She watched him, trying to keep hold of her annoyance, and wishing she didn't find him so damned attractive.

Stacie stood up and put on her boots and coat, while Dan waited at the door for her. They headed out and Dan closed the door behind her. They walked down the corridor toward the staircase. As they arrived at the top, Stacie looked ahead seeing the dimly-lit corridor continue on.

"What's down there?"

"Just more rooms," he said.

She glanced back at Dan, seeing him starting down the lavish staircase.

Dan acknowledged both the receptionists. The younger of the girls, her breasts bulging out of the top of her tight blouse, stood up as they approached. She winked at Dan and he walked over to her, kissing her on the cheek. Stacie felt acid jealousy swirl in her guts. She wanted to say something, but how could she? He wasn't hers.

She stood waiting for him as he had a quiet word with the receptionist. Stacie turned her head away, hating the fact she was green-eyed. She saw the corridor that led down to the left where Angel's office was, noticing a large wooden door to the right with a huge handle. A little further around there was another area with seats and two massive double doors in solid dark wood.

"Coming, Stacie?" She heard Dan's voice and then, wearing a long leather coat, he walked past her to the double doors on the right and opened them. He waved to the receptionist. Stacie scowled, turning her head to look at the girl, who positively glowed, a happy smile splitting her face.

Through the door was another long corridor, lined with silver Louis chairs upholstered in cream. The walls were adorned with cream flowered wallpaper, and hung with large pictures of flowers and leaves. Like the corridors upstairs, many unmarked doors led off.

They turned left at the end of the corridor to see yet another stretching before her. This one had small tables dotted at intervals, bearing bowls of fresh flowers. The house truly was stunning. Dan opened another set of double doors at the end of this corridor, which opened out onto the garden.

# Chapter Three

Stacie stepped out, the winter air hitting her. To her left was an impressive conservatory. Through the windows, she could see a black grand piano sitting in the centre, the walls lined with chairs shaped like musical notes. At the far side of the conservatory there was a bar.

Outside there was a weed-free block-paved patio with silver tables and chairs punctuated by outdoor heaters, and yet another building beyond that. She was surprised at how extensive the club was. It was far larger than it had appeared from the front.

They walked between the conservatory and the other building into a large garden. Mature trees rattled their naked branches, and the garden was well-stocked with a variety of bushes and conifers.

Dan walked ahead, then stopped and waited for her to catch up as she stared around her. "Everything okay?"

"Yes, just being nosy." She shook her head at the sheer opulence.

"It is stunning, isn't it? It has just recently been decorated. Angel has spent a fortune on it, but the place is doing well, so why not?"

They continued to walk deeper into the garden—everything looked gloomy and dismal. Winter truly held sway here. The cold air bit at her nose. Stacie wished she had brought her gloves and a scarf, not just her coat. She tagged a little behind Dan, following him through the grounds. Her thoughts turned back to the receptionist. *Has he slept with those girls?* She found it hard to understand her own anger. They were colleagues after all. Maybe they were just good friends. *Why do I find that hard to believe?*

She walked down the pathways, inhaling the winter-cold air, wondering what she would be doing if she were at home? Probably working or doing housework, cooking for one and being miserable. Instead she was at Desires getting herself jealous, and following a very attractive young man around a miserable, dull, cold garden.

Dan led her across the lawn to what appeared to be an unbroken hedge. But, as they approached, she saw it was an optical illusion. One hedge overlapped another behind it, creating the appearance of an impenetrable barrier, but in actual fact, there was a narrow gap which led to a secret garden, walled, with bushes and conifers hiding it from onlookers. A few sheds and outhouses lined the pathways. Dan led her to a sheltered wooden arbour where they sat down.

"You okay?" he said.

"I'm just thinking how beautiful this place is."

"It looks stunning in the spring and summer," he said, leaning back in the seat next to her and taking a deep lungful of the fresh air. She could smell his scent. It intoxicated her. She wanted to snuggle up next to him, but she knew he would not welcome it.

They sat in silence. Stacie hated it, wishing she could find out more about him, but she knew she would be wasting her breath.

What should she do? She knew the sensible option was to leave Desires and never come back. Dan would never give her what she wanted. Her feelings for him would never be reciprocated. He was doing his job, that was all. But then, when she had almost decided to leave, the thought of never seeing Dan again sent her into a blind panic. She wanted him, no, she needed him—not only emotionally, but practically. She still needed what she had come here in the first place for, to gain confidence in herself sexually. Wasn't it better to learn from Dan, who understood her needs? Whilst leaving Graham had been a big decision, all that Stacie had really needed was to wake up and smell the coffee, but Dan…he was something else, inexplicable.

Her mind wandered in circles, not knowing which direction to take. She admitted to herself she had enjoyed the sessions so far and she was desperate for him to take the next step, for him to be intimate with her. Couldn't she separate the physical from the emotional? Men seemed to do it easily, and even some women.

She turned her head to look at Dan, to find him staring at her. Stacie smiled, he responded likewise.

She was about to speak, when she heard a loud moaning sound of pleasure. She turned toward the direction of the sound. A woman was leaning up against one of the large trees in the garden, her legs spread and her skirt lifted to her waist. A man was on his knees in front of her, licking her pussy. Shocked, Stacie instantly looked away. She glanced at Dan to see his reaction. He merely raised his eyebrows and smiled an inscrutable smile. Curiosity got the better of her and she looked back. As the woman's moans got louder, Stacie felt guilty for seeing and hearing them, unsure where to look.

She was horrified to find herself beginning to be turned on by the display. She clenched her inner muscles and felt the familiar trembles begin, but mixed with the arousal was revulsion that they were having sex in broad daylight without caring that anyone could see them, or hear them. She watched the couple swap places. The woman knelt down and pulled his penis from his trousers, sucking it with obvious eagerness.

Stacie struggled to handle what she was witnessing, along with her reaction to it. She looked away, disgusted with them and with herself. When she looked to her right she saw another woman heading their way wearing a PVC mini-dress and black thigh boots, and following behind her was a naked man on his hands and knees, collared and leashed, the woman holding the other end of the lead. Stacie could hardly believe what she was seeing. They came closer and Stacie could see the man's shrivelled penis and balls dangling as he crawled.

As they approached, the woman stopped. Stacie didn't know where to put her eyes. "Sit!" the woman ordered the man.

He responded instantly, sitting back on his knees, his genitals dangling. Stacie felt sick. She wanted to stand up and walk away, but instead turned her head to look at Dan. *What the hell am I letting myself in for? That's humiliating, embarrassing and just horrid.*

The woman took a seat alongside Dan. They exchanged a few words, but Stacie didn't pay much attention to the conversation. She was trying her hardest not to stare at the man's genitals. They weren't attractive, and he looked frozen.

"Come on," the woman commanded, standing and jerking on the lead.

The pair left. Stacie couldn't help staring at the man's bottom as he crawled away. The two white hairy globes bobbed up and down, his balls and penis dangling beneath them. She shuddered. Stacie was relieved when they had gone. Even the other couple, now having full sex by the fence, seemed tame by comparison.

"That was disgusting," Stacie commented, shaking her head as she sat back in her seat.

"That's what he has requested."

She turned her head to gape at him. "You have got to be joking."

"No…that's what he's paying for."

She gazed where they had disappeared.

"Why would anyone pay for that? Why would anyone even want that treatment?"

"It's a fetish. He enjoys that kind of behaviour. He wants to be treated in that manner. Some people like the vulnerability of someone else being in full control."

Stacie couldn't see it and didn't want to even understand it. "Is that the kind of thing that goes on here?"

"Depends what you want. Everyone has different needs. His is to be treated like a dog. She is clearly his Mistress."

"Don't you find that strange?" she needed to ask.

"Personally? Yes, very. But that's what he has requested."

"Have you had any strange things like that?"

"No, not quite like that."

"Would you do that?"

"Of course, if he or someone else requested it."

Stacie looked at him, shocked. It was hard enough just to try to get her head around the whole scenario. But for Dan to say he would give that kind of session…she just shook her head. And she thought she was strange for coming to the club just wanting to be taught how to have sex. Now she felt her request was almost normal.

"What kind of strange things have you done?" she asked him, bracing herself for whatever bizarre answer he might give.

"Well, I've had an old woman request that I masturbate in front of her."

Stacie felt suddenly sick, wishing she hadn't asked. "Stop, I don't want to hear any more."

She stood up and began to walk away from him down the path.

"Is there a problem?" she heard him say as he easily caught up with her.

Stacie continued to walk fast away from him, trying her hardest to quell the hideous picture that he had just painted. A worse one arose, unbidden, of him having sex with some wrinkly old granny. Her stomach turned. This whole thing was getting a little too much for her, beyond degrading.

"Stacie will you slow down?" she heard him say.

She had no intentions of slowing down. She intended to do nothing but pack up her belongings and leave the building. Clearly, she had misunderstood what went on here.

Stacie rushed toward the conservatory, but two women came out blocking her path. As she waited impatiently for them to move out of her way, they began to kiss each other and grab one another's breasts. She glanced around. Dan was coming up fast behind her. The women looked at her and giggled, one of them waggling her eyebrows at her as if in invitation to join them.

"Stacie, please," Dan said.

Stacie wasn't interested. She barged past the women, wanting to get to the room and pack as quickly as possible. How could Dan want to perform a disgusting act in front of an old woman? How could he? She rushed as fast as she could down the corridors to the foyer. She didn't even look at the receptionists, racing up the stairs and down the corridor to the room.

Another man came hurtling out of a room. They crashed into one another. "Hey, slow down," he yelled at her. As she began to fall, she felt an arm taking hold of her and she twisted her neck, to see Dan holding her up. Stacie snatched her arm away and continued a little more sedately back to the room. She heard the man calling out behind her. She ignored him. Her mission was to get back to the room, get her stuff, and get the hell out the building.

"Open the door, please," she commanded Dan.

Without a word, Dan unlocked the door and she flew through.

"What on earth is the matter?" Dan asked.

Stacie rushed to grab her bag, and started stuffing her clothes in.

"Why are you leaving?"

"I just can't handle it, okay? I didn't realise what I was letting myself in for." She headed into the bathroom to gather all her beauty products, then rushed back to her bag and threw them in.

"What do you mean?" he said, following her around the room as she darted about collecting all her personal belongings.

"It doesn't matter, I just need to go."

Dan took hold of Stacie's shoulders. "Just stop, for one second. I need to understand what the problem is. What do you mean, you didn't realise what you were letting yourself in for? Please Stacie, explain. I want to help you," he said.

She stopped to look at him. Confusion and concern shone from his eyes.

"I'm not into that kind of behaviour. I find it repulsive—"

"I know you're not, and I wouldn't expect you to be. You're here to regain your confidence and self-esteem and bring back your love for sex, nothing more."

"Well, I've decided I don't need it any longer."

"Really?" he said, releasing her. "Very well, then. I cannot make you stay here. But before you go, I want to tell you something. People come here for fun, to be free. They come here to have a good time, and not to be judged. For many people this is the only place where they can come and relax."

"I am not judging anyone." Stacie bristled.

"Yes you are. Do you think they're bothered why you're here?"

She stared at him, gazing into his gorgeous brown eyes. Her desire to leave weakened. Her heart raced, her knees turned to jelly.

"You're here for help regaining your confidence, but they're here for their fetish. It's a sex club, Stacie. What did you expect? We are all individuals and have different ideas of fun."

"But I just want to learn to have normal sex, not that…that…" she brandished a hand at the window, unable to find the word.

"And there is no one more than myself who wants to help you."

"I mean, for heaven's sake, I get embarrassed just being naked in front of you, let alone what they were doing."

"Trust me, you have a great figure. You're just lacking in confidence."

"I just…I do want fun and to enjoy myself…but…" she said, attempting to look at him.

"Only you can make the decision to continue or not. I cannot and will not coerce you. I can offer you all the guidance you require, but the drive needs to come from you. So what that he likes being treated like a dog. So what that the couple were having sex against the tree and the fence. And who really cares that the girls were playing with one another. That is what they can do here. That's why they come. And you, Stacie, are here because you want to feel good about yourself. Hold your head high, you have nothing...and I mean nothing to be ashamed about."

He continued, "It's hard for everyone initially. I bet those guys out there took some courage to come here like you. I bet they hammered for days, weeks or even months to take the plunge. Desires is a place where you can experiment with your sexual fantasies without censure. Here, you can be whoever you want to be without shame or stigma." His eyes were compelling in their intensity as he tried to make her understand.

"This is starting to sound like a lecture and I'm sorry. But it's important that you understand before you decide. I look at Desires as a box of treasures for us all to enjoy. No one is judged. No one even really cares about your fantasy, whether it's extreme fetish or just plain damn good love-making. No one here would ever judge you for what you do or don't do."

"Do others come here for guidance like me?" she asked, sitting down on the bed.

"Yes, all for different reasons. Some come because they have no idea how to arouse themselves. Now that, you are getting good at," he told her, a sideways smile appearing on his lips. He waggled his eyebrows at her. Stacie felt herself blush and she looked away.

"Hey, don't feel ashamed," he said, sitting next to her on the bed and lifting her chin to look at him. "You have the right to hold your head up high. You've already done the hardest part, just deciding to come here. It's not easy I know, and I bet it took you ages to decide."

"It did."

"And who's to say those guys out there didn't take ages?" he said. He took hold of her hand and patted it. His touch made her shiver.

"Can I ask you a question?" Stacie said.

"Of course. Ask away."

She dropped her gaze to their joined hands. "Did you enjoy masturbating in front of that old woman?"

Dan paused. "I didn't personally get any pleasure from it, but she was a client, and sometimes we all have to do things that we don't enjoy. And it made her happy, so that made me happy to be able to help her. Look Stacie, I want to teach you. What I have done in the past and what I will do in the future is my job. Yes, I will enjoy some clients more than others, but that's the nature of my job."

"Should I be expected to have that attitude?"

"No, absolutely not. You are here for your own pleasure and it is my job to make you happy. Just as it was my job to make her happy."

"Do you think I'm a prude?"

"I think you need to discover who and what you are, and no I don't think you're a prude. I feel you're scared and I can hardly blame you. Coming here is a big step for you, and Stacie," he said, holding her hand tighter, "I want to help you."

Stacie lifted her head to meet his eyes. They were full of care and compassion. "Can I have a few minutes, please?"

"Of course." He let go of her hands and stood up. He walked to the door and glanced back at her once, smiling briefly before leaving.

Stacie sat on the bed, trying to figure out what to do. What he said made sense. Her eyes had been well and truly opened in the last hour. She had seen things she hadn't even considered might exist. She had been repulsed and disgusted. The things she had seen were things she would never consider doing. But if it made the people happy, and no one was hurt, why was it so bad? Who was she to impose her norms on other people? Yes, she wouldn't want to be led around collared and leashed, but who was she to tell that man he shouldn't?

Of course he couldn't do it out in the street, which was precisely why he came here. So he could pursue his fantasy in a safe place.

If she didn't want to see it, all she had to do was stay out of the public areas. She could just come here to the room, and be with Dan, and not have to see anything that the other people got up to.

She lay back on the bed, and let out a deep breath. Having made her peace with the nature of the club, there was only one more thing worrying her. Could she deal with her growing feelings for Dan? It was pointless to deny them any longer. She had developed a major crush. It wasn't love, of course not. They didn't have any kind of relationship except for a sexual one. So, maybe she could just enjoy it while it lasted, let him teach her what she needed to now and enjoy his hot young body. At least she would leave with some sweet memories and hopefully a slew of techniques so, when she finally did meet someone, she could be a tiger in the bedroom for him instead of a mouse.

Emotionally drained, Stacie closed her eyes. It seemed only seconds later when she jerked them open at the sound of the door. Dan popped his head in.

"Have you had time to think?" he said, coming into the room. In his hand he held a bottle of wine and a piece of paper.

"And?" He walked over and put the bottle of wine on the table.

"I have decided to stay. For now," she said and couldn't help smiling in response to the grin which flashed over his face.

"That's wonderful, Stacie. I'm so glad we'll still be working together."

He came over to the bed and handed her the paper. It was the menu for the evening meal.

"I thought you might like to take a look at this. We can eat downstairs in the restaurant, or have room service. What do you fancy?"

Panic at the thought of going into any of the public areas flooded Stacie. "I think it would be nice to eat here, just you and me," she said, hoping her feelings were not evident.

"Fine with me," Dan said. "Do you want to order now for later?"

Stacie perused the menu. "Can you recommend anything?"

"Everything I've had here has always been excellent."

"Well, you're no help, are you?" she teased.

"Sorry."

Stacie enjoyed their relaxed easy banter as she dithered over the choices. She finally decided on duck à l'orange with baby roast potatoes and trimmed beans. Dan rang the orders through, ordering a seafood pasta medley for himself. He then opened the bottle of wine and filled their glasses, bringing one over to her on the bed. Dan smiled and she fully expected him to sit beside her on the bed. But instead he seated himself in one of the chairs by the small table and watched her thoughtfully.

"How are you feeling?" he asked.

"Fine. I was just wondering what the next session will be."

His eyebrows flew up. "Do you feel ready for the next session?" The look in his eyes made her blush but she kept her eyes up this time, determined to ride it out.

"Yes."

Dan stood up and came toward her, placing his wine glass on the dresser and taking his usual seat on the stool. Stacie swung her legs over the edge of the bed to face him. He took the glass of wine from her, and placed it next to his on the dresser, before turning back and taking both her hands in his.

"Well, if your demonstration in the bath earlier is anything to go by, you have learned the initial lessons well. Do you feel more comfortable masturbating now?"

She replied with a nod and an, "Mm-hmm," as she stared into his eyes. Even if she didn't she would have answered in the affirmative, desperate to get on with the next step.

"Well," he continued, stroking his thumbs over her skin, "feel free to say if you're not ready for this yet, but I thought we could move things along with a little kissing and touching. Me, that is, touching you." Stacie's eyes widened and a shiver ran straight from her hands where he touched her, to her pussy, which quivered in response. A grin split her face. "Do I take that as a yes, from your smile?"

Stacie firmly schooled her expression, not wanting to seem too keen. He couldn't know she wanted him to touch her more than anything.

"I think I could do that," she said.

He picked up their wine glasses and passed hers over. She all but gulped it down, eager to begin. Dan drained his glass of wine and put the empty glasses back on the dresser. Stacie wriggled back on the bed, lying down eagerly, leaving him plenty of room. He came back and eased himself onto the bed beside her, propping himself up on his elbow. She mirrored his posture, staring into his eyes.

If he'd just rolled her over and taken her right then, without preamble, she wouldn't have complained. She was so ready for him it hurt. She wanted him to strip her clothes off and lick her all over.

"We will begin with a little kissing," he was saying.

Kissing? Okay, kissing. She could wait for the rest. Stacie licked her lips, longing to taste him. Never had she been so impatient.

He moved closer to her. His face got nearer. Her body responded, vibrating to his presence like a harp string. She closed her eyes, awaiting his arrival. Stacie could feel his breath on her face then their lips touched. The kiss was feather-light and whisper-soft, but it sent tingles to places she'd forgotten existed. She kissed him back, wanting to touch, but scared in case he backed off. She wanted to press her body against his, to feel his urgency. She felt wanton...and it felt good.

Stacie opened her eyes to make sure she wasn't dreaming, that it really was Dan kissing her. It certainly was. He pulled away to smile at her then moved back close. She closed her eyes once again, craving the feel of his lips pressed so delightfully against hers. The kiss turned more passionate, his lips became firmer and more urgent and he wound one hand around her waist, pulling her closer.

She shivered at his touch, the anticipation heightening her arousal. Dan deepened the kiss, touching his tongue to her lips. She opened in mute acceptance, her own tongue seeking his.

Stacie felt him move his body even closer to her. His pelvis touched the tops of her thighs and his hand wandered round to rest on the curve of her bottom. She pressed herself to him shamelessly, feeling the heat of his body through her clothing.

Dan pulled away for a second. Stacie opened her eyes to see him staring at her, his eyes almost black, before he descended on her again, kissing her fiercely, hungrily. Stacie felt his tongue at her lips. She opened her mouth without hesitation, allowing his tongue to glide inside, feeling it circling around hers. Stacie joined in rolling her tongue around his, tasting him, enjoying the intimacy. This was the moment she had been waiting for, the taste, the passion.

The hand on her bottom began to wander, caressing up and down her spine. Each tickling touch made her quiver and tremble. Impatient, Stacie took control, plunging her tongue deeper into his mouth, swinging her leg up over his hip in invitation, wanting more and more. Yearning for more, she thrust herself at him, but Dan pulled away. He gently removed her leg and placed it back on the bed. Stacie flushed, knowing she had done wrong by taking the initiative. She began to roll away from him, embarrassed, but he pulled her back, holding her close to nuzzle into his neck. She felt his breath on her right ear and then he began kissing and pulling at her ear lobe, leaving her shivering through her entire body.

He rolled her onto her back and hovered over her, supporting his weight on his elbows as he gently touched her cheek with his hand, running his other hand through her hair. He slid his tongue back in her mouth. She accepted eagerly. She'd never tasted anyone so good. Stacie craved to touch him, to feel his body, but that wasn't what this lesson was about. If she did, he would almost certainly stop, and that she definitely didn't want.

He transferred his weight to one elbow, running his free hand down to her waist and then further to her hip, his lithe fingers tickling and teasing. Stacie leaned her body into his touch. He brought the hand to her chest and she barely breathed as he ran his hand over the top of her breast. She longed for him to touch her bare flesh. He pulled away from her then, kneeling up to tug at her top. She sat up to assist and he pulled it up over her head, discarding it on the floor next to the bed. She pushed her chest out invitingly and met his eyes.

He lowered her back to the bed and kissed her neck and shoulders, her whole body quivering in sensation as his gentle hands and lips teased her body. It had been so long since she'd felt so desired.

As Dan kissed a trail round her neck, he began flicking his tongue out, blowing on the wet marks he made. Stacie shivered with every blow, throwing her head back on the pillow. He moved his lips down toward her breasts and she thrust them toward him. But he bypassed her breasts completely, shifting his body down to continue his kisses down her stomach. Nearly growling with frustration, Stacie forced herself to lie patiently. Dan arrived at the waistband of her jeans and paused.

Stacie lifted her head up to glance at him. Dan met her gaze with a waggle of his eyebrows and a quirk of his lips. A rush of desire seized her and she barely managed to resist thrusting her crotch in his face. He ran his finger round her waistband, slowly undoing the button and then the zip. She raised her hips to allow him to pull her jeans down. Her world was Dan and this room. The only thing she wanted right now was for him to take her, fill her, empty his seed within her. She would have done anything. Stacie widened her thighs in welcome as Dan positioned himself above her. She could feel his jeans against her bare legs, his erection beneath the denim pressing into her yearning pussy. He lay over her, gazing at her breasts. She quickly thrust her boobs up toward him, desperate for him to touch her.

Shifting his weight to one elbow, his other hand slid up her slender torso to cup her breast in its lacy covering. He dropped kisses across the top of her boobs and ran his thumb over her hard nipple poking through the silky material, eager for attention. Stacie jiggled her hips, almost beside herself with desire and longing. How much longer would he make this last? Transferring his weight to his knees, Dan sat back a little, caressing both breasts and pushing them together. He put his face in the cleavage he had made and kissed first one breast, then the other, inhaling deeply. Stacie dropped her head back, closing her eyes.

Dan slid his hands around to her back to unclasp her bra. She lifted up on her elbows, allowing him to remove it. He peeled it away and it joined her top on the floor. They both stared down at her naked breasts for a second before Dan descended. He didn't suck on her nipples as she had expected. Instead, he pressed his lips gently against them, kissing them all over, but avoiding the nipple area. Stacie cupped her boobs together feeling his lips all over them. She closed her eyes, forcing herself to wait, anticipating the moment.

He toyed with her breasts for a while, kissing around them, then down to her stomach. He kissed all over her hips and waist and back to her breasts. He pushed them together and then, without warning, he pinched both nipples at the same time, sending her screaming in pleasure as pulses raged through her body. She thrust her pelvis into his groin, feeling her juices soaking her thong. He sucked on her right nipple, whilst pinching her left one, adding a gentle pull and twist. Her body ran wild, all her nerve endings sending urgent flashes to her pussy, craving for more and more. Dan teased her nipples, sucking one then moving quickly to the other, making her body spasm and buck.

She wanted to grab his cock, wondering if he was as hot as her—she was burning. Instead, she reached behind her to grab the bedhead, pushing her body up to him in a mute plea. He gripped her left nipple with his teeth and gave a gentle tug. She collapsed on the bed, thrusting her pelvis into his. He kept firm hold of her breasts, pushing them together, licking from one nipple to the other. Stacie bit hard on her lower lip, trying not to cry out with pure excitement.

Dan worked his way back down her body, kissing all the way down her soft skin until he arrived at her pubic mound. He kissed all around the triangle of her panties, sodden with her juices. He ran his tongue down one inner thigh, then back up again, stopping just short of her pussy. She let out an involuntary mew as he skipped over to the other side and repeated the action. Stacie clenched her pelvic muscles and wriggled beneath him, resisting the urge to beg.

She felt his breath on her mound as he blew over her pussy. His lips pressed against her panties and his hands ran up and down her thighs. He hooked one finger into the front of her panties and pulled them all the way down. She felt him roll off her, but he didn't go far. She opened her eyes and saw him lying next to her, just taking her nakedness in. She lay before him, smiling, unashamed, wanting to give him the gift of her body. Soon he was back, covering her body with his, kissing her urgently, his hands roaming her body as if they didn't know where to go first.

He kissed down her body, sucking and nibbling on her nipples until she was breathless, then continued down to her pussy. Dan spread her thighs wide and positioned himself between them. She closed her eyes and felt his breath hot on her as he kissed all over her mound.

Stacie lay back on the bed, trying her hardest not to direct him. Whatever he would do to her it would make her wail with delight. They'd probably be able to hear her at the other side of Desires.

She waited, tense with anticipation. Then, she felt his tongue hot and wet within her labia. Stacie cried out as the sensation rampaged through her entire body, hitting every nerve ending possible.

His fingers swiped her clitoris, which was aching with need. She lunged her hips off the bed, pushing herself against him. He flattened out his tongue and lapped at her, as she grabbed her breasts, toying with her nipples. Then she felt him slide two fingers within her, pushing in and up. She squealed aloud as the point of his tongue taunted her sensitive folds of flesh and his skilful fingers played her like a violin.

He was driving her mind to captivity—this young horny, sexy man who had certainly had the right touch was commanding her body. She craved him, wanting more. Her body was sweating, and her mind transported by what Dan was doing to her.

Stacie felt herself beginning to lose control. Dan's tongue dipped in and out of her pussy, alternating with his fingers, while his other hand tormented her clitoris. Her whole body was taken over, sweat blossomed on her skin. She clenched her inner muscles around Dan's fingers, trying to wring maximum feeling from them. She was sure he had managed to slide a third finger in her slick tunnel. She was past caring, lost in pleasure, thrusting frantically against him. As his fingers kept up their steady rhythm, his lips surrounded her clit, sucking lightly as his tongue flicked over the bud. Stacie screamed out as her clitoris burst with sensation, her hips rising off the bed as her orgasm swept over her. She clung to the bedhead, letting her body buck. It seemed to go on forever, then finally began to ebb.

Stacie relaxed onto the bed, quivering with the after-effects. She felt Dan sit back on his heels on the bed, but she couldn't muster up the strength to open her eyes. Her heart pounded and her breath came in shuddery gasps. She could feel wetness trickling down her thighs and pooling on the duvet. Had that all come from her? She felt the bed creak and dip as Dan got off and then she heard the bathroom door open.

She opened her eyes in time to see Dan disappearing inside the bathroom, closing the door firmly behind him. Stacie stared after him for a few seconds. When he didn't come back quickly, she climbed off the bed, pulled the duvet back and slipped beneath the covers. She put her fingers down to her inner thighs, feeling the moisture still trickling from her. She puffed up the pillows and got comfortable while she waited for Dan to come back. Stacie stretched, cat-like, feeling her body relax into a delightful torpor.

The bathroom door soon opened and Dan came out. She watched him head over to the large flat-screen television. He picked up the remote and turned the television on, putting it on mute, before coming over to the bed to sit on the end.

He turned to look at her. "How are you feeling?"

"Wet," she replied, giving Dan a naughty smile.

"Is there anything in particular you'd like to do now?"

"How about just chilling for a bit," she said, imagining them snuggled up together in bed, watching mindless television and talking. She wondered what his next plan with her would be.

"Sounds good. Would you like some more wine?"

"That'd be great," she said, not too bothered about what happened for the next ten minutes, as long as she got close to him.

Stacie watched him pour out another two glasses. Her gaze roved his body, she yearned to touch and caress him. Her response to him surprised her. She had never experienced the feeling of being hungry for sex. Sometimes it had been nice, but nothing special, and she'd never been that bothered really. If it hadn't been for Dan, that would still have been the case.

He passed her one of the glasses of wine and the remote control to the television, and then flashed her a smile before leaving the room. Stacie shot up in bed, panicked. Where was he going? She thought they were going to snuggle up in bed together. But, wait, he'd poured himself a glass of wine. He couldn't be going far. Stacie made herself relax back against the pillows. She flicked through the channels, not finding anything interesting so she switched it off. She climbed out of the bed to make her way over to the large window. There wasn't much to see. It was dark outside now, the winter night looming. Winter was her least favourite time of the year, cold, wet and miserable, nothing to be cheerful about. Then there was Christmas fast approaching, a very expensive time of the year. Graham had always seemed to go out of his way to make Christmas miserable. Roll on spring.

She wandered to the bathroom to clean herself up while she waited for Dan. Stacie gazed in the mirror seeing her breasts gleaming with sweat. Her tummy seemed flatter. Must be all the exercise she was getting. Stacie hadn't stopped sweating since she met Dan, but she certainly wasn't about to complain. She grabbed the robe of the back of the door and was coming back into the bedroom as Dan entered through the other door, carrying two bottles of mineral water.

"I wasn't sure if you preferred still or sparkling so I got both. I don't want you getting a headache from all that wine," he said, brandishing the bottles before placing them on the table.

Stacie's heart somersaulted. He was so thoughtful.

"So, which would you like?" That sweet half-smile was back as he watched her watching him.

"Hmm? Oh. Still, please." Best watch that. Can't let him see how much you like him. Keep it together, girl.

Stacie sat back on the bed watching Dan pour the water. She wished she could find out more about his personal life, about the man himself. How much was off-limits? Maybe it was time to find out.

"How long have you been working here?" she asked him, not sure if he would answer.

"Eight months," he replied. He walked over to the bed and passed her a glass of water. He sat down on the bed, half-lying facing her, propped up on his elbow. She was a little disappointed, hoping he would have got into bed with her. But he was fully-clothed still.

"You obviously enjoy it?"

"Yes I do," he replied.

One question sprang into her mind. She remembered that every time they had had a session, he disappeared off by himself. She'd wondered why, but now the answer seemed clear. How could she have been so stupid? She hesitated before asking, but decided to bite the bullet.

"Were you masturbating in the bathroom after you finished me?"

Dan turned around to stare at her and for a second she wished she hadn't asked. *A bit personal, Stacie*, she said to herself.

"Yes, I was," Dan replied, not seeming too bothered.

She looked at him, not sure if she was more shocked by him doing it, or that he'd admitted it. "Why didn't you do it with me?"

she asked in a small voice, not at all sure she wanted to hear the answer.

Dan just smiled. "Because that comes later."

Stacie felt her smile bursting to come through. She wanted to jump around the room with excitement, knowing she was going to get her toy boy. It couldn't come soon enough. She wanted the evening to suddenly speed up and get on with the next lesson immediately.

Trying to calm down, she asked the first question that came into her head. "Do you normally get excited after a session?"

"With you, yes."

"What about with other people?"

He paused. "Confidentiality, remember," he told her, moving further up the bed alongside her.

*Confidentiality, my arse*, she thought, remembering how he had happily told her about masturbating in front of the old woman. But then she also remembered how she had reacted to that revelation. Perhaps she should just stop asking him about his experiences with other people.

"So, what's my next lesson?" she asked, keen to hear his reply.

"Well, if of course it's okay with you—" he said, turning his head to look deep into her eyes "—I thought I could teach you oral."

She stared at Dan and he gazed directly back at her. Stacie felt her knees trembling. "You mean—"

"Yes, on me."

Finally, she would get to see his cock, maybe even see him naked. She wriggled with delight, the thought already turning her on.

Dan sipped his water and reached for the remote. His hand brushed the skin of her arm as he picked it up, raising goosepimples. She couldn't believe how much she reacted to even the tiniest of touches. He put the television back on and flicked the channels until he found a sports channel.

"Do you mind if we have this on for a bit? My team's playing," he said.

"It's fine," Stacie replied, touched that he'd asked her. When Graham put football on she would leave the room and head off doing something completely different, but with Dan, Stacie didn't care as long as they were together.

She sipped at her water and lay back, closing her eyes, thinking about her life and where she wanted to be. Her job was important but she needed to have her life back. She needed to socialise more, go out, have fun, be slightly extravagant, let her hair down and be free. Once she had finished the sessions with Dan, hopefully she would be able to do just that.

\* \* \* \*

Stacie's eyes flicked open with a start. Dan was still watching football. She scrubbed at her eyes, not believing she'd dozed off. Dan turned around and smiled at her. "Did you enjoy your snooze?"

She didn't answer immediately, still getting her bearings and a bit dozy. She had dreamed about Desires but she was with someone else, not Dan. She shook her head slightly. It was only a dream and she was here with Dan in this gorgeous bedroom.

"Yes, I did, thank you," she replied.

"Good."

Stacie smiled at him in response. She slid out from under the duvet and headed to the bathroom. She flicked on the mirror lights and gazed at her reflection. The woman looking back at her was someone she didn't recognise. This woman looked replete, content, and very, very pleased with herself. Was this what good sex did to you?

A smile crept onto her face as she thought about Dan, and Stacie watched her reflection get a dreamy look on its face. She would never have thought that she could feel so comfortable in such a short space of time having a very sexy young man show her how to masturbate. She still didn't approve of the behaviour she'd witnessed in the garden, and as for him masturbating in front of a woman old enough to be his grandmother, that was disgusting…

*Stop! Stop thinking about it.* Stacie watched her reflection frown. She stared into her own troubled eyes, wishing the thoughts would stop. After all, he wasn't her man and would never be. She signed a contract and needed to realise Dan was being paid to teach her.

Why would a gorgeous young man like him need to work in this kind of place? And why on earth did he not have a girlfriend? Maybe he did and she didn't mind, or didn't know. No. What woman in the world would be happy with her boyfriend having sex with other women for money? Stacie was desperately curious, but knew Dan wouldn't answer any of her questions. He had his life and she had hers. He was her tutor and that was the way it must remain.

She cleaned herself, then brushed her hair, and freshened her makeup. Satisfied, Stacie headed back out. The football had finished and they were on the post-match talky waffle. Dan muted it as she came out and sat up to face her.

"Did you win?" she said, sitting on the bed.

"Yes, 2-1," he said, with a grin. Stacie smiled. At least he would be happy now. Graham used to grump and stomp about for hours whenever his team lost. "So…" Dan said, drawing out the word, "when would you like to begin the next lesson?"

*Now!* she wanted to scream but managed to paste a nonchalant look on her face. "Whenever."

"How about now?" Dan's eyes were dark and intense. *Oh boy!*

"Okay," Stacie managed. Her body started to quiver in automatic response.

"Are you sure? If you feel I'm going too fast—"

"*No!* No, I mean, it's fine…it's been quite a while since…"

"I don't want you to feel pressured. I know it's hard for you, and just being here is a big thing for you." Dan lay back on the bed, crossing his ankles and pillowing his hands behind his head. "If you would rather wait, I understand."

"No, let's do it. I want to," she said, her gaze dropping involuntarily to the bulge in his jeans.

"If you change your mind at any time—"

"Understood."

"In this lesson I will be teaching you how to a pleasure a man, both orally and by sexual touching." The words were clinical, but coming from his mouth they sent shivers down Stacie's spine directly to her pussy. There was just one thing she had to make clear.

"Can I just say at this point, I'd really rather you didn't, you know, come in my mouth."

"No problem," he replied easily. He knelt up on the bed and moved closer to her. She closed the gap between them. They came face-to-face, and he smiled tenderly. Stacie closed her eyes and awaited his touch. Soft lips touched hers and a hand went round her back pulling her closer. Their torsos pressed together and she could feel his warmth even through the thick robe.

Stacie kissed him back hungrily, opening for his tongue when she felt it touch her lips. He was a nice kisser, gentle and respectful, not plunging his tongue down her throat.

Stacie placed her hands on his back grasping his T-shirt with both hands. Dan pulled her even closer. She could feel his heartbeat bounding. Dan pulled her robe apart, exposing her breasts. She pulled his T-shirt out of his jeans and slid her hand inside, finally feeling his naked flesh. She ran her hands up the complete length of his back. His skin was soft and warm. Stacie grasped the bottom of his T-shirt, releasing his mouth as briefly as possible, just long enough to lift his shirt up and over quickly, before rushing back to his lips. She could feel his naked chest pressing against her nude breasts. Her robe hung open all the way down—she knew she was on show to him completely.

Dan kissed her with more urgency than he had before. His hands slid beneath her robe, hot on her back, pulling her to him. Stacie wished for a second she was allowed to do more than just accept his advances, then she remembered that she could. He had given her permission to touch him sexually. Stacie pulled away from his lips to move to his perfect cheek bones, nibbling and kissing, tasting the saltiness of his skin. She kissed her way toward his ear, nibbling slightly at his soft ear lobe. She heard his faltering exhale, almost a moan. There wasn't an inch of his body Stacie wanted to miss.

She kissed and licked around his ear, then slowly made her way down the sensitive tendons of his neck, her hands caressing the wide flat muscles of his back. His hands were not touching her, which pleased her. She wanted to totally concentrate on him, to make sure she was giving him pleasure, not be distracted by her own.

Stacie nibbled along his clavicle, dropping a kiss in the hollow between his collarbones. His pulse beat strongly beneath her lips. She reared back to look at his chest before going any further. A sprinkling of dark hair lay in the valley between his pecs. He wasn't overly muscular; he was lean, but well-defined. He was beautiful. Tracing his pecs with her fingertips, she leaned in and kissed around his flat brown nipples which rose obediently. She ran her flat hands down his flanks, allowing her thumbs to trace the subtle bumps of his abs. Her fingertips arrived at his belt, resting there gently while she pressed her lips gently on his naked chest, inhaling his scent.

She sat back on her heels and regarded him. His eyes were slitted, watching her. Her gaze dropped to his jeans and, greatly daring, she brushed a hand across the front. There was a definite bulge there, so much so, her mouth went dry at the thought of what lay beneath. She traced his outline with her fingernails, glancing up as she did so. His eyes were closed and his head thrown back. He drew in a shuddering breath and she detected a definite pushing of his crotch into her hand, as if in invitation. Slowly, keeping the anticipation going, she unfastened the belt. She knelt up, kissing and nibbling his delectable lips as she undid his button and unzipped his fly.

Resisting the temptation to dig right in and pop that cock out, Stacie instead reached around to cup his rear. She felt him tense to her touch and dug her fingers into his firm cheeks, pulling him to her. Through his jeans she could feel his hard cock against her pussy as he ground himself into her, the denim delightfully rough against her skin. His hands went under her robe again, grabbing her bottom in return, pulling her close. Mouth to mouth, chest to chest, crotch to crotch, she could have pulled his cock out and jumped right on. But this one wasn't about her.

Stacie slid her fingers between his jeans and his trunks, sliding the jeans down to his knees oh so slowly. His trunks seemed moulded to his flesh, his bottom rounded and firm. She trailed her hands around to the front, and sat back on her heels once more, leaning forward to kiss his chest and stomach, deliberately ignoring the rampant bulge that reared up for her attention.

She could smell him, the scent of sex hung heavy in the air. It filled her nostrils and befuddled her mind. She let her gaze rest on the thick shaft clearly outlined behind the thin material. She put two fingers on the end and slowly grazed her nails down the length of him. His breathing was ragged. She allowed the fingers to continue, making a delicate pass of the soft sac beneath the shaft, before heading back up again. She stretched out the waistband of his trunks, allowing his cock to spring up from its nest. It was long and thick, extending past the waistband once released. She reached in with her other hand and wrapped her fingers firmly around the thick shaft, rubbing her thumb over the end. She looked up at him for confirmation she was doing okay. His eyes were closed and his face wore a look of beatific rapture. His penis pulsed in her hand and she moved her hand up and down a couple of times.

Dan abruptly pulled away but before Stacie could question it, he slipped off his jeans and trunks and dropped them on the floor. He lay on the bed, his cock rigid against his abdomen. Stacie shucked her robe and made her way across the bed on her hands and knees, smiling to herself to see Dan's gaze drop to her breasts, which swayed as she moved.

She straddled him, looking down at his cock, mere inches from her pussy. Stacie took hold of it, finally able to run her hand up and down his length. Her pussy ached with longing. She could just kneel up and slide it on in, but he hadn't allowed that yet. She took a shuddering breath and forced herself to move down his body. She wriggled down the bed until her face was level with his cock.

"Have you ever sucked a cock before, Stacie," she heard Dan ask.

"Once, but I wasn't very good," Stacie confessed. *And I didn't like it much.* She'd wanted to oblige her first boyfriend, but he'd held her by her hair and thrust into her mouth without finesse, finishing by coming down her throat without warning. She'd thrown up in the sink and refused to do it since.

"Well, I want you to pretend it's your favourite lollipop," he said, a smile in his voice.

*Favourite lollipop? Okay.* She gave a mental shrug. She took a deep breath, poked out her tongue and licked the full length of his manhood all the way down to his balls. He tasted clean, and smelled of soap. She licked back up again and ran her tongue around the ridge at the base of his head. He let out a tiny noise and took in a shaky breath.

"Good, Stacie. Now, put your mouth around the head and suck gently." Stacie obeyed, wrapping her lips around the bulbous head.

She was a little taken aback to taste the saltiness of the fluid leaking from the small hole, but she gamely licked it off, rewarded by a shudder and a moan.

"The balls. Play with the balls," she heard coming from above as she sucked diligently on his rounded head. She cupped her hand around his sac, gently squeezing and stroking. She felt him thrust further into her mouth, and she responded by sliding her lips down further, then back up and down again.

"Christ, Stacie," she heard him exclaim.

She popped her mouth off the end in alarm. "What? Is it not good?"

"Not good? Stacie, you're doing fantastic. Carry on."

Happy, Stacie lowered her face down to his cock again, sucking more firmly on the end. She felt his hands in her hair, but gently, not forcing her to stay in place, just caressing her head. She flicked her tongue over the end of his cock and smiled to herself to hear the groan that accompanied it.

She slid her lips down the shaft, wondering just how much of him she could take. She felt his cockhead rub against her soft palate and his deep moan as he thrust further into her mouth. She lifted her head up, bringing her lips to almost off the end, and dove back down onto him again, feeling his body judder in response. She glanced up at him as she held his dick in her mouth, to see him watching her, his eyes on his cock where it slid in and out from between her lips. She felt herself start to dribble and popped her lips off the end with a slurping sound, continuing to masturbate him as she wiped her mouth.

"Do you like to watch?" she asked.

"God yeah. Nothing sexier than a sexy woman sucking your cock."

She looked again at his cock, admiring it, long and stiff, rubbing itself eagerly between her hands.

Dan moaned. She bent down again and sucked the tip of his dick followed by licking down the length, using her mouth and hand simultaneously up and down his shaft. She felt his hands on her head again, moving her hair out of the way where it obscured his view.

"Suck my balls," he instructed her breathily. Stacie raised her eyebrows. This one was new, but he was the teacher. She took her body slightly down the bed, kneeling between his legs. She trailed her fingernails up his thighs until she arrived at his balls. She took hold of them, massaging them lightly then bent forward and licked gently. They felt different on her tongue, not as smooth as his cock, but not unpleasant. Stacie eased her lips around one of his balls and took it into her mouth, hearing him cry out. She sucked carefully, aware that this part of a man's body was the most delicate. She ran her tongue over the skin, feeling the smoothness of the pebbles within. She wondered if she could get both of them in and spread her lips wider gently easing the other in.

It went in, but there wasn't much room for manipulation, so she simply added a little careful suction before releasing him.

"Good?"

"So good!"

She gave his balls a final tender lick, and then moved back to the full length of his penis, licking all the way to the tip then filling her mouth with his cock as far as she could, covering his dick in her saliva.

"I need to come," he gasped out. Stacie pulled her mouth off his cock and he rolled her over in a slick movement, then straddled her, pushing her breasts together and sliding his cock between them. He pumped repeatedly, the tip of his cock coming close to her mouth each time. She licked the leaking end with every thrust, then clamped her lips shut at Dan's gasped warning. He grabbed hold of the headboard and his body jerked as he covered her breasts in his cum. She heard a faint, "Aaaah," then he rolled off her and collapsed on the bed.

She looked at his diminishing penis, then up at his face. His eyes were closed. Stacie stared down to her chest, seeing her breasts covered in his cum. She climbed off the bed trying her hardest not to get any mess over anything and headed to the bathroom to clean up.

Dan was getting dressed as Stacie returned to the bedroom. She caught a glimpse of his bare bottom as he pulled up his trunks.

"Was that okay?" she said, picking the discarded robe up off the floor and slipping it on.

He turned around to look at her. She walked toward him, feeling her face splitting in a smile. "Not bad," he replied as he pulled up his jeans. "How was it for you?"

*Only "not bad"?* Stacie felt as if he'd slapped her across the face. She swallowed before speaking. Well, she could do nonchalance as well. "All right, I suppose."

"You're doing well," he told her as he pulled his T-shirt over his head.

Stacie sat on the edge of the bed facing away from him, wondering what she'd done wrong. She'd done everything he asked, and he seemed to be enjoying it. Heck, he'd come hadn't he?

"Are you ready for some food yet?" he said.

She'd been hungry, but her appetite suddenly seemed to have disappeared. "I guess."

Stacie glanced at him as he came round the end of the bed. Could she have done better? Stacie honestly thought she had done amazing considering the last and only time she had a man's dick in her mouth was years ago. Stacie went over all his instructions in her head. He'd seemed to enjoy himself. Maybe it was because she'd needed to be guided rather than knowing what to do for herself. But wasn't that what he was meant to do, to teach her?

"Are you all right?" he said, coming to sit next to her on the bed. She didn't look at him.

"I'm fine."

"Is something the matter, Stacie?"

"No," she replied, standing up and picking up her clothes from the floor where she tossed them before.

"Yes there is. What's the matter?"

"Nothing." She didn't bother moderating the sharpness in her voice.

Dan moved over to her. She started snatching clothes up off the floor, anything to avoid looking at him. She couldn't let him see how upset she was.

"Stacie, what's the matter?" he said again.

She threw the bundle of clothes onto the bed and wrapped her arms around herself.

"I just…I just thought I had done better than *not bad*," she told the floor.

She heard a long exhale behind her and felt his hands patting her shoulders. "Stacie, can you turn around please, and allow me to explain," he said, trying to turn her to face him. She resisted, not wanting to look at him and endure yet another lecture. "At least come and sit on the bed."

Reluctantly, she moved over to the bed and sat next to him, staring at her hands twisting together in her lap.

"Look, Stacie, you did fantastic. You really did. I'm sorry I didn't give you the answer you wanted. It's my fault. I didn't realise just how inexperienced you were, and how much I'd need to direct you. You did great for a beginner, and you will improve so much as we work on your technique. I'm sorry I upset you. Forgive me?"

Stacie looked up at him, somewhat mollified. So, she hadn't done great, but she'd done okay for a novice. Maybe cock-sucking was like any other skill. Maybe she just needed a little practice.

And maybe, once she got better at cock-sucking, she would finally feel his cock in her pussy, where she longed to have it.

## Chapter Four

Dan rang the kitchen to confirm they were ready for their food.

"It'll be about twenty minutes," he said when he put the receiver down. "I'm going to take a quick shower."

Stacie got dressed while Dan showered, then she poured herself the last dribbles of wine from the bottle and daydreamed about Dan naked and washing his body. In her mind, she imagined herself going in to help him, lathering him up, getting in with him, hearing him say, "Stacie, I want you."

She jumped with a guilty thrill when the bathroom door opened and then had to stop herself from staring as he came out wearing just a towel around his waist. Water dripped down his lean torso, and glistened on his arms. His hair was damp and tousled and he rubbed it with a second towel, oblivious to her longing. Then, with a naughty waggle of his eyebrows at her, he whipped the towel away, draping it over the dresser stool. She stood, open-mouthed, virtually drooling. He was magnificent, like a Grecian statue come to life. His body was perfectly sculpted and each muscle begged to be licked and nuzzled and tasted. Stacie had to turn away, flicking on the television and pretending to be interested in some mindless show.

She heard rustling behind her and, when she turned to peek at him, he had pulled on his trunks and jeans and was just picking up his T-shirt. *Down, girl!* she told herself firmly. *You'll get your chance.* But she couldn't help staring as he pulled the T-shirt over his still-damp hair and settled it. He was such an enigma. She wished she was able to get a little more information out of him about his personal life.

Dan cleared the table of their lunch detritus, putting it by the door, and got a candle from the bathroom, which he placed on a small candle plate he got from one of the dresser drawers.

A knock at the door announced the arrival of their meal. One of the female staff entered, rapidly setting the table with cutlery, napkins, and glasses. She placed the cloche-covered plates on the wicker mats, and an ice bucket containing another bottle of wine on the floor, before piling their lunch dishes on the trolley and leaving.

"More wine?" Stacie queried.

"You don't have to drink it."

"No, it's okay – the food will soak it up anyway." Stacie was already feeling happily merry. Maybe she could get Dan squiffy enough that she could persuade him to advance the sessions.

They sat down and Dan removed the covers from their plates. The smell was divine and Stacie set about her duck with gusto.

"How's your food?" Dan said, spearing a mussel.

"Delicious. Yours?"

"Good. I've had this before, it's one of the chef's specialties. Have you ever tried calamari?"

"Squid?" Stacie shook her head, screwing up her mouth in disgust.

"You should." He held out a ring of something that looked like white rubber. "How do you know if you like it or not if you don't try it?"

His tone was severe, like a parent chastising a child for refusing to try something new. Stacie considered. She'd always been grossed out by the thought of trying squid, or snails or anything weird. But she liked prawns and fish, so why would squid be any different.

"Okay, but just a tiny bit," she said.

Dan cut a section off the ring and offered it to her. She tentatively closed her lips round it and slid it off his fork. She chewed.

"Well?"

She swallowed. "Not bad actually. A bit chewy. It doesn't really taste of anything much."

"At least you tried it. More?"

She shook her head vigorously and Dan chuckled. They spent the meal in idle chit-chat. She discovered that he enjoyed football, both playing and watching and that he supported Liverpool. She told him about her work and regaled him with funny stories from the office.

She couldn't stop herself. She knew she was becoming dangerously addicted to him. She couldn't get enough of his smile, his facial expressions, the way he raised his eyebrows, the way he ate his food, the way his stubble made him so utterly delectable. She forced herself to concentrate on the banal chatter, but all she wanted was to feel his hands on her.

Stacie shook her head at herself. She'd known him less than twenty-four hours and was smitten, craving him. After Graham, Stacie had sworn that she would never fall into that trap again. She had vowed to remain wary and careful about her friends and the men she spent time with, yet here she was, sitting with a man who had trapped her without him even realising it.

What on earth was going on in her mind and her body? Dan was like a lightning bolt, striking her common sense numb while her emotions whizzed and sparked, and her body trembled like a schoolgirl with her first crush, willing to do anything and everything to be noticed and get his attention. She felt free and rebellious, wanting to break every rule in the book, be a naughty girl, do things that would have horrified strait-laced Graham. Stacie wanted everything from Dan, sex, love, devotion, and passion and to be seduced in more ways than she had ever imagined. She wanted to find the other side of Stacie, the side that had been locked away for years. It was time she had some serious fun, and allowed her body to let go and enjoy everything he could throw at her.

She watched the way he speared his pasta, staring at his hands, firm and brown. She trembled as she imagined those hands wandering freely around her body, not missing a single inch of her skin. The thought of his lithe fingers caressing her, teasing her, taking her to another planet, made her jiggle with excitement. He could use those hands to tie her to the bed, to lay her completely open to his whims. *Now where did that thought come from?* Stacie delicately cut another piece of duck, chewing thoughtfully. She had never had the urge to be tied to the bed before. But the thought of having Dan in complete control of her, doing whatever he wished to her, made her feel quite faint.

The little she'd learned of him during their light conversation had served only to increase her interest, not satisfy it. The most insistent question on her mind was, *Is he in a relationship?* Maybe this was Dan's secret life. Maybe this was how he got his kicks. Certainly, Stacie knew she would never be happy with any boyfriend of hers working in a place like this. Why did a young, sexy, intelligent, kind man allow old women to watch him play with himself? Stacie struggled to understand why he would do this kind of job.

"Is everything all right?" she heard him ask. Caught in thought, she looked up, startled.

"Great," she replied, faking a smile.

"You seem to be miles away."

"Do I?"

"You do. What are you thinking about?" he asked.

Stacie cast about in her mind. "Oh, I was just wondering what my next lesson's going to be."

He smiled at her. "Is that the first excuse you could come up with?" he said, loading his fork with pasta. Stacie raised her eyebrows. Was she so transparent? "You want to find out more about me," he said, pointing his fork at Stacie before popping it into his mouth.

Stacie just stared at him for a second, her mouth working like a landed fish. How did he know?

"Go on, get it off your chest, as my mother always says."

She cut another piece of duck and chewed slowly, debating whether to tell him and be honest, or just let it lie. It didn't matter what his answer was, really. Despite her feelings for him, they couldn't ever be together, girlfriend or no.

She finally looked up and met his calm gaze. The pit of her stomach lurched. "I just can't figure out why a good-looking guy like you is here doing this line of work." Well, it was part of what she'd been wondering.

"I enjoy it, especially when I get stunning clients." His mouth curved in a half smile.

The food she'd just put in her mouth turned to dust and she had to force herself to chew. What did he mean by that? Was he referring to her, or did he mean the other clients he had pleasured? Her mind rapidly went from picturing his hands running all over her body, to imagining him caressing other women, gorgeous women, begging for him to make love with them. She was shocked at the surge of black jealousy that filled her.

Stacie stared back at him as he filled his mouth with another forkful of food. "How can you do this without feeling some kind of emotion?"

He regarded her coolly as he emptied his mouth. "It's all about the money, honey."

"Yes, but you said you had stunning clients."

"Some are more attractive than others. Some are, *shut your eyes and do your job, Dan*. I cannot and will not have emotions for my clients," he told her bluntly.

"What about what you want?"

"What do you mean by that?"

Stacie stopped to think. Questions whirled around her head. She had a feeling this wasn't going to work out well. Was she smitten with a man who purely loved himself? He was waiting and she struggled to work out how to answer without sounding like she had feelings for him. "Don't you owe yourself more respect?"

"Why? I am happy, Stacie, doing what I am doing. It's great having sex with women knowing they aren't going to expect more from me. Out there," he waved a hand vaguely at the window, "you get clingy women who are always wanting more. Here, I can have fun without that attachment. I don't want commitment…I want fun. This club gives me security. The contract ensures that."

Stacie put her knife and fork down. She wasn't hungry any more.

"Is the food not good?"

"It's excellent. I'm just full."

Stacie understood. He was no better than any other man, just wanting as much sex as he could and nothing deeper than that. And he was gorgeous enough to be able to actually get paid for it as well. Stacie didn't want to confront him anymore—she'd heard enough. His looks weren't compatible with his outlook on life, but wasn't it always the good-looking ones that were full of themselves and selfish.

"Do you have a girlfriend?" she asked, not caring any more what he thought of her.

"I cannot answer that question."

"Do you often get nosy women?"

"Not usually."

"What do you normally do with your clients?"

He grinned. "Have sex."

"Am I a new experience?"

"Kind of."

He clearly was going to give the shortest answers possible. "Am I boring?"

"No one is boring, Stacie," he said, his expression changing to a look of mild censure. She stared at the food on her plate, wishing she'd never started this pathetic question time.

Stacie stood up and walked toward the large window. She stared out at the dark winter evening, wishing they could have a proper conversation. "It's not easy for me, being here."

"I know. You're doing really well."

Stacie began thinking about her time with Graham and how cheap he'd made her feel. When they married, she didn't have a clue what mind games he was capable of. He'd manipulated her and that was just the beginning. She had been brainwashed until there was nothing but crap in her head, being told so often she was worth nothing that she came to believe it. She became his servant—*If you loved me you'd want to look after me*—lost everyone who was important in her life—*You should only want to spend time with me. You're supposed to love me*—lost her glamorous beauty—*Who do you need to dress up for? I don't want other men looking at you*—and had become a woman who was so low on self-confidence, she was afraid of everything and everyone.

"What are you thinking?"

Stacie gave a short, humourless laugh. "Just thinking about my husband."

"Do you want to talk about it?"

"What, tell you how pathetic and blind I was, not seeing what mind games he was playing with me. How he left me with nothing and how stupid and naïve I was?"

Stacie's breath began to come short, closing her eyes and picturing Graham in her head, standing over her, shouting down at her, telling her she was a stupid fucking cunt as she curled up in a ball at one end of the sofa, her hands over her ears. He'd always made it seem like it was her fault, that it was something she'd said or done that made him lose his temper. If she tried to get away from his vicious tongue, he'd follow her. One time he'd followed her to the bedroom to continue his tirade, only to barricade the door with his body when she tried to leave, preventing her from getting out. And then, every time she told him that was it, she really was leaving him this time, he'd cry, tell her he was sorry, tell her he'd try harder next time. And she always gave in, always believed him, ignored that tiny voice telling her she was stupid, that he'd never change,

She tried to calm her panicked breathing. It was over. He couldn't get her any more. Dan was waiting. "It was a friendship that progressed. I met him through a friend. We all used to go out as a foursome. It was great. Fun, fun, fun was our language—nightclubs, expensive weekends away, even a holiday. It was a fantastic time. I was having the time of my life. I was young and madly in love. He would do anything for me. When he proposed it was like a fairy tale. Two dozen red roses, the best champagne, a stunningly gorgeous ring. I jumped around for months, bouncing around like a mad woman, so excited, getting everything prepared. I even bought my dream dress. It was so expensive, but I looked amazing." She smiled, remembering how she'd looked in her stunning satin gown, with a chapel-length train, her hair curled and pinned on the top of her head and crowned with a tiara.

"I bet you did." Dan's comment was so quiet she hardly heard it.

She continued. "The day was totally hectic, everyone running around me like I was a queen. It was a fabulous day—you just couldn't get me down the aisle quick enough. The venue was perfect and in the evening we drank champagne all night. I just couldn't stop staring at him, planning our future in my head. Our honeymoon was incredible. I just knew that he was the perfect man for me and that I would live the dream of a happy and fulfilling marriage. Boy, was I wrong.

"I couldn't believe how it had turned into such a disaster. It was like my world had shattered. No one else saw it. My family, friends, everyone loved him and thought he was the bees knees. No one could fault him. He was helping, caring, considerate...the perfect son-in-law. But behind the front door, he turned into a monster."

She dared a glance at Dan. His eyes were sober, full of compassion.

"The first time was the worst. We'd just got back from our honeymoon. I had been at work all day and I was heading home. I was so excited to get home to my husband. I walked through the door and rushed into the kitchen to see his face full of anger. I asked him what the problem was and he went mental, screaming at me, waving his fists, and then he hit me and, guess why?" she asked Dan, knowing full well he wouldn't know the answer.

"Why?"

"Because I didn't wash the breakfast dishes before going to work," she said, ignoring the tears streaming down her cheeks. "I couldn't believe it. I fell to the floor begging and pleading with him to stop, but he began kicking me. I was crying and screaming, but it didn't help. He called me names, useless bitch, stupid tart and fucking useless whore, told me no man deserves a useless lazy wife. Once he stopped, I could barely move. I managed to sit up and curl myself into a ball. I had no idea what had happened. I spent the night trying to make head or tail of it, but it was as if he was a totally different person. I even attempted to talk to him, but he wouldn't even look at me. The following day I called my mum, and do you know what she said after I told her what happened?"

"What?"

"She asked, what did I do to provoke him?" Stacie spat the words out. "It must have been my fault, obviously, as Graham wouldn't behave that way. What chance do you have if your own mother isn't on your side? I cried a lot, but then after a while I began to wonder whether it was me and how I could prevent that situation in the future. Maybe he'd just had a bad day and it was a one-off.

"He was furious I'd spoken to my mum. The next day I walked in the house and he was fuming. He rushed over to me, pinning me to the wall with his face right in mine, telling me if I ever mention him hurting me again, he would beat me black and blue so no one would recognise me. After that he used to give me a list of jobs he expected me to do, so me being a complete mug and with my mum saying a wife should look after her man, things just went on from that evening."

"Why did you not leave him straightaway?"

"Why indeed? I asked myself that same question over and over. But I didn't want to admit that I'd failed in my marriage. And

I guess I thought this was something we could work on together. I wanted to help him with his anger problems, support him, not just walk away from him. Isn't that what a wife is supposed to do, support her husband? And I was so in love with the nice Graham that I figured I could put up with the nasty one. I know how silly that sounds. I shouldn't have had to put up with that from my husband, but it's amazing what you tell yourself."

"Have you never told anyone about it?"

"No…I just kept it all inside. I never really knew who I could talk to."

Stacie wiped away the tears, limp with remembered rage and burning humiliation. She wished she had done something at the time, but she'd continued to take the pain and the brainwashing. And, after a while, she had started to believe what Graham told her, that it was all her own fault. That if she hadn't said such and such a thing, he would have no cause to lose his temper.

She sat back at the table and took a gulp of her wine. "Listen to me going on about all my boring problems."

"How can you say that, boring problems? My God, Stacie, he really did a number on you, didn't he?"

"Yes, but you don't need to hear about it." She cradled her wine broodingly before taking another gulp. Maybe she should just get totally hammered.

"Why shouldn't I hear about it? You've been to hell and back. You deserve to have your life back. He needs to be locked up. How can a guy hurt a woman like that? Bloody hell Stacie— boring? And of course I need to hear about it, it will help me to better understand your needs. Stacie," he leaned forward and caught her hand. "I want to help you. You can't live your life believing what he did was your fault. He was the one with the problem not you. Did he work?"

"At first, but he got made redundant after we got married. He said he was looking for work, but every time I asked him about it, he got angry. Then I think he just stopped trying, if he was ever trying to begin with. He used to say we were quite the modern couple, me being the breadwinner and him being the househusband."

"My God, what a selfish…Oh my God, Stacie," Dan said, almost sputtering in his anger, compassion and pain for her shining from his eyes.

"You haven't heard the worst."

"Tell me, Stacie."

Stacie swallowed, turning her head to look at the floor as she pictured that day. She didn't really want to relive it—she'd tried her best to forget it. But she couldn't pass up this the opportunity to talk to someone. Maybe talking would release the pain she had suffered since it had happened.

"I'd had a really shit day at work. It was raining and I got totally soaked waiting outside all day to do an interview, only for the person not to turn up. When I got home, thankfully, Graham was out. Probably with his mates drinking and doing drugs that I paid for. I did all the jobs that were on his list, made the house sparkle. I had a hot bath, and chilled out in front of the television waiting for his arrival. It got late and I wasn't able to keep my eyes any longer open, so I headed to bed. I was woken by the front door slamming, and heard more than just Graham's voice. He'd brought friends round. I wasn't impressed as I was so shattered, I needed to sleep. I headed downstairs to ask them to keep it down and was told to *fuck off back to bed*, so I did."

Stacie drew in a deep breath. Nausea roiled as she remembered the events of that night. "I listened to them all laughing. They were being exceptionally noisy but I couldn't be bothered to confront them, so I stayed where I was and dozed a bit. I managed to nod off then I heard the bedroom door open. I thought it was Graham, finally coming to bed. But usually Graham slept to my right side and this evening he was getting in on my left. I just figured he'd been drinking and was more than likely pissed."

A lump rose in her throat and she began to shake. She took another long draught of the wine. Dan reached across the table to take hold of her hand. "He began grabbing my breasts, pulling up my nightie. That was what he always did, he got into bed and started to fondle me and then we would have sex. But then I heard his voice. It wasn't Graham. As I was about to scream he filled my mouth with a cloth. He got on top of me and pinned me down with my hands above my head, with one hand. I struggled, and tried to knee him, but he was stronger than me. He used his spare hand to put his dick into me and then started grabbing at my breasts, squeezing really hard. I had never been so petrified. I just wanted him to stop."

Stacie stared down to the table. Tears dropped onto her abandoned plate and she forced herself to continue. "He started calling me names, whore, slut, bitch. I couldn't defend myself, I felt so weak. Then I remember hearing the bedroom door open. I saw Graham. I thought he'd come to rescue me. I thought he'd pull his friend off me and punch him, or something. Instead he stood there watching with his other mate. They were laughing and calling me names, encouraging him to rape me. Then he pulled out and I thought it was over, but he moved up and knelt over my chest. He jerked himself off for a few seconds then came all over my face. He climbed off and they were all laughing at me. I pulled the gag out. I felt I was about to throw up, but I had to get past them to get to the bathroom. They made me squeeze past them, making cheering noises as I passed. Graham grabbed my breast and the other one slapped my bottom."

She scrubbed her tears from her face. "I went to the toilet and was violently sick."

Dan moved round the table and stood next to her, pulling her to him where she sat. He stroked her hair as she nestled into his abdomen, her arms curving round his back.

"Abominable. There is no other word for it."

Stacie closed her eyes and snuggled into him, feeling his warmth, and the rise and fall of his torso as he breathed. He bent over to kiss her hair and stroked her back with one hand. Tears streamed down her face and she let out a shuddering breath of release.

"He was a bastard, a man who didn't appreciate something so special."

"I know that now. It's taken me all this time to realise it. Just telling you about that night has made me see what I suffered. I was so vulnerable and I was an idiot for putting up with it for so long."

Dan dropped down to kneel on the floor next to her, lifting her chin to make eye contact. "You cannot blame yourself—he had you brainwashed. They all should be locked up and hung by their balls. Men like that make our society criminal. You're brave, and haven't anything to be ashamed of, nothing in the slightest. My

God, Stacie, to think you have gone through all that and you are still here. He was lazy and a coward, relying on you to do everything and then—bloody hell—to allow his mate to rape you while he watched. He was sick and evil."

Compassion glowed from his eyes and Stacie bowed her head.

"And he didn't just work his evil on you, but also your family. I cannot believe your mother's reaction. He controlled you utterly and made you afraid of everything."

"That's what he was good at, he had me captured, a player in his sadistic, vindictive game. The worst thing is that he's probably still up to his tricks with some other woman."

"But you saw sense and for that you need a bravery award. You are the bravest woman I have ever come across and you deserve my full respect."

"I'm hardly brave."

"No, you listen to me. What you have been through and what other women are going through needs to be recognised. Women aren't servants, you aren't here to be at a man's beck and call, you should to be treated with respect. We live in a new century and men who treat women like that should be made to change their ways." He dragged his chair round close to Stacie's and sat in it so their knees touched. He took both her hands in his. "You're amazing, Stacie, you truly are. You should be proud of what you managed to do to get yourself out, not ashamed of the circumstances that caused it. I would imagine it's probably the hardest thing you had ever had to do. I gather there are no children?"

"No," she whispered. "But there nearly was. He beat me again and I lost it."

Dan's head dropped and he could not look at her. After a minute, a tear dropped to their joined hands. "I have no words. I can't begin to imagine what you went through," he said finally, looking up, his eyes red-rimmed.

Stacie felt a sudden surge of rage against Graham blacker than she had ever felt. Why didn't she see the signs before? Why had she left it so long? She should have gone after that first beating.

After a while Stacie raised her head and looked into his sad brown eyes. "I'm sorry. I never meant to burden you with all this."

"Don't ever apologise. I'm humbled you have told me. You deserve something in return. I could lose my job over this, but you deserve nothing less than total respect and honesty."

"You don't have to tell me anything."

"I want to. I believe I can trust you, and I want you to trust me. He robbed you of your confidence and for you to come back from that at all shows me what type of person you are. I think you're the bravest person I have ever met and it deserves to be recognised."

"I didn't tell you for sympathy."

"I know. You told me because you needed to talk about it. Sometimes it's easier to talk to a stranger."

He poured them both a fresh glass of wine. Stacie took a sip of hers, then jumped up.

"If you've finished, I'll just clear away these dishes," Stacie said, unsure where to take the conversation next.

"No, it's okay. I'll do it," Dan insisted, taking her plate out of her hand.

Stacie watched him for a second before standing up to go to the bathroom.

Stacie wetted a tissue and scrubbed at the mascara stains under her eyes. She looked a mess. Dan was an enigma. One minute he seemed like a typical selfish man with all his talk about just wanting sex with no commitment, the next he was kind and considerate, holding her and listening as she sobbed her heart out over Graham. But then maybe he was just a normal young man having fun with his life, and her sense of what was normal had been warped by her experiences with Graham. Weren't all young men sexually selfish to some degree? Was it selfish to not want to settle down too young? And what right did she have to judge his choices anyway?

What did he want to tell her? She was eager to find out more about him, especially as it was forbidden. But what was the point, if there was no possible chance of a relationship or even friendship at the end of the weekend? At least she'd had an opportunity to talk to someone about Graham, although that wasn't why she'd come. Or maybe it was. She'd come here to regain her confidence sexually, and maybe talking about what had caused her to lose that confidence was part of it. Poor Dan—he hadn't signed up to be a counsellor.

# Chapter Five

Stacie headed back into the bedroom. Dan had moved to the bed, lying back against the plumped-up pillows with his glass in his hand. She saw he'd put hers on the bedside table on the other side. She climbed on the bed to sit next to him, and picked up her own glass.

"I don't have a girlfriend."

Stacie tried hard to stop her relief from showing on her face. "You don't need to tell me."

"I want to tell you. My day job is IT support and computer repair. It's not very interesting. I do this job for some fun extra cash. I do enjoy it, although it has its moments like any job. And when I'm not working I hang out with my mates, play football, and drive my car. That's all. I'm quite dull really."

They sat on the bed talking. Dan regaled her with stories about his childhood, school-days and university. Stacie listened avidly.

"At university, I had an alter ego called The Yellow Ninja. The only person who knew it was me was a friend," he said.

"And what did The Yellow Ninja do?"

"Basically, The Yellow Ninja would go places he wasn't supposed to, and my friend would take a picture of me in these places and then we'd post it on my website," Dan said, a smile cracking his face. "It all started when my friend bet me I couldn't climb onto a roof. I didn't want to get caught, so I borrowed a costume from the drama department when they'd done some mad play with a custard monster in it. So there was me dressed in yellow trousers and a yellow jumper wearing a yellow balaclava doing *The Thinker* on the drama studio roof. My mate posted it on the SU website and it went viral. Everyone was sharing it and the university management went ballistic. They demanded to know who it was and of course no one knew. I thought it'd be funny to take a few more pictures of The Yellow Ninja in a few more places and it really took off. I created a website and I started to get issued with challenges."

"What do you mean, challenges?"

"Well, one time someone wanted me to gatecrash their lecture so I dressed up and ran screaming through the lecture hall. I have pictures of me pretty much everywhere in that university I wasn't supposed to be."

"What was the scariest one?"

"Breaking into the Vice-Chancellor's office," Dan said promptly. "That was pretty cool though—I got a picture of me lounging at his desk doing a thumbs-up."

"And they never caught you?"

"Nope. The Yellow Ninja was a legend. And to this day no one knows who he was, except me and my mate. And now you."

"That's pretty awesome." Stacie shook her head in admiration. "The maddest thing I ever did in university was get absolutely rat-arsed one night, roll up to lectures the next day still drunk and fall asleep on the desk."

"This one time…" Dan glanced at her, then stopped.

"What?"

He pulled a face. "You might not approve."

"Try me."

"Okay, well this one time, someone put a challenge on the website, if I managed to break into a certain place at a certain time, this girl would suck my cock."

"And did you?"

"Hell, yes."

"And did she?"

"Oh yeah!"

"And she never knew who you were?"

"Nope. I was fully masked the entire time." He sighed. "Good times."

Stacie's childhood had been mixed. Her mother had left her father, which had naturally caused upheaval within the family. Stacie missed her father tremendously and would have preferred to live with him, but it would have broken her mother's heart. She did get to see him at weekends, but her mother made it difficult. Then her mother found a new partner, Ray. He was okay but Stacie never allowed Ray to replace her father, which made things awkward with her mum, who wanted them all to play happy families together.

She never really got on with her sister, Samantha. They seemed to be always fighting, causing bad atmospheres in the home. Samantha fawned over their mother, and could never do anything wrong in her eyes. But it was all show and Mum fell for it. Samantha was mercenary, constantly after her mother's money. Stacie distanced herself from the two of them. Better to let them sort it out between them. Once she met Graham, her relationship with her mum improved and she helped Stacie to organise the wedding and decorate the house. But then, once Stacie left Graham, it all changed for the worse again. She was lucky if she heard from her mum once a month. And even then, it was usually only if something was wrong.

Her father remarried and had another child. Stacie was devastated. How could he replace her so easily? Bitterly disappointed by both her parents, Stacie resolved to get on with her life and do what made her happy. She learned how to fake it, to make nice and smile for family occasions, but for the most part, she would rather have nothing to do with any of them.

Dan made her feel real again. With him, Stacie could be herself, her real self, not the fake Stacie that laughed at other people's jokes but didn't really care.

She'd always had difficulty making new friends. Taking that first step was nerve-wracking, then she struggled to trust enough to allow them get close enough to be a true friend. Most of the time, it simply wasn't worth the hassle, especially with Graham demanding to know why she needed friends anyway. But with Dan, it was easy. She didn't have to try. It just…happened. And he made her feel safe.

"Do you fancy getting some food? I'm starving," he said.

"More food? But we've only just had dinner."

"Dinner was three hours ago."

Stacie looked at the clock, startled. Had they really been talking for that long?

"Just have a snack. Let me show you downstairs."

"Downstairs?" Stacie began to panic. What might she see downstairs? Would there be other people? The thought of leaving their haven was disconcerting.

"It's okay." Dan had accurately read her expression. "If you see anything that makes you feel uncomfortable, we'll come back up again. Promise."

Dan opened his wardrobe and pulled out a tuxedo. When she'd packed to come here, Stacie had thought they might go out to eat, so she'd put in a nice dress. When they'd ordered room service, she hadn't bothered to get changed, but she was glad she'd packed it now. She hadn't realised it would be quite so formal. She watched him get dressed, eating him up with her eyes. She'd rather have him than more food, but she was curious to see downstairs. She could have him later.

"How do I look?" he asked, posing in his tux.

"Awful. I think you should just take it all off."

She giggled and he grinned. "Maybe later." He gave her a wink and her stomach lurched. God, she could just jump on him. *Later,* she reminded herself sternly. She pulled her dress out of the wardrobe where'd she'd hung it and went into the bathroom. She quickly freshened her makeup and pulled the dress on, running a brush through her hair and twisting it up in a fountain before coming back out.

"You look nice," he said as she twirled for him.

"Thank you."

"Shall we?" He held out his arm and she took it.

They walked down the corridor toward the staircase. She could almost pretend they were a proper couple, in a nice hotel somewhere, walking down to the restaurant.

Until, that is, they passed a couple walking up the stairs in PVC fetishwear. *You wouldn't see that in a posh hotel*. Stacie tried not to stare. They smiled at her pleasantly as they passed, and she managed a smile back. Stacie turned her head to watch them as they walked down the corridor.

"You're staring," Dan murmured to her.

"Sorry." Stacie's head spun back to face front and they headed down the stairs.

She was surprised to see a gang of people all dressed in cowboy and cowgirl outfits in the reception area. She'd never seen this place so busy. Dan guided her round the edge of the crowd, but Stacie resisted.

"Can you just wait for me here," she said, turning to him. "I just need to speak to reception about something."

His eyebrows rose in query, but all he said was, "Sure." He sat down on one of the leather sofas and waited. Stacie took a deep breath to calm her nerves before proceeding through the crowd, trying to get to reception. Someone grabbed her bottom and she whirled around to see who it was, but there were so many men around her it could have been any one of them. Certainly no one was owning up. Huffing, she turned back and continued fighting her way through, trying to be polite. By dint of much excusing herself, and finally just shoving, she finally made it to the desk.

There were a number of people waiting to speak to the swamped receptionists. Stacie attempted to wait patiently, tapping her feet and silently urging them to hurry up so she could get back to Dan. She glanced around the area, for the first time noticing how revealing the outfits were. One girl had more material in her hat than in her outfit.

She felt a hand on her bottom and a voice in her right ear. "That's a very sexy dress you're wearing." The hand gave her rear end a slap and she bristled. "Which party are you from?" the voice asked.

Stacie turned her head to her right, seeing a leering young man dressed as a cowboy. "I'm not with a party." She reached behind herself and removed his hand from her backside.

"That's a serious shame. I could imagine you and me having so much fun," he said to her cleavage.

"Well, you just keep imagining, as it won't be happening. *Excuse me!*" she called to the receptionist, wanting to get away from these people, before any more of them got any ideas. She moved around the desk, doing everything to get the receptionists' attention, barging her way to the other side.

"Sorry, can I help?" asked the receptionist, arching her brows at Stacie.

"Yes, I hope so. Can you tell me if Dan is available tomorrow afternoon and evening?"

"Let me have a look," she replied. Stacie watched her pressing a few buttons on the keyboard. "Can I have your code, please?" she asked. Stacie gave it to her. "You are with him now?"

"Yes."

"I will have to contact him," she said, looking up at Stacie.

"What, right now?" she asked.

"Yes, just to make sure he has no plans."

"Oh." Stacie wasn't sure why, but she didn't want Dan to know she was considering booking him again. Not yet anyway. "It doesn't matter," Stacie said and turned to fight her way back through the crowd.

She arrived back to where Dan was waiting.

"All done?" he asked, standing up as she approached.

"Yes."

"What did you want to speak to them about?"

"Nothing exciting," she replied. "Shall we go?"

Dan led her round the crowd and down a corridor she hadn't been down yet. A discreet plaque on the double doors at the end proclaimed it to be the restaurant. Stacie peered curiously round the door as Dan swung it open for her, but saw nothing but smartly dressed diners dotted around the room. Dan smiled at the look on her face.

"Disappointed?"

"Not at all." *Liar,* Stacie told herself. *Come on, you wanted to see something a little spicy.*

"This restaurant is mainstream. There are others where you might see something a little more…interesting. But I thought you'd prefer it here. I ordered while you were in the bathroom. I didn't know what you wanted so I just ordered a selection of starters for us to share."

A girl wearing a tiny waitress's uniform came forward to greet them. As she turned to lead them to their table, Stacie could see her frilly white panties peeking out from underneath her barely-there skirt. Suspenders held up fishnet stockings, and she wore impossibly high heels on her feet. She and Dan exchanged pleasantries and her rippling laugh grated on Stacie's nerves. They'd only been seated a couple of minutes before she was back with a trolley laden with plates and another bottle of wine.

The waitress leaned over the table as she set out the plates. She had very large breasts that were almost falling out of the low-cut top she wore. Stacie could have sworn she could see the edge of the girl's nipple. Dan was smiling at her and his eyes definitely flashed to her boobs. Stacie could hardly tear her own eyes off them, but for very different reasons.

She poured them both a glass of wine then sashayed across the room. Stacie watched her go.

"The food looks good," Dan commented.

"Yes, it does," she said absently, not looking at it.

"You okay?"

"Yes fine," she said. Had Dan been intimate with that girl? They seemed very chummy. She caught herself. They were probably just colleagues. And that's just the uniform she has to wear—it's not her fault. And anyway, what did it matter if he had? She had no claim over him.

"How are you feeling?" she heard him ask.

"Fine." She brought her attention back to Dan and the table. The food did look very nice. Maybe she could manage a little bit of something. Those stuffed mushrooms looked delicious.

"Good. So, what did you talk to reception about?" he asked her.

"Nothing."

"It must have been something."

"Why does it matter?"

"It doesn't, not at all. I was just curious." His phone rang. "I'm sorry, I have to answer this," he said leaving the table to stand by the window as he took the call. "Hello," he said. Stacie shamelessly eavesdropped on his conversation and admired him in his suit. "Oh right," she heard him reply. "Yes…no problem…okay…no that's fine…speak to you soon, bye." She started to add a selection of the starters to her plate as he came back to sit down.

"You've only booked me till lunchtime tomorrow, haven't you?" he asked, sitting down and covering his lap with his napkin.

"Yes, but I was hoping to extend it till dinner," she said, forgetting her reasons for not telling him in her sudden panic.

"Ah, I see."

"Why, would that be a problem?"

"That was reception on the phone."

"With a booking? For tomorrow?"

"You could say that," he said.

Stacie sat back in disappointment, staring at the dark window. She had just missed out on having him all day tomorrow. Why hadn't she allowed the receptionist to get in touch with him? Stacie wondered if she should book him for the following weekend, before anyone else had the opportunity.

Stacie managed to make small talk throughout the meal, such as it was. She picked at the dishes and drank too much wine, angry at herself for not having the courage to book him for the whole day tomorrow. She couldn't help but think about the woman who would be with him. She hoped it would be somebody disgusting, so he would wish it was her instead. But then, why would she assume he liked her? Yes, he had opened up and told her a few personal details but, wasn't that part of her therapy? It didn't mean he liked her.

"Dessert?"

Stacie looked up, surprised. She'd been so lost in thought she hadn't noticed that Dan had finished. "Sorry?"

"Would you like dessert?"

*Only you.* "Not for me, thanks. I'm stuffed."

"Do you want a drink? Or we can go to one of the party rooms."

Earlier she'd been curious, but now she just wanted Dan. Knowing he'd be with someone else tomorrow made her want to not waste a second of the time they had.

"Can we just go back upstairs?"

"Of course."

He escorted her back along the corridor. Thankfully reception was empty again. They must have come down just as a party was arriving.

"Do they often get parties here?"

"Frequently, usually at weekends. Groups can either book a private room, or mingle with other groups in one of the larger rooms."

"And these are…sex parties?"

"Naturally."

Stacie shook her head at her own innocence. It was a whole other world.

Dan put on the television, flicking through the channels. There was nothing on but rubbish. Restless, Stacie wandered around the room trying to burn off some of the food she'd eaten that day. It had been delicious, but not as wonderful as her Dan-shaped dessert later would be. Her mind wandered and she found herself leaning against the dresser, staring at him foolishly. Her eyes drifted over the planes of his face, his cute dimple and the soft curls on his head, which her fingers ached to run through.

She started in embarrassed surprise when he looked up at her, then warmth flooded her belly when he smiled and patted the bed next to him. She sat on the bed, staring at his profile, wanting to get close to him. She wanted him to touch her in a way no other man ever had. He turned his head to look at her looking at him. This time she didn't look away, meeting his gaze.

He looked at her for several seconds, the expression on his face looking as if he were trying to decide something. Stacie's heart began to beat rapidly. Was this the moment she had been waiting for? She felt suddenly, inexplicably shy and more than a little anxious.

Dan shifted his body round to face Stacie. He took hold of her hand and raised it to his lips. He kissed each knuckle one by one, still looking at her. His lips felt soft and his eyes were huge and dark in the minimal light cast by the dimmed wall-lamps. He lowered her hand, then leaned toward her. Stacie closed her eyes and darted her tongue out to moisten her lips. She felt his lips pressing gently on hers. She kissed him back lightly, a tiny kiss, over the instant it had begun. He cupped her cheek with his hand and she leaned into it. This time his kiss, when it came, was more urgent, more passionate. His hand moved round to the back of her head and he held her close, his tongue dipping and tasting along her lips. She opened a little to welcome him and he slid his tongue in, not too far, just far enough to touch hers.

She shivered and inched closer to him. He matched her movement until they were both kneeling up on the bed, their torsos crushed together. His hand was on the back of her head, hers were trailing up his back under his jacket. They deepened the kiss, their tongues playing catch-me-if-you-can until Stacie was quite breathless.

She pulled away, just for a second. His eyes devoured her. She put her hands beneath the front of his jacket and pushed it off his shoulders, tossing it onto the floor beyond the bed. He pulled her back to him and kissed her deeply, one hand tiptoeing down her leg to pull up the skirt of her dress. She felt his fingers on her bare thigh, then both hands on her bottom, pulling her close.

He sat back on his heels and sat her down so she knelt straddling his thighs on the bed. She could feel his erection pressing for her attention beneath his dress trousers. Tremors of arousal shot through her pussy and she trembled in his arms.

She wanted him now, yet wanted it to last. He cupped her face in his hands, stroking her cheeks with his thumbs. He kissed her forehead, then her nose, then both cheeks. He moved across to her ear, licking delicately around the earlobe and nibbling with gentle teeth before kissing down her neck and across one bare shoulder. She hooked her arms loosely around his shoulders and let her head hang back as he continued down toward her breasts. He nuzzled her cleavage, seeming to breathe in her scent. One hand caressed a breast, pushing it up to meet his eager lips, while the other explored under her dress, just brushing her moist mound with his thumb. She wriggled on his lap and cried out, grinding her pussy into his bulge.

Dan brought his head back up, kissing her deeply, his hand still exploring her breasts. Stacie untied his bow-tie and began to fumble at his shirt buttons, undoing them as quickly as she could. He quickly shucked the shirt, exposing his flawless chest. In return, he unzipped her dress and pulled it down to her waist. She knelt up on the bed and pulled it down further before sliding her legs out. Dan tossed it onto the floor and sat back, looking at her.

His hands ran wild over her body, brushing across the tops of her breasts, then down her stomach and along her waist while he kissed her passionately. They stopped briefly at her bottom, cupping it greedily before one hand came round and rested on her thigh. He trailed his hot fingers down to her knee and back up her inner thigh. Her body tensed for his touch, but he stopped short of her pussy, leaving her aching.

Dan eased his fingers into her bra cup, peeling the lace away from her breast. Her nipple emerged into the air, erect for his attention. He took it greedily into his mouth, sucking and licking. She felt his hand once again on her thigh, trailing higher. She had to stop herself shamelessly thrusting her pussy at him. *Touch me,* she begged in her mind, hoping he would pick up her thought.

When his fingers finally brushed the ultra-sensitive skin between her thighs, she almost jumped ten feet in the air. She groaned and leaned into him, pushing herself into his fingers, welcoming him. He used just the very tips of his fingers, tracing a trail down the damp material. She almost cried when he moved his fingers away again.

He moved his attention then to her right breast, slipping the bra cup down. Stacie reached behind herself to undo the bra, but her fingers met Dan's. He unclipped the bra expertly, lifting it away from her breasts and dropping it on the floor. Then he wrapped both his arms round her back and began to kneel up, forcing her to shift her weight backward into his arms. He lowered her to the bed and lay on his side next to her, his gaze roaming her body leisurely.

He kissed between her breasts, shifting his body as he dropped a trail of kisses like breadcrumbs down her belly. He nibbled along the soft curve of her belly just above her panties before he started plucking at them.

"I think we can get rid of these, can't we," he said, inserting a finger from each hand inside them.

Stacie could do nothing but nod jerkily and lift her bottom so he could slide the knickers slowly down her thighs. She spread her legs like a wanton when he came back up. He knelt between her thighs, just staring at her for a second while her breath caught in anticipation. He took her calves in both his hands and pushed her legs out and back, spreading them wider before lying down on his belly on the bed, supporting himself on his elbows.

Stacie closed her eyes and lay back. She could feel his breath on her pussy as he moved closer, then his thumbs spread her apart and she exploded at the first touch of his tongue on her clit.

Her hands went to his head, holding him in place, her pelvis thrust into him, incoherent noises emanated from her mouth as his tongue did such things to her as she had never imagined. The tip of his nimble tongue swirled around her clit and she felt him dipping his finger into her wet hole. She wriggled and mewed, clenching her pussy muscles around his finger, wanting more.

Stacie felt him insert another finger hard into her pussy as his tongue continued its torturous tickling. She cried out loudly, thrusting her hips high off the bed, grabbing her own breasts and squeezing them together. Stacie moaned, tossing her head from side to side, losing herself in his mind-blowing touch.

He pulled his fingers out and she opened her eyes, watching him as he licked them clean.

"You taste divine," he told her, before bending once more to his task. Stacie's eyebrows flicked up in surprise. Graham had always refused to go down on her, said all girls smelled, and tasted, like rotten fish.

Then all thought of Graham was gone as Dan flattened his tongue and licked slowly down her pussy. He pressed the tip of his tongue to the entrance of her vagina and she held her breath as he pushed it in as far as he could. She closed her eyes again, surrendering herself to his expertise. With his clever hands and tongue, he brought her close to the edge half a dozen times, leaving her screaming with frustration each time he stopped.

Stacie felt her whole body being taken over by emotion and madness. She hardly knew where to turn.

Then Dan moved. She felt him climbing up her body, kissing her stomach and breasts *en route*. He arrived at her mouth, kissing her deeply. She could taste herself on his mouth. She couldn't help feeling the bulge in his trousers. He did nothing so crass as to grind it into her, but she wished he would. She dropped her hand to him and gently caressed it, moving her fingers up and down the length of him.

She thought she'd done something wrong, and half sat up in panic when he moved completely away from her, climbing off the bed. But his smile reassured her and she lay back, watching him. Dan headed around to the other side of the bed and opened the top drawer of the bedside table. When she saw him bring out a condom, she could barely contain herself. Finally!

Dan undressed slowly and deliberately, teasing her no doubt. He pulled his leather belt out from the belt loops, running the black leather through his palm. Stacie inhaled sharply, imagining him trailing that leather belt over her body, tickling her with it. God, the things she'd love him to do! A quirky smile crossed his face, as if he were thinking the same thing, but he rolled the belt up and placed it on the bedside table. She watched him undo his trousers and lower them to reveal his black Calvin Klein trunks. The outline of his hard penis showed clearly through the material. He turned around to lay the trousers carefully over the end of the bed and his cute sexy bottom worked as he walked. Stacie wanted to grab it and squeeze it hard.

Dan came back to the bed. Stacie couldn't keep her eyes off the outline of his cock. God, she wanted it! She was shocked at her own greed, her own craving. She'd honestly never felt this way before. He knelt between her thighs, and carefully lay on top of her, taking the weight on his elbows. She could feel the length of his almost naked body on hers. His Calvin Klein-covered cock pressed into her aching pussy. She wrapped her legs around him, holding him to her. Surely he would take her now.

Dan's face hovered over hers for a moment before he bent down and kissed her gently. His lips felt soft and warm and her tongue came out to meet his. His hand cupped her cheek and his thumb stroked her skin as his tongue sought entrance. She opened to him and quivered as he kissed her deeply. She ran her hands down his chest, dancing delicately over his stomach before coming to rest at the waistband of his trunks.

Dan kissed her one last time, then knelt up. His eyes gave Stacie her answer. She lifted her body into a sitting position, reaching out her hand to trace the outline of his penis. She stretched the waistband over his jutting cock, touching her tongue to the end as soon as it hit the air, tasting the saltiness seeping from the end. As each inch came into the light, she took it into her mouth, until she had as much as she could take. She pulled down his shorts to his knees and then abandoned them, returning her hands to busy themselves playing with his balls. He groaned and thrust into her mouth, resting his hands on her hair. Stacie smiled around his cock, pleased to hear him enjoying her pleasing him. She looked up at him, saw him watching her through slitted eyes.

She slid her mouth off his penis to lick the whole length of his shaft, rolling her tongue over his tight skin. She began to jerk him off, adding a little twist to tease him, wanting to hear him cry with hunger. A deep groan came from above. She glanced up at him. His eyes were shut tight and his face frozen with ecstasy.

He pulled away from her then, lifting his knees one by one to remove the trunks from where they still lay around his knees. She lay back on the bed, waiting for him. Considering she never normally found men's bodies attractive, Dan was definitely something else. Even his penis was nicely-formed, smooth and well-coloured, his balls tight and round.

He opened the condom packet and rolled it on. It was a shame they had to use it, *sex was much better bare,* she mused, for both of them. But, no point taking chances. Rubbered up, he dived on her almost with a growl, positioning his cock between her thighs. Even latexed, she still wanted it.

He was there, at her entrance. She needed him, she wanted him, she pushed into him as much as she dared, hoping he would get the message. Instead he leaned over and kissed her again. Stacie almost cried. *Just do it,* she thought. He took his cock in his hands and rubbed it up and down between her labia. She shivered and whimpered when he rubbed it over her clit, running her hands over his bottom, pulling his pelvis close to hers.

"You ready?" he whispered.

Stacie meant it to be a yes, but it came out as a high-pitched moan. Dan repositioned his cock at her entrance and slowly, slowly sank it into her, immersing himself totally in her wet passage.

The feeling sent her crazy, she reached behind her and grabbed onto the headboard whilst his cock took her to complete heaven. He withdrew and penetrated again, all her nerve endings went wild. But it was too slow, too gentle, she wanted more. She thrust into him shamelessly, her hands squeezing his firm bottom, urging him on. He picked up on her need and began pumping her till her boobs jiggled. Stacie screamed wildly. Surely it had never been this good before.

He stopped after a minute or so, breathing heavily as he moved off her, rolling his body around to her right side. He turned her over into a spooning position, her bottom tucked into his tummy. He lifted her right leg and then glided his penis back into her. She bent her leg backward as much as she could and wrapped it over his hip. He was even deeper inside her than before, if that was even possible. Dan reached around and took hold of her breast, squeezing and pulling. Stacie reached her hand down to where they were joined, feeling his cock sliding in and out of her. Her thumb glanced over her own clit and a jolt of feeling shot through her. She began to rub with earnest, then she heard Dan tutting in her ear as he removed her hand, and replaced it with his own.

Dan kept sinking his cock in her, sliding his manhood deep inside, hitting that sweet spot deep within her. She wasn't sure where to concentrate, on him, or his penis dipping in and out of her excited vagina, or the way he was stimulating her clit. Stacie was in pure heaven.

He pulled away again, this time putting her onto all fours. He came in close behind her, taking a firm hold of her bottom. She reached under and helped him into position, then felt his cock tormenting her lips before he sank deeply, hitting her G-spot. Stacie cried out, twining her fingers in the bedsheet. He reached around and resumed his playing with her clitoris, thrusting in and out of her sodden shaft. Stacie screamed, feeling her build up. She could hear the sound of his moaning—he wasn't far behind.

She buried her head in the pillow, surrendering to the inevitable. Her entire body felt hijacked, it jerked and fired in all directions. Her body became overwhelmed with a hot sweat and all her nerve endings erupted. Dan cried out as he thrust, penetrating faster and harder into her juicy pussy. He groaned and held his position as Stacie erupted into oblivion. She felt his cock pulsate with his orgasm, even through the rubber. His hands flexed on her hips, holding her in place as he spasmed inside her. Aftershocks rocked her body.

Stacie held her position feeling his body against hers. Her body trembled. His hands relaxed on her hips and she felt him lean over and kiss her back.

The he carefully withdrew and she collapsed on the bed, rolling over to face him, attempting to catch her breath. Dan lay on his side opposite her. His smile was enigmatic. Stacie didn't bother trying to read him. She lay looking at him, her breath beginning to slow, taking in the magic that had just happened. Never in her life had she felt so much hunger for a man, or climaxed with so much pleasure.

"How was that?" Dan asked her, discreetly pulling off the condom and wrapping it in tissue from a box on the bedside table before throwing it neatly into a bin next to the bed.

Stacie was surprised her grin didn't split her face. She could feel herself glowing with pure ecstasy. She was wet with sweat and she could feel her pussy was soaked with her own love juices. Her body craved for more of him. Dan was her man, well for tonight anyway. He might be a stranger, but he had taught her more about the sheer pleasure of sex in the last twenty-four hours than she had learned in her entire life.

Dan sat up and plumped up the pillows.

"Would you care for a drink?"

"That'd be great."

Stacie watched him climb off the bed. His rounded bottom dimpled as he walked over to the dresser. He stood unashamedly naked as he poured their drinks and brought them back to the bed. His body was divine, his muscles perfect. God help her, she wanted him all over again.

"What are you thinking about?" he asked, a cheeky smile on his face. He passed her glass to her and got back onto the bed, holding his glass carefully. It hardly mattered if he spilled it, the bed was soaked with her juices anyway.

"Guess," she replied, pulling the sheet up from the bottom of the bed to cover her body.

"I assume you enjoyed it?"

"What gives you that idea?"

Stacie made herself comfortable in the bed, arranging the pillows behind her so she could sit up straight. She didn't want to meet Dan's eyes. She felt a little embarrassed now by her reactions. She took a sip of her wine, not tasting it. Dan's stare was almost tangible. She stared straight ahead, realising she had a problem she couldn't put off any longer. She was beginning to finding him more attractive. And it wasn't just physical either. That was great, but it was more than that. The thought had been prodding her for some time and she knew she was going to have to face it. She was falling for him. It was hopeless, she knew. She couldn't have him. *That damn contract!* Stacie wished she could grab it and rip it to shreds.

"What are your plans after leaving here tomorrow?" he asked her.

"Back to my flat and housework, I guess. Terribly boring," she replied, finally managing to bring herself to look at him. His lips were delicious. "Is your client tomorrow a regular?"

"No, well yes...she's just started," he said, sipping his wine.

She looked at him, confused. "What do you mean?"

"She's only been coming a short time. She's a little older than me."

"Oh right. Is she pretty?" Stacie asked, wishing she hadn't.

"Not bad, I've certainly had much...much worse," he said. The pit of Stacie's stomach began to ache.

"Yeah, the old woman?"

"Yes definitely, but this woman's unique in many ways. I have to say I'm looking forward to her. You could always book me next weekend, if of course you want to. I could give you a few instructions to keep yourself going," he said, his expression inscrutable.

"Oh right," she replied. Her heart felt like it had been pulled out her body and ripped apart. This was why the contract existed, she savagely reminded herself, so stupid women like her wouldn't go and fall for their instructors. Which was precisely what she had gone and done. She got up, intending to head to the bathroom to clean up, not looking at Dan. It wasn't his fault. He was just doing his job. It was her fault.

"Are you okay?" she heard him ask.

"Yes, of course, why?" She felt her eyes brimming with tears and dashed them away, horrified. *Just let me go to the bathroom and cry!*

"Stacie, it's you."

"Who is?" she asked, hesitantly turning to look at him. He was smiling.

"Tomorrow. My client. My afternoon and evening," he said.

Stacie shook her head, not understanding. "How come?"

"You went to reception to book me."

"Well, yes I did, but I—"

"Yes...and the receptionist was ringing to see if I was available for you." He got off the bed and moved close to her, smiling. "You know, I almost got the feeling you were jealous."

"Did you?" she whispered, her knees suddenly wobbling so hard she had to sit hurriedly back on the bed.

"Yes." He sat next to her, lifting a gentle thumb to wipe away the tear that overflowed.

"I'm aware of the rules," she said, looking away from him.

"Ah yes, we must always remember the rules," he said, kissing her cheek before standing up. He went to the bathroom while Stacie sipped her wine. A smile cracked her face as she remembered what he'd said. "I'm looking forward to her." Did he mean it?

Her mind's cogs began to churn. She had to try her hardest not to become flattered with the few sweet comments he had made. This was his job. He could be just keeping her sweet, saying what she wanted to hear, so she'd carry on coming and he'd keep on getting paid. But would he be that cruel, letting her fall in love with him, just for money? One would have to be a consummate actor in this line of work, never letting the client see if you were disgusted with them, or what they wanted you to do.

She sat on the bed, staring hard at the bathroom door, waiting for him to return. She couldn't help it, she wanted desperately to see his sexy smile, in fact to see him, full stop. The way he walked, the way he talked, the way he touched and the way he made her feel. He was everything she had ever dreamed about in her perfect man. There was simply nothing that she didn't like about the guy—except, perhaps, his chosen line of work.

He came out the bathroom and flashed a smile at her. His cock was limp but he was still gorgeous. Did he know, this handsome young man, what effect he was having on her life?

"Are you okay?" he asked her.

"Wonderful. You?"

"I'm great…I am just going to pop out for a few minutes, get a little air," he told her. He went to the wardrobe and pulled out some jeans and a T-shirt.

Whilst vaguely wondering why he was going out in the dark, she didn't answer him other than an, "Mm-hmm," of acknowledgement. He really didn't need to answer to her about anything. She returned his smile as he left the room, stretching with pleasure, content in the knowledge that she would have him all day tomorrow as well.

## Chapter Six

Stacie opened her eyes, hearing movement in the room. She must have dozed off after Dan had left the room. She turned her body slightly to see Dan sitting on the bed.

"What time is it?"

"Nine thirty. You were fast asleep."

"You must be wearing me out," she replied, stretching out while kicking off the sheet. The air hit her body and she realised she was completely naked. She grabbed the sheet and covered herself back up. "How was your fresh air?"

"Not bad, it's freezing out though."

Stacie climbed off the bed picked up the robe that was still beside the bed and headed into the bathroom. After combing her hair, Stacie refreshed her makeup then headed back out to Dan who was resting on the bed. Stacie went over to the wardrobe pulling out the grey jeans and red sweater she had been wearing before, then sat on the end of the bed, staring at the television, seeing what Dan was watching.

"What do you fancy doing?" he asked, switching the television off by the remote.

"How about we go out for a walk? I fancy stretching my legs and getting some air."

Dan jumped off the bed and started to put on his shoes. Stacie slipped hers on also and started to move toward the door. Dan got there first, opening it for her. She brushed past him deliberately, feeling a *frisson* just from that slight touch.

They walked down the corridor hearing music—it got louder as they approached the staircase. A couple came hurtling out of a room laughing and groping one another. They seemed pretty drunk. Stacie watched them losing their footing, falling all over the place. Dan took hold of her hand to keep her moving. Stacie glanced back at the drunken pair, they had fallen to the floor with him landing on her.

They arrived at the top of the staircase. The music belted out from below. Stacie loved a good dance, it reminded her of the good old days hanging out with her friends, leaving college, and quickly getting ready before hitting the pubs and nightclubs. She always loved dancing, standing out from the others, moving her feet to the beat and swaying her hips, hoping to be noticed by the men. She swayed to the music as they walked down the sweep of stairs.

The receptionists were sitting and chatting. They both smiled at Dan and said, "Good evening." Stacie frowned, trying to analyse their smiles. This was a sex club. Did they all shag each other indiscriminately? Who knew what went on here? Dan replied cordially, letting go of Stacie's arm.

Stacie walked over to the large double wooden doors from where the music was emanating. She wondered what was behind it. Where was Dan? She looked back to see him laughing with the receptionists. Quelling her ridiculous jealousy—they were just colleagues—she opened the doors a crack.

The semi-darkened room was like a night club. The dance floor was full of party-goers, jigging and writhing, their hands in the air. That was something Stacie certainly was in the mood for. She went inside and glanced around. The hall was huge and grand with old Georgian features, a decorative ceiling, large canopies, and gleaming chandeliers. There was a bar at one end and comfortable-looking seating areas surrounded the dance floor.

Then Stacie looked at the other end of the room, which was dominated by a large stage. It was a live sex show! There were several couples having sex right there on stage—there was even one woman lying on a cushioned bench being penetrated by several men from all directions. Alongside the grand old chandeliers, cages hung from the ceiling containing naked women and men dancing seductively.

She felt her arm being grabbed. She turned to see Dan, who was indicating her to follow him out the room. She did so, feeling almost disappointed. She told herself she was disgusted by the sex show, but she couldn't help feeling curious also, and a little turned on.

Dan let the double doors close behind them. She followed him down a corridor, past a room with an opened door. A voile curtain covered the doorway and moaning came from within. Stacie stopped. Dan continued to walk ahead of her down the corridor. Curiosity struck Stacie. Dan had no idea she had stopped. She moved closer to the voile and moved it aside to see naked bodies scattered all over what looked like a huge inflatable mattress covered with piles of scattered cushions. The mattress virtually filled the room. They were penetrating and being penetrated indiscriminately...*an orgy!* Stacie's eyes widened in disbelief. Quickly, she sped up to return to Dan.

On the way, she heard more music coming from behind another door. Stacie stopped at another door, unsure whether she should open this one after the shock of the last. Curiosity won out. She opened the door to see a room containing tables and chairs with both men and women watching strippers on a small stage. Dan turned around to look at her as she shut this door, shaking her head. Stacie looked at him with a reluctant grin, wondering what kind of place this really was.

Dan waited for Stacie outside the door to the conservatory she had seen before. When they went in, Stacie saw the musical note-shaped chairs she had seen before were now arranged in small groups around tables set for eating. The lighting was dimmed and small candles gave the room a cosy feel. The conservatory, or restaurant, as it was now arranged, was decorated in fetching colours, dark purple wallpaper beneath the windows, patterned with large silver leaves. A few lights shaped as women's basques hung from the ceiling. Stacie noticed a painting of chandeliers and pianos hanging behind the small bar.

Several couples were sitting at the tables eating, and other people stood at the bar, either ignoring or blatantly watching the antics of the other people in the room. There was one couple openly having sex in a corner, and a woman's naked bottom poked out from underneath another table. She was clearly giving a blowjob to the clothed man at the table who was fondling the breasts of another woman, also naked, who sat next to him.

"Drink?" Dan said, walking over to the bar.

"Just lemonade," Stacie said, following him. She'd had enough wine for now. The bartender passed her and Dan their drinks and then he and Dan chatted while Stacie stared round the room, feeling faintly disgusted. A woman—clothed—was playing the large piano. Stacie wondered how she could stand it, but she was probably used to it. The couple having sex began to cry out as they reached their climaxes. Stacie tried her hardest not to stare too much, but surely they shouldn't be doing something like that while people were trying to enjoy their meals.

Two loud girls came hurtling through the doors, dancing and singing. One girl was tall, skinny and pretty, wearing a revealing top which barely covered her breasts and a skirt which was more like a belt. The second girl was shorter with curly hair. Her very large breasts plunged out of the top of her very tiny dress. The thin girl pulled the other girl's dress down and started to grab her breasts. The curly-haired girl pushed the other into the corner and raised the girl's brief skirt. Curlytop ran her hand up Skinny's thigh and pulled up her skirt, showing the room that she wasn't wearing any underwear. The shorter girl dropped to her knees and started to lick her out. Stacie turned her head, she did not want to watch the two girls having sex with one another.

"Still want that air?" Dan asked. Stacie nodded. She took one more curious look at the girls and felt sick to her stomach.

Stacie followed Dan back out of the room. They walked down the corridor and Stacie spotted yet another couple having sex up against the wall. She wondered if there was anywhere she could look without seeing people having sex?

They came out at the back of the building. The cold air hit her, sending shivers down her spine. She hadn't quite expected it to be quite so cold, but she needed air. She followed Dan onto the patio, where a few people stood smoking under the heaters. Stacie expected Dan to pull a cigarette out and have a smoke—that would have put her completely off him. But he just continued sipping his drink.

They stood under the heater for a while. Dan was uncharacteristically quiet. Stacie was frozen, covered in goosebumps despite the patio heaters. She stood as close to Dan as she could, trying to get some of his body heat. She wished he would hold her close. Stacie glanced into the garden seeing two men spit roasting a girl on a bench. Even in this damn freezing cold weather they couldn't control themselves.

She turned away, looking at a wall while taking a few sips of her lemonade.

"Dan! How you doing, mate?" Stacie heard a male voice say. She turned around to see a man wearing a smart suit approaching.

He was with a woman wearing a blue sequinned dress, looking far too elegant and pretty for a place like this.

"I'm great, and you?" Dan said. The two men shook hands and Dan gave the woman a kiss on the cheek while the man planted a kiss on Stacie's right cheek.

"Wow, you're beautiful, babe. What a sexy girl, Dan."

"Yeah she's not bad," he said, laughing.

"What you been up to, or shouldn't I really be asking?"

Embarrassed and uncomfortable, Stacie pasted on a fake smile as the men talked. The man pulled out a cigarette, lighting it up and began dragging on the fag.

"What you up to now?" the man asked.

"We're just getting a little air," Dan said.

"You going back into any of the rooms?"

Stacie was disgusted. She certainly wasn't going anywhere in those rooms. The thought that these people thought she was here for that kind of behaviour appalled her.

"No, we're not going to be doing that," Dan said.

"Well, do you fancy getting together with us? We could have our own little fun." The man waggled his eyebrows up and down at Stacie and grinned at her breasts.

Horrified, Stacie turned and ran back into the building. She could hear Dan calling her name behind her. Stacie kept running. She dashed down the corridor and somehow took a wrong turn. She opened door after door, then found herself in the night club room by the stage. She felt a surge of relief. If she could only get to the other side of the room, the double doors would bring her out to the reception area, and then she could get back to their room, to safety. But the room seemed to be wall-to-wall with people. She began to *excuse-me* her way through the crush, but they ignored her. She was knocked about and pressed against bodies.

Head down, elbows out, she barged through. She had to get away from all this sex. Was there no one here who could talk or think about anything other than sex? Stacie charged her way through the crowd. Hands grabbed her bottom and her breasts. She felt sick—he crowd seemed never-ending.

She'd never been claustrophobic, but the horde was stifling. She'd managed to make her way to the dance floor when a big drunken giant of a man staggered against her and knocked her off balance. Arms flailing, she tried to grab onto him to stay upright, but he took it as an advance, and turned around, his gaze dragging down her body, then up again, landing on her breasts.

"Well, hello!" he slurred, reaching out to pull her close.

Stacie shrieked and took a lurching step back, falling to the floor. A shoe stood on her hand and she cried out in pain.

"Wait," the big man said, holding a hand out to her, but she scuttled away on her hands and knees, landing up against a table and chairs purely by chance. Sobbing, she managed to pull herself to upright again, cradling her painful hand with the other. Over the heads of the mob, she saw the double doors. The crowd thinned briefly and she charged for them. She dashed through, to be confronted by yet another large group of people filling the hall and the reception area. Stacie stared at the stairs where people sat with tongues down each other's throats. She thought quickly…scanning the area, thinking fast…the main front door! She shoved her way through, hearing people behind her calling her names. She ignored them. Her stomach was in knots, and her chest felt like she was being suffocated.

She could hear her name being called out, but she didn't bother to stop, keeping her mind on her target, the front door. Stacie grabbed the door handle and opened the large heavy door. The cold clean air hit her immediately, and she took a deep breath, feeling it fill her lungs, displacing the tainted air of the club.

Stacie closed the door behind her and just stood for a moment, ready to drop. Her body was drenched with sweat and her breath came in heaves. She took the few steps across the porch and sat on the top step, staring at the car park. At least here she wouldn't have to see anyone having sex. That kind of behaviour wasn't allowed outside the main door. The cold air brought her goosebumps back. She wiped away her tears and took a few moments to think.

Visions of the rooms and the people stalked her. Why did those people behave in that manner? Sex should be something beautiful and private between a couple. These people made it into some kind of sport or sordid entertainment.

A few tears escaped when she thought about Dan, visualising his face, reliving her experiences with him. He was a good looking guy, who seemed intelligent. How could he could blank out the intimacies of sex and keep it professional? But then, she considered, when Graham treated her like meat, didn't she do something similar, just blank it out. Maybe that was how Dan coped.

Stacie raised her head, and stared out at the bleak wintry landscape. She shivered, but had no desire to re-enter the building. She needed to clear her head, gather her thoughts, and give the reception area time to be cleared up of bodies.

She heard the slight noise of the door opening behind her. "Stacie?" A woman's voice spoke. Stacie wasn't sure whether to be relieved or disappointed than it wasn't Dan that had followed her out.

Stacie turned to see one of the receptionists coming to sit down alongside her. "Are you all right?"

Stacie replied with silence, unsure how to answer the question.

"What happened? Dan said you stormed off and doesn't understand why."

"I just couldn't cope," she answered, looking over at the car park.

"What couldn't you cope with?"

"Everywhere I looked, there were people having sex."

"But that is what Desires is all about. People come here to explore their fantasies with no strings attached."

She paused, as if to give Stacie a chance to answer. When she was met with only silence, she went on.

"We all enjoy different things, whether it's craftwork, reading, sports, or sex. Some people never have the opportunities that Desires offers. We're all individuals and live life differently. It doesn't make anyone bad, Stacie. Desires is very professional, nothing happens without anyone's say so."

The woman paused again. Stacie's mind whirled with thoughts. What the woman was saying went against every moral fibre of Stacie's upbringing. She seemed to be saying that what went on in there was okay, so long as it was agreed to.

"Look Stacie, Desires is all about fantasies and sex, whether it's love-making, bondage, play or just a damn good night out. I'm not saying you have to change your life or ideas, we all have our own opinions whether you agree or disagree. But that's what Desires is."

Stacie understood what she was saying. Whether Stacie wished to take Desires' open-minded view or not, was another matter. If everyone was entitled to their own opinions, surely she was too. People having sex with strangers, having sex in public, openly displayed their nakedness and being proud of their open-mindedness! Stacie had been brought up to respect herself and love the person she was. But wasn't that the problem? She wouldn't be at the club if she loved herself. Stacie didn't like the person she saw in the mirror at all. A woman who ran around all day, working, not spending any time on herself, needing to decide where her life was going.

"Are you not freezing out here?"

"Yes I am. I just needed to get some air, where I didn't feel I was going to bump into people having sex everywhere."

"I understand what you mean, it can be a bit in your face. Friday and Saturday nights are always the busiest though. If you come during the week, it's a whole different place. It's the same for everyone, work during the week, play at weekends."

Stacie sat and stared at the cars, seeing hers, debating whether to leave or not. But then there was Dan.

"Shall we head back inside?" the woman said.

"I don't know. Is it still busy in there?"

"I'll have a look. It should have quietened down now. We'd just had a couple of parties arrive at once when you came through." She got up and opened the door. "There are still a few people, but it's not as bad as it was," she reported.

"Okay, I'll come back in. It is a bit cold," Stacie said, a violent shiver juddering her body.

She stood up. The receptionist held the door open for her then followed her into the warm building. Stacie saw Dan standing ahead of her in the reception area, his face etched with concern. The receptionist strode up ahead and Stacie fell in behind her.

A few people were still standing in the reception area, but it was a great deal less crowded then when she had left. The receptionist took her place back behind the desk and Stacie felt exposed. Dan stood before her. Stacie didn't dare to look directly at him, but held her head low, staring at his feet. They moved closer to her.

"Are you all right?" he asked.

"I'm fine," she told him. His feet moved closer still and she felt him put his hand under her chin and lift her face up. She glanced at him briefly then moved her gaze to the side. "Can we head back to the room?"

He released her face. "Okay."

He led the way to the staircase and Stacie began to follow when she saw Angel standing at the foot of the stairs, staring at her with sharp eyes. She was wearing a PVC microdress and thigh-high heavily buckled boots with towering spike heels. She held a cat-o'-nine-tails in her hand.

"Is everything okay, Dan?" she said, still looking at Stacie.

"Everything's fine," he said. Stacie moved quickly to Dan's side, putting Dan between herself and the other woman.

Stacie could feel Angel's stare as they started up the stairs, but couldn't meet her eyes. Angel was intelligent and aware. Stacie knew Angel would have picked up on the fact that there was a problem.

"You know, I think you should look at your life." Stacie heard a man's cutting voice coming from behind her. She turned around to see the guy from the patio that had offered the foursome. "Desires is all about sex. No matter what your opinion is, we love it and personally, I don't think you belong here."

Dan moved back down the steps to confront the man. "That's enough. She isn't here for that business."

"No mate, it isn't enough. She's looking down her nose at us, the stuck up bitch. I couldn't give a damn about her reasons for being here. She has no right to be fucking looking at us like shit."

"That's enough, James. I'm sure she never meant it that way." Dan turned around heading back toward Stacie. He took hold of Stacie's hand and began to pull her up the stairs.

"Stuck up bitch," came the yell from downstairs. Dan's hand clenched hers hard. "People enjoy sex, go fuck yourself, bitch." Stacie swallowed, trying not to get upset.

Dan stopped at the top of the stairs and released her hand. Stacie felt her heart beating overtime, sensing something was about to kick off. "Wait here," he commanded, then she watched in horror as he headed back down the staircase. "Don't you dare call her a bitch. You know absolutely nothing about her."

"I couldn't give a shit, and if you're doing your job correctly she wouldn't be glaring at everyone like they're dirt. You should be fucking her, show her what the real world is."

Stacie listened to the confrontation from the top of the stairs, horrified but oddly excited at the same time. James advanced on Dan, pointing his finger at him, when Stacie noticed Angel move in.

"James, don't you have a client to attend to?" Angel said, her posture oozing authority.

Stacie saw James scowl at Dan then he looked up at her, giving her an evil glare before he walked off, his face murderous. Stacie watched Dan turn around and come back up the stairs. She stepped back as Dan arrived at her side, his face set in angry lines. Stacie wasn't sure if she should say something. She felt guilty now for storming off the way she had. She could hardly believe Dan had just confronted James on her behalf.

Back at the room, Dan opened the door and went in first. Stacie watched Dan storm over to the bathroom, slamming the door shut behind him. She walked in the room, closing the door behind her. She was unsure what to do other than hide under the bed. Visions of Graham's tempers came back to her—she was terrified of Dan's reaction. She was paying him to teach her sex, not fight her wars for her, and she wasn't paying to be scared of his anger.

Dan came out from the bathroom, his face wet. She watched him pull off his soaking wet top and launch it at the floor. He rushed toward her and she panicked, moving out of his way and cowering to the bed for protection. Stacie's heart skipped beats as Dan opened the wardrobe door and pulled out a clean top. He turned to look at Stacie as she stood next to the bed, scared stiff.

"What are you doing?" he said. He stared at her, then advanced on her, frowning. Stacie backed away. "Hey, come here," he said, holding his arm out.

Stacie's eyes filled with tears and she ran to him. He wrapped his arms around her shoulders, cuddling her tight.

"I'm sorry," Stacie said, bursting into tears.

"Hey," he said, running his hands up and down her back. She snuggled into his bare chest, hearing his heart beating fast. "I'm the one that should be sorry. He had no right whatsoever to prejudge you like that. He needs to look at his attitude, not get annoyed when someone refuses him." Dan stood holding her tight to his chest. She felt him kissing the top of her head then he stiffened and leaned back, looking searchingly into her eyes.

"Oh my God…Jesus, no. Bloody hell, Stacie. I am so, so sorry…God…" he said, holding her tighter than ever. She guessed he had just worked out the reason for her terror. They stood for a long moment, him holding her so tight it was almost painful, but comforting at the same time. "I know what you're looking for." she finally heard from above. *What did he mean by that?*

Stacie drew back a little from his chest, reluctantly pulling away from his comfort and scent, longing to remain there forever. "What?"

"You need someone to love you."

*But you can't do that.* The words remained unspoken. They were unnecessary. They both knew what the contract said. Stacie released him, stepping back to look deep into those brown eyes, which looked calmer than when she last saw them. She stepped back a few feet, seeing a smile on Dan's face. *Time to change the subject. That thought's far too scary to contemplate right now.*

"Do you think I am a stuck up bitch?"

"No, don't be silly. I think you're a woman who needs direction," he said. He pulled the clean top over his head. "Don't allow him to manipulate you, he's just pissed off you didn't fancy having sex with him."

"I'm not into that."

"I know that, but you stormed off and never gave me a chance to answer him. I was going to say no, but you ran off."

"I am so sorry, I just didn't think. I was annoyed that every direction I looked people were having sex and then he kind of finished it off."

"Don't worry about it. Unfortunately, there's no real safe place in this building unless of course you keep hiding out at the front door," he said with a laugh, then shot her a wink.

They both sat on the bed. Stacie looked at Dan, analysing him, the way his dark hair reflected the light. Slowly, her gaze moved to his shoulders, they weren't broad or overly muscular, they sloped slightly, his dark T-shirt not giving much of his body away. Every time Stacie thought about having sex with him, a *frisson* set her pussy atremble. She felt reborn and blown away with excitement. The way he touched her, caressing her body in the manner she loved, soft and gentle, then the way he kissed her…

She reached out, placing her hand flat on his back and then trailed her fingers down the ridge of his spine. She tucked one foot under her and knelt up, leaning forward to kiss his bare upper arm, just where the material of the T-shirt ended. Her fingers gently massaged all the way down to the waistband of his jeans. He turned to look at her, a quirky smile tilting his lips.

"What are you thinking about?" he said.

"Guess."

In response he turned and kissed her deeply, his left hand cupping the back of her head. His right hand supported her back as he lowered her to the bed. She closed her eyes, lost in his kiss, welcoming his tongue as it politely requested entrance. He covered her body with his and she wrapped her arms round his back and held him close.

"Do you think I need some fun in my life?" she said to him when they came up for air.

He replied with a smile; the sexiest smile she had ever seen. Stacie was trapped in the pleasantest of snares. There was nothing in the world right now her heart desired more. Stacie pushed her right hand into her jeans, sliding it down into her panties, feeling her own arousal. She couldn't seem to control her bodily functions when Dan was around.

Stacie slid her middle finger between her labia, feeling the dampness there, yearning for his throbbing cock. She glanced at him, seeing him looking at her, his face alight with pleasure and desire.

Dan leaned in—his lips almost touched hers. She opened to him, preparing to indulge in his mouth, when he turned and kissed her on the right cheek. Stacie inhaled his aroma, sweet and indulgent. She placed her hands onto his back, sliding them down to his buttocks. Dan kissed her around her cheek, his kisses soft and delicate. They only excited her more—she wanted to touch him all over.

His lips moved to her ear, kissing around her earlobe—he nipped at her lobe with gentle teeth, making her shudder. He used his tongue to tease and manipulate her till she longed to indulge and tease his body the way he was hers. Dan slowly drifted down her neckline where he pressed his soft luscious lips on her throbbing pulse. She tossed her head from side to side on the pillow, needing Dan more than ever, craving his cock. Why on earth did Dan have to be so good? There must be some magic inside him, keeping her at the club.

He pulled her jumper up and turned his attention to her breasts, kissing and nibbling along the soft curves. She held his head in place, inhaling the scent of his clean hair. Dan was divine, but something inside told her she was going to have to unlock her mental doors and allow her body and mind to relax more when it came to sex. Dan would no longer be in her life once she stopped coming to Desires—her whole life would change. Her thoughts drifted to the orgy room, with all those guests having sex. How did they get the confidence to be naked around complete strangers? Stacie hugged Dan to her, leaning down to kiss his springy hair.

Dan paused in his ministrations to her. Stacie looked down to see him looking up at her, an odd expression on his face. Suddenly he rolled away from her and climbed off the bed.

He headed over to the table and poured himself a glass of the wine that was still there.

"Have I done something wrong?"

Dan didn't reply but gulped down the entire glass of wine. The phone in the room suddenly rang. Dan picked it up, and took the receiver through into the bathroom. Stacie sat up, puzzled, trying to make out Dan's side of the conversation through the bathroom door. She lay down again trying to look natural when he came back in and replaced the receiver in the cradle.

He looked at her. "Sorry, I'm needed downstairs for a while," he said, walking to the door. "I'll take the key." He opened the door and left. Stacie lay still for a moment, her mind whirling. One minute he was making love to her, the next he had done a runner. Nothing seemed to make sense.

Stacie sat alone and bewildered, trying to figure out what she'd done wrong, if anything. Had it been because she'd kissed his hair? *Surely not.*

She climbed off the bed and wandered over to the dresser. Stacie sat on the stool staring hard into the mirror, glaring hard at herself, gazing deeply into her own brown eyes, seeing a sad woman, who felt lost and who couldn't figure out her direction in life. She wanted love like Dan said, but she knew it didn't come easy and it certainly didn't come knocking on the door. She must open her mind.

Clearly, spending time with a young sexy man had made her realise what she had been missing in her life. Graham might have brainwashed her, but she could only be trapped while she allowed herself to be. Stacie straightened her back and stared hard at herself, pulling her hair away from her face and pouting her lips. She brushed her hands through her hair and down toward her breasts, smiling to herself.

Stacie licked her lips then opened the dresser drawers. She was sure she'd seen a few makeup bits in one of them earlier. There they were. She went through the collection, finding a bright red lipstick, much redder than she usually wore. She applied it to her lips, pouting at herself in the mirror. She ringed her eyes with black kohl, making them look smoky and alluring. She rummaged farther into the drawer, finding a bottle of perfume. She sprayed herself, then brushed her long hair, and looked at the results. She pulled a face. Jeans and a roll-neck jumper weren't exactly sexy.

Hadn't she seen some clothes hanging in the wardrobe Dan had been using? Stacie stood up and went over to the wardrobe. She opened it and saw a small collection of female outfits shoved over to one side. They were more like costumes, she thought as she looked through them. There was a nurse outfit, a policewoman, a waitress and several others. She stared for a long moment at a baby doll outfit sandwiched between a pair of *lederhosen* and a schoolgirl outfit. Gauzy red material flowed down from its heart-shaped cups. It tied with a red ribbon between the cups, allowing easy access with the open front, if necessary. There was a matching red string thong, a large red heart covering the essentials. It was new, the tags still on. Stacie pulled it out and held it up in front of herself in the full-length mirror. *Stuck-up bitch* resounded in her head. Maybe it was time to discover who was right. Maybe meaningless sex with strangers was what she needed to loosen her up a bit. Who knows—it might be fantastic. Everyone here seemed to be enjoying themselves. Maybe she was missing out.

She stripped off and put on the skimpy outfit. She put on her black patent high heels and found a black satin robe hanging up in the wardrobe. She slipped it on, leaving it hanging open at the front. Stacie looked at herself in the mirror, staring at a whole new Stacie Clifford. Her cleavage looked amazing, inviting attention, her lips stood out with the brightness of the lipstick and her eyes seemed to smoulder.

She turned around and peeked over her shoulder, moving the dressing gown aside and was smugly pleased to see her bottom looking tight and perky. She looked at her reflection thinking about the orgy room, feeling a flutter of excitement mixed with several tons of nervousness. She thrust her chest out, pulled in her tummy and decided she needed to live.

# Chapter Seven

Stacie opened the top drawer of the bedside cabinet and grabbed a sheaf of condoms, slipping them into the pocket of the satin robe.

She inhaled a deep breath as she reached for the door handle. She opened it and stared out at the deserted corridor. Niggles of doubt shot through her brain. She ignored them. *Just do it*, Stacie told herself. It wasn't as if she actually had to do anything if she didn't want to. Just going out there dressed like this would be a start.

She pulled the door closed behind her, the soft clicking it made marking the start of her new life. The corridor was empty as she walked toward the staircase. Nonetheless, she swayed her hips sexily as she walked, wanting to feel sexy.

She arrived at the top of the stairs and stood tall, looking down at the reception area. There were a few people hanging around. She gulped and looked back around to the door of their room in the distance. The urge to go back crossed her mind, but she couldn't anyway, she had no key. Stacie glanced down the stairs, then lifted her shoulders and thrust her breasts out in the sexy babydoll. She straightened her back and neck and walked slowly down the staircase.

One man stood staring at her as she walked. She glanced at the receptionists to see them watching her as well. She didn't break her stride as she reached the bottom of the stairs, continuing through reception.

She could hear the loud dance music coming from the night club, but she focused on her direction. She walked through the double doors to the right and down the corridor. A couple approached her. He was wearing only boxer shorts, she wore a basque and thong and whopping high heels. Instead of scuttling past in embarrassment, Stacie smiled and said, "Good evening." She saw the orgy room ahead as the material of her babydoll blew in a light breeze coming from a slightly open window.

Goosebumps sprouted all over her body, but she kept putting one foot in front of the other, trying to swallow down the nerves.

She arrived at the door feeling sick with nervous anxiety. She was seriously considering stopping this stupid behaviour and just being who she was. But she didn't want to be that person any longer.

Stacie stood at the voile curtain blocking the doorway. The breeze from the window wafted it aside, allowing her to see inside the room. Her whole body was numb and her mouth had gone dry. She took a deep breath and grabbed the curtain, pulling it all the way to the side, and entered.

She could hear people moaning with pleasure and fulfilment. As her eyes adjusted to the dim light, she could see naked bodies scattered everywhere. One woman was on all fours, her breasts dangling, a man taking her from behind, his face contorted with pleasure and her wailing out with delight whilst he rammed her.

She took a few more steps into the room. The room was dark, and she edged her way round the large inflatable mattress which took up most of the floor space. Stacie took her heeled shoes off, not wanting to puncture it. She stepped onto one side, not wanting to get in anyone's way, picking her way round the cushions, unsure what to do next. Stacie stood in the midst of the action, observing people having a good time. She felt a little embarrassed for watching them, knowing she wouldn't enjoy having an audience. But then, she reconsidered, they probably didn't care that she stood watching. If anything, they enjoyed it.

As she looked around, she saw two familiar faces. Curly and Skinny, the two girls she'd seen in the conservatory earlier, lay on a pile of cushions. Curly lay on her back, her eyes closed and her head thrown back in enjoyment, as Skinny enthusiastically licked her pussy. Curly was screaming with pleasure and Skinny's hand came up to caress her breasts as she continued her attentions. Stacie wanted to find it disgusting but instead she was intrigued. A matter of hours ago she'd seen those two girls kissing in the bar and found it degrading. But after listening to the receptionist and having a lecture from the arrogant James, she was beginning to find the whole thing interesting. What a difference a good word could make.

She watched the women for a few minutes then her attention was caught by a trio of two men and a woman. One of the men was lying on his back, the woman kneeling between his legs. She was sucking his cock, her bottom stuck high into the air. At the same time, the second man was fucking her from behind, reaching around to play with her dangling breasts. Despite herself, Stacey found herself getting turned on. She reached up and began to caress her breasts, feeling her nipples erect and sensitive through the material of the cups.

Her whole body twanged to the sexual vibe of the room. The room was hot and she was tempted to remove her dressing gown. She tore her eyes away from the ménage to see a woman giving a man a blowjob, his face full of glory. Stacie turned her head around, seeing bodies all over the place, men on women, women on men and woman on woman. It really was a room for fantasies.

She glided her hands down to her waist and hips, followed by moving her hand across her stomach. She wanted to move her hands further. Did she dare to start playing with her pussy in front of these people? They surely didn't care.

Bottling out, for now, instead she moved farther into the room. She noticed one man smiling at her. Stacie grinned back as he shoved his penis into a woman who was clearly almost floating in delight. She saw a large cushion a few metres away. Carefully she made her way over to it to sit down. Stacie found herself positioned next to a couple about her own age. The man was broad, muscular with a rather sexy bottom and dark hair. The woman wore a white crotchless playsuit, open at the front. Her large breasts swung freely out of the playsuit as he penetrated her. She was pretty with long red hair and looked like she was enjoying herself immensely.

The woman opened her eyes, looking at Stacie whilst grinding her pelvis back and forth making sure she got the best of her man. Stacie was so close she could see his cock plunging in and out of her. He watched Stacie avidly, while he was thrusting deeply into the redhead. Stacie turned her head, feeling embarrassed to be watching the couple having sex, yet, curious, she looked back as they continued.

Stacie tried to hold back the temptation to play with herself. She could feel her own arousal, her pussy was spasming and sending wild bursts of feeling throughout her body. Meeting the man's gaze, she daringly caressed her breasts, lifting them and pinching her nipples through the material.

Suddenly, she felt heavy breathing on her neckline, lips pressing gently on her flesh. Her heart began to race, butterflies fluttered in her stomach. Was some stranger touching her? Did she really want this? Was she ready? The lips pressed lightly against her naked neckline, and she felt a hand touching her shoulder. She turned her head frantically, to see Dan. Her dream boy had arrived. Suddenly, the room melted away. All she wanted was Dan.

She threw her arms around him and he captured her lips. His hands ran over her body, beneath the sheer babydoll. His touch ignited tiny fires on her skin. She removed her robe, Dan helping her as she tugged at the satin material. Their mouths remained fixed together, Stacie tasting all she could of him. Dan lowered her down onto the cushion she'd claimed and began to kiss her neck, adding flicks of licks from his tongue, before blowing on the wetness his tongue had left, sending tremors of excitement throughout her body. His body covered Stacie's, his leg lapped over hers whilst his hand caressed her cheekbone. She held onto him tightly, putting her hand onto his naked back.

Stacie looked down—all he was wearing were his trunks. She closed her eyes, concentrating on the feelings he stirred in her as he kissed her shoulder, and ran his hand down to her stomach, which ached with desire. She trembled as he traced the curved top edge of the heart on her thong, but then his hand came back up to rest on her waist as his kisses went lower.

Stacie ran her hand up and down his back feeling his soft skin before deciding to take control. She rolled her body away from him. Dan sat up to look at her in surprise. She smiled and swung her leg over him to sit on his lap. She could feel his hard cock beneath his trunks pressing into her pussy. She glanced around. The smell of sex was thick in the air and sex was everywhere she looked. But far from disgusting her as it had before, it was turning her on. She pressed her hands flat on his chest and pushed, making him lie down on the large floor cushion as she straddled him. She bent over him and kissed him before trailing her lips over to nibble at his ear. He moaned and she felt it vibrate through his chest. He thrust his pelvis beneath her and she ground into him in answer.

Stacie kissed and licked down his chest, tasting the slight saltiness of his skin, not wanting to miss an inch. She licked around his nipples, feeling them pucker beneath her lips. He shuddered and hissed his breath in. She slid her body down his, moving down to his navel, dipping her tongue in then kissing down the fine trail of hair to the waistband of his trunks.

Dan's hard throbbing cock was jerking inside his trunks, straining for release. Stacie kissed all around the area, deliberately avoiding the crucial area. He pushed up at her, evidently wanting her to pay some attention to his member. Stacie grinned, feeling empowered. She looked around the room full of panting, screwing people, feeling a sudden slight hesitation. Would he mind her getting his cock out here, in front of everyone? *Don't be silly, Stacie*, she admonished herself. *He works here. He's surely done it before.*

Nonetheless she watched his face as she began tugging on his trunks, just in case. He simply raised his buttocks up, allowing her access. Stacie pulled his undergarment down revealing his cock, stiff and huge. She came back up, kissing along his inner thigh, until arriving at his genital area. Again, she deliberately avoided his penis, wanting him to enjoy the anticipation. She kissed all the way round his genitals. Above her, she could hear him groaning and feel him attempting to grab her head, but she managed to avoid him. She wasn't going to let him to have any control. She licked and teased him as his cock bounced and thrust.

She raised her body up, staring down at him, defenceless, turned on and about ready to burst. Stacie waited for him to look at her. He opened his eyes sleepily and gave her a slow, intimate smile. Suddenly it was as if the room was empty, it was just her and Dan.

Stacie glanced down at him. His penis throbbed and Stacie licked her lips. She looked back into Dan's eyes and inserted her middle finger into her mouth, sucking and licking it like a cock, covering it in her saliva. She stared into his dark brown eyes, knowing she was teasing him. She dove down, finally taking hold of his penis and took it deep in her mouth. Stacie deep throated him as much as she could, hearing Dan cry out aloud as he thrust into her mouth.

She slid her lips back up, twirling her tongue over the sensitive tip before sliding her mouth off his cock, then licked the full length of his shaft before taking it deep into her mouth again, hearing him moaning in pleasure.

Stacie moved back up to the tip of his dick to flicker her tongue over the end, before teasing him with delicate teeth. He wailed and shuddered. Stacie could taste his excitement, licking up the salty droplets of pre-cum greedily. She rolled her tongue around the tip of his dick and then took his whole penis back into her mouth. She could feel her own juices running and moved her hand down under her thong to dip her fingers inside, shuddering at her own touch.

Stacie glanced up to see Dan's face full of excitement, his expression desperate and needy. She moved up to sit on his lap, positioning her craving pussy over his swollen cock. She leaned over him, letting gravity take her breasts. Dan grabbed for them, squeezing and pushing them together eagerly. Stacie swallowed, taking a look around the room again. Many people were busy with their own pleasure, but she could see eyes on her and Dan, both male and female. *Come on, girl!* Taking a deep breath, she pulled on the baby doll strings so the top fell open, revealing her large swollen breasts. She swung them in his face and he took hold of them both, pushing them together into a cleavage. He began sucking on the right nipple first, then moving from one to the other. He made noises as he suckled, using his teeth to tease and tantalise. Her whole body erupted in sparks.

She felt his cock between her legs, rubbing against her dripping pussy. She wanted him, she needed him. Dare she fuck him here? The urge to lift herself up and slide down onto his thick cock was immense. Dan continued to inhale her nipple, holding and grasping her breasts, squeezing them hard. It should have been painful, but it was exquisite. Stacie tilted her pelvis desperately. She wanted his cock into her juicy slit and she wanted it now!

She lifted her rear, positioning her entrance directly over the tip of his cock. She could feel his movements stop as he became aware of her intentions. If she did this, she would be actually having sex in front of a roomful of people. It would be so easy. She was slick and wet, his cock was there and ready. The expression of warning on his face gave her pause for a second, before she saw the condom in his hand. She'd almost forgotten! He rolled it on expertly, then she slowly lowered herself down, his cock slid in, past the tiny thong that was no barrier. She sat back, feeling his penis fill her deeply, satisfyingly, luxuriously. She could feel him within her, filling her soul, satisfying her hunger, setting every nerve ending on fire by the simple physical connection.

Suddenly Dan sat up, grabbing her by the waist to turn the situation around. In a blink he was on top, fucking her urgently, driving his penis deep inside her. She splayed her legs as wide as she could to welcome him, reaching blindly behind her, grabbing handfuls of the cushions as her vision blurred. His fingers teased her clitoris, sending Stacie into oblivion. She couldn't concentrate, she screamed aloud, lightning flashing behind her eyes.

He withdrew his penis, making Stacie whimper like a baby who'd lost its dummy. But before she could protest, he was sliding down her body, tugging at her sodden thong and pulling it down past her feet. She spread her legs and he dove between them, licking and sucking on her clitoris, causing her to squeeze every muscle in her body. She felt his tongue dipping between her mounds of flesh, she burned with desire. Stacie grabbed the top of his head forcing his mouth more into her, his tongue flicked over her nerve endings making her cry aloud.

She could feel her orgasm approaching. Half of her wanted to dive into it, allow it to crash over her, the other half wanted to put it off, to prolong the deliciousness as long as she could. She broke into a sweat then her entire body erupted. She lost control, screaming with abandon, her body jerking and juddering beneath Dan.

Stacie took her time coming back to the real world, then she felt Dan burying his penis back into her deep, hungry hole, penetrating her, hitting her G-spot. He fucked her hard and fast, animal-like, then moved off her, turning her around onto all fours before sliding back into her. His body moulded perfectly around hers as he thrust. The new position played havoc with her nerve endings as he hit her G-spot every time. Stacie tilted her pelvis allowing deeper strokes. He leaned forward, cupping her breasts into his hands, squeezing and pulling as he glided in and out her dripping pussy. Stacie couldn't take any more, her whole body was losing control. She buried her head in the cushion and screamed as her second orgasm racked her body, her knees shaking and her pussy quivering.

Dan's thrusts became quicker then he stiffened and cried out. Stacie felt his cock pulse within her, filling the condom with gushes of liquid. She clenched her muscles around him as he came, feeling him react with gasps. They held the position for a few moments before dropping down onto the cushion. Dan moved with her, keeping their bodies locked firmly together while he held her tight. She loved the feel of him holding her, feeling his heart beating rapidly against her back. She heard him attempting to catch his breath—her own breathing was still erratic.

Stacie felt sated and euphoric, not just because she'd just had the best sex ever with a young adorable man, but also because she had just stepped into a whole other world of sex.

Slowly she opened her eyes seeing bodies still coupling all around her. No one was looking at them now, and even if they were she wouldn't care. Never in her life had Stacie thought she would be having sex in a room full of people, but what an amazing and exciting experience.

They remained still, Dan holding her close. She savoured the feeling of being held, and not shoved to the side and forgotten about. Although Dan wasn't for keeps, it didn't stop her from enjoying the thought that one day she'd have this with some other man, who might just give her the love and time she desired.

"Do you fancy getting a drink?" he whispered in her ear.

"Okay."

Dan pulled out of her slowly, kissing her shoulder. Stacie rolled onto her back watching him deal with the condom then bend down to pick up his trunks. His muscular bottom flexed as he pulled them up. God, she was getting turned on again at the sight.

Dan retrieved the rest of his clothes from where he'd left them as Stacie pulled her thong back on and tied up her babydoll top. He came back and passed Stacie her dressing gown, helping her on with it before he quickly put on his own clothes.

They headed for the door, Stacie making sure she snagged her shoes from where she'd left them. She slipped them on her feet and Dan dropped the condom in a bin by the door then he took her hand and led her down the corridor to the conservatory bar. It was busier than it had been before. They made their way toward the bar where a couple were standing waiting to be served. Stacie returned the woman's smile before she realised it was the couple she'd been watching for a few minutes after she found her place on the large cushion. Stacie looked at the floor, suddenly too embarrassed to even look at her.

The couple were served and then Dan placed their order. Stacie ordered a white wine and Dan a pint. If ever a drink was deserved it was now, after their workout. Stacie found herself buzzing, was it Dan that kept her going?

"Evening," said the woman, moving to stand beside her. Stacie forced her gaze up to meet the woman's friendly smile. The image of her with her breasts swinging being shagged by her partner rose up in Stacie's mind.

"Evening," Stacie managed.

"Have you had a good night?" the woman asked. She clearly wanted to make conversation.

Stacie gulped before replying. "Er, yes thank you, and yourself?"

"Absolutely fantastic evening. You can't beat coming here to Desires. I love just being able to let go and relax for once. Have you been coming long, I don't remember seeing you before."

"No, this weekend is my first time."

The woman's eyes gleamed with curiosity. "So what do you make of Desires?"

"Well I have to say it's a little scary," Stacie said, wondering if honesty was the best plan.

"I bet it is to a new person, all these naked people having sex in random places. It's not something you would come across on a regular day," the woman said, with an understanding smile.

"No, definitely not." Stacie started to relax a little. "Have you been coming long?"

"Five years."

Stacie raised her eyebrows, a little surprised.

"We try and come at least once in every two months," replied her partner. Stacie looked from her to him. Were they a couple, then, and not just here for random sex?

The man continued, "It gives us time away from the children and to be just a couple. It makes us feel human," he explained. Stacie glanced at his wedding finger, seeing a ring. She felt relieved. At least these two were a proper couple, not just hooking up.

"Would you both care to join us at a table?" the man asked Stacie.

Stacie turned to see what Dan thought of the invitation. He smiled his agreement. "That would be lovely," she said, deciding that it might be nice to talk to someone about Desires. It would be interesting to get an inside look from a different point of view.

They took their drinks and headed toward a table to one side. The women sat on the couch on one side of the table, while the men sat opposite on two of the musical note chairs.

"I'm Chrissie," the woman said, "and this is my husband, Jason."

"Stacie and Dan," Dan said. Stacie smiled at the sound of her name on his lips. The way he introduced them almost made it sound as if they were a proper couple. They all shook hands. It all seemed oddly polite and civilised considering she'd seen them having sex less than half an hour earlier.

"What do you enjoy about Desires," Stacie had to ask.

"I love the fact that we can be a couple and have fun without anyone judging us," Chrissie said. "You two looked as though you were having an amazing time in the orgy room. You both look so in love and happy," said Chrissie.

Stacie looked at Dan, feeling ashamed and a little embarrassed at Chrissie's assumption. "Sorry, we're not lovers. Dan..." *Now, how best to phrase this?* "Dan works here."

"Well, good for you," she said to Stacie, not missing a beat. "You didn't half bag a corker. Younger too, well done you, girl." Stacie smiled at her then looked at Dan who was joining in the laughter. He didn't look in the least abashed.

"I bet you're getting what you paid for," Chrissie said in an aside to Stacie, still laughing.

Stacie laughed with her, wondering if she was joking or being serious. "You certainly could say that, he's fabulous."

"So how long have you worked here, Dan?" Jason asked.

"A little less than a year," he said, flopping back in the chair, holding his pint.

"I bet you see some sights," Jason said, his eyes curious.

"I certainly do. Some you do your hardest to forget." They all laughed again. The door opened and a couple walked in the room wearing absolutely nothing. Stacie stared for a second before looking quickly down. She glanced at the others, who were relaxed and not reacting at all.

"You know, what other place could you walk around like that?" Chrissie mentioned, gesturing with her glass at the couple. "We can't even do that at home. We have two small children and a close family, who are forever calling in unexpectedly. If we walked around even in sexy underwear we would definitely get caught. That's why we come here to chill and relax. This is the only place where we can actually do what we want to do without being judged, or running the risk of getting caught. Also, it's nice to spend some quality time together. It's too easy to forget about each other when we're at home."

"Yes," Jason agreed. "You come in from work every night shattered, looking after kids, family visiting, it just never ends. So once every two months we come here to enjoy each other."

Stacie listened to them. She was beginning to see another side to Desires. It wasn't just randoms hooking up for sex with anyone, there were couples here, just trying to have that all-important quality time together. Chrissie and Jason seemed like a nice, normal couple. Who cared if their sexual tastes were a little out of the mainstream? Was it so wrong if their got their kicks having sex in front of others? For the first time, Stacie began to wonder whether her views might be a little narrow-minded.

"What about you?" Chrissie asked Stacie, who shied away from the question. "What brings you to Desires?"

Stacie prevaricated, wishing Chrissie hadn't asked.

"Come on, it can't be that bad."

"It's quite embarrassing—"

Dan interrupted her, "No it isn't, be honest."

Stacie looked at him, hesitating. Should she be honest? Lying probably wouldn't help her, especially if this couple were wild and possibly looking for another couple to join them. "I am here to start from the beginning, to find my confidence again." She paused. "I was in a very violent marriage and sex was pretty much an ordeal every time. So, Dan is helping me find pleasure in sex again."

"Bless you. That must have been a scary decision to make," Chrissie said.

"It was. I was stuck in a complete rut, sick of being lonely but not confident enough to go out and meet other men."

"No, I think that once you've been in a violent relationship it does make you wary of stepping into another relationship with someone else. I bet he scared you bad...well done to you for taking the plunge," Chrissie said. Stacie sat up straighter.

Stacie found herself listening to Chrissie as the other woman told her all about how she met Jason, how they were both career people, and that having a family meant the whole world.

"We only have sex with each other here. We don't allow others to touch us," Chrissie said. "Some things are meant to stay between the couple and that to us is important. The thought of another woman touching him intimately would make me angry, and likewise, Jason wouldn't want another man touching me. It's on our contract...unless we choose to change it." Stacie was intrigued. *Choose to change it?*

Chrissie continued. "We come to the club strictly to have a fantastic time together and make love, whether it's in our room or around the building, we like to wander about and watch other people."

"Aren't you bothered about others seeing you naked?" Stacie needed to ask.

"I was at first...I always think the first time is the worst. It was something I'd always been intrigued about, but never had the guts to actually do. I was nervous as hell. But no...not now...I enjoy it. I love the fact we can wander around Desires in as little clothing as we like without people staring strangely and thinking it's disgusting. But you were very brave to go in the orgy room on your first weekend." Chrissie said. "It took me about three times coming here before we went in there."

"It took quite a bit of Dutch courage. I did hesitate, but decided I cannot and will not allow my ex to control me anymore."

"Many people wouldn't achieve what you have."

Chrissie looked over at Dan, who was sitting chatting to Jason. She lowered her voice. "So, is Dan to your satisfaction?"

Stacie leaned in and replied likewise. "You could say that, he's so amazing and understanding. I've known him a day and he understands exactly what I need. I spent a good number of years with my ex and he never truly knew me."

"Well, he just wanted to manipulate you. He was evidently not remotely interested in your pleasure or happiness. You're a very beautiful woman and I honestly thought you and Dan were a couple—you both looked so amazing together."

Stacie gazed at Dan as Chrissie spoke. Dan looked at her and smiled. His eyes overpowered her.

"Yes, but he can never be mine," Stacie said when Dan turned back to resume his conversation with Jason.

"Would you have him?"

Stacie kept staring Dan, her body vibrating to his presence, feeling the urge to hold him tight in her arms and have him make passionate love to her.

"Yes, I would. But he has to be nice to me, don't you think. I am paying for him after all. It's not real."

"It's true that you're paying for his time, but you can't help who you fall in love with. I see something in his eyes when he looks at you. If you and he are meant to be together it will happen. I am a great believer in things happening for a reason," Chrissie said softly.

Stacie stared at Dan. He glanced at her and sent her a little smile. "He's gorgeous," Chrissie whispered in her ear.

"Yes...yes he is..."

Chrissie moved closer to Stacie so her voice could be heard quietly at her ear. "Does he make your knees go weak?" Stacie nodded. "Does he make your heart skip beats?" *Nod.* "Does he hit all the right spots?"

"He certainly does."

"I'm guessing you signed the contract?"

"Yep!" Stacie fervently wished she could hold that document in her hands right now and rip it to shreds.

"Between me and you, what the fuck is in that contract? Who's to stop you and him getting together outside this place?"

Stacie paused for a long time. "Nothing, I guess," she said, not wanting to look at Dan. Unbidden thoughts raced around her mind, them out together, like a real couple...going back to her flat, undressing him, him working his magic.

"Did you sign before you saw him, and discovered just what a fantastic man he is in all departments?" Chrissie said.

"I did, and no I never clapped eyes on him before the signature…bloody hell—"

"What?"

"My stomach aches," Stacie said. Her tummy felt like there was an entire tentful of butterflies in there, and her heart galloped.

"Love is amazing, isn't it?"

"I've never felt this way."

"Tell him."

"I can't."

"Of course you can. Are you going to allow him to get away?"

Stacie felt more confused than ever. She stared at Chrissie, horrified, panicking.

"If you want him, have him, go and get him girl. Life's too bloody short to be living with regrets. By the sound of it you've done enough with your ex." Stacie gazed at Chrissie, her heart beating rapidly. "I'll tell you what, I'll give you my mobile number, call me sometime. Do you live locally?" Stacie nodded. "Give me a call and we could meet up and have a damn good chat. Do you have any close friends?"

"No, not anyone I could pour my heart out to," Stacie said, feeling the urge to share her experience with Dan.

"Well you do now. Call me and we'll arrange to see each other." Chrissie scribbled her number on a napkin, and pushed it across the table at Stacie. Stacie wrote down hers also and gave it to Chrissie, feeling as if she'd found a friend in the most unlikely place she ever would have expected.

## Chapter Eight

Stacie found it difficult to sleep that night after they had settled down. The conversation she'd had with Chrissie kept running through her head. Should she tell Dan about her feelings? She wanted to, but the contract kept wandering through her mind. "Emotional involvement with your tutor or tutors is strictly forbidden." Here she was breaching that very contract. Maybe it was just the fact that Dan was the first young man to catch her eye and treat her with respect. He might not even care for her in that way. She might just be another client to him, someone he had to put up with, and be nice to, to get his money. Was she making a fool of herself, having her head turned?

Her head ached. Nothing made sense. She sat up in bed looking down on his sleeping body. He was lying naked. His breathing was calm and even, no snoring. He looked defenceless and sweet, at peace with no worries in the world. If only he knew what Stacie was going through, wondering how she was going to make it through the day.

Stacie sat trying to figure out what to do. She was acting like a schoolgirl with her first crush. Was that what Dan was? A crush? Or was he someone who had stepped in after too long putting up with her own company, moping about her flat feeling sorry for herself. Stacie often listened to sad songs, and drank alone, cooking an exciting meal for one, having no one to share her day with. A sane conversation was something she would enjoy, a night in front of the television, glass of white wine, box of chocolates and a man wrapping his arms around her keeping her warm, followed by an evening of rampant passion.

Just thinking about how lonely she really was left Stacie depressed. She spent all her cash on herself, with no one to lavish it on, which was probably why she could afford Dan. Okay, she had a nice clean flat, new car, dressed well, ate for one, shopped for one and lounged around her flat without a care in world, but her life was empty. Stacie had wallowed in self-pity long enough, she was determined the experience at Desires would change her. It certainly couldn't make things any worse.

When the hands on her watch turned to seven o'clock, she crept out of bed and headed to the bathroom where she stood scowling at herself in the mirror. *Get a grip, girl. You've got the opportunity to move on with your life.* She only had herself to blame for allowing Graham to have so much control over her, and he wasn't in her life anymore.

Stacie put her hair into a clip and had a quick shower, trying to scrub away the worrying thoughts. She went back to the bedroom where Dan was still sleeping peacefully. She put on her jeans and a fitted T-shirt then wandered over to the window to open the curtains slightly. The rain hammered at the desolate garden, making everything look as depressed as she felt.

She closed the curtain and turned to look over to the dresser. The room key lay next to the phone. She decided to leave Dan in bed and go downstairs to get some breakfast and a strong cup of coffee. She took the key and left the room being as silent as possible so as not to wake Dan. She wandered down the quiet corridor, even the girls on reception were nowhere to be seen. She headed to the restaurant where they'd had supper last night. There were a few people sitting and having breakfast so she went in.

She chose a cosy spot in a corner near the open fire and sat, looking through the menu. There was plenty to choose from, toast, croissants, a full English breakfast, fruit salad, and scrambled egg, which was her favourite. Very soon a man came over to her. He was tall and thin, wearing a white shirt and black trousers.

"Good morning."

"Good morning," she replied. "I'll have the scrambled egg please, with a cup of coffee."

"Are you eating alone?" he asked while writing her choice down.

"Yes."

"It'll be about five to ten minutes," he said, then left.

Stacie glanced at the other people in the room. She was the only one alone. Maybe the man thought someone else was coming down, hence the question.

A few people in the room acknowledged her as she gazed round, she smiled back at them. The waiter arrived with a tray bearing her cup of coffee, with a small jug of cream and a bowl of sugar. "Aren't you the girl who's with Dan?" he asked her as he put everything on the table.

"Yes, why?" she asked, arching her eyebrow at the question. What business was it of his?

"No reason, just wondered." He walked off leaving her curious as to why he asked, not that it was any of his business who she was at the club with.

She prepared her coffee to her liking, then sipped thoughtfully. When her breakfast arrived, Stacie ate with relish clearing the whole plate. Evidently, sex was good for the appetite. She felt much better after she'd eaten something.

Stacie then saw Angel walk in the room, looking more soberly dressed than she had the night before. In fact, she had to look twice to make sure it was she.

Stacie watched her standing at the bar, her long black hair hanging straight down to her shoulders. She was wearing a satin jacket over a white vest, which she'd teamed with skinny jeans and ordinary black boots. A chunky gold chain hung round her neck. She looked stunning. Mind you, Angel would look stunning in a binbag. Stacie saw her looking in her direction. She turned away quickly, pretending she hadn't noticed her.

Her heart beat wildly as she stared in the opposite direction, watching a couple reading a newspaper.

"Good morning, Stacie. May I join you?"

The pit of Stacie's stomach churned. She turned her head to see Angel standing before her. Angel looked pretty and almost normal, but Stacie felt more afraid of her in these clothes than in her PVC.

"Sure."

Angel folded her long legs into the chair opposite Stacie. "No Dan?"

Stacie noticed her makeup was very well applied. Her lips were red and luscious, and her eyes dark with purple eye-shadow. Stacie sat feeling like a complete mess, no makeup, her hair untidy.

"No, he's sleeping."

"So you're enjoying your own company?"

"I guess so."

"How are you finding Desires?"

Stacie felt anxious, unsure how she should answer the question. Angel frightened her. In Stacie's job she was used to powerful people who constantly talked down at her. She usually just ignored them and got on with her job. Angel intimidated her in a different way. She was gorgeous, powerful and ran Desires. She must need a strong hand, authorising and commanding all the time. She wasn't the kind of person to get on the wrong side of. As she pondered her answer, the waiter brought Angel a cup of black coffee. His manner was anxious and deferential, with none of the almost insolent impertinence he had shown Stacie.

"It's different," Stacie said, when the waiter had gone.

"It certainly is, thank goodness, or I'd be out of a job! Dan tells me you are doing very well."

Stacie took a sip of her own coffee, feeling her chest tightening, thinking about the performance in the reception area last night, which Angel had seen.

"I'm really pleased to hear that," she added.

"Even after yesterday?"

"You mean that whole thing with James? I wouldn't worry about it. We're all entitled to our own opinions. Personally, I was more bothered about what he said to Dan. He shouldn't be judging Dan's fantastic work." Now that comment Stacie certainly couldn't argue with. "I don't accept that behaviour, especially when it involves someone who works here. If Dan was bad at his job then I would have certainly looked further into the situation, in private, but as I know Dan is amazing then I don't have to. James was badly in the wrong. If anything, he needs to be examining his own attitude."

"Do you actually run this place then?"

"Yes. The people who come here have been coming for years and I enjoy seeing the same people as well as meeting new people. My mother used to run it. Now, she just sits in the back and watches me run around screaming the orders which amuses her! I enjoy being in charge, maintaining Desires' good reputation. And I love bossing people about," she said, laughing.

"I bet. Have you been running it long?"

"About four years. When my mother used to run it, I spent quite a few weekends here watching her and occasionally having the odd dabble."

"Did you work here?" Stacie couldn't imagine any mother running a sex club and employing her own daughter as a sex worker.

"I used to help out with the admin side of things, but nothing else. If I indulged, it was strictly for pleasure only," Angel said. "I also heard that you are a bit of a dark horse yourself."

Stacie looked at her, concerned. What was she talking about? Stacie was no dark horse. Her life was dull, dull, dull. There certainly wasn't anything for her to be a dark horse about. "What do you mean?"

"I heard you went into the orgy room last night." Stacie stared at her. Her heart started to jack-hammer and her stomach roiled. "Don't look so frantic, I know about everyone in this building, no one escapes my clutches, I can tell you. So what did you think?"

"Sorry?" she answered, as her mind tried to process the horror of Angel knowing.

"What did you think?" Angel repeated.

"It was okay." She paused, wondering if Angel thought she had slept with someone else other than Dan. "Dan joined me."

"So, you enjoyed it then?" Angel said with a grin.

"Yes, it was okay," she answered yet again. Why would Angel ask? Maybe she was doing a little customer satisfaction research. Impishly, Stacie wondered what Angel would do if she gave negative feedback.

Stacie didn't wish to tell Angel exactly how much she blanked everyone else in the room out and just concentrated on Dan. The orgy room wasn't exactly what Stacie would have thought an orgy room would be, people swapping partners and experimenting with others, but then Stacie was learning that Desires wasn't exactly what she might have thought it was at all.

"Tell me, Stacie," she said, taking another sip of her coffee as the waiter arrived with a rack of toast and a small tray with little pats of butter and tiny pots of various spreads. "What turns you on the most?" Angel spread a slice of toast with jam and took a bite.

*Dan.* The answer sprang instantly to the forefront of Stacie's mind. Stacie hesitated, wishing she could just not answer. But Angel was the boss and knew most of her personal details anyway. She sat there, looking at her, waiting for the answer.

There is no way she could tell Angel how much Dan turned her on. The shrewd woman would no doubt divine that Stacie had developed feelings for Dan and she would probably be escorted off of the premises. Her heart raced faster. God, she had to think of something, just to get Angel off her back.

"I enjoy having my clitoris sucked," she finally said weakly. It was true, very true in fact, just the thought made her wild and hot. Better still if Dan was doing the licking.

Angel smiled. "God, yes that is fucking amazing. I have a slight confession to make," she said, wiping her mouth with the napkin. "I have to have that at least once a day, it's my addiction. I'm not all that bothered about cock, but the clitoris, fucking hell…what an explosion, I just love the build up and sensation, fucking hell…" she paused. "Mind blowing or what?"

"Yes, I must admit I'd forgotten how amazing it is."

"I'll tell you what, I'll make sure Dan gives you one of our 'keep it quivering' leaflets, regardless if you come back or not." She paused and took a sip of her coffee. "Are you coming back?"

"I'm not sure," Stacie said, taking a sip of her own coffee to hide her sudden confusion.

"Does all the testosterone put you off?"

Stacie almost choked on her drink as she attempted to answer her quickly, "No."

"It can get too much, that's why I'm pleased there is plenty of girl on girl action here also. Has Dan shown you around Desires?"

"Only a little," she replied. Over Angel's shoulder she saw Dan walk into the room. Stacie's heart began to race and she firmly quelled the smile that threatened to spread over her face. Angel turned around to see what had caught Stacie's attention.

"Dan, come here," Angel commanded Dan. He obeyed with no hesitation.

"Good morning, Dan," Angel said, then glanced at her watch with a quirky smile, "Only just, mind. Stacie said you needed your beauty sleep, so she left you to it."

"You should have woken me," he told Stacie, taking a seat at the table to Stacie's left.

"Sorry, I just thought I should leave you."

"Nah, wake him up, get his cock hard and shag him senseless for breakfast. A bit of sausage is much more appetizing than scrambled eggs."

Stacie looked at Angel, shocked at the way she spoke about him. Then she looked at him. His face was impassive, she couldn't tell if he minded or not—or even if he enjoyed it or not.

The waiter arrived taking Dan's order and cleared the table.

"Anyway, I have work to do. Enjoy the rest of your time here at Desires, Stacie, and I hope you will come back," Angel said, before standing up and leaving them alone.

Stacie was left wondering what on earth to say to Dan when his coffee arrived. They sat making general chitchat, but Stacie found it hard work. She had to work hard not to let her emotions show and she was struggling to put what Angel said about having him for breakfast out of her mind.

"What would you like to do today?" he asked her as his full English breakfast arrived. She watched him squirt the ketchup all over the place then dive in with his knife and fork.

"Not really sure, anything you suggest." A question was playing on her mind. Best to get it out in the open. "When did you speak to Angel about me?" she blurted.

"Last night. She caught up with me when I was getting some air. Why?" he asked, looking at her as he filled his fork again.

"Just wondered."

"Angel knows everything about everyone in this place, it's her job to make sure everyone's happy," he said. "You look tired." He put the fork into his mouth.

"I didn't sleep much."

He swallowed. "Was the bed uncomfortable?"

"No, I just couldn't sleep. My mind was working overtime," Stacie said. She watched him eat his food. Just the actions of him filling his fork and putting it into his mouth were fascinating to her. At least he had good table manners, not talking until he'd emptied his mouth, not like Graham who would happily talk through a mouthful of food, spraying bits everywhere.

"I hate that, all you want to do is sleep and your brain begins thinking about anything and everything," Dan said.

The conversation drifted to a halt. The only thing on Stacie's mind couldn't be said, and anything else she thought of was just inane small talk.

"I might just step outside while you eat. I need some air," she told him in the end. His mouth was full so he just nodded.

Stacie almost ran from the room. How long could she hold out before he started noticing her weird behaviour? She wandered down the corridor until she got to the back door leading to the patio.

She opened the door and the cold air hit her. Stacie stepped outside, everything looked sad and cold. She walked across the patio and toward the deserted garden. Stacie stood on the frosty grass inhaling the cold winter air. She filled her lungs then released, seeing her breath cascading out into the air.

Hearing voices, she turned to see a man and woman come out. They stood under the heaters and lit cigarettes, beginning to gossip. Stacie paid little attention to anything but stared unseeing at the garden, thinking about Dan and what she should do. She didn't feel that saying anything would help the situation, because of the contract, that damn fucking contract. Maybe she should step back into the real world and see where it took her?

After about ten minutes of serious thinking and no conclusions, Stacie wandered back into the building. It had started already. There were many more people hanging around in raunchy outfits than there had been before. She made her way back to the restaurant to find Dan chatting to the barmaid. Stacie walked in and smiled.

"Hello there, I was just about to come and find you," Dan said.

"Were you?"

"Yes, of course," he said and took a step closer. "You okay?"

"Fine. So, what are we doing today?"

He started to walk toward the door and she fell in step beside him.

"Do you fancy the grand tour?" he asked, opening the door for her.

"You mean there's more I haven't seen yet?" Stacie walked through, out into the corridor.

"Lots."

"Why not."

Dan took hold of her hand. The intimate gesture quickened her breath, but she barely had time to savour it before he was leading her toward the back of the building. Instead of turning to the patio she had just come from, he went through another set of double doors. This corridor was dimly-lit and there were many anonymous doors leading off. He took her straight past them before finally stopping at one that looked no different from the others. He opened it to reveal a staircase lit with candle-bulbs in black iron sconces.

At the bottom was a corridor which led off in both directions. The wall was bare brick with yet more doors. The same candle bulbs and sconces were placed between the doors, and the floor was bare concrete slabs. She followed Dan down the corridor past at the large wooden studded doors. They almost looked like dungeons. Stacie guessed that was the intention. They had probably been storage cellars at one point in the mansion's history.

It was cool and clammy down here and she shivered. She saw Dan up ahead holding a door open and hurried her steps toward him.

"Come in," he told her. She entered the room.

The eerie flickering bulbs lit brick walls and a cold concrete floor. At Dan's encouraging, she stepped further in and saw a bed with shackles and a neck brace, a cast iron cage hanging off the ceiling and restraints left, right and centre.

The other equipment in the room she couldn't begin to identify, but Dan pointed out a stool spanker, a punishment bench and a sex swing. There was a wall full of bondage equipment, whips, paddles, handcuffs, chastity belts for him and her and ropes in all different colours. Stacie couldn't believe her eyes, there was everything, dildos, nipple accessories, gags, chains, feathers and bondage clothing including masks. Stacie was freaked out all over again. She was just coming to terms with Desires, but being faced with evidence of some of the things people liked to do to each other was disturbing.

"Have you used this room?" she asked, picking up a grooved paddle.

"Only to get equipment out of," he told her. He reached behind him and picked up a whip. "Come here."

"No, I don't think so," she said, stepping back away from him.

"I will not hurt you, I promise. If I do, you can have the weekend free on me. Trust me."

Stacie stared into his eyes, seeing nothing but calm reassurance there. She moved closer to him, still a little anxious, but wanting to trust him. Maybe he could show her what people saw in all this.

"Bend over the bench," he said with her looking deep into his eyes whilst he ran the leather strands through the palm of his hand. Stacie positioned herself over the bench, tensing up and closing her eyes. She heard the gentle whistle of the whip as it approached and cringed away, scared it would hurt. To her surprise, it was soft and gentle, almost like a caress. Dan trailed the tails of the whip up her back, then whipped her bottom again, a tiny bit harder. Shivers ran down her spine and Stacie wriggled on the bench. She felt Dan moved closer behind her, then felt his hands on her, undoing her jeans. She froze and he stopped.

"Trust me," he said again.

Stacie relaxed. He wouldn't do anything to hurt her. He certainly wouldn't want to jeopardise their friendship. *Or his earnings*, the cynical part of her interjected.

Dan pulled down her jeans. The cool air hit her flesh. She felt his hand caressing her bottom, running his hand softly over her skin. His hand moved away and Stacie clenched her buttocks, anticipating his next move. Surely it would hurt more without the protective denim covering her tender skin. Dan put a light swing into his wrist with no force at all and again gently lashed. Stacie felt no pain, only a light burning sensation, heating her skin.

"Well what do you think?" she heard him ask.

"It's not too bad."

"Not all bondage involves pain. I just thought I would show you." He put the whip back and she pulled her jeans back up, a little disappointed the demonstration was over. "And in here," he told her, while walking through to an adjoining room, "is the cell." Stacie looked into the cold cell with cast iron restraints set in place. It looked evil, freezing, not inviting at all. There was even a small metal bed pan situated in the corner.

Dan closed the door and crossed over to the other side of the room, opening another door. There were more of the ubiquitous flickering lights, which illuminated a St. Andrew's cross against the far wall, complete with handcuffs and feet restraints, and another wall full of various bits of equipment she couldn't begin to imagine the use of.

"This is exceptionally extreme," he said to her as she reluctantly stepped in.

Stacie walked up to the cross, Dan coming up behind her.

"This can be used for all different kinds of fetish. Have a go," he said, stepping past her and pressing his body against the cross, putting his hands and feet to the restraints.

Stacie stared at him. "What, you want me to tie you up?"

"I am all yours. Restrain me and use whatever you choose, feathers if you like. Sometimes it's nice to be out of control. Try it."

"Can I pass?"

"You can if you wish, but it's not all about pain. Try something sensual."

"I'm not sure," Stacie replied, looking around the scary room, then back at Dan.

"Go on, what harm will it do? Use that blindfold, so I don't know what's coming. That's always exciting."

"How can that be exciting? I could just tie you up and leave you here."

"Oh, I see," he said with a twinkle, removing his body from the cross. "So you would restrain your partner and walk away and leave him to be punished in that manner."

"Absolutely, especially if he is driving me loopy."

"I'd better give that one a miss then." He walked toward her. "I don't actually think you would leave me there though."

"And what makes you think that?" she said. His smile was too cocky.

"Well, that would be wasting your money."

"Not if I tell them you were rubbish and you promised not to hurt me with the whip and offered it for free."

Dan moved his mouth to her left ear. His hot breath warmed her cold flesh. "You're evil, Miss Clifford."

"Little me?" He reached for her, but she slipped neatly away, turning her attention to the items on a nearby table. She picked one up, trying to work out what it was.

"It's a butt plug," he told her. She stared at it then quickly put it down. "Not your cup of tea?"

"Hardly, I don't find anal sex nice at all. Graham liked it sometimes, but I didn't enjoy it. I found the whole event painful."

"You either like it or you don't." He regarded her thoughtfully. "I know what you would like," he said, and walked over to a chair with a hole in the middle of the seat, which again had handcuffs and shackles attached.

"Pull down your jeans and panties and sit on the chair," he commanded her.

Stacie looked at the seat, trying to figure out what exactly the purpose was. It looked like some kind of commode, not exactly sexy. She obeyed, sitting on the chair, feeling embarrassed.

Dan dropped to the floor. He lay on his back, then moved under the chair. Stacie watched him disappearing underneath. Then, to her shock, she felt his tongue prodding her pussy. Stacie clenched her muscles in shock, becoming stimulated just by the touch. She instantly jumped up, with him still under the chair and pulled her garments up.

Dan came out from under the chair. "Did you enjoy that?"

Stacie didn't answer. She was too embarrassed to tell him the truth that she could have easily stayed there.

"Honestly? I felt like I was on the toilet."

Dan smiled. "Sometimes that's what it's used for." Stacie looked at him, not understanding. "Some men enjoy having girls..." he paused "...well, having girls evacuate themselves on their face."

Stacie stood still, certain he was teasing her. "Not really! That's...that's just disgusting. I mean, really, really foul."

"Well, some people are weird that way."

"You're bloody telling me." Stacie shuddered at the thought. Wild sex, yes, that she could understand, even exhibitionism, but what Dan was describing was beyond repulsive. She made her way back into the bondage room hearing him following her. Dan caught up with her at the door. He opened it and they went out into the corridor, just as a number of people arrived to use the facilities. They all wore leather or PVC clothing. One man was just wearing a thong.

They left the way they'd come. Stacie was relieved when they came back up into the top corridor. They went down a little way, then Dan stopped at another door.

"This room might shock you a little, but some guys like it." Dan opened the door and put the light on.

The room was decorated like a nursery, with blue teddies on the wallpaper and white nursery furniture, including, Stacie was shocked to see, a massive adult cot. A stack of adult-sized nappies sat on a changing table the size of a hospital trolley, and empty feeding bottles and large dummies waited on shelves to be used. Stacie was completely stunned, and walked back out, her stomach churning.

Dan took her into another room containing what looked like a cross between a boxing ring and a large paddling pool. There was a small bar, along with tables and chairs. "Bitch fighting," he explained. "They fill the ring with custard, mud, jelly, you name it. They put two girls in dressed in tiny bikinis and they fight to rip each other's bikinis off."

They walked further down the corridor, arriving at another door. Stacie felt apprehensive, wondering if this tour really was such a good idea. What perversions might be hidden behind this one? However, Stacie went in to find nothing more sinister than a large table with many chairs surrounding it. "This is the main function room. Sometimes they hold business meetings in here, but most of the time it's the feast room."

Stacie turned to stare at him. "Feast room?"

"They cover each other in food and eat it off one other."

She turned her head to look at him, bizarre images filling her mind

"Have you ever...?" she asked.

"Yes." He walked back out the door. Stacie's head was filled with visions of him covered in whipped cream and fruit, and her licking him clean. Or her covered in sweet delights and him slowly eating everything off her. That might be quite nice actually. Stacie began to feel that warmth that was becoming familiar. She started at Dan's voice. "Everything all right?" He was standing at the door holding it open for her, and looking at her quizzically.

"Fine," she answered, walking past him into the corridor.

They continued, arriving at another outside door where the corridor made a ninety degree turn. He opened the door to show her a large patio dotted with hot tubs. "These are extremely popular in the summer. I have to confess I wouldn't mind one in my back garden." He closed the door on the hot tubs and they turned down the new corridor. Dan took a swift right turn into another short passage, which ended in a door. Dan opened it and went in. Stacie followed him. It was just an office, with a woman sitting behind a desk.

"Hello Dan."

"Hello Lucy, how are you doing?"

"Fantastic, now." She grinned at Dan. *No doubt an admirer of his*, Stacie thought.

"Have you got a booth for about five minutes?"

"Of course," she answered, passing him a key.

"Thanks, gorgeous." Dan winked at her and she positively glowed.

There was another door off the office. Clearly wherever they were going, they had to go through this woman first. Dan gestured Stacie through the door and she walked into a semi-circular passage with numbered doors off it. Dan unlocked door number six and held it open. Stacie entered first. The room was tiny, not much more than a cubicle. It was unlit, but in the light that came in from the hallway she could make out a lone chair.

"Take a seat," Dan said.

Stacie obeyed. A large roller blind covered the wall in front of her. Dan closed the door behind them. She heard the rustle of him moving and then the blind slowly began to open. Behind the blind there was a large window, but it was what she saw through the window that caught Stacie's shocked attention. It opened onto a large, brightly lit room containing a circular bed, on which a man and woman were joyfully and rampantly having sex. The light from the room illuminated Dan as he stepped back and stood beside her, watching the couple.

"How many people are watching them?" she said after a moment.

"There are eight booths opening onto the room."

"And they don't mind people watching them?"

"Well, they wouldn't be in there if they did, would they? Some people enjoy putting on a show, it gives them a thrill. And some people enjoy watching them. Here, everyone's happy, the exhibitionists and the voyeurs. Anyone can go in there, couples, groups, a man or a girl stripping and playing with themselves, sometimes two girls, or occasionally two men. If being watched is their thing, here's where they can go."

Stacie sat watching the couple. She found herself becoming turned on as the man sucked on the woman's clitoris. Stacie felt her own nerve endings throb with arousal, here in this darkened room. She slid a hand down between her thighs, rubbing her pussy through her jeans and wriggling on the chair. From behind, Dan's hands rested on her shoulders, bringing her back to herself. Shocked at her own loss of control, she stopped and leapt to her feet. She wrenched open the door and fled back to the office.

"Leaving so soon?" Lucy said.

Stacie stared at the girl. Lucy's face lit up and her gaze drifted to look over Stacie's shoulder. She knew without looking Dan was right behind her. Lucy was looking at him like he was made of chocolate, and when she turned, Dan was smiling back at her. Shaking her head, Stacie continued with her stomp, sweeping out of the room without another word. For God's sake, had he shagged every woman here?

Dan was close behind her. "What happened there? I thought you were getting turned on?"

"No, what made you think that?" she said, continuing to walk at a thousand miles per hour. They passed the orgy room. The voile curtain had gone and there was no one in there but a couple of cleaners.

Stacie approached the reception area. Angel was standing talking to the receptionist—it was the same woman who had come out to talk to Stacie the night before. Angel turned and smiled at them. "Hello there, how is everything?"

"Fine, thank you," Stacie answered.

"Dan," Angel said in acknowledgement.

He barely nodded back to her.

Stacie looked at the way Angel's eyes ran down Dan from top to toe. She looked as if she was undressing him. She looked at

Dan, unable to read the expression in his eyes. He didn't look happy though. Curious.

"Dan has just been giving me a tour," Stacie said into the charged silence.

"Wonderful, and what do you think?" Angel asked.

"Could do with more sex…" Stacie said, trying to be funny. Everyone looked at her strangely. "Joke," she explained. The receptionist gave an uncomfortable giggle.

"Anything take your fancy?" Angel said.

Stacie thought for a second, trying to think of something. "The feast room looks good."

"Feel free to use it whenever you like. Or if you prefer, you can have anything ordered to your room."

"Thanks," she answered. The receptionist stood up, her eyes fixed on Stacie. Stacie glanced at her, feeling a little uncomfortable with the intensity of her regard. The receptionist turned then, and walked into the rear office off the corridor behind the reception desk, but just as the door was about to close, she turned back and gave Stacie a smile.

Angel left also, sweeping off in the direction of her office. Stacie felt Dan's hand creeping into hers.

"Come on," he said. "Do you want to head back to the room?"

Dismissing the curious behaviour of the receptionist, she said, "Yes please."

## Chapter Nine

"Do you mind if I take a quick shower? When I got up this morning I came straight down to find you," Dan said once they were back in their room.

"Really?"

"Really." He kissed her on the cheek then headed off to the bathroom.

Stacie plumped up the cushions and sat on the bed. She flicked on the television, but couldn't concentrate on anything on the screen. Her head whirled with thoughts about what she had just seen. She was beginning to realise that her sex life so far had been extremely tame. Certainly much of what people did here, Stacie would not want to do, but if it made them happy, what was the harm? The baby room took her more by surprise, but then, if someone wanted to be a dog like she had seen on her first day, then being a baby was not really any weirder.

She struggled more to understand the bondage room. How could people find pleasure in pain and humiliation, either giving or receiving? She had liked the whip Dan used, but he had been very gentle with her, there was no pain. She wanted to try and understand these fetishes, but some of them made no sense. And the toileting one—well that just defied understanding. Surely apart from anything else, it was very unhygienic.

She was determined to try to understand some of these bizarre practices. It all seemed so extreme. Stacie enjoyed being held and made love to with passion and desire. Maybe some people don't like the emotional side of sex. Everyone liked different things, not just in sex, but in all aspects of life. Some people liked watching gory horror films, the bloodier the better. Stacie preferred a soppy romantic comedy. But it didn't mean that everyone had to like the same films or books she liked. She could respect people's choices in films or books, why not in sex?

She heard the shower stop and her thoughts turned to Dan. Visions of what she could cover Dan's cock in arose in her mind's eye, whipped cream, chocolate sauce, treacle. Her mouth began watering at the thought of sucking and licking his cock clean.

He came out the bathroom, a towel around his waist and another in his hand. She lay back and took in his exquisite body, shining with moisture. She could just pull that towel off and dive on his cock, suck him to stiffness, then ride him into submission.

Dan turned around and saw her staring at him. Unabashed, Stacie didn't look away, letting her gaze drop deliberately to his groin area. He smiled.

"You're getting to be quite the little minx, aren't you?" He scrubbed the towel over his wet hair and then dried his body. Stacie drank in his every move, watching the play of his muscles as he rubbed the towel over his skin. She considered making a move on him but decided against it. He would come to her. She'd just watch for now, knowing that she could have his delicious body very soon.

He put the second towel back in the bathroom and came back into the bedroom, sitting on the stool to watch Stacie watch him. He didn't smile, just watched her as if considering something. After a few moments, Stacie began to feel uncomfortable. She stood up, trying to get away from the burn of his eyes. She moved over to the table. Dan swivelled on the stool, following her with his stare. She could feel his eyes on her. Her heart began to flutter, although she had no idea why. She poured some water and took a sip. Why the hell was he staring at her? She wished he'd stop.

She glanced back. He was still staring at her, but now a cheeky smile lifted the corner of his mouth and he sat back on the stool. Stacie relaxed. She recognised *that* look. She'd make him work for it though. Call it punishment for freaking her out. She deliberately walked back to the bed, shimmying her hips a little as she went, and keeping dirty eye contact with him. She lay down on her tummy, propped up on her elbows and crossing her ankles in the air behind her. She knew without looking that her T-shirt was gaping at the top, showing her cleavage.

Why wasn't he coming over? She fastened her gaze on his lips, thinking about licking, nibbling, tasting and sucking them. Kissing had never been so good. Dan seemed to know instinctively how she liked it, soft and gentle, yet firm just the right time. She wanted to taste his skin, to smell him, to feel his cock stiff and ready in her hand, that smooth velvety shaft, hard, yet soft at the same time. She wanted him to take her, to cover her body with his, to slide it in and…

"What are you thinking?" he asked her.

"Nothing!"

His smile told her she wasn't as opaque as she hoped. "Is there anything you fancy doing?"

"Maybe," she replied, darting her tongue out to lick her lips. Dammit, was she going to have to spell it out for him?

His cock peeked out from under the towel, which had shifted slightly as he'd moved. It was quiescent, looking meek and inoffensive in its flaccid state. Stacie imagined taking it whole into her mouth, teasing it to attention.

"So what's the maybe?" Dan asked.

Stacie dragged her attention off his cock to look back at his face. "We could go for a walk," she replied teasingly.

His face dropped. "You're joking, right?"

"No, I thought the cold air would cool you down," she said, giggling to herself.

"Okay, fine, I'll get dressed and we'll go for a walk."

"Okay," she replied. Dan remained seated on the stool, not making any attempt to move. His cock looked lost, in need of somewhere warm to put it. "You know, the view's rather distracting," she told him.

"Don't you like it?"

"I didn't say that. Although, I prefer it when it's stiff and hard." She rolled the words around her mouth with relish. "No offence, but limp willies aren't the most attractive thing in the world."

"Women on the other hand, have gorgeous bodies all the time. It's not really fair is it?"

"What's your favourite part of a woman's body?"

The look that spread over his face was reminiscent of a small boy being asked what his favourite sweeties were. "Boobies," he said finally. "I love boobies. I could happily play with tits all day."

"Ah, a boob man," Stacie said, glancing down at hers, suddenly insecure. Were they big enough? Did he prefer massive ones?

"Oh yes! I love looking at them, and playing with them, and squeezing them, they're so lovely and squashy. And I love that girls love it too. We both get pleasure. I love summertime when girls walk down the street in little skimpy bikini tops and I can have a good stare behind my shades."

"Pervert," she said jokingly.

"Well, girls shouldn't have them on display if they don't want them looked at. I like the look and the feel," he said, raising his hands to squeeze a pair of invisible boobs. "I could happily play with yours all day, they're perfect," he said then.

Stacie's gaze flicked up to his and they locked eyes. What was he saying? Was it just a simple compliment, or something more? After an intense moment Dan broke eye contact and rearranged his towel, hiding his cock from view.

"I mean it, you know. In fact, you have a stunning figure all over, not just your boobs," he said.

"I do for now," she answered, pausing before continuing her thought. "Until I have a family, that is."

"You want children?" he asked, sounding surprised.

"One day, absolutely, and my clock is ticking. Don't you?"

"I suppose so. It's not something I have thought about."

"No, I guess not, you're still young."

He grinned. "Exactly, still young and selfish."

"I wouldn't say that," Stacie said.

"Wouldn't you? Why not?"

"Any man who can make a woman feel the way you make me feel couldn't be described as selfish." Stacie dropped her gaze, embarrassed, then rushed on. "With regard to kids, you're still young, you're only twenty three, you have plenty of time."

"Is that what you're looking for?" he said, his stare intense.

"What?"

"A man to have a family with?"

"Maybe, eventually. Why?"

"Just wondered."

Had she scared him off with the talk of a family? She would love nothing more than to find a man and settle down and live a life of love. She'd hoped for that with Graham. It hadn't worked out with him, but it didn't mean it couldn't with someone else. She hadn't looked at Dan before as a man to have a family with, just for some sex and fun. But now the thought was there, it didn't seem to want to leave. Stacie scolded herself mentally at the turn her thoughts were taking. It was bad enough that she thought he might return her feelings. Now she had to start fantasising about settling down with him? *Get a grip, girl!*

A knock at the door interrupted her mental castigations. Dan turned, looking at the clock, then stood up, tightening his towel around his waist. Stacie sat up on the bed and watched him answer the door.

"Come in, come in," Dan said to whoever was out there. "Just give me a minute to get dressed."

A man walked in the room. Dan went into the bathroom and Stacie looked at the man. He was blond, tall, fairly muscular, with a look of one who spent time in the gym. He wasn't bad-looking, but she preferred Dan. She glanced at the bathroom door, wondering why this man was here. Dan came out, fully dressed, his hair still damp. "Stacie, this is Mike," Dan said.

"Hi," Mike said. He made his way to the bed and held out his hand.

"Hi," she replied, shaking it.

"Wow, you're a sexy treat," he said, his eyes roving over her body, lingering on her breasts. Stacie recoiled and turned to look at Dan. "Christ, Dan, you got a looker."

"I certainly did," Dan replied.

Mike sat next to Stacie on the bed and turned slightly toward her. Her heart began to pound frantically. What the hell was going on? Did this character think he was in with a chance? He shuffled closer to her and Dan just looked at her, his face impassive.

Stacie leaped up off the bed. "I don't think so," she told them.

"Can you give us a minute, mate?" Dan said to Mike, who shrugged and walked out the room. Stacie turned around to glare at Dan. "Stacie, I want you to have sex with him."

"You've no bloody chance," she blurted in petrified anger.

"Look, I'm not going to be with you, out there in the big world. You need to have experience with another man. Mike is the best man for the job. He knows your background and he'll not do anything to upset you. Please, Stacie," he said, taking hold of her hands. "I need you to do this for yourself."

Stacie glared at him, seeing his eyes full of despair. Did he really want her to have sex with this stranger? Or was he doing it to hide his feelings, if there were any? God, she was confused.

"Stacie, please, I'll just be sitting here, at the table. I'm not leaving the room."

"No, Dan! No! I can't do it with him. How could you ask such a thing?" Her heart felt like it was being wrenched out of her chest. His words rang round her head. *I'm not going to be with you, out there in the big world.*

She didn't know what to do for the best. Could she bear the thought of another man touching her, seeing her naked, licking and kissing her body, being as intimate with him as she had been with Dan? Stacie quivered, the whole thought made her stomach turn. But Dan had a very good point. He was only available here at Desires. Being out there in the real world would be another story.

"Stacie, please." His quiet voice rang like a shout in the silent room.

She sucked in a deep breath. The pit of her stomach ached and she sat heavily on the bed, overwhelmed with emotion, trying to decide what was best. Dan sat next to her and picked up her hand, holding it between his two.

"You're going to be here?"

"Yes…I will watch every single move," he said. Did she imagine that his voice sounded unsteady?

"And you aren't going to join in?"

"No…unless—"

"No," she said, needing to make that one clear.

"That's fine."

How far had she come already, here at Desires? In such a short space of time she'd done things with Dan she'd never done before. She'd even had sex in an orgy room, with other people watching. She watched other people having sex, and enjoyed it. It might not be as bad as she feared. She might actually like it. Mike was quite good-looking. And Dan wouldn't let him do anything she didn't want.

"Okay," she whispered, watching Dan's face. He didn't look happy, as she expected he might. In fact, he looked quite desolated. He leaned over and kissed her on the cheek.

He got up to let Mike back in. There was a quiet conversation at the door that Stacie couldn't quite hear, then Mike came in, grinning hugely. Stacie's heart ached and her tummy did back-flips. She had a sudden urge to do a runner, but then her time at Desires would have been a complete waste of time. She was at the club for a confidence boost. Maybe Dan knew better than she did what was good for her. She had to admit that doing everything her own way hadn't worked awfully well for her so far, had it?

Stacie sat back on the bed against the pillows. Mike lay down beside her, propping himself up on an elbow. She watched Dan pull a chair from under the table, positioning it so he could keep a close eye on everything. Maybe she could use this to her advantage. Would Dan get jealous?

Mike shuffled his body closer to her, raising his hand and placing it onto her knee. She quivered, scared, wanting to get through this for her own benefit. His hands stroked her leg slowly, moving up to her thigh, and came up toward her chest, her breasts clearly on show beneath the tight T-shirt she'd put on for Dan's benefit.

"Wow, you have fantastic tits," he told her, cupping her right breast, then her left, caressing and stroking. She froze, holding her entire body stiff, not wanting to enjoy his touch.

"Hey relax, babe," he said. "Lie down." He paired his instruction with a gentle push to her shoulders. She lay down obediently, the position reminding her of the times she'd assumed the position for Graham while he did whatever he wanted to her. At least she knew she'd be able to endure this, if necessary. Mike's hands ran up and down her body, kneading her boobs like they were dough. Stacie turned to look at Dan over Mike's shoulder. He was smiling at her encouragingly. Stacie didn't smile back. Right now she hated him.

Mike pulled up her T-shirt, kissing around her tummy and licking in her navel. He pulled away from her taking off his tight top, revealing a six-pack with plenty of chest muscle and a few tattoos. He flicked his shoulder-length blond hair back then stood up and undid his fly. He was going commando, his cock popped out as soon as he lowered his trousers. Stacie stared at it, revolted.

She looked again at Dan, glaring at him. He picked up a glass of water to take a sip, not looking at her.

Mike came back on the bed, crawling up her body. He undid her jeans and pulled them off her. It was all happening in such a rush. She felt cheap and tawdry. At least with Graham, they had been married. He tugged at her T-shirt, lifting it up and over her head. She didn't resist, she couldn't be bothered to argue with him. She lay on the bed, wearing her bra and thong. Stacie wished she wasn't wearing sexy underwear, it gave an appearance that belied her feelings. It seemed wrong to be looking sexy while feeling nothing.

He moved over to her right side, so Dan could see everything. He kissed her on her lips. She didn't kiss him back. Mike quickly moved down to her breasts, pulling down the cup on her bra and inhaled deeply on her right nipple as his other hand twitched her left nipple, pulling and tugging at it. He licked and sucked intensively on her right bud till it was erect, then moved across to the other one.

"Wow, your boobs are amazing," she heard him say.

He moved suddenly, coming up on his knees, positioning his cock next to her face. Erect, it swayed before her. Mike took hold of his cock and placed it next to her lips. Stacie closed her eyes, and opened her mouth. She could easily bite the damn thing but knew that wasn't going to solve anything.

Mike placed his dick into her mouth. She sucked on it mechanically while he played with her breasts. He reached down, pulling her thong to the side. His fingers dipping in her pussy caused her to squeal and wriggle. She was still sensitive from her earlier arousal with Dan, when he sat with his cock on show. Mike took her noises as encouragement and dug his fingers in farther. Had Dan just been putting on an act to get her in the mood for Mike?

His finger flicked over her clitoris while Stacie sucked his dick. He swung his leg over her head, putting them into a sixty-nine position. She stared briefly at his dangling balls and arsehole in her face before shutting her eyes tightly. She just lay with her mouth open, not even bothering to suck anymore, letting him fuck her mouth while he licked and teased her clitoris and inserted his finger into her hole. She couldn't help making involuntary noises when his finger entered. He made circular movements with his fingers deep inside her. Her body jerked slightly, and he thrust his cock deeper into her mouth, making a loud groan.

He pulled out and moved off her. Stacie turned to look at Dan. He wasn't even watching, but staring at the bedside cabinet. Could he not bear to watch Mike shagging her? Or was he just not bothered?

Mike lay down on his back and quickly rolled on a condom. "Come and sit on me, babe," he invited her, his latex-clad cock rearing up.

Stacie turned around so her back faced Mike. At least she didn't have to look at him. She gathered up an amount of saliva and lubricated herself like she used to have to do with Graham. Slowly, she lowered her pussy onto his dick, feeling him deep within her, then began to thrust herself up and down on his cock. She closed her eyes, wanting to allow herself to attempt to enjoy the sex session. Maybe she could get beyond the emotional and just concentrate on the physical. She rode his dick hard, feeling him fill her.

"Oh God, yeah, baby. You're so good, you're so into it. Fuck me harder, baby. Make your tits jiggle."

She leaned back and felt Mike's hands grabbing at her breasts as he thrust up to meet her.

"You feel so good, baby, so hot and wet. Turn around, I want to see you."

Stacie pulled herself off him and turned herself around. She reinserted his cock and leaned over him, so her boobs jiggled in his face. He grabbed at them, sucking desperately on her nipples like a giant baby.

"Lie down, sweetheart. I'm gonna fuck you so good you'll come like you never did before."

Stifling a sigh, she moved off him, lying flat on the bed. He moved over the top of her, and shoved his dick in, thrusting deeply. Stacie looked at his face. He was clearly enjoying himself. Probably the best way to get this over with was to pretend to be enjoying it too. Mike began to thrust harder and faster, hurting her a little. Stacie grabbed the bed sheet, doing her best to make noises like she was enjoying herself when really the opposite.

He came with a groan and she matched his noises, jerking her body as if she was coming. She looked over at the chair to see Dan gone.

Mike climbed off her and pulled the condom off, tying it up and wrapping it in a tissue. Dan appeared bringing her a robe from the bathroom. She took it and pulled it over her body.

"Thank you, Mike," Dan said.

"No hassles, she's a beauty. Was that good for you, babe?"

"Great," she replied, not even bothering to fake a smile. He obviously wasn't that brilliant at his job if he didn't notice she didn't get excited. She blinked back tears. She felt cheap, dirty and disgusting.

Mike pulled on his clothes and Dan saw him to the door. Stacie sat up on the bed, tying the robe tightly around herself. She hated Dan, hated him!

Had he seriously expected her to enjoy that? Stacie lay on her side and curled up into a ball as Dan stood outside the room talking to Mike. He was exactly the same as the rest of them, no respect whatsoever. How could she have thought he might love her? My God, she'd even been considering him as husband and father material. He'd done her a favour by getting this Mike involved. It was probably time for her Desires experiment to come to an end.

Stacie climbed off the bed and went into the bathroom to clean up. Only an hour ago she had been so happy. Now she just felt empty. Tears of self-pity came and she sat on the toilet seat and sniffled for a few minutes. How stupid was she? For the first time, Stacie considered the possibility that maybe the contract was there for her own protection. Certainly getting emotionally involved with Dan was bringing her nothing but misery.

Stacie headed back into the room. Dan was sitting on the bed. She didn't say a word to him or even favour him with a look, but instead headed to the wardrobe, getting out her overnight bag.

"What are you doing?" he asked, standing up and moving toward her.

"Leaving."

"Why?"

Stacie didn't reply, pulling her things out of the wardrobe and stuffing them in her bag.

"But you have paid until seven. I thought we could go downstairs and get something to eat and then come back here and—"

"What…and shag? I don't think so." She pulled up the bag by its handles.

"What's wrong?" he asked, sounding puzzled.

"Don't give me that. Look, I have things to be doing back at home, I need to get ready for work, sort a few things out. I have wasted enough time this weekend."

"What do you mean? I thought…" he said, standing up, coming close to her. Did she imagine the pain in his face?

She pushed past him, dragging her bag through into the bathroom and started gathering up her toiletries. He followed her and stood at the door. "You thought what? That I'm a slag and need a good fucking? Was I wearing you out? Did you need to bring in someone else to help you?" Stacie laced her voice with generous amounts of venom.

"No, not at all. I can't believe you're thinking that. I brought Mike in to allow you to experience another man, not to make you feel you're a slag. I obviously made the wrong decision," he said, his voice becoming a little high-pitched with panic.

"Damn right, you did that all right," she said, pivoting to scowl at him. Adrenaline pumped and she began to shake. She wrapped her arms around herself and glared.

"I'm so sorry, Stacie, I never meant to make you feel that way. I honestly thought I was doing the right thing. You should have said something before if you weren't enjoying it."

"Oh, right, so it's my fault is it?"

"No, I didn't mean that! I thought that bringing in another man might just boost your confidence, I never even thought it would make you suffer the way you are. I swear Stacie, I'm so, so sorry, I cannot apologise enough to you. Please, stay a little longer."

Stacie stared at his beseeching face and exhaled, resenting his pathetic apologies. "I do need to go," she said in a calmer tone. "I need some time to myself. I need to think about things."

"I just thought it might help. I never wanted to cause you pain."

"Just forget it. I have obviously taken it the wrong way. You're only doing your job," she said. She picked up her last few bits and put them in the bag, zipping it up, then dragged the bag back into the bedroom. She picked up her clothes from where Mike had dropped them.

"Will you come back?" Dan asked her.

"I'm not sure."

"Okay, wait here, I will just go and get you a leaflet." Stacie quickly got dressed while he was out of the room and wandered over to look out of the window. Grey rain lashed the dismal gardens. Stacie looked around the room, wondering if she had truly just over-reacted to the whole situation.

He burst back into the room, out of breath, a tri-fold leaflet in his hand. She walked back over to him and he thrust it at her. She took it, not looking.

"It's some suggestions of things you could do at home, you could buy a few vibrators, clitoral stimulants, oils, that kind of thing."

Stacie stuffed the sheet in her handbag. "Thanks. Well, I should be off." She didn't look at him, didn't want to see the look on his face.

Dan carried her bag down to the bottom of the staircase. The receptionists looked at her as they came downstairs, then exchanged a significant glance.

This was it, then. She turned and took her bag off Dan. She raised her eyes to his briefly. He was smiling, but it wasn't convincing. She tried not to read too much into it, that was what had got her into trouble to begin with.

"Goodbye," he said, leaning to give her a kiss on the cheek.

"Goodbye, take care," she replied, accepting his kiss, but not returning it.

Stacie turned and walked to the main entrance. She wondered if Dan was watching her go, or had he just disappeared. She looked back. He was still there, at the bottom of the staircase, watching her walk away. She opened the inner porch door, holding it open as she looked back one more time. He gave her a little wave, but he wasn't even pretending to smile any more. She could stay. She had paid till seven after all. But it was time she accepted it, Dan wasn't her future. It was time to move on with her life.

She let the inner door swing shut, and opened the outer door, the rain on her cheeks mixing with her tears as she left Desires.

## Chapter Ten

Stacie's flat was freezing when she arrived home. She dropped her bag on the floor and headed straight into the kitchen to switch the heating on. She turned on the lights and drew the curtains, then plumped herself on the sofa and stared round at her cold empty flat. It would take ages for the heating to warm the place up. She turned on the gas fire in the living room and stared at the flickering flames, feeling their heat warm her face.

Wine might be a good idea. Wine and some music. She went into the kitchen and opened a bottle of Cava, pouring herself a glass then put on her favourite CD. Stacie sat cross-legged on the fake sheepskin rug in front of the fire and sipped her wine. She drained the glass and poured another, gulping it down, feeling the strength ebb from her limbs. Dan's face floated in her mind's eye. How did he feel about her? Really? He had seemed genuinely devastated that she was going. He hadn't been able to watch Mike and her having sex, yet he had engineered it. If he had no feelings for her at all, he wouldn't care that she was leaving, he was still getting paid after all. He wouldn't care that she and Mike were having sex, in fact he would probably enjoy watching. All the evidence suggested that he did genuinely care for her.

She jumped to her feet and dragged her bag into the kitchen. She pulled out the clothes and began to sort her washing, trying to keep her mind occupied. She put a load in the machine, then did the washing up that had been there since before the weekend, scrubbing at the crusty plates with a scouring pad till they sparkled. She dried them and put them away, then looked for something else to do.

She decided to make something to eat and opened the fridge door. She stared at the shelf full of meals-for-one that constituted the entirety of the contents of her fridge and closed the door.

She wandered back into the living room, which felt a bit warmer now, and sat down on her sofa. She stared around the empty space, for the first time feeling alone. She had never felt this way before. Usually, she loved her own company, especially since leaving Graham. She enjoyed not having anyone to clean up after, being able to do everything her own way. But now, she felt incomplete.

She scrabbled in her bag and found Chrissie's mobile number. She could call her. Chrissie was the only person who knew about Dan. But what could she say to her? *I fucked up. I allowed him to slide through my bloody hands. I walked out on him before our time was up.* She stared at the clock, annoyed at the fact she still could have been at the club with him, gazing into his brown eyes, holding him tight to her body, caressing his divine body, feeling his cock…

Stacie shivered as she became aroused. What the hell had she done?

It was pointless any longer to deny the fact she was in love with him. Her heart felt punctured and crippled, her legs were like jelly. She didn't know what to do, she couldn't stand these feelings. She yearned to go to bed with him, feel his body pressing against her, his breath on her naked flesh, bringing her to ecstasy.

"Bloody hell Stacie, get a grip. Forget him. You paid him for sex and got it, now shut up." She grabbed a cushion and hugged it to herself, tears sliding down her cheeks. She wished she hadn't walked out, wished she'd had the courage to talk to him. "Stop it Stacie! Stop thinking about him. You fucked up, you live with it."

\* \* \* \*

Her alarm blared. Stacie rolled over and hit it into silence. Her head ached. Last night she'd polished off the remainder of the bottle of wine, along with several bottles of pear cider left over from her divorce party. She didn't even like pear cider, which was why they were still there months after the party. Stacie tweaked the curtains and winced against the bright sun streaming across her bed.

She had to get up, though. It was just lucky she hadn't been so drunk as to forget to set her alarm. Work wouldn't wait. She dragged herself into the shower, grimacing at the state of her face in the mirror, streaks of mascara trailed down her cheeks from her self-pitying crying jag the night before.

She drank about a pint of water and took some painkillers to try to get rid of her headache, before getting ready and heading off for work, hoping she didn't get pulled over. She wasn't entirely sure she'd pass a breathalyser. The traffic was manic and she arrived late.

"Good afternoon, Stacie," said her boss, leaning back and crossing her arms.

"Sorry, traffic," Stacie explained.

"You should leave earlier."

"Sorry," Stacie mumbled again.

She spent the day in and out of meetings, trying to organise the next magazine, but her mind was all over the place.

That evening Stacie put on her favourite chick flick, *Bridget Jones's Diary*. She was turning into a real Bridget Jones herself useless at everything, falling for the wrong men, sitting at home necking wine and listening to sad songs. Where was her Mark Darcy? She didn't want to be like that any longer. Stacie put the DVD away, determined that the next time she watched it, she would have a Mark Darcy of her own. Time to take charge of her life.

\* \* \* \*

She worked late the next few days at work, trying her hardest to get organised and snap back into action.

Sitting at her desk one morning, analysing an interview, she jumped when her mobile phone rang. Stacie frowned at her phone, not recognising the number.

"Hello?"

"Hi, Stacie?" said a cheerful woman's voice.

"Speaking," Stacie said.

"You forgotten about me already?" said the woman, sounding bubbly.

"Sorry?"

"It's Chrissie, from Desires."

"Oh God…I am so sorry. Yes, I had forgotten, I've been busy with work." Stacie was surprised at how pleased she was to hear from the other woman. She'd shoved the napkin with Chrissie's scribbled number into her bag when she'd left Desires, but then totally forgotten about her intention to put it in her phone.

"I can't talk for long, but I was wondering if you'd like to meet up for some lunch, or dinner, if you're not busy?"

"That would be great, I could do dinner tonight," Stacie replied, a smile cracking her face. Finally she had a social life.

They made arrangements and hung up. Stacie tried not to think about what she was going to say about Dan.

Stacie spent the afternoon running around making sure that any all loose ends were tied up. She wasn't working late tonight.

She left work, feeling pleased to have someone to meet. At least one good thing did come from Desires, she met a friend if not a lover. She went home and got changed, taking off her confining work suit and slipping into a long flowing jersey dress. She touched up her makeup and got a taxi to the restaurant.

On arrival, she was heading over to the bar when she heard her name called. She turned around to see Chrissie standing at a table, waving at her, a beaming smile on her face. She walked over and Chrissie kissed her on the cheek, then enveloped her in an unexpected hug.

"How the devil are you?" Chrissie said.

"I am fantastic, and you?"

They ordered their food and began to chitchat, just gossip about work and the latest soap stories. It was so nice to have a pleasant conversation with someone.

The food was delicious and they'd managed to polish off a bottle of wine between them. Stacie was just beginning to feel merry when Chrissie put her knife and fork together on the plate and leaned back in her chair.

"So, go on then. What happened with Dan?"

"Oh don't. I fucked up, he fucked up. I have no bloody idea what happened," she replied, holding her face in her hands.

"Come on, explain," Chrissie said, moving closer and wrapping a comforting arm over her shoulder.

"I have no idea. Well I just have no clue…I was all ready to say something, I had it going around in circles in my head and then, well…I just—"

Chrissie interrupted, "You never told him how you felt about him?"

"I was going to, but then he brought in this other guy to have sex with me, and after that I hated him."

"I see," Chrissie said.

"If he had any feelings for me, would he have done that?"

"Maybe he had no choice. Maybe because it's his job, he had to be professional. Do you still love him?"

"God, yes. I haven't stopped thinking about him. He did say a few things that made me think he might have feelings for me."

"Like what?"

"Well," Stacie felt her face heating at the memory. "He said I had fantastic breasts, he could play with them all day, and then he said I have a stunning body. Would that mean anything?"

"He could have been just flattering you."

"But there was more than that. It was more in the way he looked at me, if you know what I mean. And he didn't look happy when I was having sex with the other guy. Not at all!"

"What have you got to lose by telling him? You don't have him now, do you?"

Stacie shook her head.

"And if you tell him, and he doesn't feel the same, you still won't have him."

"But I'll feel stupid and embarrassed."

"Isn't it worth feeling stupid and embarrassed when you think about what you'll gain if he does feel the same? You only live once Stacie, life's too short. Have you arranged to go back?"

"No."

"Have you got the number?"

"Yes, it's in my phone." Stacie began digging about in her handbag. "Oh, I must have left it at home when I rang the taxi."

"Come on then, back to yours," Chrissie said, standing up and gesturing for the bill.

They got a taxi to Stacie's flat. Stacie's heart skipped and her body ached with excitement, praying and hoping he hadn't been booked up. The phone lay innocently on the hall table. Stacie grabbed it up and they rushed into the living room. She brought the number up on her contacts list and just stood there staring at it.

"What's wrong?"

"I can't," Stacie whispered.

"Why not?"

"I don't know."

"Give it here!" Chrissie grabbed the phone and hit the call button, passing it back to Stacie as the ring tone began.

"Hello, Desires?" came the voice.

Stacie opened her mouth but nothing came out.

"Hello? Hello? Is anyone there?"

Stacie looked at Chrissie, who made urging gestures with her hands. She took a deep breath.

"Sorry, hi. It's Stacie Clifford. My number is 7029."

"Good evening, Stacie. How are you?"

"Fine thanks. I…I…I was wondering if I could book Dan for the weekend?" Stacie said in a rush.

"Just one moment please." There was a pause. "He's not scheduled to come in, but I can contact him for you, if you wish."

"Yes, please!" she said in excitement then remembered to tone down her enthusiasm. "That's fine, if he can't do it, don't worry about it."

"I'll give you a call back as soon as I get in touch with him, okay Stacie?"

They said goodbye and hung up.

"Well?"

"They're ringing him and getting back to me," Stacie said, bouncing on her toes with anxiety. "Chrissie, what have I done?"

"I think wine is called for," Chrissie said, taking hold of Stacie's shoulders and propelling her into the kitchen. "Do you have any?"

Stacie shook her head. "I drank the last of it the other night," she said, shame-faced.

"Didn't I see a corner shop just down the road?"

Stacie nodded.

"Don't go anywhere. I'll be right back."

It seemed Chrissie was gone only two minutes before she came back bearing a bottle of sparkling wine. She expertly popped the cork with a giggle and poured them both a glass.

They went back into the living room and sat staring at the phone.

Stacie sipped her wine and fidgeted, silently begging the mobile to ring, tapping her foot on the coffee table leg, while Chrissie chewed her fingernails. Stacie had never felt so anxious about waiting for a phone call, not even when it was her solicitor about her divorce. But this call was a whole different situation, this was about getting between the sheets, and possibly more, with a gorgeous, delicious, sexy, irresistible young man.

"I feel like a schoolgirl," Stacie said, trying to breathe naturally.

"Good, isn't it?" Chrissie answered, sounding almost as excited as Stacie did.

"Definitely. But what happens if he isn't free?" Stacie asked in panic.

"Then book him for the following weekend."

"But Christmas is looming and everyone is busy."

"Stop panicking. Wait till they call you back, then take it from there."

Stacie knew Chrissie's words were wise, but she struggled to calm her racing mind. Again they stared at her bright pink mobile, when suddenly it rang. They froze, looking at it.

"Well answer it," Chrissie said aloud.

"I can't. What if it's bad news?"

"Then we'll deal with it. Answer the damn thing."

Stacie picked the phone up, glancing at Chrissie. She pressed the accept call button and placed it to her ear. "Hello," she said with difficulty over the nervous lump in her throat.

"Hello. Is this Stacie?"

"Speaking," she said, trying to calm the tremor in her voice.

"We have contacted Dan, and he says no problem. He can be here from eight on Friday night. Is that okay for you?"

Stacie sat in shock, her stomach churning in sheer relief. Chrissie's face showed concern and Stacie let her smile show.

"That's great…I mean fine…yes!"

"I will confirm that with Dan and book you in. We will see you Friday at eight," said the receptionist, sounding inviting.

"Thank you," she said, grinning like a schoolgirl who had her first date.

She hung up and they began dancing around her lounge skipping like girls in the playground.

* * * *

Stacie bounced out of bed on Friday morning. She'd already packed her overnight bag, planning on changing clothes at work before she left for Desires. She didn't want to turn up in her boring work stuff. She'd packed a killer outfit of a tiny black dress with a plunging neckline, teamed with towering heels. Dan wasn't going to know what hit him. She had a quick shower and grabbed a bit of toast for breakfast, then jumped into her car in good time. She arrived at work early for a change, meriting a sardonic eyebrow lift from her boss.

She grinned around the office, calling out merry greetings to people. Even a day packed full of dull meetings couldn't dampen her enthusiasm. She floated through them on a cloud, dreaming of Dan and what they would do that night.

Then all hell let loose. One of the directors decided it would be a good idea to change the format of the magazine, and called a late meeting. Stacie kept watching the clock. Time ticked away, the hands turning slowly from six o'clock to seven. Nothing was being decided, no one could agree. The editors were arguing with the directors, who were in turn adamant that their way was the best. Eight o'clock came and went with no sign that the meeting was coming to an end.

Stacie excused herself, nipping to the toilet to call Desires, explaining that she was going to be late. Once again she had to put her social life on hold for her damn job. Stacie wouldn't mind but the director had nothing to go home to and was a complete spoilt bitch who always managed to get her way with everything, regardless of the consequences. Stacie never had seen eye to eye with her. In fact, she couldn't stand her. She walked around like everyone else meant nothing, and she had to be centre of attention. Stacie really didn't know why they bothered holding these stupid meetings as she always won.

She returned to the meeting, staring at the clock, watching the hands moving, imagining what she could be doing right now to Dan. The hands ticked to nine o'clock. Still nothing had been resolved. Stacie was no longer paying any attention to the damn meeting. As far as she was concerned, what was being said could have waited until Monday. Instead she was sitting here in this dull, dull, dull meeting, when she could be warm in Dan's arms. Her stomach began to rumble—she hadn't eaten since breakfast. She'd expected to be wining and dining with Dan now, not listening to people arguing with no conclusion in sight. Suddenly, one of the girls stood up.

"I'm sorry, but I have to leave."

Stacie burst into life, standing up with her, "Yes, I have somewhere I should've been almost two hours ago."

The boss finally got the meeting moving, suggesting a vote on the issues which had been discussed. Stacie sat back down holding her head in her hands. Surely this could have happened earlier. It was as if they were being punished. The vote was made. No one wanted to change the format, so the director decided to stomp about like a toddler who wasn't getting her way. Stacie stood up. She wasn't going to spend any more of this evening listening to a spoilt cow having a tantrum.

"I really have to go," Stacie told everyone. She collected her bag and left the room, ignoring the director's stunned expression. Halfway down the corridor, she heard the door open. She cringed. Were they going to call her back? She glanced over her shoulder, and saw everyone else streaming out of the room also.

"Good for you, Stacie," said one of the other girls. "Thought we were never getting out of there."

Stacie ran to the car park, and leaped into the car. There was no time to change, she just wanted to see Dan. She floored it out of the car park, squealing down the road. Her heart skipped about in her chest and she grinned the entire journey.

She turned the familiar corner and Desires appeared. She pulled into the car park, smiling to see a huge lit Christmas tree outside the porch. Stacie parked her car, then put on the light and checked her reflection in the mirror. She looked tired. It wasn't surprising, it had been a long day. Maybe Dan would wake her up. She collected her overnight bag out the boot of her car and made her way to the main entrance. She punched in the key code and was ready to open the heavy door as soon as she heard it release. She almost skipped down the corridor.

"Good evening," Stacie said, approaching the reception desk.

"Good evening, Miss Clifford. How are you this evening?" asked the receptionist. It was one she hadn't seen before. This one had blonde hair, tied tightly back. She was wearing a white blouse which plunged at the front, showing her ample boobs.

"I'm fine, now I've finally made it. God, the boss sometimes," she said. The young woman smiled at her. Another receptionist came from out the back office. It was the one who had come out to talk to her out front after she had stormed off last weekend. She gave Stacie a broad, happy smile which went on for just a little too long.

"Your bill, Miss Clifford," she heard the first receptionist say.

Stacie handed over her credit card. "The feast room is open for delights this evening," the woman told her as she processed her payment. Stacie noticed the other receptionist lick her lips provocatively. "The booth rooms are both going to be having sessions with couples," she said, handing Stacie a sheet with the times on it. "The music hall is holding a ball tomorrow evening, wasn't sure if you are interested in going. And the lounge room is available for pole dancing."

"Er, thank you," she said, distracted by the other girl walking sexily back to her desk, holding eye contact with her. She took hold of her bag and turned to the stairs.

The girl suddenly spoke. "If you need anything, Stacie, please don't hesitate to ask me, my name's Bailey," she said. "You can ask for me any time."

"Thank you, Bailey, I might do that," Stacie replied cautiously, continuing toward the stairs.

At the top she glanced back at the receptionist desk seeing Bailey watching her, she smiled again. Stacie couldn't make up her mind about Bailey, something didn't add up. She dismissed her concerns with a shrug. Bailey was probably just being nice, as she was the night she talked to her on the front step.

Stacie continued her journey down the corridor, her steps becoming lighter and faster as she approached the door. She knocked lightly and in a matter of seconds the door opened. Stacie saw Dan's face split in a glorious smile. Her own lips widened involuntarily and she smiled back.

"Hello," he said. He stepped forward at the same time she did and held her in a tight hug, before coming toward her to kiss her on the lips, a kiss of such sweet deliciousness, Stacie's knees felt quite wobbly. She felt his hand relieving her of the bag and he pulled away, gazing down at her with radiant eyes. "How are you?"

"Wonderful, now I'm finally here."

"I got your message," he said, moving into the room. Stacie followed him, hardly believing she had managed to finally be with him.

"I'm really sorry about making you wait."

"Don't worry about it, it was well worth the delay," he said, closing the door behind her.

He put her bag on the floor next to the wardrobe and headed toward the small table, which held an ice bucket with a wine bottle poking out the top, and two crystal glasses.

"I thought you wouldn't mind me ordering a bottle," he said, popping the cork and filling their glasses.

"No, not at all," she said, taking the glass from him and taking a sip. She felt the effects instantly on her empty stomach and closed her eyes, feeling the warmth spreading through her body.

"Are you hungry?" he said softly.

"Totally starving."

She drank half the glass then walked to the bedside cabinet, putting the glass on it. She took off her coat and hung it in the wardrobe, then started to unpack her bag. She had just hung the final item up when she felt Dan's arms creeping round her from behind, stopping her in her tracks.

"What are you starving for?" he asked, his hands moving from her waist to her hips. She licked her lips and felt her body tremble. She pressed her body back against his, feeling his body heat through her clothes. His hands moved forward, sliding over her tummy, and started to unfasten the buttons of her jacket.

"You look gorgeous, by the way," he murmured in her ear. "This whole businesswoman look suits you." He slid the jacket off her shoulders and laid it over the end of the bed.

Stacie turned around, missing his touch even for the one brief second it took for him to come back to her. He was wearing a black shirt with only one button done up, teamed with black jeans. She grabbed his belt and pulled him back to her.

His eyes were full of cheek and they glowed, sparkling in the subtle light. His stubble was just the right length to be sexy and not scruffy. His hair was slightly tousled and begging to be rumpled. It really didn't matter what he wore or the way he looked he still made her go weak.

"There is only one thing I am starving for," she replied, pushing him back onto the bed. Off guard, he fell. Stacie lunged forward, landing on him, her skirt riding up to her waist as she straddled him. It was time she took control. Stacie took hold of his hands and pulled them up above his head, restraining him. She stared down at him, then leaned forward, pressing her lips against his.

Stacie kissed him deeply, tasting him, dipping her tongue into his mouth, rolling her tongue around his. She'd never been aggressive in bed, and she began to wonder why not. She sat back up, staring down at his face. She glanced down at herself. Her suspenders and lace-topped stockings were fully on show, and it was clear Dan hadn't missed them either.

All week Stacie had pictured him, impatient to see his face, craving to have his body respond to hers. She had a sudden urge to ring Chrissie to say thank you. If it hadn't been for her Stacie might not be here with him captured underneath her. But perhaps not right now.

She stared down at him, so glad she had finally got up the courage to come back. Her whole body tingled with excitement. She clenched her inner muscles and wriggled, feeling him beneath her. He smiled up at her, making no effort to free himself. It was clear he was quite enjoying being her captive. Stacie moved back down onto his lips, kissing him lightly then moved across his cheek, before proceeding to his ear lobe, nibbling it. She released his hands, to run her own through his hair, feeling the soft curls as she kissed his neck. Freed, his hands immediately went down to her thighs, caressing the skin above her stocking tops. She sat back up and gazed down at him, trailing her fingers down his chest. She felt his fingers move up, to caress the crease where her thighs and buttocks joined. She shivered as he came within a hairsbreadth of her pussy, then wandered away again. Then his hands grabbed her bottom full on and he flipped her over onto her back, her feet dangling over the side of the bed.

He knelt over her and pulled her skirt fully up to expose her satin panties, surrounded by the lacy garter belt. He very deliberately traced one finger lightly up the satin triangle. Stacie couldn't help letting out a moan. He moved across to the suspenders, running his finger down the elastic to where they joined her stockings.

"Have you been wearing these all day at work?"

Stacie nodded with a grin.

"Have you been thinking about me?"

She nodded again.

"And have you been thinking about what I'd do to you when I got hold of you?"

"Fuck, yeah," she breathed, pushing up to him invitingly. He took hold of her satin panties and slid them down over her stockings and off her feet, still wearing her high heels.

"Stockings and high heels. Sometimes the old ones are the best," he said, as he stared down at her smooth, fresh pussy. She smiled delightedly as she watched his reaction. She'd shaved the night before. He knelt down on the floor before her and spread her legs wide, just staring before he dove in. Stacie reached behind her and grabbed handfuls of the bed cover as his agile tongue licked and stroked and sucked. His hands cupped her bottom and he lifted her up to him, as if he were trying to take her whole pussy into his mouth at once. He flicked his tongue over her clit, then down her sensitive lips to her pussy entrance, diving in as deep as he could before coming out and repeating the process.

He kissed down one inner thigh to her stocking top, before coming back up again and down the other side. He came back to her pussy and inhaled deeply.

"You smell so good," he said before burying his head once more between her thighs.

Stacie wriggled and moaned, her hands blindly opening and closing. She thrust her pussy shamelessly into his face, feeling her crest approaching.

"Not yet, baby," he said, coming up for air. She wriggled up the bed, her head on the pillows. Dan hovered over her before taking her face in his hands and kissing her. She could taste herself on him, that curious tangy sweetness that was like nothing else. He started to unfasten the buttons of her blouse. Her hands went to his shirt, undoing the one button that held it shut. He kissed her breasts as he exposed them, rising in creamy mounds out of her black lace bra. He peeled away one cup, popping her nipple out, and fastened his mouth over it, while he caressed the other, stroking and gently squeezing her nipple.

He sat up to take his shirt off, and Stacie took the opportunity to wriggle out of her blouse and unclip her bra.

"You're still far too overdressed," he said, looking down at her skirt. Stacie lowered the zip and lifted her bottom so he could pull the skirt off. She went to unfasten the garter belt, but his hand stayed her. "You can leave that on," he said, a twinkle in his eye.

"Aren't you a little overdressed also?" Stacie said, eying his jeans.

"Well, why don't you do something about it?" he said, kneeling up.

Stacie knelt up to face him, naked but for her garter belt, stockings and high heels. She pressed her breasts against his chest and her hand rested on his belt.

"What's in it for me? Do you have anything interesting under there?"

"Well, that depends on how you define interesting. Is this interesting enough for you?" he said, taking her hand and putting it on his cock. She moved her fingers delicately up and down the length of him, feeling his girth, his bulk clearly outlined through the denim.

"It might be," she said, slowly undoing his belt. She popped the button and drew down the zip, tugging his jeans and shorts down to his hips to release his towering penis.

"What do you think?"

"Well, it's quite interesting," Stacie said, sitting back on her heels as she wrapped her hands around his cock. "But what were you planning on doing with it?"

"What would you like me to do with it?"

"I'd quite like you to make love with me."

"I can do that."

Stacie reached behind her and tugged off her shoes before lying back on the bed. Instead of diving in, Dan went back down to her pussy.

His mouth engulfed her clitoris, sucking and licking hard. Still twanging from before, it sent jolts throughout her body. His tongue manipulated and teased, and he slid two fingers inside her, pressing upwards to hit her G-sport.

She thrashed her head wildly from side to side on the pillow, grabbing at her own breasts, pinching her nipples. Dan continued his manipulations, ramming his fingers in and out as his clever tongue sent her inexorably down the path to bliss. Stacie tried her hardest to hold out but she screamed wildly as her whole body erupted into an electrifying spasm, forcing her to thrust her hips high off the bed, jerking her body spasmodically as her orgasm crashed through her.

Stacie's body was quivering with aftershocks when she felt Dan lift his body up and over hers. She jerked as he thrust his penis into her hyper-sensitive pussy. He plunged his cock in and out of her, filling her deeply, urgently. He took hold of her right leg and lifted it in the air, hitting her G-spot with every pound. Stacie moaned without inhibition, watching his facial expressions as he concentrated on his rhythm. She took her hand down to where they were joined, feeling his penis moving in and out of her soaking pussy. A mere touch of her hand on her quivering clit had her almost there. Dan clasped her close to him, his plunges becoming more urgent and forceful.

He moved her hand away, replacing it with his own. He rubbed her clit hard and Stacie closed her eyes, welcoming the crest. She wrapped her legs around him and screamed her rapture to the walls, as Dan juddered his own orgasm, gasping in her ear as he dropped on top of her.

# Chapter Eleven

Stacie woke up and stretched. A lazy smile spread over her face as she remembered where she was, back at Desires. She turned over but the other side of the bed was empty. She sat up to look around the room but he was nowhere to be seen. Stacie worried for a second, but then lay back down again. He wouldn't have gone far.

She snuggled back down into the duvet, remembering last night. She had forgotten, well actually never really knew, just how wonderful and fun sex could be, and how incredible an orgasm felt. All those years with Graham just shoving his knob into her, her only thoughts being, "Here he goes again," or passing the time counting the cracks in the ceiling. She felt alive again.

Her mobile phone gave its text message chirp from inside her bag. Stacie leaned down and hooked her finger under the handle, dragging the bag up onto the bed and digging about till she found it.

*Hiya hun, how did it go? Xxx*, Chrissie had texted her. Stacie smiled, wondering how she could adequately describe last night in only a text. She decided to call her instead.

"Hello lovely, and how's you?" Chrissie said.

"Oh, not so bad…" Stacie teased.

"Well?" Chrissie said, clearly impatient.

"Well what?"

"You know bloody what. Spill!"

"Fucking hell, Chrissie, Wow, wow, wow, bloody hell wow. I think I'm still leaking."

"Nice one, good girl, you go for it."

Dan appeared from the bathroom soaking wet, towel draped round his hips, looking more ravishing than ever. "Oh my God," Stacie said, stretching out on the bed and looking him up and down.

"What? Tell me!"

"He has just come out of the bathroom, dripping wet."

"Well darling…there's only one thing for it…Go and feast."

"Oh I will. I'll be in touch," she told Chrissie then hung up. She crossed her arms and aimed a severe glare at Dan, who looked at her in surprise. "You are aware you could cause serious health problems wandering around like that?"

Dan grinned. "Really?"

"Oh yes. Come here."

Dan came around her side of the bed, removing his towel from his waist. He stood there naked, his cock already semi-hard.

Just then the alert on her phone bleeped. Frowning, Stacie reached for it and looked at the display.

"Oh, bugger!" she said, looking at Dan in horror.

"What?"

"I can't believe I forgot!" Stacie leaped out of bed, and started pulling on clothes.

"What is it?"

She turned to him. "It's my mum's birthday. I completely forgot. I need to go, I have to get her a present and go and see her."

"Will you come back?" Stacie's heart gave a little flip at his plaintive tone of voice and she went over to him, zipping up her jeans.

"You just bet I will." She stood on her toes and kissed him, tasting his toothpaste and reaching round to grope his naked bum. She gave it a cheeky slap, then went into the bathroom to quickly wash her face and brush her teeth. She went back through into the bedroom and pulled a high-necked sweater out of the wardrobe, pulling it over her head before dragging a brush through her hair at the dresser mirror. "I'll only be a few hours," she said, sitting on the bed to put on her boots. "What are you going to do while I'm away?"

"Miss you," he told her, sitting next to her and planting a kiss on her lips. "I will watch television all alone, trying not to think too much about you and what we could be doing."

"You're making it very hard for me to leave," she said, kissing him back.

"I want to make sure you come back," he replied.

"Just try and stop me."

"There's a ball tonight, do you fancy going?"

"The receptionist mentioned it, have you been to one before?" Stacie stood up and went to the dresser to put some make-up on.

"Yeah. It's usually a good night," he said, turning on the bed to look at her.

"Yes sure, go on then. Do I get to wear a ball gown or do I need to go naked?" she asked him, waggling her eyebrows at him in the mirror.

"Totally up to you, but I don't think you will make it out of the door if you go naked," he said.

"Listen, I'd better go, otherwise I'll never go and my mum won't get her present." She blotted her lips on a tissue and came over to him, leaning over to kiss him lightly so as not to ruin her lipstick. "I'll see you in a few hours," she told him. He hugged her round the waist, planting a kiss on her tummy. She rested her hands on his head, feeling light-headed and giddy with delight. These were not the actions of a man who was just being paid to spend time with her. The more time she spent with Dan, the more she was convinced he returned her feelings. She just had to get up the courage to ask him.

"No problems," he replied. She reluctantly walked to the door and opened it. "Missing you already," he called.

Stacie looked back. He sat sadly on the bed, pulling a puppy-dog face. She gave a little wave and left, letting the door swing shut behind her. Her smile could have rivalled the sun as she danced down the corridor and trotted down the stairs.

"Morning," Stacie heard as she walked past the reception. She stopped as she saw Bailey's head popping up from under the desk.

"Morning," she replied, giving Bailey a smile then continued walking to the main door.

Stacie got in her car and looked back at Desires for a moment, thinking about Dan. She analysed every look, every word, every gesture, for meaning. Every time she convinced herself that, yes, he did like her, that little voice in her mind squashed it, reminding her that she was paying for his company, paying for him to be nice to her. But Chrissie was right, the only way she would find out would be to ask. Whatever the answer was, at least she would know. But when was the right time?

She drove reluctantly out of the car park, heading into town. She browsed awhile before picking out a nice necklace and earring set and a card. On the way back to the car park, she passed by a shop that sold kinky underwear and sex aids. She'd passed it many times, always hurrying by, embarrassed. When she and Graham had come into town together, he had always expressed his disgust at the shop, and the people who patronised it. Today, she stopped and came back to it, deeply curious. She'd heard mention of various stimulatory toys and oils, but she actually had no idea what they were talking about. About the only thing she'd even heard of was a vibrator. She glanced up and down the street. What if someone saw her going in? She walked past, pretending to be looking in the window of the jewellery shop next door, until the street was relatively empty, then darted in.

The first few racks were full of various types of lingerie, bras, panties, matching garter belts, in a rainbow of different colours and a myriad of different styles. After the first few racks of frilly underwear, simple bras and panties gave way to more seductive ensembles. Satin garters dangled from ruffles of black and crimson lace, and tiny strings hung below curtains of gauze sewn to bras with holes in the front, clearly designed to show nipples.

In one alcove, a rack full of bemusing garments made of leather and decorated with studs caught her eye. There was even a riding crop displayed prominently next to the display. Stacie shied away from the racks of scary leatherwear that looked like something you'd put on a horse. She picked up a black and pink garment that looked like a bra – but had no cups! It was as if someone had cut out the entire cup from the bra, leaving just the wire, and then decorated it with a bit of ribbon and lace.

She needed something dainty and pretty, yet sexy at the same time. She daringly picked out a pink open nipple babydoll with crotchless panties. Browsing farther into the store, she was stunned to see the variety of kinks that were catered for, right here on the high street. If it hadn't been for Desires, she wouldn't even have known what half these things were. Remembering what Dan had said about being tied up, down in the dungeon, she chose a blindfold, lace handcuffs, and tickle ties.

A display of rainbow bottles and tubes caught her eyes and she was shocked when she saw bottles of something called Dick Lick. Picking one up, she discovered it was pretty much what it said it was. You put it on your guy's dick, and lick it off. She picked out a bottle of the strawberry-flavoured one and added it to her basket. She gave the inside of the shop one more glance before going to pay. Time was running short, but she would definitely have to come back here.

She was glad the assistant put her purchases in a plain brown paper bag, though. She might be becoming more sexually liberated, but not enough to parade her purchases through the town centre. She'd had her mum's present gift-wrapped in the shop. She sat in the car and wrote out the card before reluctantly heading to her mum's house. She'd much rather be going back to Desires.

Her mum loved her present, but Samantha spent the entire time talking about her perfect life and her wonderful kids and when was Stacie going to start looking for another man? She'd already let one slip away, and she wasn't getting any younger, you know. Stacie tried to hide her distaste for her sister's lack of any social graces, but managed about half an hour before she stood up.

"Sorry, Mum, I have to go. I'm meeting someone."

"Who?" Samantha demanded. "Who's more important than Mum on her birthday?"

"It's a man actually," Stacie hadn't intended to reveal anything about Dan, but her sister's pointed comments about her failed marriage and letting Graham 'slip away' like he was such a good catch, had stung.

Samantha was actually speechless. For about ten seconds. "You? A man? Where did you meet him?"

Now *that* she definitely wasn't going to reveal. "Um, a friend introduced us. It's early days yet. Listen, I'm sorry Mum, I do have to go. Enjoy the rest of your birthday." She got up and kissed her mum on the cheek. "Bye, Samantha."

As Samantha blustered behind her, Stacie grabbed her bag and swept out the door, almost running back to the car.

She couldn't get back to Desires quick enough. Once parked, she opened the boot and smiled in anticipation as she grabbed her bag of raunchy gear. She couldn't wait to show Dan. Stacie flew through the hall to reception. Bailey was seated behind the reception desk.

"Hiya," Stacie said.

"Hi, Stacie, how are you?" Bailey answered, a happy smile on her face.

"I'm great. I was wondering is there anywhere I can go to get changed before I go back up to the room?"

"Of course," she told Stacie. "Follow me." Bailey got to her feet and led Stacie to a door that said *Staff Only*. She opened it to reveal a very elegant powder room, decorated in red and cream, with shoe shaped chairs and a dressing table with a huge mirror. "Would you like anything else?" Bailey asked. Stacie turned around to look at her, seeing Bailey's eyes glowing.

"No thank you," Stacie replied with a polite smile, waiting for her to leave the room.

As soon as Bailey left, Stacie stripped off her clothes and put on the babydoll and crotchless panties. She toyed with the idea of just wearing these to go up to the room. A powerful jolt of arousals weakened her knees at the thought. She'd worn that red babydoll last weekend and paraded through the club. But this one had her nipples and pussy on show. And last weekend she'd had about two bottles of wine inside her. Sober, it was a little different. Picking up her long winter coat, she covered up her ensemble.

She touched up her makeup and smiled at her reflection, seeing nothing but excitement in her face at the anticipation of seeing Dan's expression.

Stacie headed back to reception. "Everything all right?" Bailey asked, smiling at her again.

"Yes, wonderful, thanks." Stacie walked up the stairs slowly, much as she wanted to run. It would do no good to be all out of breath and sweaty. With every step down the corridor, Dan was getting closer and Stacie was getting more turned on.

Stacie knocked on the door. It opened barely a second later. She walked into the room, deliberately brushing her body past him.

"How did it all go?" he asked, closing the door and turning to watch her.

Standing with her back to him, Stacie slowly unbuttoned her coat and let it drop, revealing her outfit.

"It went very well, thank you," she told him, glancing over her shoulder to see his reaction. It was quite satisfactory. His eyes widened and he looked as if his birthday and Christmas had all come at once.

"Wow," he said, whilst Stacie shot him a naughty smile. She turned around, revealing her naked nipples, stiff and erect with her arousal. She was tempted to go straight to him, but the urge to tease came over her and she shimmied past him to the table, while his jaw dropped to the floor.

The bottle of wine from last night was still in the ice bucket, although the ice had long since melted. Stacie poured herself a glass and took a sip. It was a little flat and not as cold as she liked, but it wasn't bad. He moved closer to her. "Is everything okay?"

"Perfect," she replied, taking a seat at the table. She leaned back in the chair and put one foot up on the table, revealing her crotchless panties. Dan sat on the bed opposite her, staring hard, his tongue was all but hanging out, while Stacie tried her hardest to act like everything was normal, and that she was not dressed so naughtily.

"So was your mum pleased to see you?"

"I guess so. You know what, I quite fancy something to eat," she told him.

"Like what?" he asked. She wondered if he meant sex or food.

"Food, I'm starving," she replied. His face dropped.

"Okay, I'll get the menu. Do you want to, er, eat downstairs, or have something ordered up to here?" he asked, keeping his eyes very much fixed to her body. Stacie considered going downstairs dressed like this, as she had considered it in the powder room.

"Here, I think."

Stacie perused the menu and decided on a light snack, not wanting to fill herself up if they were going to the ball later. While Dan ordered for them both over the phone, Stacie lay on the bed, assuming a seductive posture as Dan turned around. He put the phone down and lay next to her. "Is everything okay?" he asked again.

"Yes, fine, I was just thinking about the ball," she said enjoying tormenting him, acting like everything was perfectly normal.

"I see," he said, turning on his side. He placed his hand onto her knee and she promptly moved it away. She wasn't about to allow him access yet. "Well," he went on, a little nonplussed. "The dress code is formalwear. I have sorted a gown out for you. It starts at eight."

"Can I have sex with other people?" she asked, watching his face keenly, wondering what his reaction would be.

His face was impassive. "If you want to, that's totally up to you."

Stacie didn't answer, not wanting him to know she wasn't that keen on having sex with others. Whatever went on tonight she would still have Dan tomorrow. "What will you be doing?"

"When?" he asked, sounding unsure.

"Tonight."

"Probably fantasising about you all night."

"Really?" she replied, stretching out her body and watching Dan's reaction. He leaned over to her and put his hand onto her stomach. Stacie picked it up and placed it back on his abdomen. As he reached out to her again, a knock came at the door. She rolled off the bed, and went to answer it. She was reaching her hand out to open the door, when she remembered what she was wearing. Glancing down, her nipples were erect and on show, and her crotchless panties didn't cover much. A *frisson* of excitement shot through her pussy. She'd had sex naked in front of a room full of people last week. She could certainly open the door to a stranger with her boobs on show.

Stacie opened the door. Bailey was outside, pushing a trolley with their food order on it. Her eyes widened and her gaze flicked up and down Stacie's body. "Thank you," Stacie said, pulling the trolley into the room.

"No problem," Bailey said to Stacie's breasts.

Stacie smiled and shut the door. She pulled the trolley over to the table and set the food up. A discreet glance showed Dan watching her constantly.

The food ready, Stacie sat at the table, one foot up on the opposite chair. Dan's eyes got wider and he licked his lips.

"Is something the matter?" she asked him. He stared at her without saying a word. Stacie picked up her sandwich and began eating, taking small bites and chewing delicately. "What do you think of Bailey?" she asked, curious. He didn't answer for a second, clearly distracted.

"Um, Bailey?" He shrugged. "She's just the receptionist."

"Does she ever get involved in the activities in this place?"

"Not that I've seen. She keeps to herself."

Stacie could tell Dan wasn't interested in talking about Bailey. She pulled a few bits off her sandwich and ate them, closing her legs and crossing them at the knee. Dan stood up abruptly.

"I think I will have a shower."

"But you had one a few hours ago," she said.

Nonetheless, he stood up, making his way to the bathroom. Looking at Stacie, rather than where he was going, he reached out for a door handle that wasn't there, as the door was already open, and almost fell into the bathroom. Stacie turned her head to cover a giggle. She was enjoying this.

She heard the bathroom door close and smiled to herself. When he came out, she planned on giving him even more of a treat.

She finished off the rest of her sandwich and headed over to the end of the bed, deciding to wait for him, wanting to give him an even bigger mind blowing image. She never thought that seeing him in despair, desperate to touch her in any way possible, could turn her on so much. The power was intoxicating. She positioned her bottom on the bed lifting her feet up so they were just on the edge of bed, then widened her thighs and began to slowly toy with her clitoris. She sucked in her breath in a gasp as she touched her folds of flesh, already slick and wet.

She dipped her finger in her vagina and drew it out gleaming with her juices. Stacie placed her finger in her mouth, tasting herself, enjoying the taste. She covered her fingers in spit, and then lathered her clitoris. Her nerve endings buzzed with sensitivity. She would never have thought that dressing up could make her so horny.

As one hand played down below, Stacie brought her other hand up to pinch her nipple, causing it to harden. She felt an answering quiver in her pussy, as if the two were directly connected. She again slid her fingers over the folds of flesh, inserting her fingers deeply into her pussy, hearing the moist sounds, wishing Dan was out here watching her toying with herself. Stacie circled her fingers inside her vagina, letting herself cry out with delight, afraid that if Dan didn't show up soon he would miss the show. She took her fingers out of her juicy pussy, using her moisture to lubricate and torment her folds of delicate flesh.

Suddenly, Stacie heard the bathroom door open. She twisted her head round to see Dan standing at the bathroom door, quirking an eyebrow at the view. He walked over to stand in front of her.

"Don't stop on my account," he said, dropping his towel to reveal a stiff cock, rearing up and ready to go.

"That's naughty," she told him.

"And what you're doing isn't?"

"No," she replied, removing her fingers from her sodden pussy, placing them into her mouth to lick off her own juices.

He reached out for her, but she rolled away again, slipping off the bed to wander over to the table. A knock came at the door. They both looked at each other. Neither moved to answer it.

"Are you going to get it?" she asked him.

He sighed, obviously not keen, with other things on his mind. He picked up his towel and was about to wrap it round his waist when Stacie called out, "Naked!" He turned around, glaring at her, but she just shot him a cheesy smile. "I'm the boss, remember. You have to do what I want."

Stacie made sure she got into a good position to watch. Another knock sounded round the room as Dan walked over to the door. Surprisingly shy, he hid his body around the door as he answered it. Stacie cracked up laughing.

"Hello Dan. Sorry, am I disturbing you?"

It was Angel's voice. "No, please come in," Stacie called out, modestly putting her knees together. For some reason, this whole scenario was turning her on, very much so. Angel appeared, and Stacie noticed the way Angel stared at Dan, evidently surprised to see him stark naked and ready for action.

"Sorry, I didn't mean to interrupt," said Angel. "I've come to see if Stacie's report is ready. I can come back if you prefer."

"No, it's okay, I'll sort it for you," he replied, looking at Stacie for approval. She inclined her head in the affirmative.

"Would you like to join me in a glass of wine?" Stacie said to Angel.

"Yes, I would love to," she replied, approaching the table and sitting down. Stacie stood up and poured them both a glass. "That's a really sweet outfit."

"Thank you," Stacie replied, handing Angel her glass. Stacie noticed Dan going for his towel again. "No, you can do the report naked," she commanded him, finding the whole experience exhilarating.

Dan turned around, displaying a massive erection. Stacie began to think maybe it wasn't such a good idea but, with Angel being the boss, she was sure she had seen it before. As the girls had taken both chairs, Dan sat down on the bed, attempting to write his report.

"So, Stacie," Angel said, looking directly at Dan. "How are you getting on at Desires?"

"It's very interesting. I have to admit I had my doubts, but I'm glad I made the decision to come back," Stacie replied, widening her legs, allowing Dan to see her pussy.

"Wonderful, I am so pleased. Are you both coming to the ball this evening?"

"Dan?" Stacie said.

He looked up anxiously. "I can't see why not. I have a stunning dress for her," he replied, then turned back to writing the report.

"I am pleased to hear it. It should be a good night. Will you try out the other rooms today?"

"I think there will be enough excitement in this room." Stacie told her, staring hard at Dan as he struggled to concentrate on the report.

"Yes, I can see."

"I've finished, Angel," Dan said, holding out the report.

Angel downed her wine and stood up, taking it from him. "Well, have fun, children," she said, then left the room.

They both sat staring at one another.

"What are you playing at, Stacie?" Dan said eventually.

"What do you mean?"

"You know what I mean. You come here, dressed like that, then you won't let me touch you. You make me do that report naked, in front of Angel, while you both sit staring at me. What's going on?"

"What do you think is going on?"

"I don't know, that's why I'm asking."

"Maybe I realised that I'm tired of the man being in charge all the time. Maybe I want a bit of control. I'm paying you to do what I want, right?"

"Right."

"Well, in that case, from now on, you are only allowed to do what I permit you to do, and nothing else. Understood."

"Understood. Is there anything you would like me to do?"

Stacie stared at him, standing there, magnificently erect, awaiting her whim. "I want you to wank yourself."

Dan began to run his hand up and down his long hard throbbing penis, while Stacie's hand dropped back down to her clitoris. It responded instantly, throbbing with intensity. She inserted her fingers into her pussy, feeling her juices flowing.

"Would you really do anything I told you to do?" Stacie asked, watching him, seeing his face screwed up with concentration as he watched her.

"Anything."

"What about if I told you to go down to the ball with me naked."

"I would do that." Dan's breath was starting to come shorter.

"What about handcuffed and tied up?"

"That too."

Stacie spread her legs wide over the chair, throwing her head back but watching Dan through slitted eyes. She brought up a mental image of a bound and cuffed Dan following her naked through the ballroom, obeying her whims. She was shocked at the intense surge of sensation the idea brought.

The fantasy changed. Now she was riding some faceless man's massive cock, watching Dan's face as he watched her get fucked. Her crest crashed over her, her body began to jerk and shudder. Stacie looked over at Dan as he ejaculated all over his stomach. Her entire body shuddered and she screamed. Dan dropped back onto the bed while Stacie jerked in the chair, thrusting her pelvis high into the air.

Stacie turned to the table, holding on for support as her breathing slowed back to normal. She felt drained, and her pussy pulsed with aftershocks. Her gaze dropped to the table top, on which sat two bowls of chocolate mousse they had ordered with their food, but never got around to eating. That gave Stacie an idea. Maybe it was time to get out the goodies she had bought.

\* \* \* \*

They cleaned up and Dan ordered up a fresh bottle of wine, pouring them both a glass when it arrived. He turned on the television and they sat giggling over some old comedy show. She loved just being near him, knowing that he was close. What would he be like out of Desires? Would he be just as sexy and pleasant? Or was he just making sure he got his wages? If he was just doing his job, and the thought made her stomach flutter with dread, he certainly would be a very difficult act to follow. How could she start again with someone else? Dan was in her mind, in her heart, and in her soul.

Dan looked over at her and smiled, opening out his arm in an invitation to snuggle close. She did so, relaxing into his chest with a sigh, feeling his arm draped over her, feeling like everything was finally right with her world.

She never imagined for one minute she would actually feel good about herself again. The few times she had gone out with friends before deciding to come to Desires, she wasn't sure how to respond around men she was interested in. It was difficult to find that balance between showing interest and seeming desperate. She never imagined eight years ago that she would be back on the singles market. Maybe she should try a dating website, but from what she'd heard it was tough trying to sift the genuine decent men from all the weirdoes and players.

How on earth had she ended up that way—alone, miserable, low in confidence and scared. Determined to get back what she had lost, and eager to show the world she was a fighter, Stacie's first stage had been a success—coming to Desires.

Stacie was proud of what she had achieved, taking such a step in an effort to sort her dismal life out. Now she needed to make her future her priority and forget the past.

She turned her head to look at Dan watching the television. Was now the time to tell him the way she felt about him? She could hear Chrissie's voice in her head urging her to go for it, but Stacie was suddenly anxious about wrecking the time she had left with him if the answer wasn't what she wanted. If he said no, there was no way she could stay another minute.

He smiled down at her and leaned down to kiss her forehead. She melted again. How could all this mean nothing?

"You okay?" he asked.

"Mm-hmm."

"Is there anything you fancy doing?"

She looked away from him, staring at the chocolate mousse on the table. She smiled as she imagined covering his cock in it.

"I do actually," she replied sitting up to look at Dan. "I quite fancy trying out the feast."

"Oh yes? Do you want to go downstairs?"

"Nope, I want to stay right here."

She climbed off the bed to get the brown paper bag that contained the items she had bought earlier. One by one she placed the lace handcuffs, blindfold and ticklers on the bed. Dan's eyes widened as Stacie picked up the lace handcuffs and climbed onto the bed on all fours. She crawled her way up to Dan, her breasts swaying. She grabbed his willing hands and he moved them up above his head to the headboard. Stacie put the cuffs on him and reached to get the blindfold. She tied it tightly round his eyes and sat back. He looked vulnerable and delicate.

Stacie climbed off the bed and admired his helpless body. He was wearing only his trunks, the bulge of his burgeoning excitement evident. She headed over to the table picking up the chocolate mousse, and then climbed back onto the bed, kneeling close to Dan.

Stacie licked her lips, looking at his eager face. She tightened her bottom, feeling her arousal already running wild around her body. Stacie moved closer, pressing her lips against his chest. She held her head up to watch his reaction. He shifted under her, and his lips parted slightly. Stacie moved her body up so her mouth was in line with his. She pressed her soft moist lips against his. Dan responded, kissing her back. She pulled away.

"No," she told him, with a *tsk* of disapproval. Stacie wanted full control of everything, including his reactions. He stopped instantly.

Stacie kissed him again, moving her lips around his, caressing them. She tasted his lips, then dipped her tongue into his mouth feeling her body responding with pleasure. Stacie took hold of his bottom lip to bite it lightly, nibbling her way along.

She started to move down, gliding down his body, kissing each nipple. He smelled of soap as she kissed down his taut abdomen. She arrived at his waistband, noticing that the burgeoning bulge she had seen before was now a full-fledged towering erection, without her having to do a thing. She smiled with great satisfaction, knowing she was succeeding. She kissed delicately around the top of his trunks, watching his body wriggle. Stacie lifted her head up to stare down at his aroused body, not quite believing she had caused this reaction in this incredibly handsome young man.

Stacie took hold of her breasts, squeezing them together, her nipples ultra sensitive. She didn't want to touch them too much, not wanting to get too excited to soon.

Stacie reached for one of the feather ticklers, wrapping it around her wrist and trailing it onto his nipples. She watched his face for his reaction. He moaned aloud. She moved the tickler over his body, watching his nipples harden, enjoying arousing him, then she drew it up between his thighs where the skin was sensitive, watching his pelvis jerk.

She watched his cock twitch inside his trunks, looking as though it was bursting to get out. Stacie licked her lips, feeling her pussy dripping with excitement. She grabbed hold of his trunks, pulling them down to reveal his thick hard penis. Stacie placed the tickler over his cock, beginning with the base then running the soft feather up the full length of his cock. His manhood rose high to the stimulation and he quivered. She repeated her actions, glancing at Dan's tense face. She took the tickler over his balls, watching as his penis continuing to bounce up and down off his stomach. He moaned aloud and Stacie smiled.

Stacie reached over and took hold of the bowl of chocolate mousse. She dipped her finger in, then coated his left nipple with the sweet dessert. She bent down and used the tip of her tongue to lick the mousse off. Dan shivered as his nipple rose in response to the stimulation. She delicately nipped at his nipple with her teeth, smiling as he sucked in a gasp. She took a heaping spoon of the mousse and laid a trail down his chest, sucking the spoon clean, before licking every trace of the mousse off him.

She slid down to his cock area. He shivered with anticipation, thrusting up with his pelvis, begging mutely. She took the spoon and slathered his whole penis in the chocolate mousse. Stacie began kissing him around his penis, using the ticklers to torment the insides of his thighs, enjoying hearing him groan.

She poked out her tongue and licked a clean trail through the mousse from the base of his girth to the empurpled tip. She flicked her tongue over the tip, hearing him groan deeply. She took the tip of his cock into her mouth, sucking strongly and using her tongue to thoroughly clean the delicious mousse off all his ridges. She took a little more in, swirling her tongue over his smooth chocolaty-tasting skin.

Stacie came up for some air, licking the whole length of his shaft, taking away the mousse, sucking and licking, her face becoming covered in mousse. She took the full length of his still smeary shaft back into her mouth as deep as she could go, rapidly moving her mouth up and down. Dan pushed his body off the bed, moaning in ecstasy. Stacie tasting a little salt mixed in with the remains of the chocolate. She sucked his penis like a lollipop, licking it from base to tip, filling her mouth as much as she could.

Once his cock was clean, she let him go, slurping her mouth off his cockhead.

"Mmm, this mousse really is delicious. You should try some," she said, smearing a generous fingerful over each of her nipples.

"I'd love to."

She straddled his stomach and leaned forward, holding one breast, aiming her nipple directly at his lips. He immediately opened his mouth sticking out his tongue, licking the mousse off and sucking her nipple into his mouth. Once one nipple was clean, he popped it out of his mouth and searched blindly for the other. Stacie obliged him, placing her left bud to his mouth, allowing him to indulge. Dan sucked hard on the nipple, nibbling with his teeth. Stacie's body spasmed and she thrust her pelvis on his stomach. He licked and sucked hard. Stacie moaned with pleasure.

Slowly, she rose up to look down on him, his mouth covered in mousse. Stacie stared for a few seconds watching him licking the mousse from around his lips. She dropped down to kiss him, licking his lips clean. He tried to kiss deeper, but Stacie instantly drew back.

She climbed off him and grabbed his shoulders, pulling him as far down the bed as the cuffs allowed, which wasn't far. She removed her crotchless panties, then placed a knee on either side of his head. She dug out a mounded spoonful of chocolate mousse, using the spoon to smear it all over her pussy and clitoris. She lowered herself down until she felt his searching tongue find her sweet spot. She grabbed onto the headboard with both hands, as he used his deft tongue to stimulate her into screaming rapture.

She moved down the bed, staring at him, his mouth covered in mousse. She kissed it off, then removed the blindfold. He squinted, flinching against the sudden light.

"You're right. That mousse is delicious," he said with a wink.

She took hold of his hands and undid the cuffs, allowing his hands to drop.

She removed her babydoll outfit and grabbed a condom from the bedside table, then climbed on board. She slid the condom on, then guided his cock into the entrance of her still chocolaty pussy. She leaned back, letting her hair dangle over his legs, taking his cock as deep as possible.

She tilted her pelvis, taking his penis even farther inside her. Then Stacie pulsed her hips back and forth on his manhood, sliding up and down, feeling him filling her to the hilt. Her body lost control, her nerve endings were under attack, her mind concentrated on her rhythm, while her body broke into a sweat. Dan took hold of Stacie, leaning her back so he could manipulate her clitoris. He thrust his cock inside her as his fingers teased her sensitive folds of flesh. Her whole body jerked violently and she cried out in pure ecstasy, feeling her juice running from her as she climaxed violently. She collapsed forward, her arms barely holding her up, her body racked with aftershocks.

Dan continued to thrust upward into her, his rhythm becoming faster. He held his breath while his body froze and he gave a groan. She felt him pulse, his cock emptying itself deep within her before he too crumpled onto the bed, letting out a whoosh of breath.

She waited until she was certain he had finished before lifting her body off his, and lying next to him on the bed. Dan lifted his arm and pulled her to him, kissing the top of her head fiercely before wrapping his arms around her and crushing her to his chest. Stacie felt a few tears well up, overcome with the exhausting uncertainty. Did he, could he, love her?

## Chapter Twelve

Sticky from sex and chocolate, Stacie decided to take a bubble bath before the ball that evening. Dan elected for a shower and Stacie lay back in the hot scented water, watching him.

He could even make a quick, business-like scrub look sexy, she mused as she watched him lather up his hair before rubbing the wash-cloth over his body. The water cascaded over his body, shining in the light. He rinsed, putting his head under the water and closing his eyes against the drops that ran down over his face. Stacie had no qualms about drinking in every single naked wet inch of him. He got out the shower and grabbed a towel, rubbing it over his head before wrapping it round his waist. He glanced at her.

"Do you want me to soap your back?" he said, walking over and sitting on the edge of the bath.

"Might be nice," she said, handing him the soap and a bath puff. He squirted liquid soap on the puff and she sat up in the water, leaning forward and resting her elbows on her knees. She felt him move the bath puff firmly over her back, moving in circles. He rinsed her off with the tumbler, dipping it full of water and pouring it over her back.

"All clean," he announced, leaning over to kiss her on her forehead. He stood up and went over to the sink. She watched him cover his face in shaving foam and begin gliding the razor across his skin. Much as she liked him with sexy designer stubble, she figured he would look equally delicious clean-shaven.

He looked at her through the mirror, smiling back at her "Is everything okay?" he asked her, swishing the razor in the water.

"Fine." She squirted some more soap on the bath puff and began to clean the rest of her body, sticking one leg out of the water to soap it up.

"Are you looking forward to the ball?" he asked.

"I guess so." Stacie soaped her other leg.

"It's great fun."

"What are the rules?"

"There are no rules really, just have a good time. If you see something, or someone, that takes your fancy, go for it, provided the other person is happy."

It sounded like the cattle market that was the local night club. Stacie couldn't help but think about her feelings toward Dan. "What about you?" she asked, a lump rising in her throat, dreading his answer. Would he be looking for someone who took his fancy also?

"What about me?" he asked, wiping away the foam from his face. He cleaned the sink, then turned around staring down at her. "I'll be hanging around. It's your night to see if there's something you fancy. Just relax and go for it, this might give you that extra confidence you're looking for."

Stacie wasn't exactly eager to bed other men, but Dan was still training her. He might be right, this might be the opportunity she'd waited for. Mike was different, she hadn't chosen him. Maybe she could find someone to have some fun with. At least at Desires there were no relationships or feelings to worry about, just pure explicit fun.

"Okay," she replied, not feeling a hundred percent sure, but prepared to give it a try.

Dan smiled and left the bathroom. Stacie soaped the rest of her body absent-mindedly, thinking about her actions and how to deal with the situation she was putting herself in. Stacie was drowning in his captivity, reading God knew what meaning into his body language. She didn't want to waste the precious time with Dan by confessing her feelings. At least she would have the enjoyment of spending the little time with him she had. The next twenty-four hours were going to mean everything to her.

Stacie shampooed and conditioned her hair. Opening one of the drawers of the small chest next to the bath, she found lady razors and feminine shaving gel. *They really do think of everything here*, she thought as she lathered up. Nothing worse than giving your man stubble rash on his torso. After her bath, clean and hairless, she wandered into the bedroom. Dan was nowhere to be seen so she decided to relax on the bed while the towel on her head absorbed the excess moisture from her hair. Images of Dan making love to her filled her mind as soon as she closed her eyes.

She opened her eyes and jumped off the bed, grabbing the remote and flicking on the television, anything to distract herself from these thoughts. She stabbed the channel button, trying to find something to watch so she could forget about him for a while. Maybe this ball was something she needed. Maybe she would meet someone who might distract her and make her look in another direction. But doubts kept entering her head. Could she voluntarily have sex with a total stranger knowing Dan was somewhere around? But if it was the key to breaking this pathetic obsession she had with Dan, it might be worth it.

Once the worst of the wetness had been absorbed, Stacie began to dry her hair when she saw the door open through the mirror. Dan walked in, two garment bags laid across his arm.

"Hello there. How are you getting on?" he asked. Then he smiled and Stacie knew she was lost.

"Fine," she said, grinning back inanely, while her common sense screamed at her from the confines of her stupid brain.

"I have got your dress here," he said, heading over to the wardrobe and hooking the bags over the wardrobe door.

Stacie laid down her hairdryer and jumped off the stool, rushing over to the wardrobe and bouncing on her toes like a little girl as Dan slowly undid the zip of the dress cover.

"Wow," she said, as he slid the cover off the floor-length white satin dress.

The bust area was thickly encrusted with diamantes and sparkled in the light. A trail of diamantes ran down to the stomach area, and the skirt was liberally sprinkled with the glittering stones. Dan turned it around to show her the long scoop back and small train. From the bottom of the garment bag Dan pulled out a shoe box, opening it to reveal matching white satin shoes, likewise decorated with diamantes.

"How did you know my shoe size?"

"I looked in your boots the other day."

"What are you wearing?"

"Just a boring old tux," he replied, unzipping the other garment bag and showing her the suit. "Do you like the dress," he said, looking anxious.

"It's absolutely stunning," Stacie whispered. Dan beamed. "But, do you think I can pull it off? I mean, I've never worn anything like this. It's like something a film star would wear to the Oscars or something. I hardly dare touch it."

"I think you'll look sensational. But then you don't need that dress to do that," he said and winked at her before flopping down on the bed and turning the television on.

Stacie stood where she was, looking at the dress, processing his comment. Was it a genuine compliment? Or was it just to flatter her to make her wear the dress? Either way, it worked. How often did she have the chance to dress up in a ball gown and look like a Hollywood A-lister?

She walked over to her bag, looking through the makeup she had brought with her. A natural look tonight, she thought, soft and shimmery, to complement the dress, not overshadow it. Stacie carried on drying her hair whilst Dan started to get dressed. It was so easy for men, Stacie thought as she watched him in the mirror putting on his trousers. All they had to do was shower, shave and throw on some clothes and that was them done. He went into the bathroom and splashed on some aftershave, the scent drifting through into the bedroom. Stacie made a mental note to find out which brand he used, and make every single boyfriend from now on wear it. It was divinely sexy. He came back through and put on his shirt and bow tie, then his shoes and jacket. He was dressed and she'd barely started. Mind you, it probably didn't help that she'd been staring at him in the mirror instead of getting ready. He straightened himself up and checked out his reflection in the full length mirror.

"What do you think," he said, coming over to her.

"Not bad. Not bad at all."

"Will I do?"

"Just about, I should think."

He went over to the table and poured two glasses of wine, bringing hers over as she started on her makeup. He watched her for a while as he drank his glass, gulping it down pretty quickly, she thought as she took a mouthful of hers before she applied her lipstick.

"I just need to pop downstairs for a few minutes," he said, putting the empty glass on the dresser. "I'll leave you to finish getting ready."

"Okay, thanks," she replied. He leaned over and kissed her on the cheek. She shivered, just the feel of his lips pressed against her flesh was enough to send her crazy.

Dan left the room and Stacie turned her attention back to her makeup and her dilemma. No matter how hard she tried to get over or ignore her feelings for him, the hole appeared to be getting deeper. Could he have looked any better tonight? Was he deliberately making her crave him?

Stacie moved over to the dress, gazing at it, imagining exactly how the dress would hang on her. She took the dress off its hanger and moved over to the full-length mirror, holding it up in front of her. Thank goodness she managed to get to a tanning studio when possible, otherwise the pure white would have made her look ill.

Stacie put the dress back on the wardrobe door, then sat at the dresser debating how to have her hair. She rummaged in the drawers and found a new pack of hairgrips, so she decided on a French pleat with a swept fringe at the front. She neatly pinned her hair up, then reverently took the dress off its hanger. She put her feet into the dress, bringing it slowly up her body until it reached her waist. She eased the bust area over her breasts, settling it low enough to give her a devastating cleavage. The dress had an almost magical inner support she found as she zipped it up the side, holding her breasts up and projecting them out quite magnificently.

She turned her back to the mirror, craning to look over her shoulder. The deep scoop at the back left her back fully naked with the train trailing on the floor. The front of the skirt sat slightly higher, so she wasn't likely to trip over it, which was a good thing.

Her breasts looked dazzling—they were certainly going to get attention. She may as well not have bothered making up her face, certainly no one would be looking at it, with those boobs in eyeshot.

Stacie slipped her feet into the shoes. The four-inch heels were surprisingly comfortable, although whether they still would be after a night of dancing remained to be seen. She did look pretty good though, she thought, giving a twirl. She heard the door open and waited till Dan was fully in the room before turning to give him the full effect. His eyes widened and his mouth dropped open quite satisfactorily, and he gaped at her for a full thirty seconds, she judged, before he managed a stunned, "Wow!" He came over to look at her from all angles. "You look sensational," he said, stealing a mouthful of her wine. "How do you feel?"

"I feel good."

"I don't think I have ever seen such a beautiful creature," he said as he admired her.

"Does that mean I normally look terrible?"

"Oh, yeah, awful. I'd be ashamed to be seen out with you," he teased, his eyes twinkling. "But there is something missing," he continued, his face turning serious.

"What?" Stacie asked, worried.

"I bought you a present," he said, drawing out a long blue jeweller's box from his inside pocket.

"A present? For me?"

"Now, don't get excited," he warned as she took the box and opened it. "They aren't real diamonds!"

"I should think not," Stacie said, as she gazed down at the stunning drop earrings and graduated bib necklace in the box. "If these were real diamonds you'd probably have to mortgage your life away to pay for them."

"Do you like them?"

"I love them. Thank you," Stacie looked up at Dan's happy face. She took a step toward him and kissed him gently on the cheek.

"Here, let me put it on."

Dan took the box off her and removed the necklace. Stacie turned back to the mirror and watched as Dan draped the necklace over her collarbones and fastened it at the back of her neck. It looked stunning, even if they were only cubic zirconias. She put on the matching earrings.

"You look absolutely amazing," Dan said in her ear. She met his eyes in the mirror. He put his hands on her shoulders. "Shall we go?"

Stacie turned and took the arm he held out to her. "Indeed."

They left the room and made their way down the corridor. Music emanated from the grand hall and Stacie began to feel excited. Another couple came out of a room. Stacie and the other woman gave each other that discreet once-over, evaluating each other's outfits. The other woman wore a bright pink strapless dress with a massive meringue skirt. She looked like a blancmange. Like

Dan, her guy was dressed in a tuxedo. Stacie indulged herself in a little smugness, feeling she had won the tacit competition. Her dress was far classier and sexier than the woman in pink. They smiled, acknowledging each other, then continued their journey down the corridor.

The music grew louder as they arrived at the top of the staircase. Stacie picked up the bottom of the dress and took the stairs carefully. She looked down at the reception desk seeing Bailey watching them both coming down the steps. Dan helped her down the last few steps and she dropped the hem back down to the floor. She held her head high, feeling sensational. Dan took hold of Stacie's arm and they proceeded to the ballroom.

Stacie stared at the double doors, feeling a sudden burst of anxiety. This wasn't just any ball. This was a ball in a sex club. What would she see on the other side of those doors? She drew in a deep breath whilst Dan opened the door. Music blasted out, it was almost a tangible force. The room was dark with disco lights flashing. Dan drew her through the doors. The ballroom was full of couples, the men looking smart in their tuxedos, perfect foils for their dazzling partners.

At the far end of the room there was the DJ, and surrounding the packed dance floor were seating areas, couches and comfortable armchairs set around small tables. Disco lights were situated all over the room, the beams bouncing off the walls, the lights flashing fast and furious to the beat of the music. A waiter approached with a tray full of glasses of Buck's Fizz. Dan took one, and Stacie followed suit.

Dan escorted Stacie around the dance floor. Her head twisted in all directions, looking at the varied costumes of the guests. Some of the women's dresses were barely there. They looked like those skimpy costumes professional ballroom dancers wore, designed to show off as much of the body as possible. They wandered through the crowd, Dan keeping close to her, not letting her go in the slightest. The atmosphere was amazing. The music was an almost tangible force in the room, people were singing and dancing around the tables, waving their hands around. As this was a sex club, Stacie was not surprised to see more than the usual amount of unashamed groping.

Stacie returned the smiles of the guests, while keeping hold of Dan's hand tight, following close behind him. He took her to the other side of the room where there were two large doors that appeared to be in fairly constant use. Dan opened one of the doors and Stacie walked in, seeing a large buffet with lots of choice. As she got closer to the table, Stacie let out a giggle. Even the food had an erotic theme, having been made to look like boobs, willies and bums! Stacie couldn't believe what she saw—sandwiches had been cut out with penis-shaped templates, cocktail sausages had been given pickled onion balls, there were small round pizzas with a central 'nipple' made from a slice of pepperoni and the small end slice of a black olive. Stacie couldn't believe the number of ways food could be presented as something sexual. The chef certainly had an imagination.

Stacie kept close to Dan, making their way toward a large bar. She could see women sucking drinks through straws topped with plastic willies, and, she looked closer, yes, even penis-shaped ice cubes.

She finished her Buck's Fizz and put the crystal glass onto the side of the bar.

"Would you like another?" Dan asked.

"White wine, please," she said, staring around the room watching people making their way around the food.

Dan came to stand next to Stacie, passing her the glass. "What do you think?"

"It's different," she said, taking a sip of her wine. Stacie couldn't help but laugh. She started to subconsciously move to the music, which surged in volume every time someone came through the doors.

"Do you want to eat something now, or would you rather have a dance?" Dan asked her.

"I would love to dance."

Stacie followed Dan around the large food table to the other side of the room, seeing the desserts, selections of cakes shaped as sexual organs, both male and female, as well as whips, and some decorated with images of erotic fetishes.

They walked back into the ballroom and Stacie froze when she suddenly saw Mike coming toward them. What should she say? What would he say? He had a woman hanging on his arm, wearing a red dress fitted to her bust and sweeping down to the floor. Stacie smiled nervously at the girl, who replied with a grin. Mike and the woman came over to them.

"Dan!" Mike held out his hand and Dan shook it, glancing at Stacie.

"Mike," he replied.

"Hi, Stacie," Mike said to her, coming over and kissing her on both cheeks. She stood still in his arms, not wanting the intimacy, but not so rude as to refuse it. "You look gorgeous." He winked at her, gazing at her breasts.

"Thank you," she said, trying to muster up a polite smile. She stood closer to Dan, taking hold of his hand. How could she get across the message that she wanted to leave.

Dan must have picked up on her wishes because he and Mike exchanged a bit of small talk then he said, "Well, I've promised Stacie a dance, so I'll see you later, Mike."

He squeezed Stacie's hand as they approached the dance floor, Stacie drinking her wine a little faster, eager to get on and show Dan her moves. Dan stood close to her. "Would you like me to take your drink?" he asked. She passed it to him and moved onto the dance floor, beginning to sway her body from side to side, wiggling her bottom and hips. Dan watched her from the side.

Suddenly, a loud raunchy song came on with naughty lyrics and a beat to blast any room away. Stacie danced hard, swaying her hips back and forth and stomping her feet on the dance floor, grinding her body to the rhythm, singing along to the dirty lyrics. She gazed at Dan feeling the wine going to her head, making her horny and ready for anything. She felt naughty, placing her hands on her breasts and pushing them toward Dan, before snaking her hips from side to side.

Stacie felt like a wild woman. More fantastic tunes blasted out, she writhed to the rhythms, caressing her body. Dan stood watching her, giving nothing away. Was she turning him on? She kept running her hands up and down her slender figure while everyone around her joined in, the women thrusting their pelvises forward, doing all they could to drive the men wild.

Another top dance song came on. The whole room exploded in a sudden exodus from the chairs to the suddenly crowded floor. Everyone started waving their hands in the air, jumping up and down to the beat and rocking their bodies. Stacie joined in, singing along to the lyrics. To her surprise, Dan joined her, taking hold of her tightly from behind, thrusting his groin into her bottom. Stacie threw her hands into the air as Dan grabbed her waist, making her move faster. The whole room was going crazy, but Stacie hardly noticed. Her world was her and Dan, their bodies locked together, feeling nothing except the warmth of his body next to her. She twisted to face him, his hands hot on her bare back. She could feel his body glued to hers, his groin pressing through her gown. His hands roamed her skin. She could feel every movement of every digit as he brought her senses to tingling awareness with nothing but his palms and his ten fingers. She trembled and her hands went up round his neck. His mouth descended and she closed her eyes. His mouth explored her lips, his tongue delicately probing, feeling it way along the line of her mouth. She opened to him eagerly, welcoming him, twining her tongue with his, tasting him. Her fingers twisted through his hair, relishing its softness. Someone knocked into her and her eyes flicked open, brought back to reality. Dan caught her before she fell and she grabbed gratefully onto his arm.

"Sorry," a voice called. Stacie glanced around. It could have been anybody. The floor was packed. It didn't matter, she wasn't hurt. This was what Stacie called a wicked night, bringing back memories of her youth, acting totally irresponsibly, just dancing like a woman possessed, singing and dancing, screaming while generally being bad. The song finished and they decided to go and get some liquid refreshments.

They head back to the bar and saw Angel. She stopped and smiled at them. Stacie smiled back while Dan kissed her on the cheek. Stacie was stunned at Angel's dress. It was long and black and plunged at the front down to her navel. Her breasts were almost totally on display; only a gem-encrusted band covered her nipples. Narrow shoulder straps kept it up and the skirt swept the floor, but showed splits up to her hips at front and sides when she moved. Angel meant business, but then she always did. Her normally poker-straight hair was artfully waved, giving her a softer, sexier appearance. She wore silver high-heeled shoes, making her even taller than she already was. She exuded an elegant sensuality.

"You look amazing, Stacie," she said, leaning toward Stacie and kissing her on both cheeks.

"Thank you, you look very sexy," Stacie replied.

"Just the way I like it. You're a great dancer."

Embarrassed, Stacie thanked her. She hadn't thought who else might be watching her strutting her stuff.

"Would you like me to show you what's on offer for the evening?" Angel asked Stacie.

Stacie turned to Dan, seeing him chatting to another guy.

"I don't mind," she said, wondering what else the place could show her.

Angel went to Dan to speak to him. Dan looked at Stacie, raising his eyebrows, and crooked his finger indicating she should go to him. As she approached, he took hold of her hand, then wrapped his other arm around her waist. "Do you want to go with Angel?" he asked.

"I don't mind," she said. She would really rather stay with Dan, she found Angel quite threatening. But maybe she should relax and trust Angel. She must be brilliant at running the place or it wouldn't be so successful. With the number of people attending this evening, it certainly had something a lot of people found appealing. "I'll go with her." He leaned toward her, kissing her on the cheek, which Stacie returned. "I'll see you in a bit," she told him.

"Okay babe, enjoy," he said. Their eyes locked for a second and Stacie's pussy fluttered.

Angel took hold of Stacie's hand and led her back into the ballroom. As the night progressed, dancing and groping had begun to give way to more overt sexual acts. The crowds dispersed for Angel, though, giving way before them like the Red Sea. A few people called Angel's name, and she acknowledged them with a wave and smile.

They exited the hall, arriving in the cooler quieter reception area. Stacie glanced over to the reception desk, seeing Bailey. They both smiled at each other. Angel took the lead heading down the corridor which led to the orgy room. Bodies were all over the place in various states of undress and sexual congress.

Stacie continued to follow Angel. They arrived at the orgy room and Angel pulled back the voile, allowing Stacie to enter first. It was different than it had been last time Stacie was here. It was set up as a sex show. Men and women sat on the cushions watching two men and one girl having sex. One of the men was lying on his back while the girl was riding his cock. As Stacie watched, the second man came up behind her, his impressive cock rigid. He began to prepare her ass, lubing up his fingers and pushing first one, then more inside, stretching her, before kneeling behind her and shoving his cock up her asshole, to the evident appreciation of the watching crowd. The two men fucked her for a few minutes before the girl started calling for another man from the audience to come and get his cock sucked. A man quickly volunteered, ready and willing and she deep-throated him, taking him all the way in. More men started to converge on the girl, touching her, fondling her, jerking off over her, until she was hidden by male bodies.

"Does she work here? Is she getting paid for that?" Stacie wondered aloud.

"No, that's just her thing. She loves to be gangbanged," Angel said. "She's a member of the club, just like you."

The girl's cries of pleasure echoed around the room. Angel took her hand, taking her back out into the corridor. They walked a little way to another room where there was a girl performing a striptease. Again, couples were watching and a few were having a personal dance. Stacie watched one girl shove her naked breasts in a man's face whilst his partner sat next to him. Stacie would have exploded with jealousy, having some girl dangling her chest in her man's face. But this couple just started fondling the girl's breasts, both the man and the woman. Stacie turned to Angel in surprise.

"I thought there was a 'no touch' rule in lap dancing."

Angel shrugged. "Not here. This is a sex club, not a lap-dancing club. Where's the fun if you don't touch?"

There was a small dance floor with a pole. Stacie watched a girl wrapping her body around the pole, tipping upside down. How did she manage to hold the position without hurting herself? It looked quite painful.

They move out of the room. A few people hurtled toward them wearing bondage PVC ball gowns and gimp masks, looking as though they were being suffocated. Angel greeted them as they passed then led Stacie to another room where this time a man stood on a stage stripping. This room contained mostly women who were screaming and yelling encouragement at the stripper.

He grabbed some whipped cream, spraying it onto his penis, then invited girls to come and lick it off. Three or four women scrambled onto the stage, fighting over his cock while he stood there, hands on hips, a big smile plastered over his face as the girls licked him clean. This was definitely a very *touchy* place.

The room next door had a massive television on the wall showing a porn film. Couples were sitting and watching on sofas, most of them having sex at the same time.

Next, Angel took her to the room Dan had said was used at the feast room. Today however, it was set up like an erotic marketplace. The room was filled with tables and stalls, all selling anything and everything associated with sex—pictures, statues, underwear and of course toys—a very large inflatable pink penis wobbled in one corner. Stacie wandered around looking at what was on offer. All the stalls were exceptionally busy.

On the first stall there were dildos, vibrators and other battery operated items. Some of the dildos looked human, but there were some she would never dare put into her vagina. One was even shaped like a cactus! Stacie moved on to the next stall which sold sex oils, liquids, and sauces. The memory of her covering Dan's body in chocolate mousse came to mind and a naughty smile crept over her face. She moved to the next stall, seeing DVDs and magazines for men and women. Some girls were chuckling over a magazine. She slipped in closer behind them, to see them looking at a man with an enormous penis. Stacie wasn't impressed. An enormous penis was all very well, but the man was ugly and looked smug and far too pleased with himself.

Stacie wandered around looking at the stalls selling underwear. There were some very sexy crotchless panties, open nipple bras, leather clothing, PVC, you name it, it was available. A few bits took her fancy, but decided she wasn't prepared to part with her money. Dan was already costing her a small fortune, although he had been worth every penny. She continued looking around while Angel chatted to a few people, leaving her to browse the room that certainly offered everything.

Stacie had finished her wander and returned to the door where Angel now stood alone.

"Had a good look?" she said. Stacie nodded. "You know, if you want to buy anything, we can put it on your bill. You don't have to have cash here and now."

"It's okay, I didn't see anything."

Angel didn't press the issue and they left the room. Angel led her down to the conservatory bar and restaurant. It was quite quiet this evening, Stacie figured most of the guests would be at the ball. Angel got them both a glass of white wine and they sat down.

"What do you think?" Angel said.

"It's okay. Great if you're with a partner and are needing to spice your sex life up."

"Yes, although we do get some singles coming also, both men and women. How are you finding Dan, you seemed to be controlling him pretty well earlier today."

Stacie giggled. "Yes, I was being rather dirty, but it was great fun."

"Good. I must confess, I wouldn't have thought you so mischievous when we first met. I'm sure you got the result you were looking for," Angel said, sitting back and sipping her drink.

"You could say that," Stacie said taking a sip of her wine, hoping Angel would change the subject.

"Is Desires working out for you as you'd hoped?"

Dan's face popped into Stacie's mind and she couldn't help but smile. "Yes, very much so. I'm feeling much more confident in myself."

"Fantastic. That's what it is all about," Angel said. "So what do you think about Dan?"

Stacie wiped the dreamy look off her face quick smart. It wouldn't do to get kicked out of the club. "He's fantastic, an excellent tutor."

"Treating you well?" Angel said showing her white gleaming teeth in what wasn't quite a smile.

"Absolutely, he really is a sexy man."

"Is he?" Angel said. Stacie started to panic. Was she digging a hole for herself?

"Well, I mean he's sexy in the way he touches and caresses, and he's good looking." *Oh God, I'm just making it worse!*

"Are you attracted to him?" Angel asked.

*Shit shit shit*! Angel's eyes peered at her sharply over the wine glass. Did she know? Was it written on Stacie's forehead just how much she was attracted to Dan?

"I mean, I wouldn't blame you if you were, he's unique," Angel added, sipping on her wine, continuing to stare.

"Only as my tutor," Stacie said, feeling that her heart must surely have climbed up into her throat. Why was Angel asking these questions? Had Stacie's answer eased Angel's mind? No…she felt there was so much more going on here. Stacie sat back in the chair, crossing her legs at the knee, attempting to act cool and pretend that nothing was going on, which was unfortunately true.

"He is sexy though. Adorable, hot, and one of my best men," Angel said.

Stacie sipped on her wine and didn't answer.

"He's a delight to have at Desires. Girls do have a tendency to fall for him, but I just remind them of a certain piece of paper," Angel said in a calm voice, staring into her wine glass before draining the last few drops.

"The contract," Stacie said. That was what this was about. Angel was reminding her about the contract.

"Exactly. I mean he isn't every girl's dream. Some women prefer men with muscles, but with Dan, you can get over that. Don't you think, Stacie?" Angel asked. All pretence of a smile was gone now. Stacie felt pinned to the spot like a butterfly on a card. Could Angel see the terror in Stacie's eyes?

"I guess," she said faintly. She drained her drink and looked around for an excuse to escape the clutches of this woman, before the truth did spill out and all hell let loose. "I…I just need to go to the toilet." Stacie got up. So did Angel.

"I'll walk with you," she said.

They both went into cubicles. Stacie wondered if she could sneak out before Angel came out. She washed her hands as quickly as possible, but Angel came out before she'd finished.

"Well," Angel said brightly as she washed her hands also. "I'll let you get back to the ball. Thanks for the chat. It's been…enlightening."

She whisked off, leaving Stacie shaken and trembling. She leaned on the vanity unit and stared at herself in the mirror, seeing terrified eyes set in an ashen face. She wished she could touch up her makeup, but she hadn't brought a bag down and Dan had the key to the room. She settled for licking her fingers and wiping away the eyeliner that had collected in the crease below her eyes, then pinched her cheeks and bit her lips to bring some colour to them.

Maybe she needed to do something to get Angel off the scent. She headed back to the bar, looking around for Dan. She got a drink, chugging it down to settle her nerves. The bar was far too crowded, so she decided to head back to the dance floor and see if she could spot him there. She wandered about a bit on the outskirts. But trying to spot one man in a tux in a sea of men in tuxes proved to be more difficult than she thought.

A song came on that she loved and she decided to dance for a bit. She went crazy on the floor, the hall was dark with the lasers and lights moving about the room, the tune belted out loud. Stacie shimmied and swayed and boogied and rocked, enjoying the admiring looks from both men and women she was getting.

An opening appeared in the crowd and Stacie saw a man watching her. Most of them men Stacie had encountered at Desires did absolutely nothing for her, with the exception of Dan, of course. But this one was different. He had something about him. He had a bit of a James Bond look going on, confident and sexy with his bow tie hanging loose and his jacket open. He stood tall with dark, very short hair. He smiled. Stacie's body hair stood up. She smiled back.

Stacie continued dancing, turning her back on him, wondering if he was watching her. Should she try to talk to the man? Not only to get Angel off her back, but also to try out Dan's suggestion of sleeping with someone else. His words came back to her, *I'm not going to be with you, out there in the big world.* He looked attractive and had sexy eyes, but he was probably here with someone. She carried on dancing, keeping the sexy rhythm going, then raised her hands above her head allowing the music to take her body.

After a few minutes, she turned slightly and glanced over her shoulder. The man had moved closer to her. He was standing a few feet away, staring at her. Stacie carried on with her movements, this time facing him, meeting his intense stare.

She began to touch her body, gliding her hands up and down her waist. He watched with evident enjoyment. She rolled her hips, swinging her bottom down to the floor, cupping her breasts, maintaining the stare. His eyes widened and he smiled hungrily at her, his eyes locked to her every move, somehow seducing her. Stacie pressed her breasts together, then ran her hands seductively down her torso to her thighs, and back up again.

He walked closer to stand before her. She froze, her body aching with anticipation. He leaned toward her right ear, "Follow me, you beauty," he commanded her.

Stacie hesitated for a moment, unsure. Her stomach was doing somersaults. A waiter passed by carrying a tray of drinks. Stacie reached over grabbing a glass of wine, gulping the whole drink down for Dutch courage. She decided to go for it, after all, this was what Dan had been trying to encourage her to do. She glanced in the direction of the man, seeing him walking away. Stacie picked up her dress and scurried after him.

She made her way out the hall, seeing him walking toward where Angel's office was. The reception desk was empty, and when she looked back, he was gone. Panic struck her, she began quickly racing down the corridor after him.

One her eyes adjusted to the dim lighting, she saw him, a dark figure in a dim corridor about halfway down. He glanced back at her. Stacie headed toward him, her stomach roiling and her pulse fluttering. He was standing outside a door, which he opened as she approached. He stepped inside the room and light flooded out from the doorway into the corridor. Stacie stopped at the open door. For a brief second, she wondered if this was such a good idea. Then she told herself sternly, *It's bloody sex club, Stacie, go for it. Find out what you've been missing.*

She stepped in and glanced around. It was a large bedroom, similar to Dan's. The bed wasn't the four-poster she was used to, but it was a king-sized bed. The sheets were rumpled and the duvet hung half on the floor. The matching curtains were pulled haphazardly across and small wall lights lit the room. A smell of male fragrance hung in the air. She took a step farther into the room and heard the door close behind her.

"You're a very sexy woman," he said, approaching her from behind. He reached round to take hold of her breasts and thrust them together. "Christ, they feel amazing," he told her, squeezing them like they were a couple of melons. "Are they real?"

"Yes," she said. He pushed her breasts together, caressing them, finding her nipples. He ran his thumbs over them and they instantly reacted, standing to a quick erection and poking through the material of her dress. He pulled the dress forward to get a good look, plunging one hand in to caress her bare skin.

"Oh, baby, you are gorgeous." He unzipped the side zip and pulled the dress down to her tummy.

She looked down at her naked breasts, the nipples hard and erect. She felt sexy and desirable and very, very naughty. He turned her around, and took hold of her boobs in his hands. Now he was closer, she saw he had dark brown eyes and short stubble. He looked a little rough but very sexy at the same time. She smiled a sultry smile at him, putting a finger seductively in her mouth and nibbling on it. He bent his head down to one of her breasts, sucking hard on her pointed nipple. Stacie threw her head back and gasped at the powerful suction, pleasurable almost to the point of pain. Her body shuddered and her knees trembled.

"These are totally fucking amazing," he told her, moving from one breast to the other, almost inhaling a large mouthful then pushed her boobs together, licking from one nipple to the other and using his teeth to bite gently.

Stacie put her hand to the pin in her hair, releasing it and shaking it out from the French pleat. She felt sexy and daring. He kept playing with her breasts with one hand, tugging her dress down with the other, till she stood there in nothing but a white thong and high heels.

"On the bed," he commanded her in a deep powerful voice.

Stacie obeyed his instruction, kicking off her shoes. He positioned her on all fours and slapped her bottom several times. He squeezed her bottom cheeks and kissed them. He got behind her and pulled her thong to the side, sticking his face between her bottom. She felt his tongue licking her pussy, and then he thrust a finger in her vagina. She pushed back at him, grinding into his face as she felt his finger thrusting into her.

"Play with your tits," he ordered her, sitting slightly to the side to watch, but carrying on finger-fucking her. She grabbed at her boob with one hand, the other being used to hold herself up. She squeezed her nipple between her fingers, and let the flesh bulge out. "Just how dirty are you?" he said, lifting her up by the shoulders to a kneeling position and grabbing her other boob. "Do you like it a little rough?"

Stacie couldn't find breath to answer. His hands were hard and hot on her, he squeezed her roughly, and she was loving it! She wanted him to throw her down and fuck her hard. He moved his hand down to her pussy and began flicking his fingers over her clitoris. She had to stop herself from spreading her legs for him and begging him to fuck her now.

Suddenly she heard the room door open. She sat up and gasped in shock as another man entered the room. She tried to cover her boobs with her hands, but her Bond man pulled her hands down. Stacie froze, unsure, her eyes flicking from one man to the other. The new man came around to the other side of the bed. He stood watching, making Stacie feel extremely uncomfortable. He was not good looking in the slightest, in fact he was quite disgusting with crooked teeth and a massive belly, a lot older and greyer than the other man.

"Don't worry, you're mine," Bond said. Stacie wasn't sure what to think. Did this other man just want to watch? She'd done it with Dan in the orgy room after all, so she wasn't exactly new. She relaxed a touch. It could be sexy. "What do you think, mate? Isn't she fucking stunning?" Bond said. Stacie preened a little, casting a glance at the new man as his eyes raked her body.

"You certainly could say that. Fucking gorgeous, those tits—wow," the old man said.

Bond grabbed her breasts, pulling them up and sucking hard on her extremely sensitive nipple. She found the presence of the older man a little off-putting, but she tried to relax and enjoy the pulses he was sending down to her pussy.

Bond turned Stacie around and lowered her to the bed on her back. She smiled and spread her legs wide. His eyes lit up. "You're one hot lady." She stretched and wriggled on the bed.

The man slid down her body and began to lap at her clitoris, before licking up and down her whole pussy then back to her clit. He slapped her pussy area and Stacie lifted her head up in surprise. That was new. It was slightly painful but not altogether unpleasant.

He hit the area a few times before sucking intensely on it using his tongue to dip in and out her pussy.

He continued to suck and lick her as she lay on the bed. She could see the other man out of the corner of her eye, just watching. Just so long as he stayed well away. She didn't want him touching her.

Suddenly, he knelt up and reached into his trousers to pull out his cock. Stacie widened her eyes. It was massive, both long and thick.

"Suck it," he commanded.

Stacie sat up, taking his dick into her mouth, as much of it as she could anyway. He grabbed hold of the back of her head thrusting her harder onto his cock. She was struggling, feeling as if she were suffocating. She tried to pull her mouth off to explain that she couldn't take it all, but his hands were hard on her head, holding her in place, thrusting it farther in.

She tried to relax her mouth and throat, it would probably be easier if she didn't struggle. He released her after a short time and she gratefully slid her mouth off his dick, wiping away the saliva that had collected at the corners.

He pushed her back to lie on the bed, pouncing on top. She felt his dick at the entrance to her pussy and before she could even think, *I'm not sure I want this anymore*, he was in. She wailed aloud as he forced his cock in deep, penetrating her hard. She screamed out as he shoved harder and faster, his balls slapping her bottom. Stacie tried to relax as much as possible, but she hadn't been ready and it was painful.

She looked up at his face as he thrust in and out. Would he stop if she told him no? She was reminded of Graham doing it even when she didn't want to, and stared at the ceiling. It would be over soon. Stacie shifted her hips, trying to give him more room to penetrate her, so it wouldn't be as uncomfortable. She closed her eyes, but opened them abruptly when she felt something fleshy against her face.

"Suck his knob," Bond demanded. The other man was dangling his hard dick in her face.

"No!" She reared away from him and turned her face. Bond grabbed her face and turned it back to face the disgusting penis. Even his pubic hair was grey and his wrinkly balls dangled low.

"Stop being so pathetic and suck his knob," Bond told her, ramming himself deeper into her.

"No...I will not," she said. She began hitting out at his chest, and wriggling her lower body with all the strength she had to dislodge him from her. "Stop it, I don't want this anymore!"

He pulled out and knelt on the bed, glaring at her with disgust. "You're a pricktease, you fucking little tart."

Mortified tears filled Stacie's eyes. "I'm not a tart!"

Bond shrugged. "Course you are," he said cheerfully. "Just like all those other bitches out there. Who gives a damn about you anyway? There're plenty more sluts who aren't so picky about who they spread their legs for. We will just go and find number nine. You've got ten minutes to get your fucking arse out of here, whore." He got dressed and the two men left the room.

Stacie burst into tears. He'd looked at her like she was dirt. She stared down at her body and bundled herself into a ball, sobbing her heart out. What had she done? Her heart ached and her self-image dropped from supreme confidence to feeling rubbish and pointless. Tears streamed down her cheeks, soaking the sheet.

She leaped off the bed, quickly finding her dress and slipping into it, wishing she had never made the decision to go with that evil man. She had been number eight. Sick to the core and totally distraught, she zipped up the dress, grabbed her shoes and fled. She pulled her hem up to her knees and ran down the corridor as fast as she could toward reception. She heard Bailey calling her name, but she wasn't stopping for anyone.

She ran up the stairs and down the corridor to her room, almost blind through her tears. She arrived at the bedroom door and wailed with horror when she remembered she didn't have the key. She leaned against the door and banged on it with her fists. Maybe Dan was in there.

"Stacie? Are you all right?" she heard a voice say from behind her. It sounded like Bailey.

"Can you get me in the room?" she begged, her tears dripping down her face and falling on the floor.

"Here," Bailey said, handing her a key.

Stacie struggled and cursed as she tried to get the damn key in the hole. Finally, Bailey took it off her and opened it easily. Stacie threw herself into the room and dropped to the floor in anguish.

## Chapter Thirteen

Stacie sensed Bailey kneeling at her side, and felt her gentle hand on her back. The touch reminded her of Bond and a wave of revulsion shook her. She jumped to her feet, kicking her shoes off, not caring where they landed. She stripped off the dress and kicked it away from her body, then yanked down her thong. She could hear Bailey asking her questions, trying to find out what had happened but Stacie ignored her, desperate to scrub away every trace of that bastard.

She rushed into the bathroom slamming the door, leaving Bailey behind. On went the shower and Stacie began feverishly scrubbing her body, needing to remove the monster from her.

Stacie scrubbed at her skin till it was raw, trying to purge herself of the filth of his touch. The words he said rang in her head. "Whore, slut, tart," the same words Graham used to use if he didn't manage to get his own way, or even when he did, he was never satisfied. She could never win—no matter how hard she tried, nothing was ever good enough for him. Now here she was back in the very situation she thought she'd escaped from, feeling dirty, meaningless, like she was only put on the planet to be ill-treated by arseholes. The words echoed over and over, as Stacie scoured every trace of his scum off her body.

She finally turned the shower off, rubbing herself dry and wrapping a bathrobe tightly round her body. She headed back into the bedroom, fully expecting Bailey to be gone, having left her to sulk on her own, but instead found Bailey sitting on the bed.

The other woman stood up instantly and came over to her. "Stacie, what's happened?" she asked.

Stacie went over to the table, pouring the last of the bottle of wine into one of the glasses. She felt physically sick, thinking about that man and his friend. She lifted the glass to her mouth, but the smell wafted to her nostrils and she ran back into the bathroom to vomit violently into the toilet. She felt Bailey's gentle hands pulling back her hair while her stomach emptied itself through her mouth and nose.

When the contractions of her stomach seemed to have stopped, she saw Bailey's hand offering a wad of tissue. She took it, blew her nose and wiped her mouth, then took the glass of water Bailey held out next. She sipped and spat, then sipped again, washing her mouth out.

"I am so sorry," she said to Bailey finally, sitting back on her heels on the bathroom floor.

"Don't be silly." Bailey helped her to her feet and Stacie headed back into the bedroom, carrying her water. Bailey stood behind her. "Please Stacie, what's wrong? I want to help you."

Stacie turned to look at Bailey, saw her face filled with concern. Bailey moved over to Stacie, reaching out to touch her shoulder. Stacie flinched away and moved over to the bed. She sat down feeling every limb in her body aching. Bailey sat next to her.

"Stacie please, I would like to be able to help you."

Stacie swallowed, trying to find the words. "I…I've just been…" She felt as if her heart was being ripped out of her chest. An image of the two men came into her mind, their leering faces, their cruel words. She dropped her head in her hands and sobbed anew, feeling Bailey move even closer, putting her hand onto Stacie's knee. "I cannot—" Stacie said feeling embarrassed and ashamed. Tears streamed down her face at the horror and cheapness. She wanted to tell Bailey what had happened, but wasn't sure how she would take it. Was it wrong to come to a sex club, and not want to have sex? Would Bailey think she was being silly? But surely no meant no, even here?

She felt Bailey's arm wrapping around her shoulder. "Stacie," Bailey said in a light caring voice. Stacie felt Bailey's breath on her face.

"I've just been treated like a whore, and called a whore," she blasted, crying, feeling disgusting.

Bailey's eyebrows flew up. "Dan?"

"No," she said, feeling utter disgust at herself.

"I thought you were with Dan. Who was it? What happened?"

"I was with Dan, but Angel took me for a tour around the place," she said drawing in a breath and moving her hands away from her face. "After, I tried to find Dan, but I couldn't see him, so I decided to have a dance. And there I saw this guy. I don't know his name, but he was the one."

"What did the man look like?"

"I think I should just pack and leave," Stacie said, standing up. "I can't stay here." Tonight was proof that Desires wasn't for her. She'd broken the prime rule, fallen for her instructor. And there was nothing else here that interested her. She'd tried to be the kind of girl that enjoyed casual sex with multiple partners, but she wasn't that kind of girl, and never would be.

"Don't do that, you've been drinking. We can sort this out. What did the man look like?" Bailey asked again only this time with anger, not directed at her, Stacie sensed, but at the man who had done this to her.

Stacie threw her hands up. "How on earth can you help? There are hundreds of men downstairs."

"Trust me. We will find out who it was. What did he look like?"

Stacie stopped to think for a minute, sitting back onto the bed alongside Bailey, really not wanting to be reminded of the evil man. He obviously knew how to manipulate a woman into his bed. She brought up an image of him in her head, sending quivers of disgust throughout her body.

"Dark hair, slight tan, a bit stubbly, has a James Bond look about him," she said.

"You mean, he doesn't tie his bow tie, wears his jacket open and has a mate he hangs about with, an older man, Malc?" Bailey asked, her voice sounding very agitated.

Stacie stared at her. "That sounds familiar. He said he can go and get number nine."

"That's Larry." Bailey shook her head. "He's a total ladies man. I don't understand how on earth he got his hands on you. He's a complete knobhead, he only thinks about one thing," Bailey said, putting her arm around Stacie for comfort.

"God, men! They're all knobheads!"

"No, not all men. But Larry definitely is."

"And my ex and Dan." Had every man she had been intimate with treated her with no respect?

"No, not Dan."

"Yes Dan. He's just screwing me for my money," Stacie said, staring at Bailey harshly, hating the way she was defending him.

"No, not in that way. He's here to help you. Dan is the most sincere man I know. He cares a lot about his clients and he has enjoyed teaching you. You should never have been left to be vulnerable to Larry's advances. Don't listen to anything he says to you."

"What on earth is wrong with me? I just want to find a nice man and be happy."

"Nothing is wrong with you. Someone is out there for you. You're a beautiful woman, and have a fantastic figure."

Stacie looked at Bailey's face, still full of concern. "I've been a fool. I thought…"

"Thought what?"

Stacie paused. She'd been about to blurt out to Bailey that sleeping with Larry might have helped her get over her feelings for Dan. But she couldn't admit that to Bailey. Nice as she seemed, she still worked for Desires. She couldn't risk that getting back to Angel.

"Do you have a boyfriend?" she asked instead.

"No," Bailey answered. Her amused tone of voice caused Stacie to turned and look at her. "I don't find men enjoyable," the other woman explained. Stacie widened her eyes, wondering what she meant. "I've been in relationships with men, but they just aren't for me."

Stacie looked at her, confused. "What do you mean?"

"I'm a lesbian."

"Oh…" *Well, that makes sense*, Stacie thought. A few things started to add up, all the smiles and advice. Maybe Bailey was attracted to her. But Stacie was not that way inclined, at least, she never had been. Maybe she was going down the wrong road—she certainly hadn't had any luck with the male of the species.

"We need to get hold of Angel and let her know. Dan too—he is going to go totally mental," Bailey said, standing up.

"What do you mean?"

"Dan hates Larry and he has just taken advantage of his client. Expect war. In fact, this isn't going to go down well with anyone. Angel will go ballistic."

What to do? Stacie really wasn't in the mood to be hanging around the club. She just wanted to pack and jump in a taxi home. She could come back in the morning for her car. She had spent a small fortune on this place to get her confidence back sexually and within seconds the whole thing was blown by one idiot man. What the hell was the point? Why did she have to decide she needed to change her life? And why on earth did she choose the sex road? Sex is one of the most intimate things a couple can do. Okay, some people seem to enjoy it purely for the physical, but Stacie had always had to have an emotional connection. Maybe that was why it was so shit with Graham, because the emotions weren't right. As she loved him less and less, the sex grew worse and worse, not that it had ever been great to begin with. With Dan…Stacie paused in her thoughts. With Dan, it was only good because she had feelings for him. No casual encounter would ever make her feel that way. The only way she was going to have good sex again was to fall in love with someone else.

The thought made her feel hollow. How could there ever be someone else, now she'd met Dan?

"How are you feeling?" Bailey asked, hunkering down in front of her and taking both her hands.

"I don't know. I feel empty, like someone has opened my chest and ripped out my heart. I feel so stupid and annoyed with myself."

"You weren't to know what Larry was about. He's a wanker, and to be honest he has been pushing his luck for quite some time. I wouldn't be surprised if Angel uses this as an excuse to finally get rid of the tosser. It makes me sick how he thinks he can use and abuse anyone."

"It doesn't matter. I'm just going to gather my bits together and leave."

"Why should you have to leave? You've done nothing wrong. He should be the one leaving, not you. Please Stacie, don't let Larry win."

"I'm not. I've decided this isn't the right direction for me."

"What do you mean?"

"This isn't the path I should be going down. I'm going to take another direction," Stacie said, her only thought now to escape the place.

"What other direction?"

"Sex isn't important to me, sex is just sex, and to be honest I deserve better." It wasn't the whole truth. Sex with Dan had been wonderful and fun. But now... Well, now, if she couldn't have Dan, she just couldn't be bothered with anyone else.

"But you were doing so well. If you leave now, you're allowing Larry to win."

The quiet sound of a key in the door fell into the silence. The two women looked at one another. Stacie quickly wiped away the tears. It could only be Dan.

Dan walked in the room, smiling when he saw Stacie. "Here you are. I've been searching all over the place for you. This was the last place on my list," he said, looking delighted to have tracked her down. He came over to the bed and Bailey stood up, her face sombre.

Dan glanced at Bailey and then at Stacie. "What's going on?" he asked, looking concerned.

Stacie stared at Bailey, her heart fluttering. How could she tell him? Bailey stared back and raised her eyebrows significantly. Stacie looked at Dan, then down at the floor. He would be so angry.

"What's going on?" he asked again, frowning.

"Stacie?" Bailey said encouragingly.

But Stacie couldn't bring herself to say it. Larry's face floated into her mind again, looking down on her, staring like she was a piece of shit. His face had gone from thrill to nasty in a split second, just like Graham's used to do. She didn't want to witness Dan's reaction, feeling the dark side of Dan was going to come out. She didn't want to see that side of him. Would he turn nasty and blame her and call her all the names under the sun? Graham would have. Larry had hurt her and she cared nothing for him. Dan could hurt her so much more—she was scared to think how much. She had laid her heart bare to him, given it to him. What would he do with it?

"Stacie, please tell him," Bailey said in a soft voice. "Dan will understand."

Stacie heard him move closer to her, then he knelt in front of her, "Stacie, please tell me what's going on."

Stacie looked down at her knees, her hair dropping around her face in a curtain. She could see his knees and his legs, but couldn't bear to look him in the eye. She flinched away when she felt his hands on her knees, hating the thought of a man even breathing on her let alone touching her.

"Okay, what's going on?" he asked in a harsher voice. "Surely it's not that bad...is it?" Worry crept into his voice. "Bailey?" he asked, when Stacie didn't reply.

Stacie felt tears drip down her cheeks. Maybe if she just didn't say anything, they would all go away. She shut her eyes and hugged herself, rocking back and forth.

"What's going on? Come on, Bailey. Stacie obviously isn't going to tell me," Dan said, sitting back on his heels.

"Larry got to her," Bailey ground out, her voice overflowing with contempt.

"Pardon?"

"Larry got to her," she repeated clearly.

"Sexually?" she heard him ask Bailey. Stacie sobbed, dreading his next reaction.

"Stacie was number eight."

Stacie watched Dan rise to his feet, standing tall. She looked at his feet, crying, worried what he was going to say to her.

"Can I leave you here to look after Stacie?"

"Of course," Bailey said. Stacie heard Dan walk across the room, and then the sound of the door opening and closing. Stacie looked at Bailey, her mouth dropping open.

"He wasn't angry with me!"

"Of course not. Why would he be angry with you?" Bailey moved to the dressing table, picking up the phone. "I'd get dressed if I were you. I think things are going to start happening pretty quickly."

Stacie grabbed her jeans and a baggy T-shirt of Dan's. She put them on as Bailey called down to reception telling them to beep Angel. There was a touch of panic in her voice. Stacie pulled on her shoes, picking up Bailey's urgency.

They rushed downstairs. The other receptionist was sitting, looking up at them with inquiry on her face as they hurtled down the steps. Bailey quickly briefed her when Angel appeared from the double doors at the heart of the club.

"What's wrong?" Angel said, looking deeply concerned.

"Larry got to Stacie!"

"Are you sure?" Angel said.

"I'm very sure. Dan's going after Larry," Bailey told her, frantic. "We need to move fast and catch Dan up or he'll knock seven bells out of him."

"I saw Dan go into the ballroom a few minutes ago," the other receptionist offered, looking from Angel to Bailey.

Stacie kept well back, not wanting all the hassle. She couldn't understand why Bailey never allowed her to simply pack her bag and leave.

"Right, you two stay here," Angel said to Bailey and Stacie. "Call security," she ordered the other receptionist who nodded and picked up a walkie-talkie. Angel spun and rushed into the ballroom.

Stacie's heart skipped beats. If she had known the problems it was going to cause, she would have kept her bloody mouth shut. She sat down on one of the squashy leather sofas in the reception area wishing she'd never come. The double doors banged open and Angel reappeared, her face like granite. She came over to Stacie and sat next to her.

"I need to know exactly what happened. Where did he take you?" Angel demanded.

"Down that corridor on the right," she answered in a whisper.

"And?"

"He had sex with me, look I didn't know. I just—"

"It's okay, Stacie. But I need the information."

"We were having sex—"

"Was it consensual?"

"What?"

"Did you agree to have sex with him?"

"I guess, at first, but then he got a bit too rough."

"Did you ask him to stop?"

"No," Stacie answered in a tiny voice. "I figured it would just be easier to get it over with."

"What happened then?"

"Then he wanted me to suck his mate's cock, I hadn't even agreed for the mate to be there in the first place. He walked in on us when I was naked. I didn't want to do that so I started to fight him off and told him to stop."

"Did he stop?"

"Yes, but then he got nasty, saying I'm a whore and a slut and that they'll find number nine," Stacie said, feeling her heart shattering into pieces, going over the sordid incident again.

"Thank you, that'll do for now," Angel told Stacie as Dan appeared, bursting out of the ballroom. He ignored everyone, storming off through the double doors, looking ready to kill. Angel ran after him.

Stacie panicked, trying to figure out what she should do. What would Dan do when he finally caught up with Larry? She felt like running out of the front door, leaving all the bizarre mess behind her. But she'd started this mess. She needed to find the confidence to face the fallout. Quickly, before she could change her mind, she got up and rushed to the double doors after them. Behind her, she could hear Bailey shouting her name but she ignored her, charging through the doors.

Stacie saw Angel heading toward the orgy room. She ran to the room and stood at the door reaching out a hand to push aside the voile, still moving from Angel's entrance.

She entered the room. Whatever the naked and semi-naked people in the room had been doing before, at the moment they were watching a different kind of show. Dan and Larry were nose-to-nose while Angel strode toward them.

"You're a fucking tosser!" Dan was yelling at Larry, prodding him in the shoulder.

"What's your fucking problem?" Larry yelled back, getting in Dan's face.

"If Angel's got any sense she'll be tossing you out on your ear. I ought to knock your fucking block off."

As Stacie watched, Dan clenched his fists.

"Just you try it," Larry sneered. "I'd have you in a second."

"Gentlemen," Angel said, her voice carrying clearly. "Can we take this upstairs, please?"

The two men glared at each other, but subsided.

Angel turned to leave, Larry and Dan following her, sulky looks on their faces, like two little boys being told off by the teacher, Stacie suddenly thought. As they passed her, Larry stared at Stacie. Dan stepped between them, pushing out his chest and glaring at Larry.

Dan took hold of Stacie's hand, but she pulled away. She didn't want to touch him or any other man at the moment. *It was his fault too!* she suddenly decided. If he hadn't encouraged her to go after another man, this whole thing would never have happened. She fell in step behind the trio as Angel led them to her office. She opened the door and commanded Larry to go in. She closed the door, shutting him in the office and then turned to Stacie.

"Is that him?"

Stacie replied with a nod. His face haunted her, especially after the amount of flirting she'd done. She felt so dirty—she'd almost begged for it.

"Just had to check."

Angel opened the door and they all trooped in.

"Sit down, please," Angel said, addressing all of them. The two men settled themselves on the sofa, sitting as far apart as they could. Stacie sat on a chair, not looking at anyone.

"Larry, can I please remind you of the rules of Desires?" Angel said abruptly.

"What about them?" he said, his attitude cocky.

"Do you remember this young lady?" Angel said, pointing to Stacie.

"How could I forget? She led me a right merry little dance. Stunning pair of fucking tits but a major attitude problem," he said, turning to glare at Stacie.

Dan exploded, leaping up and getting right in Larry's face. His face was purple. "This woman's my client and you have just fucked up two weekends of hard work, you tosser."

Larry's face altered almost comically. "Oh, and how was I supposed to know that?" he rushed out, with an edge of sarcasm. "She was flirting with me, virtually throwing herself at me. I thought she was up for it." A slightly panicky edge crept into his voice, as if he was just figuring out that he'd royally screwed up.

"She came here for help with her confidence and thank you for fucking her up and setting her so far back I don't know if she'll ever recover. You are pathetic. Men like you need—"

"Thank you, Dan," Angel interrupted. Stacie huddled into a corner, sinking away into the background.

The room filled with shouting and aggression. Stacie switched off, wishing she could just vanish. She understood why Dan was aggravated. All his hard work had basically been pointless. However, it did sound as though Larry knew which girls he could touch and which he needed to keep well clear of.

"She was on her own. I had no idea she was with you, Dan. I am truly sorry. Please," he said, staring at Stacie, his face finally full of remorse. "I swear...I had no idea who you were and I cannot apologise enough." He stood up. Dan stepped between them protectively. "Please, I'm so sorry. Will you please accept my apology?"

Stacie was unsure where to look. The devastation he had wrought hadn't gone. Her body ached and her mind roiled with mixed feelings. She didn't reply. She didn't want to forgive him. She wanted to hate the man. But maybe she was partly to blame. She had flirted with him, she had willingly gone back to his room and she had wanted it, at first. And he did stop the instant she asked him to.

Stacie glanced at Larry. His face looked pathetic and his eyes sad. She actually didn't think he was genuinely sorry, only sorry he got caught. The basic attitude he'd displayed to her in the bedroom was still there. He thought women were sluts, whores, there to be used. He had shown no interest in her pleasure while they were having sex, only his own.

"Stacie, do you accept his apology?" Angel asked.

She stared at Larry, and then looked at Dan. Everyone was waiting for her answer.

"He needs an answer. If you don't accept his apology, his account will be closed and he will not be allowed back here."

Larry stepped up his crawling a notch or ten. "Please Stacie. I am so, so sorry. If I had known you were Dan's client I would never have touched you. How was I to know? I made a big mistake. I should have checked my list. But I hadn't seen you with Dan. Please," he said, almost batting his pathetic eyelids at her. "Please, I am begging you, I need this club..."

*I bet you do*, Stacie thought. No women out there in the real world would put up with the way he treated them. But then, Desires was a sex club, designed to cater to everyone's desires, not just the ones Stacie approved of. She was not sure who was in the wrong but it probably wouldn't do him any harm to wait with torture for a while.

Stacie stood up and moved to the office door, taking one more look at the whimpering man, looking pathetic and desperate. She couldn't stand it any longer. She walked out the room, heading back to the reception area.

"Do you still have that spare key for my room?" she said to Bailey.

Bailey dug it out of her pocket and handed it over. "What—"

Stacie put a hand up, stopping her. "I can't talk about it right now. Sorry. Thank you, for everything."

Bailey smiled. "No problem. If you want to talk, you know where I am."

Back in the room, she collapsed on the bed. She glanced at the clock. It was gone midnight. She hadn't even realised how late it had got. She debated calling a taxi and going home, but the bed was comfortable and her eyes were drooping. She may as well stay here tonight and get off first thing tomorrow. She took off her jeans and got into bed with just Dan's T-shirt on, snuggling into the pillow. She couldn't sleep. The events of the evening whirled in her head. She was still tossing and turning half an hour later when the door quietly opened and Dan came in.

"I'm not asleep," she said, as he tiptoed across the room. She twisted round and turned on the bedside lamp. He sat on the bed and regarded her kindly.

"Would you like me to go and find another room?" he asked. "I don't mind, if you'd rather be alone."

"No, it's okay. You can stay in here," she replied. He got undressed and got into bed next to her. He leaned over to kiss her, but she shied away. She couldn't forget how he had encouraged her. He had to shoulder at least some of the blame for this disastrous evening.

"Is there anything I can do? Do you want me to hold you?" She looked at him. He looked woebegone, like a puppy that had been told off by its master. Her heart-strings twanged.

"No. Thank you. I'm okay. Let's just try to get some sleep."

"Goodnight then."

"Goodnight."

## Chapter Fourteen

Stacie woke the following morning, feeling as if she had barely slept. She looked over at Dan. He was sleeping soundly, snoring a little. She had stayed awake for a long time last night, going over what had happened, trying to decide what to do, whether to leave Desires, or give it another go. Even when she had dropped off, it seemed she'd woken up pretty much every hour. She stared at Dan. God, he was so sweet and adorable. She had been hard on him last night. It wasn't his fault she had got mixed up with Larry. He had just been doing his job. If she'd stayed with him, he would have warned her off Larry. It was her own fault for going off by herself. And Larry's for being such a knobjockey.

She climbed out of bed, heading to the bathroom. She took her phone with her, deciding to give Chrissie a call. Maybe Chrissie could offer her some support and help her make a decision.

"Hello you, how's everything going?" Chrissie said, sounding chirpy.

"Where on earth do I begin?" Stacie answered, hearing her voice wobble.

"Oh God…the beginning. What's happened?"

"It all started so perfect. Me being naughty, dressing up, having the most amazing sex—and I do mean amazing. Then we headed to the erotic ball. It was incredible. Dan got me the most gorgeous dress. Everyone looked fantastic, the girls were dressed in stunning gowns and the men in tuxedos," Stacie said.

"Yes, it's a great night. We went a few years ago, had such a laugh."

"I kept engaging naughty eye contact with Dan, we were having the most amazing evening. Then Angel took me for a grand tour, showing me the rooms and the stalls."

"It's amazing what you can buy there. They have everything."

"Anyway, afterwards, Angel took me to the bar and, well, she started asking a few awkward questions."

"Like what?"

"About Dan. She subtly reminded me of my contract and told me girls have fallen for a certain tutor before. I got the impression she was warning me off him," Stacie said, turning her head and trying to keep her voice down. He was only the other side of the wall.

"Oh no! What did you say?"

"Well, I tried to reassure her nothing's going on, but I'm not sure she was convinced. But then again, I'm still here," Stacie said with a smile.

"True," Chrissie said, giggling.

"Anyway after Angel left me," already Stacie's heart was skipping beats at the memory, "I couldn't find Dan. So I decided to dance alone and have a good time. I saw this one guy. He was really good-looking, James Bond type. We flirted on the dance floor. Dan had suggested I should try out other men. He told me he wouldn't be with me in the outside world. So I decided to go with this man—"

"And…?"

"Oh, Chrissie, it was awful," Stacie sniffled. "He treated me like a whore. He brought in another guy without telling me and then when I said I didn't want to do it anymore, he called me all sorts of names," Stacie said wallowing.

"The fucking bastard. Oh God, babe, you're still there?" Chrissie asked, concern in her voice.

"I'm still here, but how I have no idea—"

"And Dan?"

"In bed."

"Thank God for that. I thought you were going to say you ditched him. How did he react?"

"Well he went crazy, I think if it hadn't been for Angel, he would've killed him," Stacie said, wiping the tears from her eyes.

"Have you spoken to Dan this morning?"

"No, he's still sleeping."

"So how do you feel now?"

"Like shit. I feel like I'm right back where I started. The whole point of coming here was to boost my confidence sexually. Now, I just feel as bad as I ever did."

"You were doing really well, though, with Dan. Try to stay positive."

"I did think Dan handled it all rather well, but he might just have been protecting his income."

"I can understand why you might think that, but I don't believe it. I genuinely believe he was protecting you."

"How do you come to that conclusion?"

"He cares for you. It's obvious the way he looks at you. Would you like Jason and me to come round? We could try to get a few answers out of Dan."

"Like he'll tell you."

"Why wouldn't he? Look, Stacie, I really would like to help you. Forget what happened last night, put it down to experience and move on. Don't allow him to win, don't give him the satisfaction. You deserve more. And I certainly wouldn't blame Dan. It wasn't his fault. He did help you build your confidence back up."

"Yeah he did and what a waste of time," Stacie said, the pit of her stomach aching.

"Stop it," Chrissie said. "I know there's more to this than he's letting on. Stay optimistic."

Stacie was still inclined to pack and go, but she would very much like to stay with Dan for the day, and enjoy him for maybe the last time. She wasn't sure if she would ever come to Desires again.

Stacie and Chrissie made arrangements for them all to meet later for lunch and they rang off. Stacie finished her ablutions and headed back in the bedroom. Dan was sitting up in the bed watching the television. He instantly switched it off as she came in.

"Hiya. How are you feeling?" he asked, looking anxious and maybe a little nervous for her reply.

Stacie exhaled deeply. "I'm okay, I guess."

She sat on the edge of the bed, wishing she knew what to do for the best. Should she listen to her heart or her head? And was it her heart speaking, or just her libido? Stacie turned to look at Dan. His eyes were so beautiful, but filled with concern. He clearly was not sure what to say after last night's events. Stacie closed her eyes, steeling herself to make the decision she least wanted to make.

She decided she was going to stay and have fun with him, but today would be her last day. After today she would never come back to Desires, and she would never see Dan again.

Her heart plummeted at the very thought of it. No matter how much she told herself he was protecting his money, she couldn't help but find herself captured by his irresistible charm. Being with Dan had changed her life. He had opened her eyes to the sheer enjoyment of sex again and she would be forever grateful for that.

Dan stared at her. His expression was unreadable, as ever. What was he feeling? What was going on behind those warm brown eyes? If he had feelings for her also, his position was even more difficult than hers. Stacie would only lose her membership of Desires, Dan would lose his job. Would he think she was worth it?

Whatever happened today, whichever way her life went from now on, there was one thing she could control here and now. She knelt on the bed looking directly at him. She got on all fours and slowly made her way up the bed to Dan who watched her with great interest. She straddled him, sitting on his lap, her face inches from him, her body pressed to his. She cupped his face with her hands, running her thumbs over his cheeks. She moved her hands up to gently caress the curls at his temples. He gave her an odd sort of half-smile, with a hint of puzzlement. She leaned in to kiss him, closing her eyes and taking her time to taste his mouth, the curve of his lips, the way his face felt under her fingers. She kissed the tip of his nose, his eyelids, then his forehead, before pressing her forehead against his and cupping his head in her hands.

"What's wrong?" he said gently, lifting his hand up to twine her hair in his fingers.

"Nothing. Make love to me."

She pressed herself against his groin, feeling the bulge of his penis through his shorts. He responded instantly, slipping his hands beneath the T-shirt she wore, his T-shirt, caressing her bare back. Tingles danced along her nerve endings and she shivered.

Her pussy throbbed and she ground herself into him, his bulge firming up beneath her. Dan's hands became more urgent, running down to her bottom and cupping her buttocks. He touched his lips to hers and kissed her deeply, his tongue probing and teasing. She hung her arms around his neck and pressed herself to him, kissing him back as hard. She moved her hand down to his groin, slipping it into his trunks to palm his cock, rubbing it heatedly into a full erection. He thrust into her fingers, clutching her back convulsively. She pulled the T-shirt over her head and threw it to one side. Dan buried his face in her breasts, sucking and licking her nipples while she pulled down his trunks. He reached over to grab a condom and she rolled it on him, then slipped her panties to one side and impaled her craving pussy on his rigid cock, groaning as she felt him fill her, and pushing herself down on him as hard as she could. Stacie pulsed up and down on his cock, feeling his penis filling her to the joyful brim. Their lips stayed meshed, kissing passionately as she slid up and down on him.

His fingers moved down to her clitoris, rubbing the delicate nub until she began to gasp and squeal. She threw her body back, letting herself go, feeling the crest come and take her. She screamed as she climaxed, covered his groin in her juices. As her shuddering sighs died down, he held her torso and rolled her back, staying inside her. He stared down at her face, touching his lips to her cheeks, her eyes, her mouth, her nose, before thrusting deeply into her. She wrapped her legs around him, pulling his head down to her, feeling the bliss of him deep within her. He filled her over and over, thrusting deeper until he gave a deep groan and she felt his passion fill her.

\* \* \* \*

After they cleaned up and got dressed, they headed downstairs for breakfast. As they walked in the restaurant, Stacie saw Angel sitting at the bar. Angel smiled as they walked in. Stacie managed to smile back, hoping it didn't look too forced.

Dan and Stacie found a table and the waiter came to take their order. Stacie glanced across to the bar. Angel was staring at her. Stacie quickly looked at the table, feeling her cheeks heat. She wanted to just forget about Angel, and Larry, everything that had happened last night, and make some last memories to cherish while she was here.

Stacie tried to forget that in a matter of hours she would be walking away from him forever. She would have to find the strength to carry on with her life and move on. But at least she would have the memories of Dan to keep her going until she managed to find herself a nice man all by herself.

Breakfast arrived and Stacie tucked in. She had to force herself to swallow the mouthful though, when she saw Larry appear in the restaurant. Mechanically she ate another mouthful, concentrating on the movements of chewing and swallowing. The food suddenly tasted like dust and she was struggling to get it down. Oh God, he was coming over to them. Stacie looked determinedly at the table.

"Hello Stacie...Dan," she heard Larry say. She didn't reply. "How are you both this morning?" Stacie looked through her lashes at Dan, who was also not paying Larry any attention. "I would like to say once again how sorry I am for the misunderstanding. I see you're still here at the club having fun. Have you forgiven me?" Larry asked, not sounding particularly sorry at all.

The pit of Stacie's stomach ached, and she put down her knife and fork, if only to resist the temptation to plunge the utensils into his stupid smug face. Finding courage to face the monster, Stacie turned to look at Larry. "My reasons for still being here have nothing to do with you. If you don't mind, you're putting me off my breakfast."

"I understand, but I really need you to forgive me and tell Angel," he said, batting his eyelids, looking pathetic.

Stacie saw the desperation in his eyes. She replied by shrugging her shoulders, then turned her head away with annoyance. She was almost enjoying this, she had him crawling, totally in her power. She flicked a glance at Dan who was trying to cover up a snigger.

Stacie knew she had Larry where she needed him, hanging on a thread. He needed her to accept his apology or his contract at Desires was history. Stacie cared nothing for Larry, or his contract. Her only worry was that if he was banned from Desires, he might take his sick attitude out into the real world and then other girls would suffer from his vileness.

She turned back to Larry, who was now going down on his knees. She shook her head, glancing at Dan who was staring out the window, trying to stifle his giggles. Stacie looked back at

Larry, wondering how far he would go to beg for her forgiveness and for her to tell Angel she had accepted his apology.

Maybe she should just keep him dangling for a little while longer. Dan had finished and Stacie left the rest of her breakfast, pushing her chair back and walking past him as if he weren't there. Dan followed her. She swept past Angel, ignoring her significantly arched and neatly-plucked eyebrow, and headed back up to the room.

They had both showered earlier, but Dan went into the bathroom to shave. Stacie watched him, with Dan looking at her through the mirror occasionally.

"Is everything okay?" he asked.

"I just like watching you shave," she replied without thinking. Shit, would he think that was weird? But, no, he just smiled at her in the mirror and went back to his shaving.

Her heart beat faster. She was desperate to tell him exactly what she was going through and about her feelings for him. Stacie couldn't stare enough at him, longing to have him holding her forever, wishing to hear the sound of his voice all the time, whispering sweet nothings, telling her how beautiful she looked. She had never thought when she entered the front door of Desires that she would meet such a man, not just sexy, but kind and sweet, and everything she had ever wanted. How would she cope with him gone? What would have happened if she had never signed that damn contract?

Dan left the bathroom and her heart collapsed as it had been penetrated with a knife.

"Get a grip, Stacie," she told herself, hitting her thighs. "He's just a man. There are plenty more out there." She needed a distraction. Maybe the afternoon with Jason and Chrissie would help.

Stacie got ready very carefully, going for the gorgeous, girl-next-door natural look. Her hair was tousled, her make-up glowing but subtle. She came out of the bathroom to see Dan dressed, sitting and watching the television.

She picked out her clothes, jeans and a tight fitted T-shirt, putting a long waterfall cardigan over the top. The room phone rang and Dan answered it. He looked up at her, puzzled.

"Jason and Chrissie are waiting in reception for us?" he said, a question in his voice.

"Oh, I forgot to tell you. I asked if they'd like to come and have lunch with us. You don't mind, do you?"

"Of course not, it's a fab idea."

Stacie put on her boots and they walked toward the door but, before Dan opened it, he drew Stacie into his arms and gave her a long, slow, delicious kiss.

"What was that for?" she said, when they finally parted.

"Do I have to have a reason?" Dan said, kissing the tip of her nose before opening the door.

"Never." *Oh God, he was making it so difficult.*

They headed downstairs. Jason and Chrissie were sitting on the leather couch waiting for them. They jumped to their feet, and all four greeted one another with kisses and hugs. At least if nothing else she'd made a friend here.

Then Angel appeared, greeting them all. Stacie felt the atmosphere take a dip, or was that just her? No one else here had a reason to have a problem with Angel. "Good afternoon," Angel said with a sparkling smile. *Crocodiles smile too,* Stacie thought. *Just before they eat you.* "I hope you are all well. I would like to take this opportunity to offer you a freebie, on the club, a room to yourself. Do as you please, and have lots of fun." It seemed to be a kind offer to valued clients, but Stacie sensed an alternative motive. She betted it had something to do with Larry.

Bailey handed them the key and they went to the room Angel had assigned them. Dan flicked the light switch and a dozen twinkling spotlights in the ceiling illuminated a room wallpapered in black, with a shiny tiled black floor, almost hidden by piles of massive cushions. One wall was dominated by a huge flat-screen television. In one corner was a DVD player on top of a black ash cupboard. In another was a well-stocked minibar in a matching black ash cabinet. Dan and Jason went over to the DVD cabinet. Chrissie moved close to Stacie. "Well? Have you told him?"

"No."

"Why on earth not? Do you still like him?" Chrissie asked.

"God, yes, more than I can say," she whispered, not wanting Dan to hear her.

Chrissie tapped her watch. Stacie knew what she meant, that time was ticking by. Suddenly her firm decision to make this the last day she saw Dan started to crumble and doubt once more crept in.

"Girls, what do you fancy?" Dan said.

Stacie's head twisted so fast on her neck she was surprised she didn't pull something. "Sorry?" she said, while her knees went weak at the look on Dan's face.

Jason waved two DVD boxes at her. "What do you fancy watching? Hardcore, or a movie style?" Jason asked.

"Hardcore," Chrissie replied, finding her spot on the scattered cushions.

Stacie was stunned for a minute. She hadn't realised they'd be watching porn. She wasn't entirely comfortable with the idea, especially with other people there, but she didn't want to appear a prude. She headed over to the cushions, joining Chrissie and making herself comfortable. Dan put the DVD on then dimmed the lights. The men came to sit down and Dan reclined next to Stacie.

"You okay with this?" he half-mouthed, half-whispered at her, gesturing with his head at the television.

She nodded, trying for a smile.

She attempted to look at the television screen, but she was acutely aware of him next to her. All she wanted to do was stare at him, to drink in his beloved face. The DVD began with a girl in slinky underwear doing a very seductive dance in front of a man.

"I heard you had an interesting night last night?" Jason said.

"You could say that," Dan replied.

"How did Stacie end up with Larry?" Jason asked.

"Angel took Stacie off to show her round, then left her on her own. She should've brought her directly back to me. It's as much Angel's fault as anyone's."

"Yes, but I could've found you," Stacie interjected. "But instead, I heard a good tune and wanted to dance, and that was when knobhead found me," she said, not quite sure why she was defending Angel. She hadn't really considered Angel's share of the blame game.

"Angel should've known better. She knows what kind of men come to those functions. You weren't to know," Dan said, sitting up and reaching over to hold Stacie's hand.

Chrissie stepped in. "Stacie wouldn't've gone off with him if you hadn't suggested she try out other men."

Stacie stared at Chrissie. Hadn't she told Stacie not to blame Dan, yet here she was doing the same thing? She hastily interrupted, not wanting this to turn into a bloodbath. "I agreed with Dan that it might be a good idea. I just picked the wrong man, that's all."

Jason spoke out, "The result was you still ended up in the wrong hands. That shouldn't have happened—the club had a duty of care to you."

Dan cut in, "Larry just goes around shagging whatever takes his fancy. He'll shag anyone who opens her legs to him, then moves onto the next one. Most of the regular girls here know what he's about. If that's what they want, then fine. If not, they know to leave him alone."

"Isn't that what you do?" Chrissie said, her quiet question falling into silence. Stacie's heart pounded. Why had she said that? Chrissie was meant to be helping her, not making the situation worse. Chrissie continued, "Only you take their money." That was something Stacie mentioned earlier to her on the phone. Clearly, Chrissie was trying to get answers to questions that Stacie was afraid of asking.

Dan paused, washing his hands over his face. "Yes, I agree I take women's money to have sex with them. However, I do it for their pleasure, not my own. I am here to make them happy, not to make myself happy. I don't just open their legs and shag them. Unless that's what they want, of course. I respect women and I hope I send my clients home smiling." Stacie looked at him while he glanced at her. "I don't come here and treat them like meat, that's the difference. Larry has no consideration or feelings for women. All he's interested in is himself. He's a complete selfish bastard. I would never do that."

"How do you manage not to get personal?" Jason asked.

"It's my job. I can switch off, but yet keep myself together," Dan said. Stacie sank further back in the cushions, desperate to hide.

"You must find yourself feeling something for a few?" Jason asked.

"No," Dan replied. Stacie's heart broke. She wanted to stand up and run away for being such a stupid fool. Dan didn't love her. She was wasting her time.

"What about Stacie?" Chrissie asked. *No, no, no!* Stacie wanted to scream at her. *Not now!*

Dan answered, "What about her? She's a stunning girl and I have enjoyed her company. I have found helping her to be very rewarding, but she's a client just like the others." He didn't even look at her when he said this.

"God, you make it sound like, 'Yeah whatever,'" said Jason. Stacie felt the atmosphere shift.

"No, that isn't the case. Stacie has been amazing and, yes, I have given her more compassion and made sure I have done my ultimate best. She's been an exceptional client and I have totally enjoyed my time with her," Dan said.

Dan turned around to look at her. His face might as well have been carved from marble—there was no expression there whatsoever.

Well, that was that. It was clear she was simply a client, nothing more and nothing less. At least that had been established, he had no feelings for her at all and she knew she had been a total dimwit.

The room fell silent, everyone watching the television. Stacie stared at the screen without seeing it. Stupid thoughts ran around her head. She had been wasting her time and her emotional energy worrying about the stupid contract. It wasn't going to be broken, that much was certain. How stupid was she for thinking a young attractive man would even look in her direction, let alone fall head over heels in love with her. It was a crazy thought, total madness. She wished Chrissie and Jason had asked the all important questions last week. She could have saved a small fortune.

On the positive side, at least there had been some fun and she'd had the privilege of having sex with a very skilled young man. Stacie daydreamed for quite some time, not paying any attention to what was on the television. Movement on the cushions roused her from her reverie and she turned to see Chrissie passionately kissing Jason. She turned her head quickly in the opposite direction seeing a girl being penetrated on the television. Embarrassed, she stared into a corner.

But the rampant sexuality in the room was affecting her. Much as she didn't like it, she still had feelings for Dan, and the DVD was starting to arouse her as much as it embarrassed her.

She let her eyes slip to the side where Dan sat, letting herself feel his presence, inhale his smell. She couldn't decide if she wanted to shag him or slap him. She turned her head to look at his face, expecting to see him looking at the television. Instead, he was looking at her. His eyes were warm, and his cheeks dimpled with a smile. She kept her face stony, glaring at him down her nose. She tried to pour out her anger through her eyes, make him feel what she was feeling. Did he have any idea how much he had hurt her? Her heart felt empty and torn to shreds. But was it his fault? Wasn't this exactly what the contract was in place to prevent?

Dan smiled and moved closer to Stacie. She looked away and down to her body, hating that her body reacted to him. Stacie could hear Chrissie and Jason kissing and the couple having sex on the television. Stacie was furious at her body for getting turned on, betraying her. Dan took hold of her hand. She pulled it away, not wanting him to think she was there for him, or that she was easy.

He again took hold of her hand, Stacie attempted to pull it away, but this time he kept a firm grip on it. Stacie kept her head low, not wanting to look at him, unable to stand the thought she had humiliated herself. Dan released her hand, then used the same hand to lift her chin. Stacie resisted, staring at the floor.

"Look at me, Stacie," he commanded her, but Stacie turned her head deliberately away to look at Chrissie and Jason. Her heart ached as she watched them caressing one another. Why was it so difficult to find someone to love? The only man she'd ever met who had been nice to her, had to be paid to be nice to her.

He leaned toward her. "What's wrong?" he murmured in her ear. As if she was going to tell him. He moved away and sighed. "Can you follow me outside," he asked her, his voice sounding abrupt. He stood up and made his way to the door without waiting for her answer.

Chrissie and Jason let each other go for a second. "What's going on?" Chrissie asked, looking puzzled.

"You heard him. I'm just a client, nothing more. I think I should just go home."

"Well, it's up to you but you should enjoy him while you have him, Stacie," Chrissie said, compassion in her voice.

"You might regret it tomorrow if you don't," Jason said.

Stacie thought about what Jason said. He was probably right. If this was the last time she'd be with him, she had to make it special. None of this was his fault after all. He was just doing his job. He hadn't asked her to go and fall in love with him, had he?

She stood up and followed Dan out the door. He was standing out in the corridor, waiting for her.

"Okay, what's going on?" he said moving close and putting his hand on her cheek. Stacie couldn't meet his eyes, feeling stupid and embarrassed. "Have I done or said something to upset you? Was it mentioning Larry?" he said. Stacie couldn't answer him. He moved away, stepping to the other side of the corridor. She looked over at him. He looked upset. What did he have to be upset about? Stacie frowned.

"I'm sorry about last night. I should've looked for you," he said.

"No, it wasn't your fault," she finally replied. "I'm just not in the mood."

"But you invited your friends. I thought that this was what you wanted," he said, looking baffled.

She laughed at herself, at her own naïveté. "I just invited them for lunch. I hadn't envisaged this." Of course, a lunch date in a sex club with two exhibitionists would be a little different from a lunch date anywhere else. They hadn't even had lunch yet.

"You look tense, would you like me to massage you?" she heard him say. She looked at him. Bless him, he was trying to help her, trying to do his job. Maybe she should just let him. A massage sounded good anyway, it might help her to relax.

"Okay," she said. He opened the door for her and they went back into the room. Chrissie and Jason smiled as they came in, then went back to kissing.

Another sex scene was beginning on the television. She looked at Chrissie and Jason, seeing them kissing and touching one another.

"Are you ready for that massage?" he said. Stacie nodded and took off her cardigan and T-shirt. She lay prone on a couple of the big cushions, using a smaller one as a pillow. Dan took off his top and took up position next to her. She noticed Jason looking at her. He smiled while Dan moved her hair to one side and began gently rubbing her shoulders. At first Stacie felt tense as he dug deep into her shoulder muscles, but she soon began to relax. She'd always loved to have her back rubbed. Graham had done it a couple of times in their early courtship, but not for a very very long time.

She closed her eyes, drifting into paradise while his hands ran over her shoulders and down to the shoulder blades, her tension draining into the big cushions.

Dan glided his fingertips up her spine, arriving at her bra fastening. He undid it, lifting the back straps to each side, and easing the shoulder straps off her shoulders. He carefully pulled the bra out from beneath her, Stacie lifting her upper torso slightly to assist. She heard a bottle lid being opened, then shivered as cool liquid was poured on her back. She could feel it start to trickle as Dan moved swiftly into action, rubbing the liquid into her flesh.

His hands manipulated her skin and eased her muscles. She felt her joints loosening and her body relaxing into contentment. His hands glided farther down her body to her waist. He tugged her jeans down a little then slid his hands down to her hips, then round and up her spine. He went back up to her upper back, then down the sides of her ribcage, just touching the outer edges of her breasts with his fingertips. She shivered, wanting him to touch her more intimately.

She lifted up her bottom then reached beneath her to unfasten the button and fly on her jeans. Dan pulled them down, leaving her wearing only her thong. She awaited his touch, trembling.

He cupped her bottom cheeks, gently squeezing her flesh and making circles with his thumbs. He poured more of the liquid on her bottom, she could feel it running down into the cleft between her buttocks. He moved his large hands over her cheeks, rubbing and caressing, then back up her back, in long slow delicious sweeps. Gentle noises surrounded her, the soundtrack from the television and, close by, the small noises Chrissie and Jason were making as they played around with each other. Earlier, when he was rubbing her back, she was so relaxed she could almost have fallen asleep, but now as he caressed her bottom and the tops of her thighs, her body was in a heightened state of awareness. He wrapped his hands round the backs of her thighs and slowly ran them up over her skin. His thumbs tickled mere millimetres from her pussy and she quivered.

The urges of her body won out. She turned over and lay on her back, staring up at Dan. She let her gaze deliberately drop to his crotch. His arousal was evident even through his jeans. Dan reached for the bottle again. It was baby oil, Stacie noticed. He poured the liquid across her breasts. It trickled in all directions, but he flew into action, gathering up the rivulets and massaging the oil into her breasts.

She closed her eyes, surrendering to his expert touch. It was hopeless, his fingers drove her crazy. He massaged around her nipples, deliberately avoiding her nipple area at first, although she pushed her breasts into his hands desperately. Her pussy throbbed with need and she tried her hardest not to wriggle her lower body. He glided his hands down and across her tummy, stroking in gentle circles around her navel.

Stacie opened her eyes to see Chrissie and Jason naked on the cushions. She looked up at Dan and saw him staring down at her.

"I want you to fuck me," she told him. He didn't say a word, simply stood up and took off his jeans, then knelt down next to her again.

Stacie sat up, taking hold of the massive bulge in his trunks. She licked her lips and moved her body into a better position, kneeling, caressing his manhood. She ran her fingers down the hard length through the material, feeling it respond to her touch, twitching and bouncing. She dug her hands in his waistband, and pulled out his cock, admiring it, caressing the velvety softness. She bent down and began kissing his shaft. She tickled his balls, tormenting them, using her tongue to run up the full length of his penis. She rolled the tip of her tongue around the tip of his dick, hearing him let out a groan. She smiled with delight that she was able to bring him pleasure also. He had given her so much.

Dan moved pulling his cock away from her. He took hold of her thong, pulling on the small piece of material. Stacie lay back, allowing him to remove her thong. Instantly, she widened her thighs showing him her full glory. He dropped down to feast on her pussy, already about to burst with hyper-sensitivity. She nearly hit the roof when his tongue touched her. She threw her head back into the pillows and thrust her mound in his face, reaching down to twine his hair in her fingers, holding his head in place. He came up for air, licking his lips before diving in again. Stacie sat up, leaning on her elbows wanting to watch him. He tormented her pussy with his tongue, she felt it roll over her clitoris, then dip into her vagina, making her cry out with pure delight.

He pointed his tongue and slid it in and out of her vagina; the sensations sent fireworks through her body, she bucked and trembled, and clenched her fists. When he stopped, she took her own hand down to her clitoris, rubbing desperately. He plunged his fingers inside her, forcing them deep. She lunged her bottom off the cushions, riding his hand. She reached behind her head with her other hand, grabbing a handful of the cushion. Then she felt it approaching, she rubbed harder and screamed with delight, riding the tsunami, letting it rock her body. She jerked over and over, thrusting her hips high off the cushion while her orgasm ran through her whole body. As the tremors settled, her body flopped, the endorphins that had just raced through her causing a delicious languor to spread throughout her limbs.

She felt Dan take hold of her hips and opened her eyes a crack. He encouraged her to turn over, moving onto all fours. Stacie glanced at the other couple, seeing Jason penetrating Chrissie. She groaned as he entered her. Dan grabbed Stacie's bottom and she tilted her hips to allow him entrance. She felt his cock end teasing her pussy. Dan rubbed his manhood up and down her labia, and Stacie quivered at the sensations his soft skin caused on her still-trembling flesh. Dan widened her bottom cheeks, but instead of his cock, she felt his tongue licking and sucking at her sensitive womanhood. Stacie buried her face in the cushions and groaned, as he added his fingers to the agile tongue manipulating and teasing her craving vagina.

He dipped his fingers in and out of her pussy, whilst he ran his tongue between her labia, tasting her juices. She couldn't control her pleasure, wriggling her hips and waist and squeezing her breasts as he rolled on a condom.

Stacie was hooked on him, he was her drug. She wanted to take all he could offer, she couldn't get enough of him. Then he was there, in her, filling her, the pure delight of his cock within her causing her to scream with pleasure. She met his thrust, pushing her body back on him, wanting to take the full length of his girth deeply into her. Dan took hold of her waist, penetrating her deeply. He dove in and out of her saturated pussy, his rhythm getting faster, torturing Stacie with unbearable pleasure.

Stacie felt his cock hitting her nerve endings. She lunged her body into him, meeting every pound, his cock hitting her G-spot. His hand reached around and began to tease her clit. She cried out, feeling her heart racing, she was almost there, and then he stopped. He pulled out and turned her onto her side facing away from him. He lay behind her and snuggled her into his stomach. He lifted her leg up and slid back in smoothly, lowering her leg to rest on his thigh. He reached round and took a firm hold of her breast, squeezing and playing while his cock penetrated her. She glanced up, seeing Chrissie and Jason watching. It made her feel uncomfortable, but she was eager to have Dan, so she closed her eyes to the company, concentrating on the sensations Dan was creating.

She felt him start to move faster. His hand dropped from her breast to her clit, rubbing and tweaking. She pushed back on his every lunge, rubbing herself against him, grinding into him, losing herself in the animal passion. The tidal wave of pleasure hit her, consumed her. She writhed and bucked on the cushions, only dimly aware that Dan was gasping and moaning behind her, as he emptied himself into her. Her body shook and trembled, her cries echoing off the tiled floor. She felt Dan's hands convulsively squeezing her flesh, the divine pain merging with the delicious pleasure to create a sensory fusion of delight.

Stacie dropped back onto the cushions to catch her breath, keeping her eyes closed, savouring the moment. She suddenly realised this would be the last time she would have him. The thought caused a stab of agony in her gut so sharp it almost caused her to gasp.

She felt Dan move away from her body and wanted to scream out *No!*

She twisted to look at Dan. He looked down at her overwhelmed body and smiled. He bent down to kiss her and goosebumps erupted over her body.

He helped her to her feet, and passed her garments. Chrissie and Jason were getting dressed as well so she and Dan quickly pulled on their clothes. They went back to Dan and Stacie's room,

Chrissie, Jason and Dan chatting. Stacie let the others order a lavish buffet lunch. It was only when Dan asked if Stacie was okay that she mentally shook herself and made an effort to join in the lively conversation over lunch.

## Chapter Fifteen

Chrissie and Jason left after lunch.

"Call me," Chrissie had said to Stacie while they hugged in reception. "No matter what happens, call me!"

Dan and Stacie went back up to the room and Stacie felt her heart emptying—her time with Dan was also coming to an end. She packed her belongings, collecting up her clothes and makeup and toiletries, putting them mechanically into her bag. Stacie caught Dan watching her from time to time—she tried her hardest not to allow her emotions to show. The last thing she needed was Dan giving her another lecture on the fact she was only his client. She knew that, boy did she know that.

She found the necklace and earrings Dan had given her, lying in a glittering pile on the floor where she had thrown them after ripping them off after the ball. She picked them up and put them lovingly in their box before laying the box in the bag. She zipped the bag up and put it on the bed. Once done, she stood in the centre of the room. Where would her life go from here? Would she meet some charming man and live happily ever after? Did the fairytale ever work out in real life?

"I'm ready," she told Dan, staring out of the window. The squeak of the bed told her that he'd stood up. She heard the wardrobe door open and then close.

"I have something for you," he said, coming into her line of vision with a wrapped present. She took it from him, not feeling the usual thrill that came with a present. This was a goodbye present and she just stared at it. "Well, open it, then!"

Stacie looked at him. His face was filled with such a child-like anticipation that she smiled in spite of herself. She ripped away the paper, uncovering a very lifelike vibrator. She gave a little laugh, "Thank you."

"I thought that it might come in useful for you," he said with a pleased smile.

"What should I call it?" She paused for a second, thinking. "How about Danny Boy?" She giggled and he smiled.

"If you want to. Have I been that good?" he asked her.

Her smile fell away and a lump the size of Ben Nevis rose in her throat. "You've been amazing. Thank you. No, thank you isn't enough, but I don't know what else to say," she said. She wished it didn't have to end. *She could always come back, but, no!* She ruthlessly squashed that thought. If she came back, she would have this heartbreak all over again. He had no feelings for her other than fondness for a client he got on well with. It was better to just rip the sticking plaster off and end it right now.

Dan stepped forward and kissed her on the cheek. "I'm glad I could help." Stacie pasted on a smile, hoping it would hide the fact that her heart was shattering inside her chest. She picked up her luggage bag.

"Come here," he said, taking her into his arms and kissing her on the lips. If there was ever a moment to stop the clock, that was certainly one of them. Stacie tried her hardest not to release the tears that threatened to flood down her face. Her entire body ached, wishing she could rewind and relive her whole time with him. Or maybe rewind and delete, then it wouldn't hurt so much.

Dan released her. Did she imagine that his eyes were dim, looking disappointed, Stacie knew she must make a move as otherwise she would spill her heart out.

She began to make her way toward the door. She looked back once seeing him standing where she'd left him, looking lost.

"Take care," she said, only managing a whisper over the giant mountain in her throat. He didn't reply. Stacie continued to the door and took hold of the door handle

"*Stop*," she suddenly heard him yell. Stacie froze on the spot and turned around. He was striding across the room toward her. "Don't go!" Excitement flooded her body, followed swiftly by despair. She'd already made her decision.

"I have to."

"Please stay for tonight," he said, reaching out to touch her shoulder. His eyes begged her.

"I have to go home. I have work tomorrow."

"Please Stacie, I will pay the club," he said. His eyes glowed with passion, begging her to stay. "I want to make love to you." Her heart began skipping around the room like an excited loony who had just won the Lottery. Stacie stared at Dan. He would pay for her to stay? He wanted her to stay, not just as a client? He looked concerned. Concerned she was going to walk away?

"Are you sure, this place isn't cheap?" she said.

"I think I know that. I want you to stay with me one more night," he said, staring longingly into her eyes, pleading with her.

"Don't you have any bookings?" she asked. Why was she trying to find an excuse?

"I do, but something more important has come up…you," he said. He took her bag out of her unresisting hand, dropping it on the floor. He took both her hands in his and drew her close. "Stacie, I want you." Her traitorous body reacted, pressing itself against him.

"What do I need to do?" she asked in a whisper. His face cracked in a delighted smile.

He kissed her, crushing her body to his, running his hands up and down her back. Stacie wrapped her arms around him, delighting in the feel of his muscles under her fingers. She let her hands drop to his taut buttocks, savouring their roundness, and pulling his pelvis close to hers. Dan pulled her over to the dresser, not relinquishing his hold on her for a second. He got the phone out with one hand and rang reception before passing the receiver to her.

"Good evening," said the receptionist.

"Hi, it's Stacie Clifford. I would like to book Dan for the night please."

"Just checking his details. Is he still with you?" she asked, sounding puzzled.

"He is," she said, turning to Dan with a smile. He smiled back at her, pressing his lips against her cheek.

"I'm very sorry, Miss Clifford, he's booked tonight."

"She says you're booked," Stacie mouthed at Dan, who took the phone off her.

"Hi, this is Dan. Sorry, I know I have a booking, but I need to cancel that client…Just give the client an excuse when she arrives and offer her someone else," Stacie listened to him saying, "Yeah I'm aware of that…okay…thank you, Shannon, you're an angel."

Stacie got the price for the night from the receptionist and put the phone down. Dan nipped out to the ATM to get the money and Stacie paced the room waiting for him to return.

It seemed like forever before the door opened and Dan swung in, flashing her a huge smile. He reached into his back jeans pocket and pulled out a wad of notes, holding it out to her.

"Are you sure about this?"

"Of course, go down and pay for me, with my money."

"Seems daft."

"Don't care," he said, leaning toward her and kissing her on the lips. Dan moved his mouth to her right ear and whispered in the sweetest of voices, "Our secret."

Stacie felt her knees crumbling and her heart skipping beats.

He whispered softly again, sending an eruption of desire through her weakened body. "Go and pay. I'll be right here."

Stacie couldn't believe how bizarre the situation was. She felt like a teenager who had been told to stay away from a certain boy and instead they were meeting in secret. Why was he keeping her here? Didn't that mean she was more than just a client? But just because he wanted to have sex with her, rather than with some client who might be horrible, didn't mean he wanted more. It didn't mean he wanted a relationship. But he was willing to pay the club, and forego his earnings for tonight, to be with her. It was so confusing. She tried not to think about it, paying the money and heading back up to the room at a trot.

She arrived back to the room to see Dan had set the room for a romantic liaison. He had lit candles around the room, making it feel cosy and warm. A fresh bottle of wine had been brought up to the room. Dan sat at the table holding a glass out to her. His face looked warm and happy. She walked over to him and took it, sitting opposite him and taking a sip. He poured himself a glass and looked directly into her eyes. Maybe this wasn't such a good idea. Maybe it was just dragging out the inevitable.

She sipped her wine, trying not to look at him. Why couldn't he just say something like, "I love you and I want to be with you. Sod the club, sod my job, you're all I want." Then she would know exactly where she stood. Instead, all she knew was that he wanted to have sex with her again. He wanted her enough to give up a night's pay, but that in itself didn't mean anything more than just sex. Stacie took a gulp of her wine, watching the candles burn slowly, flickering in the cosy light and casting dancing shadows on everything. But sex was a powerful force. Men, and women, would do all sorts of things for sex, not always the right or the sensible things either.

*Oh boy!* Stacie gave in, turning her head to look at him, drowning in the hungry look in his eyes.

"How are you feeling?" he asked her.

"Fine," she whispered.

Dan stood up, closing the short distance between them. He stopped in front of her and held his hand out. Stacie stared at it. This was new territory. Nervous didn't begin to cover it. She took hold of his hand and stood up. Dan led her to the bed and sat on the edge, patting the duvet next to him. She sat and he held her hand tightly.

She turned her head, looking deep into his eyes. He drew in closer and she closed her eyes, anticipating his kiss. She felt his breath cascading over her face, sending shivers through her body. She inhaled his scent then felt his lips against hers. He kissed her gently, tasting, nibbling, as if for the first time. He put a hand on her knee, lightly stroking and she ran her hand up to his back.

His hands moved up to her face, cupping her cheeks. His fingers slowly moved over her skin, as if learning her contours. His kiss was tender, delicate, yet at the same time, one of the most passionate she had ever experienced. How could such a light touch ignite such desire? She lifted her hands to his head, feeling his hair beneath her fingers. She could stay in this kiss forever.

He released her lips, only to touch his lips over her face, covering her skin in tiny kisses. She filled her nostrils with his scent. She'd heard of pheromones, but she'd never become aroused by someone's scent before Dan. More than cologne, more than aftershave, it was simply—him. He kissed across her forehead, then the tip of her nose, before coming back to her lips, a delicate touch first, then a deeper investigation. She opened to him eagerly, their tongues circling in a duel of delight.

She indulged herself in him, yearning to have him completely. She rolled her tongue around his, moaning at the sensations flowering within her at the mere touch of their lips together.

Dan ran his hands up and down Stacie's back. Shivers blossomed and she fell back onto the bed. Dan followed her, keeping his lips connected to hers, half-covering her body with his. His body heat penetrated her clothes and when he rested his hand on her waist, her body trembled. She wrapped her leg around his and her arms around his back, clinging to him, holding him close. She never wanted to let him go.

He insinuated his right hand under her top. His fingertips were freezing and she shivered, aware of her nipples peaking. Dan moved his lips away from hers, moving across her right cheek, then slowly to her earlobe, gently using his teeth and breath to inflict delicious torture. Stacie kept her eyes firmly closed, feeling him wandering down to her neckline. He skipped past her breasts—despite her almost thrusting them in his face for attention—sliding down her slender body. He lifted her top and she shivered in anticipation, holding her abdomen tight. He began to kiss around her navel and her breath came short.

Impatient, she sat up and pulled off her top, throwing it randomly across the room before lying back down on the bed. Dan pressed his lips gently against her tummy, moving up inch by torturous inch. When he reached her breasts he again went past them, lifting his body up. Stacie almost cried with frustration. Far, far too slowly, he kissed all the way from one shoulder, down her clavicle to the hollow of her throat, kissing around the little ring of bone there, flicking his tongue over it. Then back up the other clavicle, so snail-like Stacie felt as if she could scream. Back over to the other shoulder, raising a crop of goosebumps as he went. She clenched her inner muscles, feeling her pussy throb.

He shifted position again, moving down her body just a little. He glanced up at her, his eyes huge and dark, then moved his gaze down to her chest. Her boobs rose out of their lace housing, quivering with every heartbeat.

Dan pressed his lips into the soft skin just above her breasts, his tongue darting out, tasting her. Finally! Stacie thrust her breasts at him. He kissed all along the upper curve of both breasts, then went back down to her tummy. She huffed out her breath, starting to get impatient. She sat up slightly, grabbing his top and pulling it up. Dan sat up also and pulled it up over his head.

Seizing her chance, Stacie knelt up then swiftly slung one leg over him, straddling his lap. He dropped back onto the bed, shooting her a knowing smile. Stacie leant over him and kissed him soundly, taking hold of his lip with her teeth and pulling it slightly before releasing it. Hunger filled her—she wanted to taste every inch of his divine flesh. She made her way down his body, kissing around his nipples before sucking, hearing him moan.

Stacie moved down his body, pressing her lips around his navel, darting her tongue out to lick the sensitive button, then moving her lips away to blow on the wetness she had left. The fine hairs on his stomach stood on end and he shivered. Just as she was about to move lower, he took hold of her shoulders and flipped her over onto her back. Excitement raced through her, leaving anticipation in its wake.

Dan slid down her body, stopping at her breasts. She watched him gaze up at her, then he plunged her breasts together and began kissing from one to the other. Endorphins raced through her and she pushed herself up to him, closing her eyes and throwing her head back into the pillow. The feel of his hands and tongue and lips on her flesh set her nerves afire and her breath caught in her throat. Dan took hold of her bra straps, pulling them down revealing her nipples, erect and ready. He took her right nipple into his mouth, licking and sucking it, and teasing it with his teeth. Stacie wailed in pure ecstasy as he used his finger and thumb to gently twist and pull her left nipple.

She was panting, lost in exquisite desire when he stood up and removed his trousers. Stacie sat up, staring directly into his groin, seeing his penis making a bid for escape from his trunks. She reached forward to touch his manhood, filling the palm of her hand with his balls then running her other hand along his long length to stroke it. He pushed himself into her hands and she reached round and took hold of his bottom, bringing him even closer to her.

She pulled his trunks down. His cock reared up, eager for freedom. She placed the tip of her tongue at the base of his manhood, sweeping it up the full length of him, feeling him reacting. Dan moaned aloud as she rolled her tongue round the tip. She cupped his balls in her hand, feeling the warm weight of them within the sac. She wrapped her fingers around his girth, delighting in his firmness. She took the tip of his dick into her mouth. He cried out with pleasure and his body jerked involuntarily as she took his manhood deeper, flicking her tongue over the end. Dan reached down to play with her nipples, pinching and adding naughty twists, sending her senses into eruption.

Dan took her hands and pulled her to her feet. He unfastened her jeans and tugged them down, pulling her panties with them. She sat her naked bottom on the bed and he pulled them off her feet, throwing them away. She wriggled backwards onto the bed, ripping off her bra and discarding it before taking up position at the pillow end. He pulled off the trunks that she'd left at half-mast round his thighs then climbed onto the bed and lay next to her. He twined her hair round his fingers and gazed at her before locking his lips to hers. She wrapped herself round him, feeling his body hot against hers—chest to chest, legs to legs, lips to lips. Kissed into submission, she lay catching her breath as he slithered down the bed, opening her legs to him.

Stacie gripped the bed sheet as Dan blissfully kissed around her mound. His lips touched her inner thighs, one then the other. His touch weakened her, her heart skipped beats. She felt his breath on her, driving her wild—she reached behind her to grab the headboard, pushing up to meet him. His tongue touched her lips, tiny licks up and down the sides—she moaned and thrashed her head on the pillow, trying to keep her lower body still for him. His thumbs parted her lips and he touched his tongue to her clitoris, just a little touch, dotting the tip of his tongue down her feminine centre to her pussy entrance and back up again, flicking and licking, sending lightning bolts around her body. She bent her knees, opening herself as wide as she could for him.

Stacie gripped the bedhead so hard it dug into her fingers, screaming out aloud as his tongue flicked over her folds of flesh, sending her to heaven. Dan's tongue played her clit like a master oboist, he circled his tongue over her most sensitive spot and she danced to his melody. He inserted his fingers into her vagina, forcing her to thrust her hips high off the bed. Dan drove his fingers in and out, wiggling them around inside her. Then he withdrew them, placing them at her lips. She opened her mouth to taste her juices on his fingers, sweet and tangy.

Dan dipped his fingers back in her vagina, sending her rocketing into oblivion. His tongue and fingers wandered her mound, dipping into her slick hole and up to her clitoris, teasing her in all areas, driving her body to heaven.

He licked and sucked on her clitoris, sending her body crazy with pleasure. Her mind was lost, feeling the build up of pleasure, concentrating on his rhythm. Her heart beat faster and her body broke into a sweat. Then that sweet unsurpassed sensation shot through her body, ripping through her nervous system. She cried and moaned, thrashing her body around, jerking wildly on the bed. Dan carefully eased off on his manipulations as her orgasm ran its course, finally stopping when she flopped back onto the duvet, exhausted.

She opened her eyes to see Dan gazing down on her, his face filled with an emotion she couldn't identify. He smiled as soon as he saw her looking, so she wondered if she had imagined it.

She reached down and took hold of his cock, running her hand up and down the length of it. He needed no further encouragement. He swung on top of her, his cock touching her dripping pussy.

"Haven't we forgotten something," she gasped, regretting the necessity.

He rested his cockhead on her pussy entrance. She moaned, desperate to feel him inside her, but wriggled back a touch. "What," he growled.

"The condom?"

An eternity passed in a second. Dan's eyes altered, seeming to grow black as he gazed at her. "I want to make love to you tonight, Stacie. Make love, not have sex. I want to feel your skin against mine, all over."

The emphasis he placed on those final two words was unmistakeable. Stacie closed her eyes and tried to fight her body which screamed out its agreement.

"Is that wise?" she said in a hoarse whisper.

"I'm clean," Dan assured her. "All the staff have regular health checks. Are you on the pill?"

Stacie nodded.

"Then, let me make love to you, Stacie. Let me feel you."

Her body and mind warred. The desperate pleadings of her libido were hard to resist. Ignoring the side of her that advocated caution, she widened her thighs to give him easy access, craving the feel of him within her. His eyes were fixed to hers—drowning her in their depths. He slid smoothly in and groaned aloud, burying his head in her shoulder as he drove into her again and again. Relishing the feel of him bare within her, she clutched his head to her. He seemed curiously suddenly vulnerable. She embraced him and welcomed him as he plunged into her with abandon. He seemed possessed, pounding without heed. He murmured her name as he sank his full length in and out of her. She wrapped her arms around his, kissing along his muscular shoulders as he rammed into her before finally slowing, seeming to lose that initial wild need. He raised his head to look down at her, that odd look in his eyes again then dove down onto her breast, sucking eagerly as he continued to fill her, more slowly now. He eased his penis in and out, sucking on her nipple as he slid one hand down to her clit, gently rubbing the still-throbbing bud. She responded instantly with a gasp and a shiver as he used her own juices to slick his thumb and bring her back to readiness. He moved onto the other breast, licking and nibbling at her tender nipple, causing her to shiver and wriggle in his arms.

He climbed off her, crawling up the bed. He turned her to face him, then pressed his body alongside hers, moulding their bodies together. Stacie lifted her left leg and wrapped it around his hip. Dan pulled her into his embrace as he slid his cock in her slick wetness. She met his thrusts, matching his need, ensuring his cock continued to hit where it gave her most pleasure. It only took half a roll for her to be on top, straddling him.

She leaned back taking his cock deep into her, feeling it hitting her most sensitive spot. She rode him frantically, rubbing her own clit. Her body spasmed and she felt her juices pooling between them. He reached up to cup her breasts as she threw her head back, screaming her climax to the unheeding walls. She shook and gasped, eventually flopping over onto his chest.

As her breathing slowed, he rolled her over onto her back, covering her body with his. He kissed her nose, and her lips, before slowly sliding into her slick wetness. She held his head close to her chest as he began to thrust into her, gently at first, then becoming more ardent. He breathed her name as, with one last frantic push, he filled her with his cream, spurting his juice deep within her, his cock pulsing with every strangulated gasp. She gazed up at him as his orgasm ended, his eyes were closed and his face wore a beatific expression. Quite unexpectedly, she felt tears well. She blinked them away, quickly scrubbing at her eyes before he saw. He opened his eyes and smiled down at her, then carefully pulled out before crumpling next to her on the bed. He pulled her to him and kissed her hair. Stacie leaned her head close to his chest, feeling his arms around her. She could hear his heartbeat slowing and his breathing ease. She closed her eyes, wishing this perfect, magical moment would never end.

\* \* \* \*

Dan's watch alarm woke them up the next morning. They leaped out of bed and began scooting around the room to get ready. Dan rang for breakfast. Stacie grabbed a quick shower and then put on her makeup whilst Dan showered.

After breakfast Stacie pulled her work suit out of the wardrobe, along with the blouse she'd worn on Friday. She held it out and tutted over it.

"What's up?" Dan said, coming over and hugging her from behind, already dressed.

"I can't wear this. The suit is okay, but I need a fresh blouse, and I don't have time to go home and get one."

"I'll sort it," Dan said, kissing the top of her head.

"How?" Stacie asked, turning round, but Dan was already disappearing out of the door. She put on her skirt and shoes and had another croissant while she waited. He was only a couple of minutes, coming back with a purple satin blouse in his hand.

"Angel keeps spare clothes in the staff room, in case anyone's stuff gets dirty for whatever reason. I just grabbed one. Will it do?"

"It's brilliant, thanks." Stacie put the blouse on, tucking it into her skirt, then put the jacket on over the top.

She grabbed her bags and they both headed down to the reception.

"Morning Stacie, Dan," Bailey said.

"Do you have a piece of paper and a pen?" Stacie asked Bailey.

"Of course," Bailey said, passing her a sheet of Desires letter paper and a ball-point pen. She raised her eyebrows in enquiry, but Stacie just took the items over to the sitting area and began to write.

"Whatcha doing?" Dan said, coming to sit next to her.

"Just a letter to Larry, telling him I accept his apology. Time I let him off the hook."

Stacie signed off and handed Bailey the letter. Hopefully it had taught him a very valuable lesson.

Dan walked her to the door.

"Well, I guess this is goodbye. Again," she said, wondering what he would say. Last time they said goodbye he had called after her, begged her to stay, *paid* the club so she could stay. What would he do this time?

"I guess so," he said, rocking back and forth on his heels, his hands in his pockets. She looked at his face. It gave nothing away.

"Well, goodbye then," she said.

"Goodbye, Stacie," he said.

*Okay. Was that it? No kiss? No hug? No nothing?* Stacie's stomach twisted and she tried not to show how bitterly disappointed she was. What could she say to that? He said goodbye without so much as a twitch of emotion. She might as well have been a stranger. She whirled and stomped down the steps, almost running to her car. The tears built in her eyes, and she felt sick. She slung her bag into the car and dared a glance back. Dan stood on the porch, watching her.

*Now.* Now should be the time where he realised his feelings for her and came rushing over to tell her how much he loved her. She waited, watching him for a second, but nothing. He just stood there staring at her. As she watched, he raised his hand in a little wave and gave her a small smile. She lifted her hand in return, and forced the corners of her mouth up, knowing now that this was the last time she would ever see him.

She got into her car, hating herself, feeling her guts were being ripped out her body. She hit the steering wheel with both hands, berating herself. She started the car and maneuvered out of the car park. Sternly resisting the temptation to look back, Stacie left Desires.

## Chapter Sixteen

It was Friday. It had been five days since Stacie left Desires. She'd gone to work every one of those interminable days, plodding through her tasks, trying to smile as much as possible. But she would find herself sitting at her desk, staring into space, imagining Dan's face all the time. Why had she never told him how she felt, or ask him how he felt? *Why*? At least then, even if it had been a negative, she would have known, instead of being in this no man's land of misery and doubt.

Everyone was buzzing at work. It was the Christmas party tonight. Stacie'd got a ticket, but she'd decided she didn't want to go. There was nothing worse than seeing other people having fun when you were totally miserable.

"Don't forget that meeting," Jayne, one of her colleagues called out brightly, tripping past Stacie's desk with an armful of files. *Bugger*! The boss had called another meeting to discuss the abortive meeting from last Friday. Stacie dragged herself off her chair and sat there for a good hour, not listening to a damn word that was said. She just couldn't shake Dan off, she spent hours picturing his smile, his eyes, his touch—it was making her crazy.

She did consider picking up the phone and rebooking him a few times. But she knew her bank balance couldn't stand it, especially with Christmas around the corner. That money was better spent on presents. She couldn't be so selfish as to spend it on her own pleasure. But then, she reconsidered, who put themselves out for her? Her family certainly never made any special effort. Dan did. Not only was he great fun and amazing in bed, he made her feel special, something she couldn't remember anyone having done, ever. Everything just felt right when she was with him, and wrong when she wasn't.

Another thought suddenly struck her. What if he was with another woman? He had cancelled a client to be with her, but she hadn't fully realised what that meant. But now she wasn't there any more, he would be with other women, having sex with other women, kissing other women. Unbidden, visions of him laughing and joking with half a dozen beautiful women filled her mind, him kissing them, touching them, fucking them, and enjoying it.

Oh God! When would this sick feeling go away? Stacie wrapped her arms round her stomach and squeezed her eyes shut. She wanted him to only have eyes for her, to hold just her, and make love over and over again to her and no one else.

"Are you okay?" Jayne said, parking her bottom on the corner of Stacie's desk. "You look quite green."

"I…I don't feel well. I feel sick," Stacie said, not having to put on a weak voice. Was this what was meant by lovesick?

"You should go home. You've been sitting there like a wet weekend all day anyway. I haven't seen you do any work. Get yourself to the doctor. I'll sort it out with the boss."

"Thanks." Stacie smiled gratefully, grabbing her bag and coat. She was sick, but no doctor could help her. There was only one cure for what Stacie had. She got in the car, her heart pounding. Destination, Desires.

She walked up to the large porch, decorated festively with Christmas lights. She keyed in her identification number and the door released. She entered the building and was confronted by a huge Christmas tree, decorated with handcuffs, plastic willies, whips, boobs, bums, anything erotic. A few weeks ago she would have been shocked. Now she just laughed, shaking her head at the silliness.

"Hello, Stacie," said Bailey, looking genuinely pleased to see her.

"Hi," she replied, bouncing up to the reception desk, a big beaming smile splitting her face.

Shannon came out of the back office and approached the desk. "Stacie, how lovely it is to see you. How can we help?"

"I am here to book Dan, please," she said joyfully.

At that moment, Angel appeared from the back office. "He doesn't work here any longer," Angel said, shooting Stacie a killing glare. Stacie gulped. Her limbs suddenly felt heavy and acid swirled in her stomach. He wasn't here? Angel must be lying. Maybe she just didn't want Stacie to see him. Or did she sack him? Why would she sack him?

"What do you mean?"

"He quit the other night," Angel replied, still scowling, then pasted on a saccharine smile. "If you like, I could find someone else appropriate for you?"

Stacie felt her whole body shattering. She was overcome with anguish and her mind turned to mush. "No thanks, I...I think I'll leave it for now," she muttered as her heart broke into small pieces. She had to force her body not to collapse into a wailing heap on the floor. "I'll give you a call later to arrange something else," Stacie managed to say, hoping Angel didn't pick up on her devastation.

"Okay, no problems," Angel replied, turning her back on Stacie and sweeping back into the office.

Stacie dragged her legs one after the other back to the main entrance. That was it. Her life was over. Dan was gone, she had no way of getting in touch with him, no reason to think he would want her to. He may as well be dead. She walked to her car, furious with herself. Why hadn't she said something last weekend? Chrissie said she would regret it, but she'd never thought it would end like this. He wasn't supposed to leave. He was supposed to be here for her whenever she wanted him.

Stacie sat in her car, tears pouring down her cheeks. She hit the steering wheel with both hands, then dropped her head into her hands, her heart aching with loss. She hadn't felt this bad even when leaving Graham. Her tears finally dried up and she sat there, she didn't know how long for, her body numb and empty.

A shiver shook her and she realised she was cold. Dragging herself together, she said, "Well, come on then, Stacie. That's that. No point in just sitting here."

She started the engine and drove out the car park. She paused at the entrance to glance back at Desires. It had been an interesting experience, but there were some happy memories. She could hardly believe her time there was over. Her eyes filled again as she realised that now, memories were all she had left of Dan.

She drove slowly, miserably, not heading anywhere in particular. She tried to remember the details of Sunday night, the way he held her, the way he made love to her, the way he begged her to stay. What had she done?

Stacie decided going back to her miserable flat wasn't on the agenda.

She dragged out her phone and called up Chrissie's details. But a phone call wasn't enough. She needed human comfort.

*Need 2cu. Can I come round?* she texted. The answer came quickly.

*Course u can. I'm in now.*

Chrissie texted her address and Stacie tapped the postcode into her sat nav. Maybe Chrissie could help sort her out. Stacie knew what her words would be, endless lectures on how daft she'd been, but at least could share this major catastrophe with her.

She knocked at Chrissie's clean shiny UPVC door and waited, inhaling a deep breath, gearing herself up for the *I told you so* lecture.

The door opened and Chrissie stood there with a huge smile.

"Hey, Stacie, it's fantastic to see you," she said, wrapping her arms around her.

"It's great to see you, too," Stacie replied, holding Chrissie tightly, already feeling better.

"Come in, come in," Chrissie said, shutting the door behind Stacie and leading her into a gleaming black and silver kitchen. I'm so pleased to see you. I was going to give you a call later once the kids were asleep."

"Sorry…have I come at a bad time?" Stacie said, worried she'd interrupted Chrissie's routine.

"No, the kids are fine and settled," Chrissie said with a reassuring smile.

"I guess I've saved you a call, then."

"You certainly have. Would you like a drink? Tea, coffee?"

"Tea please," Stacie said, settling her bottom on one of the bar stools, relaxing in Chrissie's comforting domesticity.

"What have you been up to?" Chrissie said as she put the kettle on and prepared two mugs.

"Not a lot really, just work," Stacie prevaricated, wondering how to broach the subject. Chrissie brought the mugs over and put one in front of Stacie. The redhead looked keenly at her. Stacie dropped her gaze to the shiny worktop, unable to meet that all-seeing gaze.

"Something's happened. What is it?" Chrissie said, ducking her head to try to see Stacie's expression.

Even as Stacie tried to form the words in her mind to explain to Chrissie, the emotions ambushed her all over again and hot tears dripped down onto the kitchen surface.

"Oh, sweetie, what is it? What's happened?" Chrissie came rushing round to enfold Stacie in a hug. She *shhh*ed her and stroked her hair, and rocked her back and forth as Stacie sobbed.

"He's gone!" she finally managed to blurt out through her sobs, her voice muffled in Chrissie's shoulder.

"Who's gone?"

"Dan! I went round to the club to book him again, and he wasn't there and Angel was cross with me and she said he's quit and I'm never going to see him again and I've been so stupid!" The words poured out in a long stream intermingled with sniffling sobs and huge gulps of air.

"Oh, Stacie," Chrissie patted her and held her till she'd cried herself out, then passed her a tissue. Stacie scrubbed at her eyes and blew her nose. "Why has he quit?"

"I don't know," Stacie said in a sulky mumble.

"You did tell him how you felt, didn't you? Is that why he's quit?" Stacie held her head down in shame, not looking at Chrissie. "Please tell me you did?" The room was silent. "You didn't, did you?"

"I thought I had more time," she said, knowing it was an excuse.

"You said that last time. You silly girl," she told Stacie. Tears came again and Stacie dropped her head to her hands. "Oh, sweetie, I'm sorry. That came out harsher than I meant." Chrissie drew her into a hug again.

"You're right. I am silly. I never thought for a second that he wouldn't be there when I wanted him. Now I've lost him forever. I have no way of finding him."

"What's going on?" Jason entered the kitchen.

"Dan's left Desires," Chrissie explained as Stacie pulled away, wiping the tears from her cheeks.

"Oh right...so he didn't get hold of your phone?" he said casually, walking in the kitchen and putting a mug next to the sink.

Stacie and Chrissie looked at one another, then looked back at Jason. "What about my phone?" Stacie asked, confused.

"Well, he said to me, while you two were chatting, that he was going to try to get your phone and put his number in it."

Stacie stared at Chrissie, her heart suddenly racing.

"Well, look, then," Chrissie almost shouted, making urging motions with her hands.

Stacie scrabbled in her bag for her phone, pulling it out and staring at it. Why didn't he say anything? What if he hadn't managed to do it? Feeling sick with nerves, she opened up her contacts list and scrolled down to the Ds. And there it was, *Dan mobile*. She looked at Chrissie and squealed, jumping off the stool and grabbing Chrissie's elbows. They jumped up and down like schoolgirls. Jason chuckled and shook his head at their antics. Stacie calmed down a little and covered her mouth. Was this real? Was it a dream? She had gone from total devastation to utter delight in an instant.

"Call it," Stacie said to Chrissie, holding out the phone.

"Me…? Why me?"

Stacie just looked at her, placing her hands together in a silent plea.

"Okay, but only because I love you." Chrissie took the phone. Stacie got back on the stool, then hopped off again. She wanted to run around the room with excitement. She didn't know what to do with herself. She felt like screaming at the top of her voice, or doing a stupid dance.

She watched Chrissie press dial and then hold the phone to her ear. Stacie stood still, anxiously waiting for an answer, praying it wasn't all a hoax.

"Hello," Chrissie said. Stacie felt nauseous with anxiety. "Is that Dan?" Stacie put her hands to her mouth. "It's Dan," Chrissie mouthed at Stacie. Joy rushed through her. She ran into the lounge and screamed at the top of her voice, jumping up and down with ecstasy. She couldn't believe she'd had his number since the weekend and had not even known. Why hadn't he told her?

She heard Chrissie chatting to him, laughing and giggling, and she ran back. Butterflies fluttered in her tummy, her heart raced and her knees turned to jelly. She bounced in front of Chrissie, making indications she wanted her phone back.

Chrissie said goodbye then handed the phone over, her own face wearing a beaming smile. She discreetly left the room, taking

Jason by the hand and closing the door behind them. Stacie waved her hands in front of her face in an unsuccessful attempt to calm herself down. She put the phone to her ear and took a deep breath.

"Hello?"

"Hello there." That was it. At the sound of his sexy voice, her knees crumbled, her heart stopped beating, and her mouth went dry. "How are you?" he asked, a happy smile in his voice.

"I'm unbelievably fantastic. Yourself?" she asked, grinning like a fool as joyful tears filled her eyes.

"I'm very pleased to be finally talking to you. I never thought you were going to call."

"Well, if you had actually told me you'd put your number in my phone, I might have," Stacie scolded delightedly. "I didn't know until Jason just told me. I went to Desires to book you and Angel said you had left," she said, her tummy aching.

"Oh I see. Was there a particular reason you wanted to book me?" he asked.

"Well, not really, I just fancied your cock," she said. They both giggled.

"Well, I decided I didn't want to be working there any longer. I've met this gorgeous brunette who made me realise I didn't want anyone else."

"Who was she, then?" Stacie teased.

"Now that would be telling," he replied.

Stacie wandered around the kitchen as they talked, trying to imagine what he was doing, other than talking to her on the phone. Was he at home? A matter of hours ago, she thought she had lost him. Now here she was, talking to him on the phone.

"What are you wearing?" she asked, going for seductive.

"I'm wearing my white Calvin Klein trunks, saying, 'Stacie, come and tease me,'" he said.

"You're very naughty," she said, giggling.

"Only when speaking to you. Now, you hot creature, with as much chocolate mousse as required, would you like to get together?"

"That would be fantastic...I mean yes. When?" she answered, her mind delirious with excitement.

"I'd love to see you right now this second, but I have a mate coming round in a minute and I have to go to a Christmas work party tonight. But I'm free all day tomorrow, if you fancy that?" he said.

She was hardly listening, just drowning in the sound of his voice. She pulled herself together enough to manage an answer. "Tomorrow's great. I have a Christmas work party tonight too," she said, suddenly deciding to go after all.

"Well, I will call you Saturday morning. Sorry, sweetheart, I have to go. My mate has just turned up," he said.

*Sweetheart*! "You'd better get dressed then. Can't go out in your scanties, can you?" she said, an image of him in his trunks dancing across her mind.

"Certainly can't. Right, I'll speak to you soon." He paused. "I can't wait till Saturday. I love you, Stacie," he said, his voice deep and emotional.

*Oh. My. God*! There they were, the words she had been dreaming of. Stacie blinked happy tears from her eyes.

"I love you too, Dan," she whispered. "See you Saturday."

She floated into the lounge where Chrissie and Jason sat chatting.

"Well, how did it go?" Chrissie asked.

Stacie flopped down onto the sofa, not caring that her face probably looked stupid with a grin spread all over it. She flung back her arms and let out a huge happy sigh. "I'm seeing him tomorrow. He said he loves me!"

Chrissie squealed, throwing herself next to Stacie and grabbing her in a huge, happy hug. "I am so, so happy for you I can't tell you!" They chatted for a short while before Stacie made her excuses. If she was going to this party tonight, she'd better start getting ready. She headed back to her flat, hearing his words in her head, repeating them over and over again. Saturday wouldn't come quick enough for her.

\* \* \* \*

She ran herself a bubble bath and relaxed into the raspberry-scented water. She jumped when her phone buzzed, indicating a text.

*Missing you already, you sexy, horny, beautiful, irresistible, delicious, cock-craving woman xxx,* she read.

# Desires

*Miss you too*, she replied.

*Wish I didn't have to go to this party tonight, but I need to do a bit of schmoozing now I don't work at Desires anymore. Would rather be with you.*

*It's ok, I understand. We'll see each other soon.*

*Not soon enough! What u up 2?*

*Just having a bath.*

*RU naked??*

*No, I thought I'd bathe with my clothes on today.*

*Wish I was there.*

*Wish you were too.*

*Well, I'll let you go, cu tomorrow.*

*Can't wait.*

Stacie grinned. How could she ever have doubted him?

She washed her hair and her body, then shaved everything in sight. She curled her hair then prowled in front of her wardrobe. What to wear? One thing Desires had done was make her aware of her own sexuality. She found she enjoyed dressing up in sexy outfits and having men drool over her. At the last Christmas party, she had been the one in the dowdy black dress while all the other girls pranced about like peacocks, getting all the attention from the men in the room. Well, this year, it would be different. Not that she would ever do anything now she had Dan, but it might be nice to show them what they'd missed out on. She'd gone shopping on Monday and bought a dress which had a white basque bodice and a ruffled polka dot skirt which fell to mid-thigh. She pulled on stockings and suspenders and a thong, and then pulled the dress on. It settled beautifully on her figure. Her breasts rose out of the top nicely and her waist looked tiny. She put on her makeup and slipped into a pair of heels, twirling in front of the mirror. She ordered a taxi and pulled on a bolero jacket when it arrived, not that she was planning on covering up her assets as she'd done in the past.

The party was being held at a hotel. People stared as she stepped out the taxi. She held her head up, feeling sexy and desirable. She would have preferred to arrive on Dan's arm, but she'd still have a fantastic evening with the girls she worked with. Stacie walked into the hotel to be faced with a large Christmas tree. Reminded of the tree at Desires full of erotic baubles, she had a private little giggle to herself. She gave her name then went to the cloakroom.

"You look nice, Stacie. Are you feeling better?" she heard Jayne call. She turned. Jayne was decked out to the nines, displaying her long legs and ample cleavage in a tiny gold dress.

Stacie ostentatiously shucked her jacket, handing it in at the cloakroom. Jayne's eyes popped quite satisfactorily as she clocked her basque dress.

"I'm feeling much better now, thanks. Must have been one of those things."

She and Jayne headed into the function room. There was a large dance floor and the pounding music was making her feet move. She glanced around the area seeing a balcony overlooking the dance floor with tables and chairs. A few of her work colleagues were dangling over the balcony waving at them. She waved back then she and Jayne got themselves drinks before heading to join the group.

They all gossiped as if they didn't see each other all day, every day, chattering about the latest celebs and what they were up to. Stacie smirked to herself. If only they knew what shenanigans *she* had been up to, they'd be beyond shocked. Although, more than likely they wouldn't believe her. She tapped her feet to the music, watching people entering the party, wanting to get her body on the dance floor.

She wandered over to the balcony and looked down. There were a lot of people here, there always were. She didn't know more than a tenth of the staff that worked at the magazine, all the departments kept to themselves. She people-watched for a while, dancing on the spot, wiggling about, allowing the music to take her feet.

"Hey there, gorgeous," she heard. She turned around to see a man approaching her. "Can I get you a drink?"

"Got one, thanks," she said, holding up her glass.

"Would you like to dance, then?"

"Sorry. I've got a boyfriend," she said, feeling a cheesy grin spread over her face as she said the words.

"Ah, okay. He's a lucky man," the chap said, raising his glass to her as he walked away.

Stacie watched the dance floor again. Groups of girls danced round their handbags, while groups of guys jiggled about near them, hoping to get lucky. Some were already coupled up, either jigging about in front of each other, or taking that next step, dancing in each other's arms. The song finished and another came on. It wasn't as good a song and there was a bit of an exodus from the floor. Then, through the thinning throng, Stacie saw the one person she never in a million years expected to see—Dan.

She went into instant shock. Why on earth was he here? Stacie cast around in her mind. He'd said he had a work Christmas party. Could it be possible he worked at the magazine? She tried to remember way back when she'd tried to get him to talk about himself. He'd said he worked in computers and IT support. Well, they had computers at the magazine. She vaguely remembered talking to him about her work one time, but had she ever named the magazine? Theirs wasn't the only magazine in town, after all.

Stacie watched him jigging about with a couple of other guys. They looked like typical nerds, sticky-out hair and glasses. As she watched, a bunch of girls came up to him, dancing close. Jealousy turned her stomach, but she forced herself to watch. It would be interesting to see how he handled this. Okay, he had made all the right noises on the phone, he had given up his very lucrative sideline for her—that was a big plus in his favour—but he could still be a rat. She barely knew him after all.

The giggling girls surrounded him. He looked pleased. Well, that was natural. It was nice to get attention, flattering. Heck, why had she dressed up like this if not to get some male attention? He smiled and talked to them. Then one of the girls got close, putting her hands on his waist. Stacie watched as he smiled and took her hands off him. She said something and he leaned close and spoke in her ear. She made a *moue* of disappointment and then said something to all her friends. Stacie could see them all going "*Awww*," and making disappointed faces. She didn't have to hear them, it was clear he had just told them he wasn't available. Not even looking at the nerdy guys, the gaggle went off in search of someone else. Dan shrugged his shoulders as his mates spoke to him and carried on dancing. Stacie smiled. He was hers. He had turned down a bunch of very pretty girls, for her. He had given up a job that brought him in a lot of money, for her.

She made her way downstairs and across the dance floor, keeping people between her and Dan the whole time. She didn't want him to see her yet. She circled round behind him and brushed her body past him, stroking her fingers across his bottom as she did so. She darted into the crowd as he turned, trying to catch a glimpse of who had touched him. He wouldn't be expecting her to be here, so he wouldn't recognise the back view of the brunette in the sexy bodice who was sashaying away from him. She hid behind a pillar and snuck a look, giggling as she saw his puzzled face scanning the crowd.

She came in again, sneaking up on him, this time she pressed her body against him, running her hands up and down his sides. He stiffened, trying to grab her hands. He spun so fast she barely had time to turn away, pretending to be dancing with another guy, who could evidently barely believe his luck at her sudden interest.

As soon as Dan turned back, Stacie grinned to herself and went off to the bar to get another drink. She could see Dan twisting his head around, trying to figure out who the mystery woman was.

She got a glass of wine and watched Dan for a while from behind her pillar. He was showing zero interest in any of the women who were approaching him, in fact, he seemed quite cross. As Stacie finished her glass, one of her favourite tracks came on. She headed back onto the dance floor, snaking her way back to Dan.

She snuggled up behind him, running her hands down his chest. This time, snake-quick, he grabbed one of her hands, holding it in a grip so firm as to be almost painful.

"Now, look," he began as he swung round to face her, his face set. Stacie was quite delighted to find that his comic double-take lasted a full five seconds, including a classic mouth-drop. She put her finger to his chin and exerted pressure.

"Close your mouth, darling," she said. "You look like a goldfish."

"Stacie? What...?"

"I work at the magazine," she said, anticipating the question.

"You don't!"

"Yes, I do. Have done for several years."

"But you can't work there. I work there!"

She gestured around. "Lots of people work there."

"But..."

She put her finger on his lips. "Shut up and kiss me!"

Dan's face split in a huge smile and he crushed her in his arms, lifting her off her feet and swinging her around. He put her down and kissed her, holding her face in his hands, tasting her lips, making sure she had no lipstick left on, by the feel of it. She kissed him back, holding him tightly, feeling his muscles bunching on his back. He released her, then pulled her into a hug again. She pillowed her head on his shoulders, closing her eyes, content to be exactly where she was, right now.

"This is Stacie. This is the girl I've been telling you about," he said to his friends.

"You've been telling your friends about me?"

"Of course!"

They all mumbled hellos and he introduced them to her but she was paying no attention to anything other than the fact that he was there, looking divine in his tux, and she was there.

Dan took her farther onto the dance floor, holding her close, locking her into his body. She could smell his divine aroma, staring into his wonderful eyes as they did the swaying-back-and-forth-holding-onto-each-other dance. It was as if the room was empty—it was just the two of them dancing around the floor, like Cinderella, except she didn't have to go home at midnight.

The rest of the night passed in a happy blur. They stayed together, permanently attached at the hand, or the arm, kissing each other constantly until their friends made sick noises. The dancing got more and more suggestive as the night went on. Dan ground his groin into her and she willingly thrust back.

"You're the sexiest girl alive," he whispered in her ear.

"And you, sir, are the hottest man in the world," she said, not sure how long she could wait till they were alone.

"You have amazing breasts."

"You have an amazing cock," she told him, sliding her hand between them right there on the dance floor, feeling his cock hardening.

His eyes almost popped out. Smiling, she twisted in his arms, taking his hands and putting them on her waist, while she danced seductively before him, grinding her bottom back into his pelvis.

"Right, that's it, woman. You're coming with me."

Dan grabbed her hand, and almost dragged her out in the foyer.

"My jacket," she insisted, detouring to the cloakroom. He helped her on with it, then they raced out the building, jumping into a taxi. Their lips were permanently glued together. Dan glided his hand under her skirt, teasing her unbearably, while she rubbed his cock under cover of his coat.

The taxi dropped them off. They stumbled down a path, their lips still sealed together. Stacie barely noticed they were outside an unfamiliar house. He unlocked the front door and they almost fell in. Stacie started to push his jacket off, when he suddenly stopped her.

"Hang on, is it Saturday yet?" he said, releasing her. She stood there, shocked, seeing him disappearing. What was he doing? Stacie followed him into a dark room. As her eyes adjusted, she could see it was a spacious kitchen. Blue digits on the microwave proclaimed that it was 23.58. "We have two minutes to go," he said very seriously.

Stacie looked at him, laughing. "Seriously?"

"Oh yes. We arranged to meet on Saturday. Where would the world be if people just met willy-nilly, whenever they felt like it?"

"I'll nilly your willy if you don't get over here right now," Stacie told him, putting her hand on her hip and tapping her fingers on the kitchen worktop.

"Well, I think maybe it's near enough the time," he said, launching himself at her. He pressed her against the wall and placed a hand on either side of her head. She closed her eyes as he dropped his head down and pressed the sweetest of kisses to her lips. "I've never had my willy nillied," he said between kisses. "What does it involve?"

"Well," Stacie said, "if you like, I can show you. You have to be naked, though."

"Well, get on with it, woman," he said, starting to undo the hooks down the front of her basque.

Stacie unfastened his bow tie, discarding it on the kitchen floor, then undid the buttons on his shirt. Dan opened her basque, revealing her naked breasts. He bent down and took her right nipple into his mouth, sucking and licking, forcing a wail of pure pleasure from her. Stacie reached down for his trousers, undoing his belt, then the fly and button. They dropped to the floor and Stacie caressed his groin, feeling his cock hardening and throbbing through his trunks. She licked her lips, eager to go down on him and indulge on his manhood. Dan pushed the dress down over her hips. It slipped down to the floor, leaving her standing there in only her stockings, suspenders and heels. Dan ran his hands up and down her upper thigh, feeling the lace at the top of the stocking.

Stacie stifled a giggle. He might be the sexiest man alive, but he did look a little bit silly, with his shirt and jacket hanging open, and his trousers puddled around his feet. He shot her a *look*, then quickly divested himself of his clothes.

He dropped down to his knees, kissing her tummy, sliding one hand under her thong to slip a finger inside her dripping pussy. She gasped, her body jerking. She sank her hands in his hair and spread her legs for him. He buried his face in her crotch, pushing the material to one side and licking her clit.

Her knees were weakening as Dan came up, dipping his tongue into her mouth. She rolled her tongue around his, tasting herself. Her hand went down to his cock. She curled her fingers and ran them up and down the length of him, teasing him.

Dan growled and took her hand, pulling her into the hallway, then up the stairs to his bedroom. He put on a small bedside lamp, and then closed the curtains. He came over to her, taking her hand and leading her to the bed. The edge of the bed creaked as he sat on it and pulled her close. He put his arms around her back and rested his head on her chest, snuggling happily. When she looked down, his eyes were closed.

"Not going to sleep on me, are you?" she said.

"Not for a second," he replied, his voice muffled. "Just enjoying the feel of my own personal airbags."

"Airbags?" Stacie wasn't sure whether to be offended or pleased.

"You're mine now," he told her, looking up at her, his chin in her cleavage. "And I'm yours. I love you, Stacie."

"I love you too."

"Okay, enough mushy stuff. Let's fuck!" His eyes lit up with a naughty smile and he dragged her thong down, tossing it away and pulling her down onto the bed. She shrieked happily. He lay her on her back, and spread her legs, his face diving into her pussy. His tongue teased her, manipulating her clitoris, using his fingers to widen her lips to allow his tongue to get further in. Dan dipped his tongue in and out her vagina and Stacie's mind wandered into oblivion. He was hers, and she was his, and they were here in his house together properly. His fingers teased her clit, forcing all thought out of her head—ecstasy ripped through her body forcing her to cry out in pure joy.

Dan took her to the edge, then left her there. He shifted position, lying down on the bed. Needing no invitation, Stacie climbed on top, facing his feet. She lowered her pussy onto him with a moan, taking his cock deep inside her. She began to slowly undulate her body on and off him, relishing the feeling of him deep inside of her. Stacie dropped her hands back onto his chest feeling the pressure inside her pussy as she leaned back. He reached up to take hold of her breasts, squeezing them together and twisting her nipples till she was gasping.

Dan put his hands on her waist and lifted her off him. Stacie acquiesced, lying down on the bed. He came up and over her, sliding deep within pounding at her till she was moaning and writhing beneath him. He changed position slightly, working a finger down to stimulate her clit. It was the only thing she needed. He quickened his rhythm while Stacie erupted, screaming her pleasure to the rafters, her body shaking and shuddering. Dan gave one last thrust and groaned, collapsing against her shoulder as his body juddered and his cock pulsed. She squeezed him with her muscles and he groaned again. Delighted, she clenched again and was rewarded by another moan and a shudder. Spent, he dropped on top of her between her breasts. She stroked the top of his head as she felt her own breathing return to normal.

Dan moved, lying alongside her. He wrapped his arms around her and locked their legs together.

"Is that how you do it then," he said, as he traced circles on her shoulder.

"Is what how you do what?"

"That squeeze that you did at the end? Is that how you nilly a willy?"

"Ah." She giggled. "Yes, that's exactly it."

"Well, I never knew that."

He kissed her shoulder and hugged her close.

Stacie closed her eyes. Could it be true that she was here in his home holding him tight, with no contract hanging over them, just him and her free to do as they pleased?

If Stacie hadn't chosen Desires to help her rebuild her life, then she would never have met such a wonderful man as Dan McVeigh. Their love had been created from a sex club named Desires.

## *THE END*

# About the Authors
# Holly J. Gill

Holly J Gill is a wife to Nigel and mum of three children, Rhys, Victoria and Alisha. She works as a care assistant at a residential home and in her spare time she writes erotic romantic novels. Her writing career started as a young child with a wild imagination and after twenty years her dream has come true. In her spare time she likes visiting friends, listening to music, watching movies and travelling the English countryside.

Twitter: https://twitter.com/HollyJGill
Blog: http://hollyjgill.blogspot.co.uk
Facebook: http://www.facebook.com/hollyjgillauthor

# Nikki Blaise

Nikki Blaise likes cats, erotic art, sex, running, music, writing and singing (badly and
drunkenly). She writes naughty stories she daren't tell her mother about and lives in London
with her collection of carnivorous plants.
Will tweet for money.

Twitter: https://twitter.com/Nikki_Blaise
Facebook: https://www.facebook.com/nikki.blaise

# Also by Nikki Blaise
## Jasmine
## A Second Opinion

# Secret Cravings Publishing
## www.secretcravingspublishing.com

Made in the USA
Charleston, SC
05 May 2013